ENOLA HOLMES

AND THE BLACK BAROUCHE

Also by Nancy Springer

THE ENOLA HOLMES MYSTERIES

ENOLA HOLMES

AND THE BLACK BAROUCHE

Nancy Springer

WEDNESDAY BOOKS
NEW YORK

First published in the United States by Wednesday Books, an imprint of St. Martin's Publishing Group

ENOLA HOLMES AND THE BLACK BAROUCHE. Copyright © 2021 by Nancy Springer. All rights reserved. Printed in the United States of America. For information, address St. Martin's Publishing Group, 120 Broadway, New York, NY 10271.

www.wednesdaybooks.com

Inspired by characters created by Sir Arthur Conan Doyle, with special thanks to the Conan Doyle Estate Ltd.
www.conandoyleestate.com

Designed by Omar Chapa

Library of Congress Cataloging-in-Publication Data

Names: Springer, Nancy, author.
Title: Enola Holmes and the black barouche / Nancy Springer.
Description: First edition. | New York : Wednesday Books, 2021. |
  Series: Enola Holmes mysteries ; 7
Identifiers: LCCN 2021015636 | ISBN 9781250822956 (hardcover) |
  ISBN 9781250822963 (ebook)
Subjects: CYAC: Twins—Fiction. | Sisters—Fiction. | Marriage—
  Fiction. | Psychiatric hospitals—Fiction. | Characters in literature—
  Fiction. | Great Britain—History—Victoria, 1837–1901—Fiction. |
  Mystery and detective stories.
Classification: LCC PZ7.S76846 En 2021 | DDC [Fic]—dc23
LC record available at https://lccn.loc.gov/2021015636

Our books may be purchased in bulk for promotional, educational, or business use. Please contact your local bookseller or the Macmillan Corporate and Premium Sales Department at 1-800-221-7945, extension 5442, or by email at MacmillanSpecialMarkets@macmillan.com.

First Edition: 2021

10 9 8 7 6 5 4 3 2 1

For Teanna Byerts, longtime friend

ENOLA HOLMES

AND THE BLACK BAROUCHE

Prologue

by Sherlock Holmes, 1889

Those of you who are aware of my distinguished career as the world's first Private Consulting Detective can hardly remain unaware of the sensational way in which another Holmes of similar ilk, my much younger sister, Enola, has lately burst upon the London scene. Many have found her unabashed capture of the public eye both scandalous and deplorable, and some question my own failure to control her. Therefore I welcome this opportunity to pen my own logical and dispassionate

account of my dealings with Enola Eudoria Hadassah
Holmes.

To absolve myself at once of any suspicions of sentimentality, let me state that I have no childhood memories of my sister, Enola; indeed, I barely knew her until
July of 1888. In 1874, when she was born, I was on the
point of leaving home and living on my own to pursue my studies; indeed, I hastened my departure due to
the most unpleasant household disruption consequent
upon her infant arrival. I encountered her over the next
few years only occasionally and only with the natural
revulsion of a gentleman towards a messy and undevel-
oped specimen of humanity. At the time of our father's
funeral, she was four years old and still incapable of
maintaining the cleanliness of her nose. I do not recall
having any sensible discourse with her at that time.

Ten years passed before the next time I saw her, in
July of 1888.

This was no normal occasion. The unexpected
and unexplained disappearance of her mother—our
mother—caused young Enola to summon my brother,
Mycroft, and me from London. As our train pulled into
our rural destination, Enola awaited us on the railway

platform, resembling nothing so much as a fledgling stork. Remarkably tall for a girl of fourteen, she wore a frock that failed to cover her bony shanks, and no gloves or hat; indeed, the wind had turned her hair into a jackdaw's nest. Mycroft and I thought her a street urchin, failing to recognize her until she spoke to us: "Mr. Holmes, and, um, Mr. Holmes?" As lacking in manners as a colt, she seemed confused by Mycroft's questions, and indeed, by the time we arrived at Ferndell Hall, our ancestral home, I thought my sister perhaps even a bit more brainless than the typical female.

Once on the scene, Mycroft and I concluded that our mother had not been kidnapped but, suffragist that she was, had run away. This did not greatly concern us, for Mother had served her reproductive purpose and was, at her age, both useless and incorrigible. However, as something had to be done about Enola, we considered that it was perhaps not too late to salvage her. Ignoring her nonsensical protests, we made arrangements to place her in an excellent finishing school, hoping eventually to marry her off.

Mycroft and I returned to London feeling that we had done our duty.

However, our sister never arrived at the school. On the journey, she contrived to vanish.

How dare she? The ingratitude of her!

For the ensuing days, I, Sherlock Holmes, the world's greatest detective, devoted all my skill to tracking a silly runaway girl, presumably disguised as a boy—but I could find no trace of her. Then, much to my chagrin, Inspector Lestrade of Scotland Yard gave me news of her.

She was masquerading as a widow.

A widow! For the first time I realized I had underestimated her. She had at least a modicum of brain, for, by becoming a widow, she had quite obliterated her face, added a decade or more to her age, and discouraged anyone from approaching her.

She was, however, in a widow's weeds, noticeable. I traced her to London, scarcely able to believe she had the temerity to venture there—and at Scotland Yard I encountered an aristocratic lad who had been rescued from kidnappers by a girl in a widow's guise! The boy informed me, however, that she was now dressed as a spinster with a pince-nez.

I redoubled my efforts to find her and save her from

the perils of London. Unfortunately, I had no likeness of her with which to advertise. No photograph of her had ever been taken. But I did have a most interesting and revealing booklet of ciphers our mother had given her. Having thus discovered that the two of them secretly communicated via *The Pall Mall Gazette* personal columns, I placed my own message pretending I was Mother and asking Enola to meet me. But somehow she saw through my ruse. Whilst I was at the British Museum waiting to pounce on her, she gained entry to my apartment and stole back the booklet! When my landlady said she appeared to be a poor huckster shivering in the autumn cold, I realized I had actually walked past her on my way out!

Even more concerned for young Enola now, fearing that she might indeed be indigent, I concentrated my search on the slums, where one freezing winter night I met the Sister of the Streets, a mute nun enveloped in a black habit who ministered to the poor. Indeed, she fed me a biscuit. Shortly thereafter, this nun delivered a swooning lady into my arms and tersely told me the identity of the villain who had harmed her. Recognizing the "mute" nun's voice, I realized to my utmost shock that the Sister was my sister! I tried to seize her, but she fended me off with a dagger and disappeared into the night. All the police in London failed to find her. Returning, defeated, to my flat in the morning, I found her discarded habit there! The brass, the nerve, the sheer daring of her, she had hidden in my own rooms while I was out looking for her!

And, by the way, in order to rescue the lady, she had quite savaged a murderous villain with her dagger. Evidently my sister, Enola, could take care of herself, but drat the girl, she could not be allowed to grow up wild on the London streets. I simply had to rescue her. Yet despite my best efforts, winter dragged into spring with nary a sign of her.

Then my attention was all seized by the inexplicable disappearance of my dear friend Dr. Watson. For a week I neither ate nor slept, nor did my brother, Mycroft, but we could not find a sign of him. Indeed, it was not we who saved him, but our sister! A message in the newspapers led us straight to poor Watson where he was being held captive in a lunatic asylum, and the message was signed E. H.—Enola Holmes.

Quite humbled, I had no idea how she accomplished this feat.

Nor did I have any idea where in London she lived or how she sustained herself day to day. But, gentle reader, please recall the swooning lady she had once delivered into my arms. Shortly after Watson's return, that same lady fell victim to a forced-marriage scheme, and I was retained to save her. This involved a surreptitious nighttime visit to the mansion where I had reason to think she was being held captive. All dressed in black, with my face darkened, I stole into the back garden—and seemingly stepped off a precipice! Hitting the bottom of what turned out to be quite a deep trench, I badly hurt my ankle.

And my pride. One does not expect to encounter a "sunk fence" in the heart of the city, yet there I was caught in one, unable to even attempt to climb out. Already my ankle had swollen so greatly that, seated on comfortless rocks, I had to take my penknife and cut my bootlaces in order to get the boot off. Struggling to do so in utter darkness, I swore under my breath.

A girlishly distinctive voice above my head teased, "Shame on you."

I am sure my jaw dropped. So great was my shock that it quite strangled me for a moment before I was able to gasp, "Enola?"

Yes, it was she, tossing down brandy and bandages to me, then swarming up a seemingly impossible tree with a rope, of all things, between her teeth. Securing it, she came thumping down like an oversized monkey on the far side of the trench in which I remained entrapped. I expected her to give me the rope so I could get out, but no, she started to go gallivanting off by herself to free the imprisoned lady, and I might be languishing in that pit to this day if it were not that the lord of the manor came out with a shotgun and fired upon us! In the duress of the next few moments I found Enola helping me out of the trench, up and over the fence, and away, my injured foot so useless that I must needs cling to her shoulder to limp along. I am sure my brother, Mycroft, will never forgive or understand why, when we reached safety, I felt obliged to let her go, but gratitude and my sense of honour compelled me. We shook hands, my sister and I, and then like a wild moorland pony she shied away, her mane of hair flying, and ran for freedom. I was relieved to note that she wore a skirt, not trousers.

Only two days later, she entrusted me with the care of the unfortunate lady after *she* saved her from forced marriage. Thereafter, I saw no more of my sister, except that quite by accident the next month I encountered her in the home of Florence Nightingale. Enola wore glasses, a mannish hat, inky gloves, and a dark, narrow dress to disguise herself as a scholar, but to my long-awaited credit, I recognized her at once. She fled. I chased her clear up to the top of the house, but she escaped through a window, down a mighty oak tree, and away like a hare.

Simultaneously angry and admiring, I went about the business Miss Nightingale had engaged me for: finding a missing woman named Tupper. I made my inquiries, then the next night I got myself up like a poor rickety old greybeard and went scrounging around a certain grandiose house as if searching the gutters for farthings. Much amazed was I when a plainly dressed but obviously aristocratic lady crossed the road in front of me, strode up the walk, and smartly rapped the brass knocker. It was Enola! Unable to stop her before she entered that dangerous place, I made shift to watch her through the windows; indeed, such was my concern for her safety that I climbed the side of the house when she was escorted upstairs. As I clung to vines, my face pressed against the glass to see within, she looked straight at me and winked! I was so taken aback, I nearly lost my grip and fell. Thereafter, as was becoming deplorably customary, she outwitted me. As the front door burst open and I was busy engaging the villain in jujitsu, Enola disappeared out the back way along with, of course, the Tupper woman, whom she conveyed to safety at the Nightingale house.

The next day, from shouted conversation through an ear trumpet, I pieced together that the pitiful, deaf, and ancient Mrs. Tupper had been Enola's landlady, and with some mental excitement I deduced that Enola might visit her at the Nightingale residence. Thereafter I lurked in wait for her, along with a companion named Reginald. Dozens of people entered the Nightingale home daily, and on the lookout for my plain-faced sister, I paid no attention whatsoever to quite a lovely lady in an elaborate cerulean gown of three fabrics—but

Reginald, my sister's longtime pet collie, whined and pulled at the leash! I let him go bounding to her, and could scarcely believe it when the "lady" greeted the dog with laughter and tears, most unceremoniously sitting on the ground to hug him! When she saw me looking down at her, she smiled up into my face and willingly took my hand to arise. She sensed, I think, that I no longer "looked down" on her in any other sense of the phrase.

Thus were we reunited. Not without complications; she gave me the slip again that selfsame day. But we remained in communication, and only a few days later I contrived to get her, in her most ladylike incognito, into the same cab as our brother, Mycroft. After spending an evening with his astonishing sister, helping her locate a missing duchess in the labyrinth of London's dockyards, Mycroft came to much the same conclusions I had already reached:

Enola did not need protection.

Enola did not need to go to finishing school.

Nor did Enola need to be married off. Indeed, heaven help any man who might be so unwary as to wed her.

The next day, Enola's fifteenth birthday, the three of us had tea and cake together at my flat. From a letter recently received, we now knew why our mother had run away: her days were numbered, she had spent them in freedom from society's dictates, and she was now deceased. Enola shed a few tears, but her smiles were manifold; her mother was gone, but she had her brothers now. Mycroft had made peace with her, and I had grown to care for her. All was well.

Or so I reflected to my satisfaction, quite blindly failing to foresee that she might go sticking her considerable nose into one of my cases . . .

Chapter the First

After my reconciliation with my brothers in the summer of 1889, I spent August quite happily with Reginald Collie, visiting Ferndell, my childhood home in the country. Moreover, after returning to London and my very safe albeit somewhat Spartan room at the Professional Women's Club, I purchased a delightful new dress, apricot foulard with slightly puffed shoulders and a narrow gored skirt, which disguised me as no one but my slender self! At last, and most fortuitously, the "hourglass figure" was going out of style—just when I no longer required bosom enhancers and hip transformers to conceal myself from Sherlock and Mycroft! Eagerly I looked forward to seeing them again as the authentic Enola Holmes.

But days became a week, then a fortnight; August became September, yet I did not hear from them.

My spirits sank. Once more I found myself too much alone, as seems to be my fate; my very name, Enola, when spelt backwards, reads "alone." I wanted to purchase a hat to go with the apricot foulard, but even contemplation of that pleasing errand failed to rouse me from inertia. So, one sunny afternoon when I could have been making the rounds of the shops, instead I was moping in the club parlour when a maid brought me a note on a brass salver. "The gentleman said he'll wait for your reply, miss."

Males, you see, gentle reader, were not allowed past the door of the Professional Women's Club.

No gentlemen ever called for me; therefore the note had to be from one of my brothers, almost certainly from Sherlock, as Mycroft could hardly ever be induced to stray from his orbit among his Pall Mall lodgings, his Whitehall government office, and the Diogenes Club. So my heart quite leapt as I reached for the note, written upon a sheet of stationer's paper, and unfolded it to read. But first I looked at the signature.

Bother. It was just Dr. Watson. He wrote:

Dear Miss Enola,

Your brother Sherlock would deplore my applying to you in this fashion, I am sure, but both as his friend and as his medical advisor I feel compelled to notify you of his alarming condition. Perhaps you are unaware that he is prone to fits of melancholia. And undoubtedly he will castigate me for my interference. Just the same, I must beg you to come with me to see him, in hopes that your presence might influence him for the better. I await your response.

Your humble servant,
John Watson, M.D.

My heart recommenced its gymnastics. Sherlock, in an alarming condition? Whatever did Watson mean?

I must needs go see at once.

Bolting to my feet, I instructed the maid, "Tell the gentleman I will be with him directly," and ran for my room to put on my newest boots—I had been wearing delicate silk slippers fit only for indoors; they would have been shredded on the street—and find a matching, decent pair of gloves, and tidy my impossible hair before topping it with a hat, and snatch up a parasol. A fashionable lady must never be without a parasol, or a fan, or at least a handkerchief, something pretty to carry, and the gentle reader will doubtless have noticed by now that I had become fond of appearing to be a fashionable young woman of society.

So much so, indeed, that I had a fancy to change my dress, but I overruled it. Rather than leave Dr. Watson waiting on the sunny pavement any longer than was necessary, I assured myself that the taffeta-and-dotted-Swiss frock I wore was quite smart enough.

When I hurried out of the front door of the Professional Women's Club, the good doctor was waiting with a hansom cab, into which he helped me with some conventional words of greeting before seating himself at my side and bidding the cabbie to convey us to Baker Street.

Of course I then had to make the usual inquiries: were Dr. Watson and his wife quite well? I liked Dr. Watson a great deal, and hoped he could hear my

affection in the warmth of my voice. Were I not so fond
of him, I would have rudely skipped these preliminar-
ies, for I quite wanted to know more about what was
wrong with my brother.

"And Sherlock? Something causes you to feel
alarmed about him, Doctor?"

The good doctor sighed, his honest brown eyes
troubled. "For the past ten days, Holmes has exerted
his amazing powers nonstop on a case concerning secret papers purloined from the Admirality, the *Princess
Alice* shipping disaster, and a rare species of Malaysian
spider. Working around the clock without pause, he has
strained his extraordinary constitution to its breaking
point, and now that he has resolved the matter, he has
plunged into the deepest depression. At the triumphal
hour when our nation's leaders praise him in the halls of
Parliament, he will not leave his lodgings nor eat, and
it took all of my persuasive powers earlier today to get
him out of bed." Dr. Watson, who had been speaking
to the floor of our cab, now raised his steadfast gaze,
making no attempt to conceal his distress. "I exhorted
him to shave and get dressed as a rudimentary step in
exerting himself towards recovery, but to no avail. He

refused me without uttering a word. He turned his head away and ignored me."

The hansom halted in front of 221 Baker Street. But after we had descended and the cab rattled away, I balked on the pavement, telling Dr. Watson, "I will not go up until I understand what I am to do."

"You are unfamiliar with melancholia?"

"Not entirely." I tried to smile but grimaced instead. "I've had such dark fits myself; I suppose the predisposition runs in the family. To me, the mood seems rooted in spleen, and I think a fine fit of temper, some cleansing anger, might be its best cure. Do you agree?"

Watson seemed a bit flummoxed by my views, but replied staunchly, "Any rousing change should surely be an improvement."

"Then I think, my dear doctor, you had better go about your business. I believe I am likely to have better luck with Sherlock on my own."

Mrs. Hudson, Sherlock's amiable, long-suffering landlady, gave me a wink and a smile as she unlocked his door for me.

Letting myself in, I found myself stepping into melancholia made manifest in the form of gloom. Draperies closed over the windows and unlit lamps made Sherlock's sitting room a dim and dusky Lethe through the shadows of which I could barely see him lounging on his settee—or at least I saw a long, featureless, motionless figure reclining there.

"Dear me, how very crepuscular we are," I chided as I crossed the room to throw open the window blinds. Daylight flooded in, and I turned to have another look at my brother. Wearing a mouse-coloured dressing gown, Sherlock lay with his lower limbs stretched out on the couch and crossed at the ankles—his bare, bony ankles seemed oddly vulnerable to me, although he had carpet slippers on his feet. Beside him on the floor stood a stack of newspapers, placed there for his diversion by the faithful Watson, I felt sure. But I saw that not one had been touched. Sherlock leaned back against the settee's pillowed arm, his long hands lying idle in his lap. He had turned his head towards me, yet hardly seemed to look at me, his gaze unfocused. With a pang in my heart, I missed his usually keen eyes. His skin looked pale, his face unshaven and haggard.

"My dear brother, whatever is the matter with you, sitting in the dark?" I said in an officious way meant to be annoying. "We have a case of the mopes and we need treatment, do we? Well, let us see to it." Setting my gloves and parasol aside, I helped myself to a pencil and a tablet of rather expensive paper from his desk. Appropriating a dining chair, I placed it beside the settee and seated myself upon it, directly in front of him, peering into his bristly face and nodding solemnly. "If you were in the asylum, they would give you chloral hydrate and black hellebore to take the spleen out of you," I said, "but I suppose we could start with a purge." I began to scribble on the tablet paper in my lap, muttering as if to myself, "Laudanum, belladonna, antimony, all highly efficient if they do not cause your untimely demise . . . I'm sure Dr. Watson could recommend something. Or we could try sweating the black bile away, Sherlock!" I glanced at him, not so much in search of a reaction as to show him my fanatically gleaming eyes, for my sense of melodrama had quite taken charge of me, and I am sure I quite looked the part of a fervid female determined to help at any cost to the sufferer. I returned my attention to my fiendish

list, augmenting it. Sweat. Turkish bath. No, total im-
mersion in *cold* water! "Tonic, sweat bath, ice water," I
gabbled, "or—" As if the lightning of genius had struck
me, I stiffened straight up in my chair. "Or one of those
new galvanic baths! Have you heard, Sherlock, they
place one in the water and pass electricity through—"

O joy! He interrupted! "Leave me alone or I'll gal-
vanize *you*."

I beamed at his stormy eyes now focused upon me.
"Galvanic belts are also available for purchase, you know,
at some of the more up-to-date shops. I could bring you
one and you could wear it until you are feeling better."

"Get out of here and let me be, Enola!"

"Let you be like a mole in the dark eating worms?
No indeed, my dear brother. It is my mission as well as
my duty to take care of you."

"Your mission be damned!" He sat up straight, his
hands clutching the couch, and, glory be, he raised his
voice at me! "Interfering female," he shouted, "what do
I need to do in order to—"

"Exactly!" I grinned at him. "Galvanization is indeed what you need to do in order to cure yourself.
And along with the galvanic belt, certainly I could

purchase you some mustard plasters. I have heard that, for melancholia, sometimes a counter-irritant—"

"You yourself are quite irritating enough! Would you please *leave*?"

I gentled my voice. "Not until I see you dressed and eating, my dear brother."

He turned away from me. "No."

"Sherlock—"

"No." He lapsed back onto the settee, his voice a monotone. "No. Go stick your head in the Thames, fancy hat and all. Let me alone."

"Sherlock," I complained, more coaxing than provoked.

He did not answer. Leaning over to peek at him, I saw that his eyes were closed, the better to ignore me thereby.

I sat back in my chair, sighing. Although determined not to give up, I had no idea what to do next. I had shot my bolt, and had no other arrows at hand— except, I supposed, my obstinate presence.

So I sat where I was.

Time passed as I listened to the silence, trying without success to think what next to do or say. Sherlock lay taut and still but not asleep; he scarcely seemed to breathe, and the clock ticking on his mantelpiece made more noise than he did, that and the traffic rumbling over the cobbles of Baker Street. After a while I heard the bell ring at the front door, and Mrs. Hudson's matronly footsteps as she went to answer it, but I gave the matter no thought—until, a short while later, I heard Mrs. Hudson again, this time ascending the stairs! She knocked at the door in her usual crisp fashion, let herself in, and said to the motionless form on the settee, "It's a young woman to see you, Mr. Holmes, all pale and trembling, so beside herself with some terrible trouble that she won't take no for an answer. I know what you told me, Mr. Holmes, but—"

Her voice choked to a halt as he opened his eyes and glared at her. That single dagger-sharp look answered her as clearly as words.

"But I can't just put her back out in the street," Mrs. Hudson appealed with distress I had no doubt was genuine.

I stood up and walked over to her. "Never mind, Mrs. Hudson." I took the card from her salver. "Send the young lady up directly. Tell her that Mr. Holmes's sister and associate will be happy to advise her."

Chapter the Second

Miss Letitia Glover, said the card in a most peculiar way; the name was typewritten rather than having been done in a print shop, and all around the edge of the stiff little paper rectangle ran a decorative border that reminded one of cross-stitch embroidery, XxXxXxX, most cleverly executed, like the name, with a typewriter.

I was still admiring this singular card as light footfalls pelted up the stairs and the door whooshed open to admit Holmes's client—or rather, mine. My brother had resumed impersonating an inanimate object, motionless, with his eyes closed, not even looking at Miss Glover. I, however, studied her with interest as I extended my hand to her. Perhaps never before had I seen grief and determination so intermingled on such a fair, young face—heavens, she seemed only a few years older than I was. With her eyes puffed and reddened from weeping but her chin lifted and her lips compressed, she returned my handshake firmly.

"Flossie simply cannot be gone from this world," she stated, her voice clotted yet vibrant with emotion. "At first I wept, all day long, but lying awake last night and thinking it over, I refuse any longer to believe it. My sister and I are twins. Possibly you have heard of the empathic bond twins share. I would have instantly sensed my loss had she passed away."

"Please, Miss Glover, be seated and tell me how I can help you." I beckoned her to a comfortable chair beside the window. As she crossed the room, she looked curiously at the supine figure on the settee, and I smiled. "I assure you, Miss Glover, you need pay no heed to my catatonic brother. In his present state he is harmless, and as deaf as the driftwood he resembles."

"Deaf?" She seated herself, placing her reticule on the floor beside her.

"Willfully so." I took my seat in the chair facing hers, both of us angled with our backs towards Sherlock, and of course I surveyed her from head to toe without appearing to do so. Rather than flaunting the usual cheap baubles and imitation finery of a working girl, she wore a mannish shirt, waistcoat, and cravat above her narrow skirt—but the cravat was cheerful paisley, the waistcoat cerulean blue, and her cream-coloured shirt made of soft silk. Her simple chignon was topped by an equally simple bowler hat of navy-blue velveteen. She could have been an eccentric suffragist aristocrat if it were not for something indefinably middle class about her speech and manner. "I can see by your mode of dress, Miss Glover, that you are no ordinary young woman. You work for your living, but with the greatest independence and dignity."

"I take great pride in my work as a typist," she replied, and I thought: Of course! Her card! As I nodded, she attempted a smile, continuing, "As you can tell by my surname, my forebears were humble glove makers, and my family's money earned in trade, but I share with my sister—"

The word choked her. "Your sister?" I gently prompted.

"My twin. Flossie." The word verged upon becoming a sob until Miss Glover paused, visibly struggling to master herself. Her voice barely trembled as she went on. "I share with her a disregard for such class distinctions, and from the day of our birth, our parents saw to it that we had every advantage of education and culture. Flossie—her name is Felicity, but we call her Flossie—she took to the arts like a lark to the sky, dancing like a butterfly and singing like a nightingale. I, however, found myself more at home with mathematics. A slide rule is my best friend." Miss Glover managed a wincing smile. "I have remained a spinster, and make my living as a typist and bookkeeper. But Felicity was born for marital bliss, or so it seemed. When our parents departed this earthly sphere, they did so happy in the knowledge that their daughter was the wife of the Earl of Dunhench, no less.

"I, too, was happy for Flossie's good fortune, although I saw her seldom and I have missed her dreadfully in the two years since she married. I have been even lonelier since our parents passed on, but I contented myself with the thought that all was well for Flossie—or at least so I thought, until yesterday."

"And what happened yesterday?" I prompted as Miss Glover hesitated, apparently struggling to go on.

Rather than speaking—indeed, perhaps unable to speak—Miss Glover bent, reached into her reticule, and withdrew a letter, which she passed to me.

It was addressed to Miss Letitia Glover of 19 Keswick Terrace, a modest but respectable London neighbourhood, and it had been sealed with silver wax bearing the imprint of a coat of arms. Unfolding the heavy, cream-coloured rag paper, I knew even before I read the embossed letterhead that the missive was from someone of rank.

CADOGAN BURR RUDCLIFF II, EARL OF DUNHENCH

DUNHENCH PARK HALL

THREEFINCHES

SURREY

In dark blue ink below, penned large in an unmistakably masculine hand, ran the letter:

August 31, 1889

My Dear Tish,

I'm awfully sorry to be the sender of bad tidings. Some news can only be stated starkly if at all, so I will be blunt: Flossie has passed away due to a sudden and virulent illness. Fear of the disease caused her mortal remains to be cremated rather than prepared for burial. As you are her closest blood relative, I will send her ashes to you in a parcel along with this letter. I am sure you will be deeply grieved as am I, but may memories of your sister comfort you.

Most sincerely,
Caddie

Once I had scanned this, I slowly and deliberately read it aloud, heading and all, for I wanted to know whether I had missed some nuance or if it was really as oddly offhanded as I thought.

Then I refolded it and handed it back to Miss Letitia Glover, and we stared at each other. She looked quite pale.

"I cannot and will not believe it," she said.

"It seems singularly lacking in details," I agreed. "What were the circumstances and exact time of your sister's supposed passing away? Was no doctor present, or did he not give her ailment a name? What were her last words? Did she convey no message to you? Who was with her? And 'awfully sorry'? Does that sound like a heartbroken husband? Altogether, it rings false."

She nodded her most emphatic agreement. "And why did I receive no telegram? The moment she became seriously ill, I should have been sent for."

"Quite."

"And no funeral? Instead, *cremation*?" The shock in her voice echoed in my own mind. A few radical social reformers had been advocating cremation as a more sanitary alternative to burial, but public opinion remained strongly against it, and the practice was far from common.

"Cremation of the wife of an earl seems quite odd," I concurred.

Her control of her emotions beginning to slip, Miss Glover wailed, "But why would Caddie write such things if they are not true?"

I leaned back in my chair, rested my elbows on its arms, and steepled my fingers. "Tell me all about your sister and this 'Caddie' person." More properly titled Lord Cadogan Burr Rudcliff II, Earl of Dunhench in Surrey, and how had a middle-class girl from London ever come to be married to him?

"Flossie—her extraordinary talents and beauty—" Miss Letitia Glover spoke haltingly in her distress, and in the midst of my patient attempts to coax the story out of her, Mrs. Hudson appeared with a tray of sandwiches and tea; I suspect she was curious to see whether there had been any change in Sherlock's attitude. Altogether, Miss Glover's tale became much interrupted, so for the gentle reader's sake I offer this summary:

Shortly after her sixteenth birthday, Felicity Glover had been offered a position as governess for a banker's three small children. The banker's social circle was an exalted one, and the beauty and accomplishments of his governess did not go unnoticed by guests; she was often requested to play the piano and sing for them. (At this point I must remark that my client, had her face been smiling rather than harrowed with grief, and had her costume been stylish, would have been quite a beauty in her own right. She and her twin differed in their tastes and talents but looked alike.) The lovely Felicity "Flossie" Glover soon found herself teaching social arts and deportment to the Marquess of Linderlea's children, the sons out of short pants and the daughters of an age to wear their dresses long and their hair up. Therefore, frequently they dined with family and guests, and while the governess's evening gowns could not have been nearly as rich as those of the ladies, her beauty and spirit so well lived up to her name (for Felicity was a happy soul) that she caught the eye of more than one young lord. And she was so well liked that only passing murmurs of scandal arose, despite the great disparity in rank, when she was courted by the Earl of Dunhench. At age thirty, the second Cadogan Burr Rudcliff, Lord Dunhench, a widower with two children sadly deceased, had become one of England's most sought-after bachelors, handsome, charming, titled, and wealthy. No doubt there was some wailing and gnashing of teeth in families with debutante daughters when he proposed marriage to eighteen-year-old Felicity Glover and she accepted. The wedding put a great strain on the bride's family's financial resources, which might have contributed to the untimely expiration, some months later, of the bride's parents. But the marriage, by all accounts, had been happy.

"Flossie wrote often, urging me to visit," Miss Glover concluded, "but I lacked the courage to brave Dunhench Hall. Even at my sister's wedding, primped and rigged as never before in my life, still I felt like a jackdaw among peacocks."

"But your sister's letters to you were frequent and cheerful?"

"Yes! And now, with no warning whatsoever—this." Grief and, I think, indignation choked her.

"A most peculiar way of imparting a matter of such seriousness. Miss Glover, is this letter in character for your brother-in-law? What is he like?"

"I am beginning to think that I do not truly know."

"But what did you think before?"

"That he must be a nice enough person because I saw no vice in him. He was a smiling, courteous, good-looking man, but now I realize that all I saw was superficial. I no more know him than—than a cipher. He has kept his true self to himself; he is like X in an algebra problem."

I agreed, but chose not to say what I had inferred from Cadogan Rudcliff's handwriting: that he had a remarkably good opinion of himself (many flourishes), that he was strong-willed (broad strokes, heavy pressure), and that he preferred action to wisdom (extreme forward slant). Instead, I changed the subject. "You mentioned a parcel of ashes."

Letitia Glover nodded as she once more reached into her reticule, pulling from it a pasteboard box from which she drew a small but very tasteful urn carved out of some pale stone—alabaster, or perhaps cream jade. This she handed to me. Lifting the stopper and squinting down the urn's narrow neck, I could see nothing.

"Have you inspected the contents?"

Clearly horrified, Miss Glover shook her head.

"We must do so, I think." Standing up, I moved across the room to Sherlock's desk to spare her sensibilities. I spread out a blank sheet of white paper, and onto this, with great care, I poured a small sample from the urn.

I saw ashes, and wondered what on earth I had been expecting—perhaps a complete set of teeth? I had no experience of cremation and no idea how to tell whether these burned remains were human.

"There are white bits that might be bone chips," I reported doubtfully.

"For the love of mercy," said a peevish man's voice, pleasantly startling me. The peevish man, Sherlock, got up from the settee and stalked across the room, carpet slippers flapping, to stand glowering down at me. He took a pinch of the ashes and headed towards his microscope, where he turned the gas lamp up for the brightest possible illumination, placed his sample on a glass slide, added a drop of water and a cover slip, then perched on a tall stool looking a bit storkish with the wings of his dressing gown trailing down. Having placed the slide in its bracket, he manoeuvred it into position, then peered into the instrument. He turned a focusing knob, peered some more, then lifted his unkempt, uncombed, unshaven head, speaking not to me, but to Miss Letitia Glover.

"Unless your sister was brown and furry," he said, "these are not her ashes."

Chapter the Third

Miss Letitia Glover sat speechless and visibly struggling against tears, whether more of relief or of consternation I could not tell.

Sherlock strode past her, opened the front door, bellowed, "Mrs. Hudson, hot water!" then without another word disappeared into his bedroom.

I applied myself to comforting Miss Glover, pulling my chair closer to hers, passing her a dainty handkerchief scented with lavender, and attempting to say something kind while succeeding only in being blunt and awkward. "You are caught in such a muddle, you must feel as if your head might explode."

Handkerchief to her face, Miss Glover nodded fervidly.

"Let us make a list, shall we, and see whether we can sort your problem out at all." Turning to a fresh page of tablet paper, and reading each line aloud as I penciled it, I wrote:

- Ashes are probably those of a large dog. Can we therefore assume Flossie is alive?

- If so, why did Cadogan Rudcliff attempt to deceive his sister-in-law?

- How many other people has he deceived, and again, why?

- If he is involved in some plot involving his wife's disappearance, what is its object?

- How did his first wife meet her demise?

- Where is Flossie and what has happened to her, if she still lives?

- How can we find out?

I stared at that final question for some time.

Miss Glover surprised me by speaking up calmly. "I should write to Caddie—all too appropriate a nickname, as it begins to appear he truly is a cad."

"But you will not yet betray that sentiment to him."

"No, I will address him as 'Dearest Caddie,' and sign my name 'Tish,' and ask questions about my sister's supposed demise, requesting details."

"Excellent." My brother's voice turned our heads. Exiting his bedroom, he walked towards us, impeccably washed, shaven, combed, and dressed in a tweed suit for traveling. Standing over us, he bowed slightly to read the list in my lap, then nodded in cool approval. "How to find out is indeed the salient problem," he said with no worse than his usual condescension, "as I must do so without exciting suspicion."

"We," I corrected him. If he thought he was going to take over this case just because it had gotten him up off the settee, he was sorely mistaken. "I take it you are going to Surrey? I intend to start in Belvidere."

I am sure I puzzled him, for he turned to me with eyebrows raised, but before I could explain, Miss Glover spoke up in the manner of a shy person facing an unpleasant matter. "Mr. Holmes, your fee—"

He turned to her and made his most gracious bow. "I shall accept none, as I greeted you, or rather, failed to greet you, in so unmannerly a fashion when you came in. Your problem has features of interest, Miss Glover, and I will give it my fullest attention. Have you a photograph of your sister?"

Apparently she did, for she bent to reach into her reticule. This interlude gave me opportunity to rise, retrieve my gloves, and make for the door. "Sherlock," I called back over my shoulder, "you may contact me through my club, and I will contact you through Mrs. Hudson. Au revoir!" Quitting the premises before he could argue, I ran down the stairs in high spirits.

A few hours later, looking quite the lady in a teal blue traveling outfit complete with tastefully matching hat,

I exited the Belvidere train station and headed towards Basilwether Park at a brisk walk, breathing deeply in appreciation of air invisible to the eye, unlike that of London. Within moments I reached the long drive that led to Basilwether Hall, where I promenaded beneath a leafy archway of old lime trees, greatly enjoying their green-scented shade and my bucolic, sootless surroundings—

Half in a dream, I heard the soft thud of hooves on grass, yet noticed the sound only in afterthought, so to speak, when an elegant horse and rider cantered out from between the tree trunks directly in front of me. My presence caused the horse to shy violently, as horses will when they discover something unexpected beneath their long noses. The rider, to his credit, kept his seat and brought his mount to a swerving halt, facing me. His spotless jodhpurs and boots, cutaway jacket and silk topper almost disguised him as a tall, grown man, but not quite. He had shot up but not yet filled out since the last time I had seen him, a year before; I saw him to be all hands and elbows and sandy hair unruly beneath his hat.

Rather hotly, as was understandable, he challenged me, "Miss, what are you doing here, on private land?"

"Why, hello to you, too, Tewky." And rather than giving him a maidenly simper, I grinned at him.

His jaw dropped, he leapt off of his horse, strode to me and shook my hand most warmly, all before he managed to speak. "You!" he gasped.

"Enola Holmes, at your service, Viscount Tewkes-bury, Marquess of Basilwether."

"So at last I get to know your name!"

"Indeed, Tewky." I had concealed it previously only to evade my brothers. On the same day that I had run away from home, coincidentally Tewky had done the same and we had met most misfortunately, both of us bound hand and foot, captured for ransom by cutthroats.

"Don't call me Tewky!" But he laughed out loud as he said it. "Still rocking the boat, aren't you!" In my efforts to use my corset stays to cut the twine binding my wrists, I had quite literally rocked the boat in which we had been held prisoner. "And I can see that you are still masquerading as a grown-up."

"As are you. Why are you not off at some exclusive boarding school?"

"I told my parents I would run away from any

boarding school, so I have tutors." He gave a whimsical smile. "They let me do much as I please, so long as I promise not to run away again. And you? Still gadding about with a small fortune taking the place of a bosom?"

He actually made me blush. "Lord Tewkesbury!" I protested.

"Please don't mind. I am far too delighted to be proper. I never imagined I would ever see you again!" Looping one arm through his horse's reins in order to lead it, he offered me the other arm like a gentleman. "What are you doing here, Enola?"

The way I took his arm was ladylike, but the way I answered was too candid for anyone's usual lady. "I came in search of illuminating gossip." I imagined my brother Sherlock was doing exactly the same by loitering in some Surrey pub, most likely impersonating a working man, with a beard on his face and a cap pulled down over his eyes, perhaps managing to steer the conversation towards skeletons in the closet of the Earl of Dunhench. Here at Basilwether Park, with my hand on Tewky's arm, I was pursuing the same end in a different way. My previous acquaintance with Viscount

Tewkesbury, Marquess of Basilwether, and the cama-
raderie we had shared for a few days on the run after
joining forces to escape the cutthroats, gave me an en-
trée into aristocratic gossip rather than that of garden-
ers and servants. It would be interesting to see which
might prove more useful.

"Gossip!" Tewky exclaimed as we walked. "About
whom?"

"Ah, that is exactly the problem. I must neither di-
vulge that information nor let you guess it. Indeed, I
must beg you to keep my nefarious purpose a secret."

"Grand and dandy!" Still boyish despite the fact
that he was now taller than I, he laughed again. "Enola,
you are a brick." And then, as we rounded a curve in the
drive and Basilwether Hall came into view, he asked,
"How long can you stay?"

"That depends."

"On gossip? Wouldn't you rather go horseback riding with me?"

I would far, far rather have gone horseback riding. But
honour forbade. I was, first and foremost, a professional

Perditorian. Just as my brother Sherlock bore the distinction of being the world's first Private Consulting Detective, I titled myself the world's first Scientific Perditorian—a finder of that which was lost. Having a client who was relying on me to find her sister—alive, it was to be hoped—I turned my back on the seductive outdoors, mounted Basilwether Hall's broad marble steps, advanced between Grecian pillars, and plied the heavy ram's-head knocker on the massive front door. The butler who responded, expressionless as all of them were, nevertheless managed to look askance at my lack of a carriage or an accompanying footman. Showing me into a front parlour to wait, taking my card upon his silver tray, and disappearing with it into the depths of the mansion, surely he expected his mistress to be "not at home." But I had written on the card a single enigmatic sentence: "We have met before." Surely the duchess's curiosity would prevail. And yes, the butler returned to show me in, revealing a certain inscrutable degree of astonishment.

The duchess awaited me in a conservatory/boudoir, its bay windows filled with potted plants, its furnishings luxurious, almost Persian. At first seated with dignity on a divan, the duchess gasped when she saw me and arose, hurrying towards me with open arms.

"Your Grace!" I exclaimed in protest, startled into an actual curtsy, which turned out to be an awkward manoeuvre in my modish skirt, narrow as was now the fashion. Her Grace, Tewkesbury's mother, wore a flounced and gathered gown that artfully flouted fashion, as was the prerogative of a duchess. All of its colours and textures—pale blue moiré taffeta, blue-grey surah, lavender voile—conspired to compliment the smooth silver-white wings of her hair above her fair and surprisingly youthful face. I would not have recognized her as the woman I had glimpsed last year, a wild-haired woman running half mad, her face harrowed by tears of terror for her "kidnapped" son.

"I did not think you would remember me!" I blurted.

"Not very clearly," she agreed cheerfully, sweeping me into her elegant arms, "but I know who you are, and what you have done for Tewky and me, and I could not be more delighted to meet you." She released me from a surprisingly strong hug. "Please, sit down and tell me all about yourself."

And so I did, over tea with marmalade tarts for the

next couple of hours. But—gentle reader, please for-give me—a great deal of what I told her were fibs and fictions. I affirmed that I was the younger sister of the great Sherlock Holmes, the world's first and only Pri-vate Consulting Detective—but, as Sherlock had never made public his birthplace and almost certainly never would, there was no risk in my telling her we came from Surrey. And I exalted our family onto the fringes of the peerage, titling our father as a knight, Sir Lucre-tius Adolphus Holmes, while my mother's cousin was a baronet. I said I had gone to a boarding school, naming one so prestigious it served as a portal into high soci-ety. One of the alumnae . . . if only I could remember names . . . she had married an earl . . .

"The Earl of Dunhench, dear?"

Yes, I quite believed that was correct!

"Caddie Rudcliff. I've known him since he was in short pants, my dear Enola, and I must say he sowed his wild oats with the best of them, and there was a bit of a shadow over the marriage. The girl was Myzella Haskell of the St. John's Haskells."

Ah. I was to learn about one of Caddie's earlier wives, not Flossie.

"Very respectable people, the Haskells, but quite scandalized, as were Caddie's relations. I did not attend the wedding, for it was private."

I blushed in genuine shock as I began to understand.

"But I heard she was quite lovely," added Her Grace charitably, "and of course a man of such rank needn't marry every girl he gets in trouble, so perhaps it was all right. She gave him two darling children, a girl and a boy, but most unfortunately they both expired, of diphtheria you know, and not long afterwards, she, also, passed away."

I expressed consternation, noted that the loss of children to diphtheria is sad but commonplace—often it has been known to take a family's entire brood—then inquired as to the cause of Myzella's demise.

"I don't know, dear, and I can't at all understand why or how it should have been a scandal, but it was treated like one. There was no funeral. She was cremated, can you imagine?"

Chapter the Fourth

Late that night—of course I had been invited to stay for dinner, for the night, for as long as I liked—quite late, after everyone was asleep, I sallied forth from my appointed bedroom barefoot, in a borrowed nightgown grand enough for a princess, carrying a candle for light. Not much noisier than a stork, the bird of prey I most resembled, I stalked along a hallway with floorboards polished to such a shine that they reflected the glow of my candle flame, then down the lushly carpeted main stairway, and thus into the duchess's library, not to be confused with the duke's library on the opposite side of the hall. The duke, by the way, despite being a duke, had been quite pleasant to me at dinner. These were very posh people, to have more than one library. I wondered whether the duke's was finer than his wife's, and almost went to see, but managed to restrain myself, exhorting myself to attend to the business of being a Perditorian.

Lighting a gas lamp with a match from the cut-glass holder standing by, I opened the duchess's rosewood rolltop desk and readily found her address book, a dainty volume covered in figured dimity and edged with scalloped lace. The duchess, I saw with approval, had kept it up to date, its alphabetized pages quite thick with tiny, formal handwriting almost as neat as engraving. Sitting at the desk to consult it, I started doing what would not have been polite while conversing with Her Grace: I took notes.

The address book provided me with full names, correctly spelt: Cadogan Burr Rudcliff number two in Roman numerals. Myzella Odilon Rudcliff née Haskell. Felicity Fay Rudcliff née Glover.

Then I started delving. Quite wanting to find out what, exactly, had happened to Myzella in case it might enlighten me concerning Flossie's whereabouts, I wrote down names and addresses of all Haskells, taking special note of those who lived in and near St. John's, very likely Myzella's relatives, perhaps even her siblings. That finished, I went on to do the same regarding the Rudcliffs of Dunhench—

The library door opened.

I had not prepared an excuse for my being there, had not planned an escape route or a hiding place, had not even been listening for approaching footsteps, and I felt inexcusably stupid. The only intelligent thing I could do by way of compensation was to carry on as if I had every right to be copying names and addresses out of the duchess's private records in the middle of the night. Therefore I managed—just barely—to keep myself from clutching my papers or jumping and squeaking like a frightened schoolgirl. I schooled my face into a merely inquiring expression before I looked up to see who had come in.

In a nightgown far plainer than mine, with his

sandy-coloured hair wildly out of control, carrying a candle of his own, the duke's son, heir, and only living scion stood over me.

Although not exactly glad to see him under the circumstances, still, I smiled. "Tewky!"

"Don't call me that! What an absurd nightgown. You look like a giraffe in ruffles."

"I quite agree, but it's what your mother loaned me."

"Couldn't you sleep in it? What are you doing out of bed?"

"I might ask you the same question."

"I came downstairs to stave off starvation by pilfering from the larder, and then I saw your light leaking under the library door. What are *you* pilfering?" He stepped closer, squinting at my notes, and to keep myself from guiltily hiding them from him, I put my hands in my lap.

"Myzella Rudcliff? I've heard that name," he remarked. "The old ladies talk about her . . . Isn't she the one who married Dunhench?" He would make as eager a gossip as his mother someday. "She was his first wife. She's supposed to have died . . ."

How blunt, how brave, how modern of him to speak that forbidden word!

". . . but there wasn't any proper funeral—"

"What do you mean?"

"She wasn't buried. The body was burned up or something. But the wagging tongues say really she didn't die; she got taken away in a black barouche."

"What does *that* mean?"

"Um, I don't know." He looked sheepish. "I thought you would."

"I do not know, but I quite plan to find out." Putting the address book away and folding my papers, I stood up. Speaking mostly to myself, I murmured, "I will need a pseudonym."

"Ermintrude," said Tewky promptly.

He spoke with such decision that, startled, I laughed out loud. "Whatever for?"

"Because you look like an Ermintrude. I haven't any cousins. You can be my cousin, Ermintrude Basilwether. It rolls nicely off the tongue, do you not think so?"

I thought it was a mouthful. "Preposterous," I said,

then regretfully declined to join him in raiding the larder; I went back to bed.

Even though I could trust Tewky to keep my dubious nocturnal activities a secret, still, I left the next morning, bidding the duchess a gracious adieu and tendering my regrets while telling her that I had urgent business elsewhere. I hurried to Belvidere Station and boarded a train.

I was going to Surrey. But as London lay directly along the way, I stopped there, first at my club to change into fresh clothing—quite a nice day dress in oak-green velveteen with a grass-green faille overskirt gathered up into scallops. A hat trimmed with wired loops of green ribbon matched nicely. I packed a few things into a carpetbag, then inquired at the front desk whether there had been any communication from Sherlock, which there had not.

My second stop was at 221 Baker Street to ask Mrs. Hudson whether she had heard anything from him. She had not. But whilst riding on the train from Belvidere I had composed a letter to him, which I left for her to give him in case he returned anytime soon. It read:

Dearest Inquisitive Brother,

Interestingly, it would seem that the first Dunhench wife, née Myzella Haskell, came to the same fate as the second one: cremation. However, it is rumoured that she did not actually die, but was sent away in a black barouche, whatever that implies. As it sounds rather sinister, I wonder whether the same happened to the second wife, Letitia Glover's sister? I intend to scrutinize death certificates for both unfortunate wives. Therefore I will be a genealogical researcher named Ermintrude Basilwether lodging at Threefinches or nearby, should you care to look me up.

Your Loving Sister

I neither signed my name nor addressed Sherlock by his. One must at least attempt to be discreet lest our correspondence stray into hands other than those of Mrs. Hudson. Having left this missive with her, I took the underground—its Baker Street station so convenient to my brother's residence! Yet, to my knowledge, he never used it. This subterranean transport whisked me to Victoria Station, where I caught the next train to Dorking, Surrey.

My journey was uneventful, and I arrived at Dorking—a market town rather smaller than I expected—in time for a late luncheon at none too fancy an eatery. After a bowl of beef stew and one of bread pudding—such was the available fare—I walked back to the station to rent a bicycle, but I was told, with raised eyebrows, that no such newfangled self-propelled transportation was to be had, and I was directed to the livery stables next door.

There, a tobacco-chewing personage with alarmingly protuberant side whiskers informed me that, while gigs, buggies, and broughams were available in plenty, no drivers were available at the moment. "'Ow in the world do yer come to be traveling by yerself, miss?" he added, not inquiring so much as disapproving.

"Upon my own two feet," I replied, rather more tartly than I should have.

"Be yer one of them suffragists?"

"Like my mother before me."

"Well, yer should 'ave a man wid you just the same for ter 'andle 'orses and such."

"I can handle a horse," I snapped. "I will drive myself." My own irritation had convinced me that this was so. After all, had I not once successfully driven a hansom cab through London traffic? And had I not read *Black Beauty* innumerable times as a child?

"No, miss, ye don't hunnerstand," said Side Whiskers in an exceedingly patronizing tone. "The driver is ter bring the 'orse an' rig back 'ere to the stable after yer gets to—where did yer say yer were going?"

"Threefinches. How far away is that?" I inquired, thinking I might walk.

"A good ten-twelve miles."

So much for walking. "Surely I will find an inn there, with stabling for the horse?" It was a pity, I thought, that horses, unlike bicycles, could not simply be leaned against a tree until needed.

Once more I saw eyebrows elevate. "At's true, miss, but to pay me by the day, an' stablin' on top of that—"

I produced substantial money, thus squelching protest, and the upshot was that I soon found myself and my minimal luggage in, or rather on top of, something called a "gig," with the reins of a horse in my kid-gloved hands. The gig stood so high on two enormous wheels that I looked down on the horse, which I supposed was preferable to viewing its posterior. It was a horse of a different colour—taupe, with a yellowish cast. "What's his name?" I asked Side Whiskers, who stood holding the bridle.

The man turned away, and not for the first time I sensed that he was hiding mirth, although for what reason I could not imagine. "'Ee's a mare," he said, "and 'er name is Jezzie, ain't that right, Jezzie?" He gave her bridle what seemed to be an admonishing sort of shake.

Then he let go of it, and we were off. Jezzie—or did the man perhaps mean Jessie; had I misunderstood? Jessie or Jezzie took matters into her own hands, or perhaps I should say onto her own hooves, stepping out immediately at a brisk trot even though I tightened the reins. Luckily we were headed in the proper direction, and almost before I knew it we were out of Dorking, speeding down a country road like a—like a whirli-gig, of course. The gig's high wheels whizzed over the rutted road, their motion and the height of my perch making me feel quite dizzy.

I hauled harder on the reins, trying to slow down the yellow mare, but her only response was to arch her neck—quite prettily, I admit—and clip-clop more smartly, lifting her feet like a Hackney. Folk working in their cottage gardens gaped as we flashed past. I am sure that Jezzie and the gig and I made quite a picturesque sight in that bucolic setting of golden fields and green hedges, but I failed to appreciate the artistic effect, not with my hat coming loose, its wide brim lifted by the wind, and with the horse foaming at the mouth so that bits of spume flew into my face like white butterflies of ill omen. Jezzie showed every sign of wanting to break into a gallop, and if she did, she would surely land us in a ditch. Even as she trotted, the tall gig swayed whilst going uphill, swooped its way downhill, and wildly slewed every time we rounded a curve. I admit that my innards quite sloshed with fear, nay, panic, and I heartily wished I had never said I knew how to drive a horse. What was the use of my holding the reins if Jezzie thumbed her nose at them?

Again, an impossible metaphor. But such scholarly

thoughts did no good; one must take action. I hauled on the reins to my utmost, and then, in desperation, I alternated them, left-right-left-right, in a kind of seesaw attempt to get Jezzie's attention.

Thus I managed to hold the willful yellow beast to her rampaging trot. But then, as we rounded yet another terrifying curve, to my hazy gaze appeared a village ahead—Threefinches, already? It had to be. Somehow I simply *had* to get Jezzie to slow down—

No, worse! I had to get the diabolical horse to *stop*, so that I could get off! Otherwise she would carry me on and on and on, to Currywort and Harechase and heaven only knew where.

Confound the horse, whose full name, I suddenly realized, had to be Jezebel! I was not to be made a fool of by a runaway mare! My worries flipped into wrath so suddenly that without conscious thought I stood up in order to prepare for a showdown. I threw my parasol and carpetbag over the side of the gig, and then, just as it reached the edge of Threefinches, I sawed at the reins with all my strength, wanting only to slow the accursed Jezebel sufficiently so that I could join my belongings. That failing, I grasped the reins with one hand, yanked them to my utmost, and with the other hand I seized the whip and hit Jezzie's impudent backside with it.

The result was gratifying, in a way. The mare bucked, kicked, and reared, interrupting her forward momentum enough for me to jump out of the gig, which, rearing along with her, would have made a projectile of me in any case. Lest I be injured by too much upward momentum, I dove for the grassy roadside.

Landing flat with a *whumph* and with my face in the grass, I rolled over just in time to lift my head, now hatless, and watch Jezebel paw the ground, reverse direction, and leap into her long-desired gallop, whirling the empty gig back towards Dorking and, presumably, her stable.

Chapter the Fifth

I laid my head sideways on the ground, just for a moment, to rest. At the same time I heard tramping feet approaching me from behind, accompanied by a babble of masculine voices.

"Sent the lydy flyin', it did."

"Could've broke 'er neck."

"Didjer see that yeller horse go?"

"That weren't no 'orse, that were a yeller greyhound."

"Is the lydy dead?"

"Is she fainted?"

Indignant, I wanted to sit up and say I was not so easily killed and I never fainted, but to my surprise my body would not obey me. I merely stirred and murmured.

"She's moving."

I saw the clodhopper boots of common men surrounding me and smelled alcohol on the breath of those leaning over me.

"Let's get 'er inside."

"Somebody go fer the doctor."

Strong hands, not ungentle, seized me by the feet and shoulders. I could have kicked and yelled—I felt strong enough now—but my mind had started to function, realizing that I was about to be carried into a pub, for only in a public house, or pub, would workmen be drinking in the daytime. And normally no woman of good repute would enter a pub, or if she did, she would be jeered at until she retreated. But, my avid brain realized, fate in the form of Jezebel had given me opportunity to spend some time inside a pub—no, in *the* pub, most likely the only pub in Threefinches!

So I closed my eyes and pretended to be rather more helpless than I was as the men hauled me inside and laid me down on a high-backed bench by the hearth. Someone brought something pungent in lieu of smelling salts, but I shook my head, pushed the malodourous hand away, opened my eyes, and sat up, acting as if it were a great effort for me to do so. A burly, bearded man in an apron, undoubtedly the publican who kept the place, came running with a pillow for my back, and I thanked him with a gracious smile.

"Will ye have a nip of brandy, lydy?"

"No, thank you. Water, please."

"Jack! Water for the lydy!" he bellowed to some underling, and he remained nearby as I managed, with hands that genuinely trembled, to remove my gloves. Their thin kidskin leather was ruined by the mauling it had taken from Jezebel's reins, and my hands were red and sore; doubtless they would bruise. Grateful for the cool glass, I held it in both hands and sipped, looking around me. Half of the denizens of the place, like the owner, stood in a semicircle staring at me not unpleasantly, while the rest did the same from seats at the rustic tables—all but one. A tall man with beard stubble on his chin and quite a shock of coarse brownish-grey hair hiding his forehead had withdrawn to a table by the wall, where he devoted his attention to his mug of ale, or stout, or whatever noxious brew he might fancy.

I said brightly to the tavern-keeper, "I believe I would like to stand up."

"Now, why not wait for the doctor, lydy—"

But taking hold of his arm, as he stood within my reach, I got to my feet with reasonable steadiness. There were muted cheers from the onlookers. Nodding and simpering at the men all around me, I lilted, "Thank you so much. Do you suppose anyone could go out and fetch my bag, and my hat and parasol? I believe they fell along the—"

Already half a dozen would-be heroes were stampeding towards the door. Yet, if I had walked in here under my own power, any request for help would have been met with deepest suspicion. Such is life: odd.

Trying not to smile too widely, not to show my amusement, I proposed to the publican, still holding his arm, "I should like to try a little walk around the room."

"If'n yer sure yer not hurt, lydy."

"I feel quite restored by your hospitality." With mincing steps I led him forward, leaning on his arm slightly from time to time to make him feel needed.

Halfway around the room I reached the vicinity of the tall, scruffy workingman (to judge by his coarse and common clothing) who was hiding his face under his forelock. Beside the table at which he was seated, I paused and said to the publican as if I had just that moment thought of it, "I suppose I am going to need a ride to the inn. There is an inn?"

"Ye mean yer traveling by *yerself,* miss?" Suddenly I was no longer a "lydy," and my doughty escort's eyebrows shot up all too much like those of Side Whiskers.

Just barely managing to retain sweetness of tone, I asked, "Why, what did you think I was doing?"

"I thought yer were having a spin, and ye got spun." At least this man had a sense of humour. "Ye can't be thinking of staying overnight at a public lodging place all by yerself—"

I interrupted somewhat less sweetly. "Why, where should I stay, then, in a haystack? Surely you can recommend a reputable inn where I shall be quite safe."

"There ain't but the one hereabouts to serve all comers!"

I am sure he would have expostulated further, but just then a herd of men thundered into the pub with my hat, my carpetbag, my parasol, and a youth who cried, "The doctor can't come! He's having a baby!"

Laughter and general hubbub ensued, distracting the attention of my escort, the publican. I took the opportunity to swing my foot at the morose-looking, none-too-clean man seated at the table beside me. Naturally, he looked up. Not at all naturally for one who has just been kicked in the shin, his grey eyes twinkled. Slowly he pushed away from his table and got to his clodhopper-clad feet.

"It ain't but a middling walk," he said in a thick country accent, as if he had pebbles in his mouth. "Ain't no trouble fer me to show yer the way, missus. I'll carry yer bag."

We waited until we got well away from the pub before either of us spoke. Then, in his normal, aristocratic tone Sherlock said, "Well done, Enola, and remarkably well planned that you should drop in at the public house that way."

I sighed, admitting, "It wasn't planned."

"Surely it is not mere coincidence that you are

wearing a green frock upon which grass stains do not show?"

I looked down at my faille overskirt, its delicate fabric shredded, and grimaced.

My brother added, "Your hat, also, looks a bit the worse for wear."

Its wired ribbons had been badly smashed, but I had restored them as best I could before putting the hat back on my head, and I considered that there was no further need for Sherlock to chaff me. "I've been made a fool of. Enough. Have you found out anything whilst lingering at the pub? Keep your voice low," I added, because as we progressed into the village proper we were walking directly in front of cheek-to-jowl cottages, their gable windows frowning out from under remarkably low wraparound roofs so that they resembled washerwomen in headscarves.

"I have found out principally that Rudcliff has the reputation of being quite a womanizer." Sherlock did indeed keep his voice low. "Very few women, however, die and are cremated because their husbands are unfaithful. Did you come here merely to accost me?"

"No. I have made my own inquiries. It is rumoured

that the first Lady Rudcliff, supposedly deceased, was actually, and I quote, 'taken away in a black barouche.'"

Sherlock gave a low whistle, and although I could not see his eyebrows under his rustic forelock, I dare say they were lifted like wings.

"End quote," I said rather testily. "What, pray tell, does the phrase 'black barouche' imply?" Quite evidently he knew.

"It would be premature for me to say without further evidence, especially as Rudcliff remarried."

"Some men like to get married, Sherlock."

He gave me a "pshaw" look. "Had he any children by the first wife?"

"Two, but neither lived."

"Then he must desire an heir. So why would he dispose of his first wife, let alone his second?" Sherlock kept his voice down to a murmur, but his tone was knife-sharp. "It is quite preposterous."

"*What* is quite preposterous?"

But not another word would he say.

Chapter the Sixth

The inn was of course called The Three Finches, as could be seen by three none-too-artistic wooden cut-outs of birds above the front door on a half-timbered wall of such antiquity that the hostel might have been there since the times of the Tudors. The stones of the front steps were partly worn away by the feet of count-less travelers.

Snatching off his cap to reveal his shaggy wig, Sherlock carried my carpetbag up those steps and into the front hallway of the inn for me, set it down there, then humbly bowed his head and tugged his forelock. Into his other, awaiting hand I deposited a few coins. "Thank you, my good man," I told him blandly, adding, seemingly as an afterthought, "What might your name be?"

"Tom Dubbs, miss." Bobbing, he spoke once more as if he had a mouth full of marbles.

"Tom Dubbs. And where do you lodge?"

"In the stables behind the pub, miss."

"Very well, if I have need of you, I will send for you. My name, by the way, is The Honourable Miss Ermintrude Basilwether." Dismissing him with a nod and a secret smile as I glanced around The Three Finches, I heard him shut the door as he let himself out.

The Three Finches showed every sign of offering rather countrified accommodations, right down to crockery dogs guarding each end of the mantelpiece. Before me rose a steep and narrow stairway. To one side of me a billiard room was visible through an open door, and to the other side a dining room with a single large table adorned by a red-checked cloth. Judging from the clatter and chatter I heard coming from the regions behind it, the people running the inn were busy in the kitchen.

A hand bell stood on the hallway table. I picked it up and rang it until the aproned innkeeper arrived. He could have looked fat and jolly as an innkeeper should if it were not that he was scowling. Perhaps I had rung the bell too hard.

As he did not greet me, I greeted him. "Hallo, my good man. Have you a room available for me?"

Although to me my request seemed quite plain and simple, the innkeeper walked up to me and stared, his scowl deepening into a frown, as if he found it incomprehensible.

So I tried again, with no change in my airy tone, which was unwise. I should have spoken meekly and evinced a tempting amount of cash. Instead, I said breezily, "I would like to rent a room. Perhaps for several days."

The man's mouth, which resembled a mail slot with jowls, moved several times before he spoke. "Where's yer 'usband?"

"No husband. Just me."

"Wot habout yer maid, yer governess, sumphin' like that?"

Beginning to comprehend his hesitation, I became testy. "Or my mother, I suppose? No. There are just three of us. Me, myself, and I."

He shook his head and turned back towards the kitchen, but I seized him by his shirt sleeve. "Are there no rooms available in this inn?"

"Not fer no single female travelin' alone. I can't be 'eld responsible fer what might 'appen."

Confound everything, I should have expected and prepared myself for this sort of attitude from an ox of a country innkeeper; I should have planned to coax, soothe, and bribe, but instead I had let my temper run away with me rather as Jezzie had done. "Do your rooms not have locks on the doors?" I quite wanted to produce my dagger and flourish it in front of the stubborn man's face to show him that I was capable of defending myself, but I knew I would be misunderstood. Instead, I sharpened my aristocratic tone. "Do you not understand who I am? You are speaking with The Honourable Ermintrude Basilwether, niece of—have you never heard of the Duke and Duchess of Basilwether?"

"Huh. Hif that's true, then stay wit some of yer hoighty-toighty friends."

"Very well, I will!" With no idea whether I was brilliantly seizing an opportunity or making myself even more of a fool than already was apparent, I demanded, "If you refuse to provide hospitality, the least you can do is provide transportation. Find someone to drive me to Dunhench Hall."

Glad to be rid of me, I suppose, the innkeeper supplied an ancient victoria with a similarly venerable horse and driver. Seated inside, I had no opportunity to talk with the latter, so I passed the time by looking about me. Surrey offered vistas of soft hills like billows on a sunny green ocean studded with cozy white boats—cottages, I mean, each with its flower garden and rose beds and milk cow, between which meandered peaceful waterways decked with lily pads. This was a verdant, comfortable corner of England where no dangers should lurk.

Or so I thought until I saw Dunhench Hall.

The moment I caught sight of its tall black chimneys

and grey stone gables looming amidst copper beeches, I thought it looked more as if it belonged amidst windy heaths, crags, and tors than here. When my driver turned in at the drive, I saw heavy wrought-iron gates supported by massive stone pillars of great age, blotched by lichens and topped by carved stone effigies appearing to be the heads of deer, although their antlers had broken off like the limbs of some of the gnarled trees that lined the drive.

The central part of the manse, when it came into view, seemed also to be of great age, except that modern windows had been installed in its thick, ivy-draped stone walls. I could see also that the wings to each side had been added more recently, along with a pillared portico above the old oak doors.

All the windows stood blank, with their draperies drawn, and on each of the double front doors hung a yew wreath ribboned in black.

At a sedate trot my victoria rounded the circular drive leading under the portico. I rather expected to see a fountain beautifying the grass plot at the hub of the circle, but instead, there on a pedestal stood a life-size statue of melodramatic manly pulchritude I took to be the romantic poet and expatriate Lord Byron. An interesting choice of subject—but I had no time to consider its implications. My rickety victoria halted; carrying my own carpetbag, I got out; my driver pulled away at once; and there in front of Dunhench Hall I stood with no one to greet me, which was perhaps a good thing, as I had no idea how to explain my presence. Had I foreseen coming here, I should have worn mourning. Even the statue of the poet, I noted with muted surprise and amusement, wore a black armband. And the bell was hung. A real brass bell suspended to one side of the double doors, it had crape streamers trailing from the clapper, which had been wrapped to muffle it so that it could not be rung.

Ascending a few shallow steps of black granite, I observed that the funereal wreaths on the doors covered their knockers. This stately residence was in mourning with a vengeance, meaning that the grieving family was not to be disturbed by anyone ringing the bell or knocking on the door. I surmised that those who had business here were to let themselves in.

I tried one of the doorknobs, and it yielded to my hand.

Well, nothing good could come of my standing out here. And to explain my presence, the most plausible way might be with portions of the truth.

Opening the door, I slipped inside, then quite naturally stopped to gaze upward, where high mullion windows remained undraped, letting in light enough so that I could see a tall peaked roof with timbers running across it. This was indeed a hoary old hall, a fitting place for Beowulf to have feasted in. On all sides the walls showed the dull glint of antique armaments—broadswords, battle-axes, pikes, cutlasses, samurai swords, and wicked-looking Moorish scimitars. Above the weaponry hung a close-ranked array of ancestral portraits dignified by swags of black crape. The most ancient ones were too small and dark to see clearly, but above a huge fireplace (its mantel draped in black) hung a large, modern oil-painted portrait of a handsome man—seemingly Lord Byron again? Softly, I walked closer to inspect the painting, peering at it, doubting that Byron had ever worn any military uniform, let alone such a vision of gold braid and epaulettes, crimson sash and saber. Even its gilt frame, elaborate to the point of being baroque, could not detract from the forceful presence of that handsome male image.

On the bottom of the frame I saw an engraved metal plaque probably naming the painting's subject. I leaned forward, squinting to read it in the dim light—

Hollow and echoing out of the shadows of Dunhench Hall spoke a sepulchral voice. "*Who* are *you*?"

I admit I leapt like a startled deer, turning in midair towards that which had alarmed me.

In the shadows, I saw first a white shirt front, and then, as the man walked towards me, an impeccably clad figure so tall it could have been Sherlock—but no. I could now see a long, deferential face with an unfortunate nose and prominent, lugubrious eyes like those of a Pekingese.

"Miss?" inquired the butler—for he had to be the butler, standing with his hands behind his back, bowing slightly.

Reassuring myself that shadows hid the destruction Jezzie had wrought upon my costume, "I am The Honourable Ermintrude Basilwether," I answered as haughtily as I very well could, considering that I wanted to smile. "And you?"

"Brindle, Miss Basilwether. I regret to inform you that the family is not receiving visitors, miss."

"I assure you, Brindle, had I been aware the house was in mourning, I would never have ventured here," I fibbed, allowing my tone to grow a trifle friendlier, "but now that I am here, I must impose upon Dunhench hospitality, as my man has already driven away."

His lapdog eyes betrayed consternation, although the rest of his face remained impassive. "I am afraid I do not quite understand, miss."

I assumed an air of high-class impatience held in check. "Might I be seated and partake of some refreshment after my long journey?"

"Indeed, Miss, er, Basilwether. Of course, miss." After taking my carpetbag and parasol to set them aside, he showed me through the tall, gloomy hall and into a parlour of less imposing size but just as gloomy, what with the drapes drawn and all the mirrors covered with black crape. Seating me at a pedestal table, he excused himself and hurried out. My chair, a tall and stalwart oaken antique, was none too comfortable, but I waited patiently, glad of a chance to think. My intention had been to stay at The Three Finches Inn, but might I not, after all, find out more at Dunhench Hall?

I had decided I most certainly must try when tea arrived. Carrying a well-laden tray, in bustled a stout, middle-aged, smiling woman who exuded a comfortable, motherly air despite her dull black bombazine dress. "I'm Dawson, the housekeeper, miss," she said, bobbing her head to me as she set down the tray and started laying out an admirable refection for me: a cup of beef bouillon, a plate of sandwiches, buttery pound cake, vanilla wafers, salted almonds, lemonade, chocolate-covered cherries, and, of course, tea. Standing by with her hands folded over her apron, she nodded approval as, drawing off my gloves and laying them aside, I ate far more heartily than a lady ought.

"Have you come a long way, miss?" she asked as she poured for me.

"Only from London, but I have been exceedingly vexed and insulted." I had decided to act the part of an offended upper-class eccentric. "I traveled to Three-finches with the simple and innocent purpose of doing some genealogical research, and I quite expected to stop at the inn, but no sooner had I arrived than they sent me packing as if they thought me a woman of ill repute! Merely because I am of age to travel without a chaperone!"

Like a large black hen, Dawson made comfortable clucking sounds. Also, she began to show signs of scuttling away, but I forestalled her.

"Dawson, could you tell me, please, who has passed away to put this house in mourning?"

Her folded hands became prayerful. "Most unhappily, Lady Felicity Dunhench, miss."

"Oh, dear! Lady Dunhench herself? I am so sorry to hear of it. Was she well advanced in years?"

Shaking her head, Dawson began to show signs of distress. "No, miss, quite the opposite. A sweet young lady she was, taken away by a fearsome fever all sudden, within a day."

I placed my hands to my mouth in feigned horror. The gentle reader will understand I had to pretend utter ignorance of anything to do with this matter. "How dreadful! When did this happen?"

"Just this Sunday past, like the angel she was."

"So recently? The funeral must have been only yesterday!"

Instead of answering, Dawson blurted, "Excuse me, miss," and bolted out of the room as if she smelled something burning. While the parlour door was still closing behind her I shot to my feet, crossed the room as noiselessly as possible, and eavesdropped, hoping conversation would ensue nearby.

It did. I heard the sepulchral tones of the butler, then the forthright voice of the housekeeper saying more audibly, "Passed her along to us from the inn, they did, afraid she might make a scandal, her with her skirt torn and her hat all knocked about like she been in a rumpus."

I confess I blushed—for I had hoped my dishevelment had gone unnoticed—but I kept listening. The butler had spoken, and the housekeeper was replying, "She seems a right enough sort. Says she's just doing some sort of gene—genie—some kind of research. But the last thing we need right now is a houseguest! What's his lordship going to say when he sees her at the dinner table?"

"Sees who?" drawled an aristocratic, sardonic voice, male, that I had not heard before.

"Your Lordship!" gasped both housekeeper and butler simultaneously.

At times, I can be as prudent as the next person. This was one of those times. Soundlessly I abandoned my eavesdropping and retreated to the parlour table where I was supposed to be. As I seated myself, slipping my gloves back on and trying to assume a ladylike languor, I considered what an ironic blessing it was that the mirrors all around the room were covered—supposedly so that the soul of the departed might not blunder into one and get trapped inside the house, and in actuality so that I could not see what a fright I looked.

A moment later, as I dreaded and expected, the parlour door opened and the Earl of Dunhench made his entrance.

Chapter the Seventh

Soberly and impeccably clad in a grey broadcloth suit with a black mourning band around one sleeve, he posed in the doorway much as he must have posed for the portrait in the great hall; even minus his military regalia I recognized him at once, and acknowledged him to be nigh on swoonably handsome. Yet I did not much like the way he coolly looked me up and down, although I suppose it was to be expected; after all, I was a stranger invading his home.

After his pause, he crossed the short distance between us. "Miss Ermintrude Basilwether?"

I arose, but rather than curtseying, I offered him my gloved hand to shake. I wanted to put him off-balance a bit. But it was he who unbalanced me. Taking my outstretched hand in his, he bowed over it and kissed it.

Hastily I withdrew it, feeling the heat of a rosy blush in my face. "My lord!" I twittered, for my voice had shot up an octave or two, and my knees folded without my permission, seating me in my chair.

"Let us have some light in here," he said, sounding impatient with the funereal gloom. He lit the table lamp, then sat across from me. "Please, Miss Basilwether, do tell me what adventure has befallen you to disorder your charming clothing?"

I heard no mockery in his voice, so why not? I told him my tale nearly in full, omitting only my actual intentions and my encounter with Sherlock. I intended to amuse the earl, and I did; he smiled at my description of Side Whiskers, grinned when I told him how Jezzie had jettisoned me in front of the pub, and chuckled over my contretemps with the innkeeper. If he were not constrained by being in mourning, I think he would have laughed out loud.

Yet I think only decorum, not grief, restrained him. While talking I had been watching his dark eyes nearly as black as his hair, and fascinating eyes they were: intelligent, lustrous, large, widely spaced over high cheekbones. His portrait did not do justice to the curious gleam I sometimes glimpsed in them; I think no painter could. Outwardly, the Earl of Dunhench, impeccably correct, crisp of collar and smiling of face, looked like a paragon of civilized good taste. But something in the glint of his eyes hinted otherwise.

That, and something in his manner, some exceeding force of self. As I explained how I had arrived at Dunhench Hall and began to apologize for my intrusion, he interrupted. "Of course you must stop here for as long as you like; what else are you to do? But I quite forbid you to wear black; you are the only bright and interesting object I have seen in days. I will instruct Dawson to take the greatest good care of you." He stood up, bowed, and left the room before I could get my mouth closed to speak.

The good Dawson commenced her care of me by leading me on a grand tour of Dunhench Hall, omitting nothing except, of course, the backstairs haunts of the servants. But morning room, main parlour, dining room, drawing room (more accurately *with*drawing room, where ladies could go to get away from cigar smoke), music room (its piano closed and draped with crape), billiard room, gun room, and library all were shown to me, and I made sure to smile, gaze, gasp, and exclaim as if I had never in my life seen any home so grand. Dunhench Hall really was in a class of its own in regard to elk antlers sprouting from the scagliola walls and bearskins on the parquet floors. But for me, the best was yet to come. We went up the rose-carpeted front stairs and into a moist, heavenly scented glass-roofed conservatory, flooded with sunlight (I suppose a greenhouse is exempt from being draped with crape) off of which opened a private parlour where, I suppose, Lord and Lady Rudcliff could enjoy the orchids in comfort.

On the walls of this pleasant room hung a number of light and airy watercolour paintings, quite a relief to my eyes after the dark and dour oil portraits downstairs. "Oh, I love watercolours," I exclaimed quite truthfully, admiring each in turn: Child with a puppy, boat beneath a willow, girl in a rose garden, woman reading, cat in a window—terribly conventional subjects, yet beautifully done with grace of line and an unfailing eye for composition.

"Who painted these?" I cried, failing to find a signature on any of them.

"Why, Lady Dunhench did, Miss Basilwether." Dawson sounded subdued, mentioning the recently dear departed. "Quite the artist she was. Shall we go on? I believe you will like way the guest accommodations have been arranged."

I responded with the requisite enthusiasm, and we worked our way down a long corridor of bedrooms decorated and designated according to all the hues of the rainbow, although the red bedroom was called The Poppy Room, the orange one was Apricot, et cetera. All were indeed marvels to behold if one fancied such a close conspiracy of the same colour in different patterns for walls, floors, drapes, lamps, and bedcovers.

"Which one would you prefer to have, dear? Um, Miss Basilwether?"

"Oh, I cannot possibly make up my mind!"

"We'll put you in The Fern Room, to match your dress."

"I quite like green," I acknowledged, "but this dress is ruined."

"Not at all, dear—I mean, Miss Basilwether. We can replace that overskirt in two shakes of a little lamb's tail." Solicitously she took me by the elbow, propelling me down the corridor, then plied a key from the ring of them she carried on her belt, letting me into yet another room—or suite of rooms: boudoir, dressing room, bedroom, decorated with exquisite taste in a range of soothing colours: peach, ecru, soft pink, cream, pale yellow, white. I saw delicate "ladies' chairs," carved, but with upholstered circular backs and seats, a couch that curved around a circular ottoman, lacy handmade lampshades. Over the dressing table hung a circular mirror framed in golden scallops. A remarkable white bedstead seemed designed to cup the sleeper almost like a boat. Even the wardrobes were painted white.

Dawson bustled to the wardrobes and opened them, but I stood still, my gaze fixed upon a large watercolour supported by an easel as if it had just been finished. "Are these Lady Dunhench's rooms?" I asked, feeling a bit peculiar at the thought, my voice sinking to a whisper as if I might disturb a ghost.

"Yes, Miss Basilwether." Dawson plucked garments from the wardrobe.

"And she painted this watercolour?"

"Yes, miss."

Indeed, Lady Felicity's boudoir might better have been termed a studio, for it was fitted out with tables, baskets, and lazy Susans full of supplies. But the painting I was studying seemed oddly unlike any of the others I had seen of hers. It depicted a woman in a russet habit riding a bay horse, with a cottage and woods in the background, but the composition was dreadful. The horse's nose nearly exited the left-hand side of the painting, leading the viewer's eye outward and away, quite an elementary mistake. Nor did the painter seem interested in what a horse looked like, or a cottage; both were crudely done. And the background was filled with woods, flat and monotonous—why not a hill or two, some distant sheep, a vista? Even the trees of the woods looked clumsy, with straight limbs jutting at odd angles instead of forming graceful curves. I frowned, trying to make excuses for the talented Lady Felicity.

"Was this done a long time ago?" I asked Dawson.

Arms loaded with clothing, she turned towards me. "That? No, the paint's hardly dry on that, miss. She did it the day she . . ." Dawson choked, failing to finish her sentence, and hustled past me without looking at the painting, seeming suddenly in a great hurry to exit the unfortunate lady's chambers. "This way, miss," she directed me, her voice quivering.

Following her out of the door, I finally realized her intention. "Surely you cannot expect me to wear the clothing of your so misfortunately expired mistress!"

"Why not, dearie? What does she need them for now?" Dawson sounded unwontedly familiar. More; she sounded, although quite calm, a bit hysterical.

"But I—I am quite tall, you know."

"It won't matter. Nothing matters."

More than a bit hysterical. I judged it best to be silent, trailing after her to The Fern Room, following, like a good donkey, where I was led. But my mind had taken off galloping in several directions.

Dawson had a footman bring up my carpetbag and parasol and sent for a maid named Jill. Listening to Dawson give Jill some rather alarming instructions, I bent over so that neither would see what I was doing, slipped my dagger out of my corset and hid it deep in my carpetbag, firmly and silently assuring myself that it was unlikely Jill would discover that my bosom was filled with papers, pound notes, and other supplies; all should now be well.

Dawson helped me out of my green dress while Jill hung up my spare dress, a ruched nankeen frock, declaring it charming but not formal enough for dinner. Then, while Dawson set to work with scissors, needle, and thread, replacing my ripped overskirt with a similar one "borrowed" from one of the purloined gowns, Jill took on the challenge of making me presentable to dine with the earl, trying Flossie's evening gowns on me.

Although they accommodated my girth, they were, as I had predicted, too short for me, and ways had to be found around this difficulty.

During these hours of sewing and fitting, it was quite natural for the housekeeper, the maid, and me to talk about fashion, and by complimenting Lady Felicity's wardrobe, I devised ways to ask questions about her. Jill and Dawson willingly and warmly spoke of her as a ray of sunshine, a songbird, and a blessed angel. Gently pressing them to be a bit more specific, I learned that Felicity liked to arrange flowers, drive her pony-phaeton around the park, and create fancy boxes out of seashells and the like. I learned that she preferred boysenberry jam on her breakfast scones, disliked kidneys whether or not they were served with beans, and adored ice cream. But as for details of her final illness and sad departure from this mortal realm, I could learn none. On that topic, the housekeeper and the maid were as indefinite as if we spoke of an imaginary person.

Most perplexing.

Nor could I blame their vagueness on stupidity, for both showed evidence of intelligence. Jill, for instance, made some of Flossie's gowns "work" on me by adding lace-up "waists" to cover that problem area. As for length, fashions had recently changed so much that skirts could now stop just below the ankle instead of dragging on the ground, so all was well in that regard, although sweeping hemlines had to be straightened.

Finally Jill costumed me to her satisfaction in a wine-red frothy confection that bared my arms and collarbone. She then placed a filmy combing wrapper around my shoulders and began to address the problem of my wayward tresses. (I continued efforts to converse, turning the talk to Lord Cadogan; was he a master with foibles and failings? But I learned little.) After brushing my hair one hundred strokes in the hope of civilizing it, Jill subdued it sufficiently to coil it atop my head, securing it there with an army of metal clips and pins. Into my coif's interstices she poked pink silk roses to match the pink velvet waist concealing the muddle in the middle of the dress like a cummerbund. After removing the combing wrapper, she looked me over and declared me "ravishing," but asked whether I wanted my face and arms dusted with rice powder. I declined. Both she and Dawson declared me pretty as a picture and said it was a pity I could not see myself, as all the looking-glasses were shrouded. (Silently I begged to differ. No one had draped the mirror in Lady Felicity's bedchamber.) Then, bobbing, both Dawson and Jill allowed themselves to be dismissed, leaving me to myself and my own thoughts.

Those thoughts were various and disturbing, so much so that I extracted paper and pencil from my fussy wine-red bosom in order to write them down. I wrote:

- If Flossie expired due to such a virulent disease that her body had to be cremated, why is her bedroom not closed off, quarantined, fumigated?

- Why is the mirror in her room, and only her room, not draped with black?

- Why does her last watercolour look so odd?

- Why are Dawson and Jill so willing to dress me up in their late mistress's clothes?

- Why are they so vague about her demise?

- Why has the earl invited me to dine? He
  should be in deep mourning.

- How am I to let Sherlock know where I am?

Even after I hid this list in my wine-red bodice,
my thoughts continued so restlessly that I could not
abide the battling green decor of my bedroom anymore.
Exiting, I wandered downstairs, found my way to the
parlour with the pedestal table, and sat at it. As on
every pedestal table in most parlours in England, there
were displayed a redoubtable Bible, a Grecian goddess
gracefully holding a plate for the collection of calling
cards, a vase of flowers, several small photographs in
freestanding oval frames, and a silver salver bearing the
afternoon post. Topmost among the letters lay one with
a typewritten address. Eyeing it curiously, I found that I
recognized the return address, also typewritten. It was
the letter Tish had said she would write to Caddie.

Exercising some mental discipline, as I had no good

excuse if I were caught riffling through the mail, I turned my attention elsewhere. On this particular pedestal table lay a sizeable item that scarcely looked like a book, for its ornate intaglio-velvet covers puffed like upholstery. But when I picked up this peculiar cushiony thing, it opened in the middle, and I found myself gawking at photograph after photograph mounted by means of decorative cardboard corners upon thick black paper. Such was my first experience of a photograph album, and a fine one it was, beginning with smeared and blotched silvery daguerreotypes that had to date back to the beginning of photography, nearly fifty years ago. They represented Larimer Trask Rudcliff, fifth Earl of Dunhench, and his wife, Olga Thorpe Rudcliff.

After lighting a lamp so that I could see more properly, I skipped over several generations of Rudcliffs to study the more recent, sepia-toned likenesses, looking for my host, Cadogan Burr Rudcliff number two. And there he was in the requisite wedding photograph, the lady being his first wife, Myzella Haskell Rudcliff, so labeled. She wore a great deal of white and seemed a bit smothered in point lace and orange blossoms. He wore a top hat and tails in which he somehow managed to look jaunty despite the need to maintain a pose for a full minute.

The next photograph was a death portrait of Cadogan Burr Rudcliff I, presumably Caddie's father, laid out in a casket so fine it might as well have been a sarcophagus.

Death portrait followed death portrait. Cadogan Burr Rudcliff III, who must have been Caddie's son, dead and swaddled in white at the age of two and a half. Then an old female Rudcliff, rather grand, who was perhaps Caddie's mother. Then a little girl, Angelica Myzella Rudcliff, surely his daughter, who had lived to be three before succumbing to diphtheria and being laid out in white ruffles and lace.

But then came another wedding portrait in which Cadogan Burr Rudcliff II stood tall beside Felicity Glover Rudcliff, aka Flossie. I recognized her at once, for she looked just like her twin, Letitia Glover, my client, although more feminized in her traditional white gown, cascades of lace, and a crown of rosebuds on her head to hold her veil.

More black pages remained to be filled, but that

was the last photograph in the album. I closed it thoughtfully.

I had seen no death portrait of Flossie.

Even more telling: I had seen none of Caddie's first wife, Myzella.

This fact disturbed me. Greatly.

Chapter the Eighth

Dinner only increased my perturbation. A footman seated me—or rather enthroned me, on an ornate, heavy chair with arms—at one end of a long table formally laden with linen, crystal, and silver. And there I waited, eyeing the empty seat at the other end of the table.

Lord Cadogan Rudcliff came in unconscionably late, carrying the afternoon post and sorting through it. As I watched, he threw one letter—Tish's letter, the only typewritten one!—into the fire without opening it to read it. Well! Caddie *was* a cad.

He laid the post aside, turned, and bowed to me with exaggerated courtesy before his footman enthroned him opposite me. There must have been a hundred candles lit, on the table, the chandelier, the sideboard, yet the room seemed dark and enormous to me, and I was reminded of Little Lord Fauntleroy's first dinner with his ferocious grandfather. I felt quite as small as that angelic child, and fully as fictitious. I knew myself to be a sham, a clown in a borrowed gown, miserably aware of my bare, scrawny arms and neck.

"Are you well this evening, Miss Basilwether?" Lord Rudcliff inquired most politely and insincerely.

"Quite well, and grateful for your hospitality, my lord."

"Please, call me Caddie."

At that exact ill-fated moment, as he offered me this rather daunting intimacy and as I was being served a bowl of turtle soup, I noticed the elegant silver-plated epergne centred on the table, no larger or more tastelessly ornate than most such fripperies, yet more disturbing to behold. Its molded stem did not depict the usual swans, shepherd boys, or cherubs. Instead, it duplicated the statue I had seen in front of Dunhench Hall! My host's table was decorated with a proud and shining miniature of himself.

I had not until that moment realized that the statue out front *was* Caddie. The existence of the statue had slipped my mind until I saw the epergne. But the combination in my mind of the statue, the vainglorious portrait in the main hall, and now the epergne—all indicated to me that Caddie fancied himself even more greatly than I had suspected.

Rendered perverse by the thought but maintaining a mask of ladylike imbecility, I peered down the candlelit table and chirped, "Oh! What a lovely centrepiece! You must admire Lord Byron very much."

"Lord Byron? Hardly!" My host reacted heatedly. "Lord Byron was a molly boy with a clubfoot!"

All innocence, I blinked across the distance that separated us. "But your epergne looks just like him."

I am pleased to say I made him blush. Even he, for all his force of ego, did not have the effrontery to explain that the object in question was fashioned after himself. He blurted, "Never mind the blasted epergne!"

But in no more time than it takes to turn the page of a book, he regained his manners and his practiced charm. "Enough about me. Tell me about yourself, Ermintrude." He helped himself to my first name as readily as he helped himself to some biscuit to go with his soup. "Where were you brought up?"

"Just about anywhere between Wales and Scotland." I tried to change the subject, referring to the excellent soup I was eating: "I have always regarded turtle soup as rather a mystery. How in the world does one skin a turtle?"

"I think that is something a lady should not really want to know. Tell me, Ermintrude, are you related to the Essex Basilwethers of Belvidere?"

Oh, dear. My choice of alias, I realized, had been most unwise under the circumstances. "Distantly," I answered, and luckily the arrival of the fish saved me from further conversation for the time being. Different wines were served with each course, but I sipped only water.

"Do you not care for wine, Ermintrude? Has anyone ever called you Trudy?"

I skipped the first question in favour of answering

the second one. "Certainly not if they wished to escape bodily harm."

He laughed far too heartily for a recently bereaved husband, increasing my unease. There was something shrewd, calculating, even predatory in the focus of his eyes and his attention on me.

"My mother was a friend of her most gracious grace, Wilhelmina, Duchess of Basilwether," he said. "Such a grand lady."

Hearing mockery in his tone, and having no idea what Tewky's mother's name was, although "Wilhelmina" seemed far too old-fashioned, I found myself in a quandary. I could not safely say I had never heard of Lady Wilhelmina, although it was entirely possible that he had made her up. So, cautiously, I said, "Of course I know the duke and duchess. Was Wilhelmina his mother's name?"

"Yes, indeed! And what relation is she to you? Your grandmother?"

"My great-aunt."

"Indeed? How very peculiar, as she never existed."

It was my turn to blush, and blush I did, furiously; he

had well and truly skewered me. "Oh, well," I babbled, "perhaps I was thinking of my great-aunt Mehitabel. I have never been good at keeping track of relationships."

"And yet you have come to Threefinches to research your family tree?"

Confound and blast! Hoist by my own petard! But I had to say something. With as much dignity as I could muster I stated, "I intend to master my own shortcoming."

He laughed again, heartily and not very pleasantly. But whilst I was trying to decide whether to take offense and make a frosty exit, the footmen came in with the "joint," meaning the meat course, which was in actuality a jugged hare accompanied by mashed turnips. Even had the fare been more to my taste, I had by then lost all appetite. But I pretended great interest in the contents of my plate, and did not look up at the occupant of the other end of the table for a considerable while.

He cooperatively remained silent, accommodating my sulk. And at last, of course, there came a time when I *had* to see what he was up to and lifted my gaze to glance at him.

He was sitting quite at his ease, elbows most

uncouthly on the table, smiling in a wolfish way. "So, my dear," he inquired in a most by-the-way manner, "Who are you, really?"

"I am not your dear," I retorted, before I even realized the full implications of his question.

"Very well, but who *are* you, sitting at my dinner table all dressed up in my wife's second-best evening gown?"

I glowered, partly because he had mentioned poor Felicity in such a tearless, offhand way, but mostly because I did not know how to answer. Never before had I found myself so ignominiously outfoxed.

Lord Cadogan grinned down the length of the table at me. I quite wanted to throw something at him.

"Let me help," he said in a way that sounded far more triumphant than helpful. "Having made a lifelong study of females, I believe you are much younger than you pretend to be. Because you are tall, you have been able to pass as a woman, when actually you are hardly more than a little girl, isn't that so? You are a runaway from a strict papa, aren't you?"

Of all his verbiage, one phrase struck me as a most curious thing to say. "A lifelong study of females?"

He ceased any pretense of being nice. "Answer me! You are a runaway, are you not?"

"Indeed I must be, as you are an expert and you say so."

"Do not trifle with me!" He stood up, and that hint of danger I had seen in the glint of his eyes now glared. I had faced many an angry man, but there was something different, something terrifying in the furious self-will of this oh-so-handsome aristocrat menacing me. "What is your name?"

Because he frightened me, I answered too pertly. "Why? What do you do with runaways?"

Lowering his head like a charging bull, he started towards me. "I lock them up until they beg to go home!"

He looked as if he intended to lay hands on me! Bolting to my feet, I reached for the dagger I always carried in my dress front—confound it! This dress had no front, and I had no dagger. Turning to flee, I collided with a footman who had just come in carrying the dessert tray. Like a chocolate-and-vanilla volcano, custard erupted onto me, him, and I hope the Earl of Dunhench, although I did not see. I only heard him order, not even loudly, "Seize her."

The footmen obeyed without the slightest hesitation, as if their master had directed them to remove a dish from the table; I wondered what unspeakable tasks they might have undertaken for him in the past.

"Lock her in her room."

Off I went lodged between the two men who had hold of me by the arms. I struggled, of course, but I could not wriggle as I would have liked, because the scanty and flimsy evening gown I wore would have slithered right off of me. And I could not scream, because the loathsome Caddie came along behind us with his hand over my mouth so tightly that I could not even manage to bite him.

But there came a moment when I would have cheerfully stopped struggling, and needed to remind myself to keep on writhing. And when they had shoved me inside the room, locked me in, and gone away, I needed to exert myself to pound on the imprisoning door, shouting after them, "You should be ashamed of yourselves! You, Dunhench, you are no gentleman!"

Then I turned up the gaslight and allowed myself to smile. It is true that I felt a degree of chagrin, having been treated so, but my humiliation was offset by elation, because I found myself exactly where I most wished to be. Rudcliff and his bullying boobies, evidently having failed to confer with Dawson, had locked me in the wrong room. Perhaps because I wore Lady Felicity's dress, and from that they had made a false assumption, they had locked me into Lady Felicity's chambers.

Chapter the Ninth

Searching has always been the passion of my life. As a child, I searched the woods of Ferndell, for whatever I might find—bright pebbles, a magpie nest, a skeleton? Now, sloughing off my borrowed finery and putting on a dressing gown, I looked forward to searching Lady Felicity's chambers in much the same spirit.

First, however, catching sight of myself in the large, circular mirror over her dresser, I stood still a moment, frowning. Surely if the lady had passed away in this room, hers would have been the first mirror covered?

Yet it seemed as if those in all public areas of the hall had been draped while this one was overlooked.

It followed, therefore, that she had not passed away, or at least not here.

Hmm.

Tucking the thought away to be brought out later, I set about hunting with no idea what I was looking for. I peeked into all the milk-glass flasks and jars on her dresser, then lifted the linen dresser scarf in case some paper might be concealed beneath. I searched beneath petticoats and stockings in her dresser drawers. I crossed to her desk, examined her inkwell, read notes she had written ("Need alizarin crimson, Payne's grey, rose madder, indigo") and examined her blotter for traces of any revealing words in mirror image; there were none. I looked through her wardrobe, then behind that heavy piece of furniture, then behind her mirror and all the pictures on her walls. I turned up the corners of her carpet. I checked the circular upholstered backs and seats of her lightweight chairs for secret pockets. I examined the solidity of her four-poster bed, got down on my knees to look under it, and even pulled out the fancy porcelain chamber pot I found there.

Crossing and re-crossing the rooms like a foxhound trying to pick up a scent, I passed in front of Lady Felicity's peculiar watercolour painting, uplifted on its easel, perhaps a dozen times, and each time I glanced at it and frowned, for something about its graceless lines tugged at the corner of my eye. Why had she painted something so—so uncharacteristically awkward, not to say ugly?

Finally I lit a candle to stand in front of it and have a closer look at it, at that oddly positioned horse, those jagged trees shaped like—

Oh, my stars and garters.

Shaped like capital letters.

Lady Felicity's painting was an exceedingly clever cipher.

Once I became aware of the letters in the trees, I saw them all at once, ranged across the top of the painting: INANE.

Inane?

I looked at the bottom of the painting for

something more, hoping for clarification. In order to define the letters in the trees, I now perceived, Lady Dunhench—no, Flossie; I had begun to think of her affectionately—Flossie had subtly picked them out with Conté crayon. How very resourceful, as Conté crayon was commonly used to emphasize shadows in watercolour. I searched for touches of Conté crayon on the lower part of the picture and at once found an *A* in the lower part of the horse's head and neck, with its reins being the crossbar. Then hints along the rider's habit and her booted foot in the stirrup showed me a rather elongated S. The horse's haunch and hock: *Y.* The corner of the cottage: L. Its door, a squared-off *U.* Its window with crisscross curtains: *M.*

ASYLUM.

Oh. Oh, please, no. But at the same time my eyes flew back to the top of the picture, seeking the missing letter, and finding it in the overlapping branches of the trees, angular like a backwards *Z* but still, I could now see, an *S.*

INANE ASYLUM? Hardly. The actual message was INSANE ASYLUM.

Oh. Oh, merciful heavens, no. I felt my entire

personage go freezing cold at the thought. But oh, dreadful fate, yes, it could be true, for this, I understood now, was the meaning of the black barouche, the baleful carriage conveying body snatchers who came in the night to carry their victims away to a fate more cruel than death.

I was still standing there, frozen in horror, when someone knocked on the door, making me jump even though the tapping sound was gentle, almost timid.

"Who is it?" I called once I had my voice under control.

"It's Dawson, Miss Ermintrude. Oh, Miss Ermintrude, I went to fold down the bedcovers for you and what did I find but they locked you in here! I had nothing to do with it, Miss Ermintrude!"

"It's all right, Dawson." Like a good and proper eccentric aristocrat, I treated imprisonment as a trifle. "I shall be quite all right if you could just bring me my own clothes from the other room. I should much prefer to sleep in my own nightgown."

Actually, I had no intention of sleeping. I meant,

somehow, to get out. But I had no wish to do so half naked, as none of Flossie's things fit me.

Dawson whimpered. "But, Miss Ermintrude, I don't dare put a key to this door. If you take advantage of me to make an escape, I'll be sacked for sure and tossed out to starve like a stray cat!"

Stiffly I said, "I promise you, Dawson, I am above trickery. I shall stand over by the windows. You may speak to me to make sure of me, then just open the door a crack and thrust the things in before you lock it again."

"All right, I—I'll try, dear."

My voice softened greatly. "Thank you, Dawson."

While she was gone, I paced the room, retracing my thoughts and questioning my conclusions, for the idea of a black barouche sweeping a lady away into the night seemed terribly melodramatic—but, in actuality, it need not be black or a barouche. A brougham, landau, victoria, phaeton, or any other carriage would serve the purpose. I had heard whispers that commitment to a lunatic asylum was all too often the fate of inconvenient women. Any man of means who wished to rid himself of a female encumbrance could have her committed for any of a plethora of reasons: nervousness, pride, reading French novels, consulting mediums, fear of darkness, failure to obey, suppression of perspiration, excessive laughter—any form of hysteria would do. All he needed in order to do so were the signatures of two doctors, one of whom could be the man who ran the hellish place. The wife thus disposed of—generally it was a wife—was then forgotten for all practical purposes.

But how could Flossie possibly have known that this was to be her fate?

Yet she had. There could be no mistaking the cipher in her watercolour. Also, now that I thought about it, although my search of Flossie's room had yielded no other clues, yet it had. The items I had *not* found were significant by their absence. In no conceivable way could certain essential feminine unmentionables have gone to the grave—or the crematorium—along with Flossie. But if she were yet alive, and had been stolen away somewhere, well, of course she would have need of certain personal items, even if she might never again wear an evening gown.

There must have been a hundred lunatic asylums in England. Where, oh *where*, had they taken her?

And how, oh how, was I ever going to find out?

The more immediate question was: How was I going to get out of Dunhench Hall, specifically, the chambers into which I was locked?

Until after Dawson had delivered my carpetbag, hat, parasol, et cetera, I could not think clearly about this problem, because I knew the sensible thing to do would be to cat-foot over to the door as Dawson opened it, overpower her, take the key from her, and lock her up in my stead.

But I had promised not to trick her.

Nonsense. All I had to do was gag her mouth so that she would not scream, and in order for her to remain gagged, I would have to tie her hands behind her.

But how long would it be before someone found her?

Nevertheless!

But what of decency, honour—

And so quarreled my mind until the chance was gone and I had thanked Dawson and let her lock the door again. Confound her for being a nice woman; she simply did not deserve to be bound and gagged, have trouble brought upon her, or be sacked to starve like a stray cat.

One would think the fray within my mental faculties would then cease, but no. *Confound you for being a fool, Enola!* shrieked a combative thought, causing me to feel upset—with myself?

How absurd. *You will do quite well on your own, Enola.* Almost as if hearing it speak from the grave, I remembered my mother's voice.

Instantly calm, I began to think clearly once again, and to act upon my thoughts.

First, I clothed myself, not in a nightgown, but in my own comfortable and modest green day-dress, newly mended. Then I put out the lights as if I had gone to bed. I stationed myself by a window, listening for any footsteps passing in the hallway. When there were none, and when my eyes had grown able to see somewhat in the darkness, I pulled open the draperies that had been shut since Flossie's "unfortunate demise," in order to peer outside.

It was quite a dark night, unlit by moon or even stars. I could see very little except the portico, which was glorified by gas lanterns flanking the front door.

The darkness could work either for me or against me, but it did not change my options for escape. I could think of four possibilities:

- Number one: Climb up inside the chimney like a sweep—and I quite liked to climb, nor did I mind dirt, but what if I became stuck? I was slender, but perhaps not quite slender enough, as chimney sweeping was generally done by young boys.

- Two: Slide down the laundry chute to the basement—but then I would still need to find a way out of the basement. And, again, sliding down laundry chutes is usually an activity for children. I studied the opening with the same doubt I felt towards the chimney: What if I became stuck?

- Three: Climb out of the window and—as my view of the portico told me I was located in the modern wing, where there were no vines to assist me down—as an alternative, could I stand on the window-sill, grasp the eaves, and somehow swing myself up onto the roof, whence I could clamber over to the old manse and its ivy? Still looking out the window, I shuddered and shook my head; extremely risky, both the swinging and the clambering. I quite agreed with Darwin that I was related to chimpanzees, but I lacked opposable digits on my feet.

- Four: Climb out the window and down. But how? I peered and peered to no avail. The stone walls were not so rough-hewn as to provide footholds. I saw no drainpipe, no

handy buttress, and alas, no ivy. How would
I ever be able to climb down?

Then the answer came to me, so ridiculously simple
that I smacked myself on the forehead for not having
thought of it sooner.

I would climb down the good old-fashioned way,
by improvising a rope out of bedclothes knotted
together.

Chapter the Tenth

Of course I had to wait until the nadir of night, when the denizens of Dunhench would be slumbering their deepest, and I could not light a lamp for fear of alerting someone to my activities, but during the hours that passed I became neither sleepy nor bored; I was busy fastening bedcovers corner to corner. Like many tasks, this turned out not to be nearly as simple as it seemed, especially not in the dark. I tied sheet to sheet to coverlet to coverlet to crewel-embroidered counterpane as best I could, pulling hard to tighten the knots, only to find that when I tested them, they parted as if by magic. No doubt, I thought sourly, my brother Sherlock had written a monologue on the superior knots used by sailors and mountain climbers, but as neither he nor his monologue were there with me in my prison, what was I to do?

Enola, think, said my mother's ghost in my mind.

I thought, and I remembered the modern "safety pins" I had noticed in the top drawer of Lady Felicity's dressing table, surely kept there for the purpose of holding things together in an emergency.

Aha.

Mentally I thanked both Flossie and my mother as I applied these formidable and reassuring pins to my knots, including those of the drapery panels I had added to my rope, and especially the all-important supporting quadruple knot I had tied to the bedpost. Then I put on my hat, secured it with the usual hatpins, fastened my carpetbag to my waist with the cloth belt from Flossie's purple dressing gown, inserted my parasol therein, opened the window and flung my approximate rope out through it, and, necessarily exiting the window backwards, I set forth.

As I am quite experienced at climbing, I scooted rapidly down sheets, coverlets, counterpane et cetera, and my celerity was fortunate, for my makeshift "rope" parted before I was quite finished with it, and I fell. Experience of similar situations previously helped me not to scream. And, as luck would have it, I did not fall very far. Almost immediately I landed on soft grass, taking the impact on that portion of my anatomy best padded to withstand such accidents. I stood up, brushed myself off, and considered my options regarding how to get back to Threefinches.

A bicycle? Ludicrous; no one was likely to have left one outdoors in readiness for me. A horse? In the stable, there would be a watchdog that would bark at me, thus rousing the boys asleep in the loft. However, I might find a horse in a pasture somewhere—and ride it bareback? So it could run away with me, like Jezzie? No, thank you.

My transportation, it seemed, would be shank's mare.

Once decided, I strode, indeed I nearly ran, towards the drive, visible by the light of the portico lamps. In passing, I made a very childish face at Caddie's statue, sticking out my tongue. Then, turning my back on Dunhench Hall, I hurried towards its gates.

The night remained so dark that at first I could see nothing except my own shadow, and shortly I could see nothing at all. I remained on the drive only by listening for the crunch of gravel under my feet and correcting course when I strayed onto the grass. Also, I retrieved my parasol from my carpetbag and waved it from side to side in front of me in case I encountered an obstacle, although I thought there should be none except the gate.

Regarding the gate, I felt no great concern. I could climb over it, although it would be difficult, partly because of the darkness but mostly because of my skirt, likely to catch on some wrought-iron doodad. Confound skirts, which seemed designed by malicious intent to prevent women from doing *anything* adventuresome, let alone climbing gates—

Wait. I could see the gate.

Backlit by some small light, the mighty filigree of metal, a masculine mockery of lacework, loomed a short distance ahead of me.

Moreover, I whiffed something that smelled of hot tin—a lantern. And as my eyes adjusted to the unexpected presence of illumination, I could make out a silhouette blending in with that of the gate, the form of a tall, thin man standing—No, as I watched he stooped, almost crouching, unmistakably furtive in his movements.

My hand crept towards the hilt of the dagger sheathed in the front of my corset. But I did not touch it, because I began to formulate some interesting notions. Reminding myself that it is a capital mistake to theorize in advance of sufficient data, I took a long step sideways to get off the lane and onto its grass verge. Then, holding my breath and stepping soundlessly on the grass, I stalked closer to the unidentified person. I could now see that his was a dark lantern, casting light on only one side that could be slid open or closed. Such was the sort of equipment a person might use who was, I could now see, attempting to pick open the padlock on the gates.

As he moved slightly, by the light of his lantern I got a clear look at his profile beneath the brim of a deer-stalker hat.

Smiling, I called to him softly. "Never mind, Sherlock. I can climb over."

I rejoiced to see him startle like a hare—which indeed he resembled in that hat with its bow on top like rabbit ears. Bolting upright, he caused a clash of metal as he kicked his lantern into the gate.

"Shhh!" he hissed as if I were the one who had created such an unfortunate clatter. But it was too late for either of us to shush. Out of the darkness sprang a thin shaft of candlelight—quite close at hand, moving towards what seemed to be a window—

The lodge-keeper's cottage!

There was no time to smite myself for being a ninny. Yanking my skirt up above my knees, I ran to the gate and scaled it in the moment it took Sherlock to slide his lantern closed so no one could see us in the night.

Nor, alas, could we see anything at all.

I felt my brother hoist me under the shoulders as I reached the top of the gate, and he hauled me over as if I weighed nothing at all. My skirt caught on something, of course. He ripped me free and ran, still carrying me quite jouncily.

"Put me down," I complained.

He did so, but only because he tripped over something and fell, hurling me to the ground in the process.

Lying on my back with the breath knocked out of me, I felt the most peculiar, overlarge tickling sensation on my face. Had the source of discomfort not snorted upon me, thereby identifying itself as a horse, I think I would have screamed once I had caught my breath. But instead, I sat up, and the beast began to eat my hat. I started to push the annoyance away, then changed my mind, took hold of its bridle's cheek strap, and hauled myself to my feet. "Sherlock?" I whispered to the night, a sudden quaver of fear in my voice—had he hit his head? Had he hurt himself? Was he lying nearby with a broken neck?

I could not see him. But, flickering through what seemed to be woods, I did see lantern light—the lodge-keeper, looking for us.

A familiar and peremptory voice ordered, "This way, Enola. Get in the cart!"

Feeling my way along the horse towards his voice, I whispered, "Are you all right?"

"Get in the *cart*!" A thin, sinewy, and surprisingly strong hand came down from somewhere above the horse's tail, grasped my arm, and lifted me. I flailed, encountered a structure of wood, and found myself sprawling approximately on or in it as Sherlock turned the horse and flicked the whip, and we trundled away.

Trundled, I say, because in the dark we could not go dashing off; indeed, I do not know how Sherlock was able to guide the horse at all. Perhaps the horse guided *him*. Horses exhibit an uncanny willingness and sense of direction when returning to their stables.

After a few minutes Sherlock stopped the horse, secured the reins, and got down to light the lanterns on each forward corner of the cart. By then I had gotten myself organized into some degree of verticality. Judging by Sherlock's actions there was no longer any need for stealth or silence, so I asked, "Whatever became of Tom Dubbs?" Sherlock wore his own hair and the country tweeds of a gentleman.

"Tom Dubbs served his purpose." Sherlock climbed back onto the cart and took up the reins again, clicking his tongue to urge the horse into a trot. "That lodge-keeper has apparently gone to report to his master," he added. "Do you think we will be pursued?"

"Doubtful. Lord Caddie hardly strikes me as

energetic. And even if he does send someone after us, we have little to fear, now that you are no longer a humble scion of the soil, but your masterful self."

"True." With a single word he acknowledged the authority of the great Sherlock Holmes.

I rolled my eyes towards the starless sky. "While you were Tom Dubbs, did you discover the circumstances surrounding the supposed demise of Lady Felicity Rudcliff?"

"No, but Tom Dubbs heard all about a mysterious young female being held as a runaway in Dunhench Hall. The hall servants could scarcely wait to make you the talk of Threefinches. And I was not sure whether I could trust Dunhench, womanizer that he is, to deliver you over to the constabulary in the morning."

"Thank you for coming to get me . . . but what were you planning to do once you got the gate open, for heaven's sake?"

"It hardly matters now, does it?" In other words, Sherlock had no idea. "I suppose you climbed down the ivy?"

"It hardly matters." Ever so demure, I tucked my chin. "However, my visit to Dunhench Hall, although brief, was fruitful. I have reason to believe that our client's sister is alive, but has been committed to a lunatic asylum, and we must rescue her before she comes to harm."

I hoped for exclamations, but I got none. Sherlock merely asked, as blandly as if he were inquiring about a misdirected parcel, "Which lunatic asylum?"

"She didn't say. And from the fact that she didn't say, I infer one of two possible conclusions: either she didn't know, or the name of the asylum would not have fit onto the painting."

"Enola," he said in what might possibly have been construed as an affectionate tone, "you have gotten into Watson's deplorable habit of telling your stories backwards. Start at the beginning, please, and give me an orderly account of your findings."

So I did, and darkness hid my blushes as I explained about the unmentionables that were missing from Lady Felicity's chambers. I also told him about the mirror that had not been covered, the death portraits absent from the photograph album, and the odd behaviour of the servants, specifically Dawson. I explained at length the message I had discovered hidden in the watercolour, and I conveyed my impression that Lord Caddie was not a very nice man. As I spoke, I watched as the swaying light from the cart lanterns showed me glimpses of fences, hedges, and grassy slopes, beyond which all remained dark.

Too much of Lady Felicity's story also remained dark in my mind. "I am very curious to see what darling Caddie has filed by way of a death certificate. The moment the registrar's office opens in the morning, I want to be there."

Sherlock said, "No need. I will take care of it."

"I want to go."

"The registrar is likely to be more helpful to me."

By virtue of his gender and his top hat this was true, which infuriated me.

"I shall go. You may come along if you like."

"Thank you," he said, his tone owlish.

"You're welcome."

Chapter the Eleventh

We stayed for the remainder of the night at the inn—
the very same inn that had so rudely turned me away
when I lacked a brother—and in the morning, after
only a few hours of sleep, we prepared to visit the registrar, unwilling to delay lest Lord Cadogan create some
sort of unpleasantness after all, once he had finished his
breakfast.

I experienced some difficulty regarding my costume. My green dress was once more and yet again
ruined. Necessarily I wore my other one, which was

buttercup yellow. However, as a female past the liberties of childhood, I could not be seen in public without a hat, and as I had only my battered one with the green ribbons, I chopped away those ruined trimmings then plopped the hat on my head in a shockingly shabby and unadorned condition, assuring myself that I could resume being fashionable when I got back to London.

Which turned out to be sooner than I expected, because of what the registrar dredged up from his records for us. Corpulent king of his paperwork empire, he responded to our requests—Sherlock's for the marriage and death records of Myzella Haskell Rudcliff, mine for the same for Felicity Glover Rudcliff—he produced the documents sluggishly enough to show us that he, and not we, ruled here in Threefinches.

No matter. In his own good time he handed them over. Judging from what I could see, marriage was recorded in a squarish format on creamy paper with quite a florid border, while death came on long and narrow paper that was dark grey and engraved more grimly.

While Sherlock stood looking over Myzella's records, I sat on the registrar's hard bench and studied Flossie's, making notes—the name of the clergyman who had married her, date, et cetera—but I felt much more interested in her supposed demise. The record of death told me that her unfortunate end had been reported by her husband, whose occupation was noted as *Earl of Dunhench* and hers as *Wife*; she had been twenty years old, and the cause of her death had been fever. The informant (Caddie) was described as *lordship in apparent good health, not yet of middle age, composed and condescending in manner* while his residence was dealt with more briefly: *Dunhench Hall.* Then, as required by law, fastened to the gloomy grey registration of death was a Medical Certificate of Death.

It listed Flossie's cause of death as fever, unspecified.

It was signed by John H. Watson, M.D.

Dr. Watson? *Our* friend Watson?

It was not inconceivable. Surrey was a short distance from London. And how many medical doctors named John H. Watson might there be in England?

Trying hard not to squeak or ogle, I got up and showed the paper to Sherlock. His eyebrows fairly levitated.

"What physician signed for Rudcliff's first wife?" I asked.

"None. A medical certificate of death was not required by law until ten years ago. Lord Rudcliff simply reported that Lady Myzella succumbed to brain fever. I think we should be on our way back to London, don't you?"

I certainly did.

We did not discuss the matter within earshot of anyone in Threefinches, and we waited until a hired hack had driven us back to Dorking before we sent telegraphs, one to Miss Letitia Glover asking her to call at 221B Baker Street sometime after four p.m., and one to Dr. Watson asking him to leave word whether he had recently, or ever, signed a death certificate for Felicity Glover Rudcliff, Lady Dunhench. Then we took the next train into London. Sherlock and I secured a compartment to ourselves.

Finally, I could speak with him privately. "You would know Watson's signature if you saw it, would you not?"

"I am reasonably sure I would, and that what you

showed me was not in his handwriting. But we must wait for proof before we discuss the matter any further."

He fell into a brooding silence, while I, never one to concern myself with propriety, put my feet up and fell asleep until we reached Victoria Station.

There we went our separate ways, Sherlock to inquire at Dr. Watson's office, and I to my lodging in the Professional Women's Club to put on a different hat! But first to have a wash, and brush my hair, and change my dress, et cetera. When, much later in the day, I reported back to Baker Street, I was irreproachable in russet delaine trimmed with muted gold, with, of course, a simply ravishing hat in the latest fashion. Worn on the back of the head, it tilted up to a peak in front with a froth of autumn-coloured flowers tucked underneath the brim.

"That thing you're wearing looks like a frigate in need of a figurehead," said Sherlock when I entered his sitting room. He, of course, wore impeccable city attire that had varied little in the past decade.

"Good afternoon to you, too. Have you heard from Watson?"

"Not yet."

"Bother." Laying my gloves and parasol aside, I appropriated a seat at his desk so I could draw a picture that I felt was likely to be needed soon. Shortly afterwards, I heard the front doorbell, and Miss Letitia Glover was shown up by Mrs. Hudson.

"Miss Glover." Sherlock took her gloved hand in his and bowed over it with utmost courtesy.

"Hello, Miss Glover." I shook her hand, and she smiled as if she appreciated my greeting more. Dressed as before, in a mannish fashion but feminine hues—on this day, plum and peach pink—she gazed at me in appeal, her face pale despite the rosy hue of her collar, her wide eyes fraught with anxiety.

Wishing only to comfort her, I exhorted, "Do not despair, Miss Glover! We have every reason to believe your sister is alive, just as you said."

"There are perhaps some slight indications," Sherlock amended, his tone most quelling. "Please be seated, Miss Glover."

She did so, but at the same time she found her voice, exclaiming as she looked from Sherlock to me and back again, "Oh! But what have you found out? Please tell me at once!"

Sherlock gave me a glance that spoke as plainly as words, assigning to me the task of speaking with the winsome young woman, as it was I who had raised her hopes.

I pulled my chair closer to our client's. Sitting nearly knee to knee with Miss Glover, I told her, "I have been to Dunhench Hall, and made the acquaintance of Lord Cadogan Rudcliff, and found him to be superficially charming but at times most unpleasant. For instance, I saw him throw your letter into the fire without reading it."

She gasped, and her gloved hands flew to her mouth.

"Also, for no particular reason he locked me into a bedroom—your sister's bedroom."

Tish Glover's eyes went nearly black, their pupils widened so. I leaned towards her to encourage her confidence. "Miss Letitia, do you paint as well as your sister does?"

"No, I could never!" Tish's hands left her mouth to describe loops and whorls in the air as she spoke of her sister's talent. "Flossie depicts so accurately whatever subject she chooses, but not only that, she has a genius for composition! She tried to explain to me about the golden ratio and how to translate it into an outward spiral like a snail shell, but I am quite incapable of understanding! Still, I can see how her paintings order themselves along graceful proportions and curves."

I nodded vigorously. "Such, exactly, was my observation of her artwork. Therefore I sensed something odd when I perceived this—please pardon the crudeness of my rendition—when I found a painting like this upon the easel in her studio—I mean, her boudoir."

Tish ogled the pencil sketch I showed her with a fair degree of repulsion. "Why, what could Flossie mean by painting that?"

"My thought exactly. But after looking closely, I saw that she had picked out certain areas in Conté crayon, thus." Holding the sketch against a book, I penciled for her its hidden letters. Standing behind Miss Glover's chair, Sherlock watched as well. As I spelled out IN-SANE ASYLUM, Tish covered her mouth again, stifling a choked sound.

Sherlock murmured, "Extraordinary."

"Yes," I agreed, "most extraordinary. She must have guessed somehow that her husband was scheming to put her away."

Sherlock quibbled, "Unless she was referring to her predecessor, Lady Myzella."

Tish choked back a sob again. "Sherlock," I told my brother with some asperity, "don't be such an egghead. I am sure Flossie is alive, on the evidence of the things that are missing from her dresser drawers."

Tish caught her breath then held it as she reached out for me with her gaze. Sherlock said mulishly, "What things, exactly?"

He thought he would make me blush? Confound him. Without hesitation I shot back, "Things that a young lady *who is alive* needs once a month."

He was the one who blushed, and his red face with its aristocratic white beak was most gratifying to behold in the moment before he turned away.

Tish wailed, "But where is she? *Which* insane asylum?"

"That, indeed, is the problem." Sherlock quickly regained control, and would have elaborated, I am sure, except that just then the front bell rang, and we all turned silent as statues, listening.

A moment later we heard boyish steps running up the stairs towards us. Sherlock went out to meet the messenger, then came back in carrying a slip of paper.

"It's a note from Watson," he said, "and it confirms both our suspicions and our hopes; he has never heard of Felicity Glover Rudcliff. Her certificate of death cannot be considered valid, for his signature upon it was forged."

Chapter the Twelfth

Tish dreadfully wanted to find her sister that very day if not sooner, begging to know the name of every insane asylum in Surrey. While quite sympathizing with her, I thought Lord Cadogan would have been more likely to dispose of his wife a bit farther from home, in London, where there were lunatic asylums (formerly called madhouses), sanatoriums, mental hospitals, and variously named facilities for imbeciles, idiots, and other defectives, in plenty. Tish reminded me that her sister had specified "insane asylum." I opined that Flossie had chosen those two words for their brevity as opposed to, for instance, Saint Marlebone's Incarceratory for the Dangerously Crazed. Or Earlswood Asylum for Idiots and Imbeciles, for instance, should not be overlooked. Tish nodded agreement but whispered, "Oh, poor dear Flossie."

Sherlock, who was perched on the settee, folding and refolding Watson's message and looking abstracted, suddenly stood up. "I will do everything in my power to find her," he said with an air of authority and finality, bowing slightly and extending one arm towards the door, signaling our client that it was time for her to leave.

But Tish remained in her chair. "I am going nowhere except to assist in the search for my sister."

"Don't be absurd," Sherlock said in that charming way of his. "Rather than gallivanting from bedlam to bedlam, it would be far more efficient to ferret out information at Dunhench, which is what I intend to do."

"Certainly, do so. Meanwhile, I intend to 'gallivant' just as you described." With thinned lips and uplifted chin, Tish faced him.

Sherlock condescended to her as if he were trying to reason with a child. "Have you a brother, an uncle, any respectable man to accompany you?"

"I have no one but Flossie, and Flossie has no one but me."

"All the greater your obligation to safeguard yourself. Have you thought what perils you might encounter, a woman all alone in such places?" His oh-so-sensible tone could not have been more annoying.

"She will not be alone," I interceded. "I will go with her."

Sherlock's manner quite changed as he turned to me, and his glare rather endeared him to me, as did this outburst: "Enola, don't be a fool!"

My heart warmed to him; I smiled. "It's rather too late for me to be otherwise, my dear brother." Standing up, I collected my gloves and parasol, then offered my hand to Tish, who accepted it as she rose to accompany me.

In heightened tones Sherlock appealed, "But what can either of you expect to *do*?"

"We shall see."

"Thank you for your concern, Mr. Holmes."

Arm in arm, Tish and I sashayed out of Sherlock's lodging.

At the nearest tea shop, we stopped to partake of that life-sustaining beverage along with a very late luncheon of fish-paste sandwiches, roly-poly pudding, and apple slices to be dipped in honey. Tish addressed me, "Miss Holmes—"

"Please, call me Enola. Or Eudoria, or Hadassah, or Tuppence Ha'penny, or anything you please." In one of my reckless moods, I spoke on. "You know, Tish, I have become quite fond of you and Flossie, even though I have never met her and I scarcely know you."

That made her smile a little despite her fears for her missing sister. "I feel honoured by your kind regard, Enola, and so would Flossie, I am sure." She stopped smiling. "I confess I have not the slightest idea how to gain entry into an insane asylum."

"Nor do I. We shall ask Watson."

"Also, I have only a very little money."

"I have a great deal, almost as much as there is

honey on my hands." By that time I had got myself quite sticky. "Think no more of it. Tell me, Tish, if I may ask, where do you get waistcoats of such lovely hues?"

"I have them especially made for me. It is my one extravagance." Tish seemed to be having difficulty eating much, although she had progressed to sipping her second cup of tea. "I started dressing this way," she added in a sombre tone, "to stand apart from my sister. If she could be so effortlessly beautiful, why then, I had to look—different, somehow. But now, under the circumstances, I feel terribly sorry for my pettiness."

"Not at all. It is only normal that one should wish to be oneself and not someone else. I feel the same way. Before I began to disguise myself as a grown-up, I was quite a shocking creature wearing knickerbockers."

Tish almost laughed.

"I should like to dress like you," I added somewhat truthfully, meaning at times, perhaps. Actually, I quite adored the new fashions, for—after decades of crinolines and bustles—verticality had at last come into style, and I was a decidedly vertical creature.

After we had quite finished our tea (and the attendant

had brought us basins of cool, lemon-garnished water wherein to wash our fingers), we took a cab to Dr. Watson's office. He was glad to see me, inquiring anxiously about Sherlock's condition, and when he heard that it was much improved, he was most solicitous to oblige both me and Tish, professing himself outraged that anyone had dared to forge his signature as a physician. He quite wanted a word with the man who had done that, he assured us. Shortly thereafter, we left with an index of London sanatoriums in our possession and admonitions of caution echoing in our ears. Had the good doctor not been attending a baby with badly corrupted nappy rash that possibly could have turned fatal, I think he would have volunteered to serve as our escort.

By then it was nearly evening, too late in the day for us to start. Also, by then, because of lack of sleep the night before, I was yawning until my jaw ached. Tish and I shook hands on the pavement outside Watson's office, agreeing to meet the morning of the next day, Saturday.

"On Saturdays I take a half holiday in any event," she remarked.

"You work at an office, then?"

"Only part-time, nowadays. I prefer to take in typing to do at home. It was a great thing for me when I had saved up enough to purchase my own typewriter."

"And make your own unique and very attractive calling cards."

Thus I left her smiling.

In the morning I dressed in a simple blouse, skirt, and jacket, like Tish, although I had neither ascot nor waistcoat to complete the similarity. Nor did I have a bowler hat, so I made do with a plain straw boater. When Tish met me for breakfast, as we had arranged, she took in my costume, smiled only very slightly, and tactfully said nothing.

We were both rather silent and sober that morning, for our day's undertaking promised to be a grim one. After we had eaten and drunk our tea, we proceeded to Our Lady of Bethlehem, a venerable institution better known as Bedlam, because there, Dr. Watson had told us, on days other than Sunday we could hire a guide and take a tour, looking at the inmates as if they were animals in a zoo.

Our cab stopped at a massive stone-and-brick main building that looked rather like a cross between a factory and a fortress. With its ranked windows, gables, towers, all in strictest symmetry, Bedlam seemed built to negate externally the disordered minds kept within. At the imposing gateposts in the tall wall that surrounded the whole, a guard halted us until we explained our purpose and produced money. He then summoned for us a guide, a buxom woman in a powder-blue nurse's uniform nearly covered with quite a plain and sturdy white apron. Her cap, however, a frilly affair with tails, seemed to indicate a rank near the top of the hierarchy of attendants, as did her complacent smile.

"Our interest is confined to the female wards," I told her. "You do separate the asylum populace by gender, do you not?"

"Yes, indeed." She took us in through the massive front doors, turned left, and after that I do not recall our visit sequentially, but only in snippets, as one might remember a bad dream. Women, so many women, blankly staring, not conversing with one another, yet making noise—moans, cries, whimpers, singsong droning sounds. Some who drooled, some with green crusts below their noses. Most of them wearing torn dresses that failed to cover them properly, and all of them barefoot.

"They cannot have shoes, poor things, because they are dangerous when thrown. Most of the time they seem to have very little life in them, yet they do fight, especially when one tries to clean them."

Whether young or not, they all *seemed* old because of their harrowed faces—that and their thin, frazzled hair hanging loose and unkempt. Some of the women in their torn and patched dresses stood like statues looking at nothing, some sat on benches that seemed no more wooden than they, and some lay in the middle of the bare floor, curled up as if for warmth, with no pillows for their heads except their own arms. Whether standing, seated, or lying, many of the women had their hands encased in large, thumbless mittens of padded leather.

"Some of them tear clothes so dreadfully, their own clothes and those of others, that we have to put them in mitts. But we try never to be unkind. There was a time when they would have been kept in chains. You'll not find that anymore."

We saw wards ranked with narrow beds, and similar beds lining the hallways.

"Our seemingly quite adequate space is sorely overwhelmed by the staggering numbers of hapless souls who come our way."

Some women huddled underneath the beds, hiding. One of them, sagging and wrinkled—so shocking, I had to look away quickly—was stark naked.

"Oh, dear." Our guide rang a bell to summon someone to the ward, then hastened to move us onwards. It may have been then that Tish and I began to hold hands.

We saw women separated from one another behind bars, wearing oddly shapeless, heavy dresses made out of quilted canvas. One declared, "I killed my baby! I killed my baby!" over and over again. Others hissed, or yowled, or shouted insults at Tish and me, whilst some screeched the most dreadful profanities.

"These ones are in a bad way, poor dears. They must be in cells to prevent them from hurting anyone, and wear the strong dresses to keep them from shredding their clothing and hurting themselves. The strong dresses are kinder than straitjackets. And in cells instead of in chains, at least they can move about."

Certainly they were moving about, some of them leaping against their bars, trying to attack us, like wild animals, and yelling in frenzy. With their hair shorn almost to the skull and their eyes dilated, they seemed scarcely human.

"Their hair is cut short because otherwise they get lice. In order to calm them enough for bathing, we must drug them. But those in the other wards are bathed weekly."

In no particular order that I can remember, we saw a laundry where some of the more trusty inmates worked, and an exercise yard where some wore bloomers and were being instructed to do jumping jacks, and a kitchen full of workers, some of them inmates also.

"The poor souls in this asylum eat better than most of the factory workers in London."

We were shown a hydrotherapy room full of variously equipped bathtubs. And another therapy room bristling with electrogalvanic devices. And a chapel.

"We must keep their Sunday clothes under lock and key so they do not destroy them."

And, I would rather forget, in one ward a number of inmates sitting or lying stock still in restraints. Head restraints, torso restraints, limb restraints.

"For hysterics."

"Hysterics?" Tish murmured.

"When they grow excited, laughing or singing unhealthily or trying to tear their hair or injure themselves, they must be restrained."

"Are there none who are recovering," I begged, "and who might go home again?"

"Yes, indeed. Those who are brought here for puerperal insanity often recover within three months to a year. Those afflicted with moral insanity sometimes rally when encouraged to read the Bible. And those driven out of their minds by overwork, unrequited love, unsympathetic husbands, or such misfortunes can often be helped by merest kindness. I have saved the most pleasant ward for last. This way." She ushered us into a room neither as bare nor as crowded as the others. About a dozen women who appeared normally dressed, albeit plainly so, occupied shabby armchairs or sat at tables. Some were sewing patches onto clothing, some were knitting or crocheting, and a few were reading.

They looked up and smiled when we came in. Our guide introduced them to us by name, and they replied courteously to a few words of conversation.

Tish let go of my hand, pulled a photograph of Flossie out of her reticule and showed it to them. "Have any of you seen my sister?"

They shook their heads most sympathetically, and one Irishwoman offered, "If it's to a place like this she's gone, miss, it's greatly changed you'll find her."

"I could have told you at once that she is not here," complained our guide.

I refrained from retorting that she could have been paid to misinform us, and Tish said simply, "I had to look for her myself. Have we seen all of the women who reside here?"

"Heavens, no. I can't take you to the barn where they milk the cows, or to the infirmary building full of fever, or to the ward for those who won't keep their clothes on, now, can I?"

I took one quick glance at Tish's face and said, "I believe we are finished here, then."

Our guide showed us out of Bedlam in heavily starched silence.

Chapter the Thirteenth

As soon as we achieved the privacy of a closed cab, Tish broke down and wept, curling up like a wilted flower to hide her face in her hands. I sat beside her and gave her a handkerchief, then put my arm around her shoulders, drew her into a hug, and patted her, trying to comfort her although a clotted sensation in my throat prevented me from saying anything helpful. After a short while, she sat up straight, applied the handkerchief to her face, and tried to say, although her voice would not quite obey her, that she was sorry for her weakness.

"Not at all." My own voice sounded as choked as hers. "I quite feel like weeping myself."

"To imagine Flossie . . . in such a . . . dreadful place . . ." Sobs shook her again.

"Shhh." I recommended my soothing gestures. "We will talk about it when we get home."

By this I meant the Professional Women's Club where I lodged, and I took Tish straight upstairs so that she need not suffer the embarrassment of being seen with red eyes in the sitting room. Once we were safely secluded in my rather Spartan room, I showed her to the washstand so that she could apply cool water to her face, rang for tea, then seated her in my one and only armchair. I myself perched on the wooden chair at my desk, reaching for paper and a pencil.

"One of your lists?" Tish asked, her voice so warm, friendly, almost teasing, that I smiled.

"Yes, one of my lists." I wrote:

TO FIND FLOSSIE

- Visit more asylums? Great pain for small gain. No guarantee we shall see her, as staff

probably bribed to conceal her. And it would
take us months to visit them all.

- Send photograph around, inquire at all
  asylums? Unhelpful. Again, Caddie would
  have bribed staff to conceal her.

- Would we even recognize her if we found
  her? How would being in such a place
  change her?

At this point I dropped the pencil and seized
my head in both hands, for a most unruly jumble
of new thoughts was rushing in, jostling my brain.
"Stars and garters, things I should have asked in the
first place!" I exclaimed. "Tish, what ward would
Flossie be in?"

"My sister does not belong in *any* ward of—"

"I mean, what sort of excuse would Caddie most
likely use to have her committed? Was her behaviour
eccentric in any way?"

"Enola, of course not! My sister was—is—an
angel!"

I realized I was asking questions of the wrong person, but wrote anyway:

- Hysteria? Any sort of excitement; catch-all.

- Moral insanity? Euphemism for adulterous thoughts or tendencies? Another catch-all for jealous husbands.

- Erotomania if she loved him?

- Frigidity if she did not?

- Hypothesizing that Caddie did the same with his first wife, Myzella, ask her relations whether they know what he committed her for—and where.

Eureka.

I asked Tish, "Are we agreed not to visit any more asylums just yet?"

"Agreed. Anyway, tomorrow is Sunday."

True. Public institutions, such as registrars, libraries,

courthouses, and insane asylums, would not be open to the public. But there was no reason why I should not go calling on the Haskells.

The next morning, outfitted in my exceedingly genteel teal-coloured traveling costume, I stopped at Baker Street to talk with Sherlock. But he was not there, and had not been since Friday, I was told, so I left word—*Gone to call on the Haskells in St. John's*, with the date—and then caught a train to Surrey. Luckily I was able to bypass Dorking (and its livery stable, and Jezebel), getting off at the next stop, where I had luncheon, then rented a horse, driver, and light carriage for the day. As the driver hitched up, I explained to him that I needed to go calling upon some Haskells in order to complete my family tree. "I hope I can still find some Haskells living in the St. John's area?"

"Yes, indeedy, miss!" A well-upholstered and genial man, he all but split his broad, florid face with his smile. "The Haskells got deep roots in St. John's and ain't no more likely to take up and leave than if they was a coppice of trees. Which one you want to see first?"

I had thought this out. Because I could not ask for Myzella's mother without starting gossip, and because male family members generally inhibit frank conversation, I replied, "I would prefer a single or widowed woman, if possible, perhaps an older one."

"Why, then, I'll take you straight to Dame Haskell herself."

I agreed, and he took me for a pleasant drive across the pretty Surrey countryside—much more pleasant than my jaunt with Jezzie! Peering out of the carriage windows, I saw St. John's to be a picturesque village and my destination—as I was conveyed off of the main road and up a drive—a large, comfortable-looking plaster-and-whitewash farmhouse. "Dame" Haskell's title was honourific, then, and I would not be dealing with people of rank.

With all due courtesy my driver left me at the front door—opening the carriage for me and assisting me out as if I were porcelain and might break—then abandoned me for the sake of chums in the barn or stable. But there was no need for me to stand knocking at the door; it opened, and a smiling gingham-clad housemaid beckoned me in.

"I am *so* glad you are not a butler," I told her.

Unabashed, she laughed. "No, I'm just Sally, miss. Why don't you walk right on through. You'll find Missus Haskell in the garden." There was no need for her to guide me, for in this forthright old house one followed a straight path from the front door to the back. The scrubbed, country feeling of the kitchen I passed through reminded me of Mrs. Lane's domain in Ferndell Hall, my childhood home, and Dame Haskell, when I found her gathering windfall pears and medlars and apples into a great basket, reminded me a bit of Mrs. Lane herself. Instead of the shriveling invalid I had half expected, I found a robust woman with the wind in her white hair, wearing neither hat nor gloves, her hands stained by juice oozing from the bruised fruit. Greedy for sweets, wasps and honeybees clung to her hands as well as to the fruit. "You'll be stung!" I exclaimed.

"I already was. Some would say it's what I deserve for working on the Sabbath. But I can't believe God will mind, being as these will make such good cider." Setting her basket down, she straightened to have a long and frankly appraising look at me, studying me from my fashionable hat to my polished boots. Rather than embarrass the condition of her hands by offering a card, I smiled and let her look.

She spoke abruptly. "You came all the way out here from the city." This sounded like a statement rather than a question.

"Quite."

"Whatever for? Who are you?"

"My name is Enola Holmes, and I would like to ask you some questions."

"You're not The Right Honourable Miss Enola Holmes?" A gentle gibe at my gentrified appearance.

"No, I'm just plain Enola."

"And why are you asking questions, Just Plain Enola?"

I wished I could answer this doughty country-woman as directly as she questioned me, but Myzella Haskell's fate was far too delicate a matter to broach straight on. I said, "I am representing the family of Felicity Glover Rudcliff, second wife of the Earl of Dunhench. He has informed them by letter that she recently passed away and was cremated. Her loved ones suspect otherwise, and thus beg to know what truly happened not only to her, but to his first wife."

Dame Haskell took a long breath, let it out slowly, then without a word she marched to a nearby pump, where she washed her hands and dried them on her apron. Beckoning me to follow, she led the way to a secluded stonework bench at the far end of the garden. Here she sat and, again at her wordless invitation, I sat beside her. But I did not venture to speak; I waited.

Finally Dame Haskell said, "Myzella was my treasure, my pride, my granddaughter. My heart burns for her sake every day of my overlong life."

Her words sounded hard and old, like stones. Undoubtedly she had good reason to be bitter for her granddaughter's sake. I waited; I kept silence; I scarcely ventured to breathe.

She went on in the same stony tone, "We fools, we simple country folk, her mother and father and brothers and cousins and I, we suspected nothing. We did not learn the truth about what had happened to her until it was far . . . too . . . late."

With each word she seemed to be finding it harder

to speak. I nodded, leaned forward to gaze into her face, and implored her with my hands to go on.

Eventually she got some words out. "How did this lady—What was her name?"

"Felicity."

"That is quite an ironic name for any woman married to Rudcliff." Dame Haskell sounded bitter but in control now. "How does Felicity's family suspect something wrong when we were so blind?"

"She left a cipher. May I tell you what it said?"

"Yes."

"Two words: *insane asylum*."

"Dear heavens above. How did she know?" Dame Haskell abandoned all dignity and distance; she turned to me earnestly. "Poor woman, she must have heard whispers of Myzella. Old Dr. Simmons confessed on his deathbed, or we would never have learned."

"Dr. Simmons?"

"Our family doctor here in St. John's. Until he spoke, it seemed the most natural thing in the world to us that Myzella—her heart, always so frail and tender— that she should follow her little Angelica into the grave—although for Myzella there was no grave, just that devilish cremation. Still, clod-witted farmers that we are, we suspected nothing, but Dr. Simmons knew all, and for nearly a decade it had weighed heavy on his conscience that he had let Lord Cadogan bribe and bully him until he signed the paper to have our sweet girl committed on account of nervous excitement."

Another term for hysteria.

"Committed *where*?" I spoke more vehemently than I should have; this could be the key to finding Flossie!

But old Mrs. Haskell smiled ruefully, understanding my eagerness as well as if I had spoken my thought aloud. "A wretched, unhealthy place along the Thames, Miss Enola. We arrived to find Myzella in the throes of mortal illness, only just in time to comfort her as she perished, God rest her sweet, so sorely wronged soul. And then—there was nothing we could do about the Earl of Dunhench, but we could and did set about having this so-called asylum condemned. It has been torn down and demolished; it no longer exists."

Chapter the Fourteenth

Dame Haskell and I sat on the bench at the bottom of her garden and talked a good while longer. She told me that her son, Myzella's father, lived in another farmhouse nearby, but I did not feel I could learn anything more by calling upon him and his wife, nor did I wish to open their wounds afresh. I concluded my visit and came away with greatest sympathy for all the Haskells, but not much the wiser as regarded Flossie.

What was I to tell Tish? No plan of action, except the unsatisfactory one of trekking from asylum to asylum in search of Flossie, came to mind. Once in my hired carriage, I sat staring at the Surrey countryside without the slightest appreciation of its loveliness, and once upon the train back to London, I watched the telegraph poles fly past my window in exactly the same way. As the train slowed to pull into the Dorking Station, I gazed unseeing at the people on the platform—

One of whom was Sherlock Holmes.

Not even disguised. He wore his country tweeds and his deerstalker hat.

At first, in my daze of gloom, I felt only the faintest niggling of recognition, and then I blinked, sensing that he was someone familiar, and then I gasped and shot up as if a pin had stuck me, running out of my compartment. Just as the train screeched and wheezed to a stop, I reached a doorway, shoved past the conductor stationed there, and—not wishing to call my brother's famous name aloud—I put thumb and forefinger to my mouth and blasted quite a clear, loud whistle.

He turned; I waved; he saw me. So, of course, did everyone else, the expressions on their faces exhibiting how aghast they were that a female quite properly clad in a teal traveling costume with matching hat should behave in such an unladylike manner. So much the worse for them. I grinned as Sherlock headed towards me, carrying a valise and, if I read his face aright, trying not to smile.

"What have you been up to now, Enola?" he asked with a mock scowl once we had achieved the privacy of our compartment.

I retorted, "I might well ask you the same thing."

"Indeed." Now he looked quizzical and—it took me a moment to identify an expression I had never previously seen on his face—yes, Sherlock looked sheepish. "But there's little enough to report."

"Please do report what little there is."

"Let me first light my pipe." Once this was done, and once he had emitted a cloud of smoke no more noxious than usual, he leaned back in his seat and commenced his narration. "I traveled out here Friday evening, and yesterday, in the guise of a reasonably sober Irishman, I applied for a station as a groom at the Dunhench stables, but I was turned down. I loitered to gossip but learned nothing concerning our client's sister. I invited myself to take tea in the servant's hall, chatting up the women, but they gave nothing away except by the rigidity of their postures and the tightness of their faces; they know something but are frightened of it."

"So you made no progress."

"Wait a moment. It gets worse. I took my leave on foot, doubled back to hide in the woods, and found a leafy dingle in which to doze until late at night when all the lights in Dunhench Hall had gone out. I then burgled the place. I need not bore you with details; suffice it to say that should I ever require another career, I would make an excellent burglar. I quickly penetrated the library and opened the safe I found hidden behind a large but unlovely oil painting of an ancestral Rudcliff. I riffled both the safe and the desk thoroughly in search of any suggestive leaf or scrap of paper, anything to reveal the whereabouts of the putative asylum to which Lady Felicity was committed, or the pseudonym under which it might have been done, but I found nothing. Not the slightest indication."

"Finding nothing does not prove there is nothing to find."

"I found rather less than nothing. Having failed in the library, I stole upstairs and into Lord Cadogan's suite of rooms, their location having been revealed to me in the course of my conversation with his servants. There, with greatest stealth, I attempted to examine by rushlight the papers on his dresser top and bedside table. However, he awoke, and I was obliged to flee."

"Sherlock! Did he see you?"

"He saw no more than something that went bump in the night, nor did anyone else, although I must say the man has an excellent pair of lungs. However, a brave lad sped off on horseback to alert the constabulary, who are scouring the countryside for suspicious persons. I thought it wise to take early leave of Threefinches, so here I am. And now, Enola, your report?"

Trying to think how best to begin, I quipped, "Might I borrow your pipe?"

"Nonsense, Enola." But he could not quite keep the corners of his mouth from twitching upwards.

"Well, Tish and I visited Bedlam, and returned much shaken in our emotions *and* our plans, for we learned it was quite possible, in any given asylum, for Flossie to be in residence without our ever seeing her."

"There were some wards to which you were not admitted."

"Exactly. Also, wherever Lord Cadogan has

committed Flossie, surely he is paying well to have her concealed."

"Have you gained any insight as to why he might have dealt with her so?"

"Wait a minute. Today I visited St. John's to talk with the Haskells. Because the local doctor confessed on his deathbed, we now know conclusively that darling Caddie's first wife, Myzella, was indeed committed to an insane asylum, where—"

Sherlock interrupted with what for him must be called considerable excitement. "*Which* asylum?"

"It doesn't matter. The Haskells had it closed down as a pesthole; Myzella among many others had succumbed there to Thames River damps. Apparently Lord Cadogan then felt free to marry again."

"And once again to marry below his station in life." Sherlock bit on his pipe stem and puffed hard, frowning—most likely because he found it distasteful to talk with a female, me, about such a sensitive topic as matrimonial union. "Enola, has it occurred to you to wonder why he wed Flossie Glover, no matter how pretty and talented she was, when he could have had . . ." Apparently overcome with delicacy, he failed to complete the sentence.

I endeavored to complete it for him. "When he could have had any available woman from scullery maid to maid of honour. I would respond that he is the sort of man who considers women fungible."

His eyebrows shot up. "I beg your pardon?"

"Fungible. Interchangeable, one much the same as another, like cattle or clothespins or checkers on a board. Our mother taught me the word to describe a certain kind of womanizer."

"My dear sister!" My candor shocked him.

"Dear brother, you know it's true. I daresay the reason Lord Cadogan did not marry a titled woman was that a woman of rank, with a powerful family, would have been much more difficult to discard when he tired of her."

"Then why marry at all?"

"For the sake of an heir, most likely. But for some reason he quickly tired of Flossie. I imagine she was rather too decent a person for him."

Sherlock puffed his pipe in silence for some time, and continued to hold it in his teeth even after it went out. I watched the view from the window—we had reached the wretched Southwark slums of London—but I saw only the disturbing images in my mind. A beautiful woman barefoot, her clothing clawed to rags, her hair half pulled out by the denizens of a madhouse. And the cad of a so-called gentleman who had put her there, who had cast her off like a rag. Lord Rudcliff riding his high horse to hounds. Lord Rudcliff in an expensive smoking jacket, smiling over his wine. Lord Rudcliff ogling the servant girl who brought him his nightcap.

As we pulled into Victoria Station, my brother blinked, roused, and pocketed his pipe. "What are we to tell our client?" he asked me. "That we have exhausted all avenues of inquiry?"

"There must be something we can do about that cad!" My vehemence and volume surprised me; I gentled my tone. "I must think, Sherlock. And I must do so without the assistance of shag tobacco."

I knew myself to be tall, like my brother, and dolicho-cephalic, like my brother, and regrettably similar to him in profile, which is to say, proboscis. But I also knew myself to be quite unlike him in many ways even aside from being female. Dr. Watson's accounts of my brother portrayed him as forgetting to eat when he was at his most brilliant. I, however, never forget to eat, and I believe a good meal being well digested is as significant an aid to the brain as it is to any other portion of my personage.

So, upon returning to the Professional Women's Club, I dined well on saddle of mutton with mint sauce and parsley, hot potato crisps, apple dumplings, and rice pudding. Afterwards, alone in my room, I seated myself at my desk and brought out pencil and paper as unconsciously as many women take up their knitting. (My mother saw to it that I was not taught to knit, crochet, embroider, or play the piano; she wanted to make quite sure that I would never become domestic or decorative.) Idly, as if of its own accord, rather like the pointer on a Ouija board, my hand started sketching, producing a nastily leering caricature of Lord Cadogan Burr Rudcliff II's ever-so-handsome face.

Warming to that subject, I drew him sticking out his tongue, then falling off a horse with posterior in the air, then with his coattails flapping as he ran after a fleeing woman, who metamorphosed as I drew her from a scullery maid to someone more like the women I had seen at Bedlam. Setting Caddie aside, I found myself drawing picture after picture of them, the so-called madwomen: barefoot, ragged, abject, slumped on benches, curled like rubbish on the floor. One of them was Flossie. Although I had never met her, I had seen her photograph and her twin sister, Tish. Filling paper after paper, I drew Flossie, thin and haggard, dressed in a heavy quilted canvas strong dress, then Flossie in rags with her long hair in a dreadful tangle hanging down, then Flossie quite lovely in an evening gown, and then Flossie in a magnificent new hat and a jacket with stylishly puffed shoulders. Opposite her I drew Tish, very smart and rather daring in a bowler, a waistcoat, a high collar, and a flowing ascot.

Usually something helpful would float up from the more obscure recesses of my mind when I went on a sketching jag like this. But I knew better than to *think* about it. I drew Flossie again, on quite a spirited horse in a riding habit, and then Tish—but I had only just sketched in her face when something quite unusual happened.

Someone knocked on my door.

Papers scattered all over the floor as I arose and hurried over, calling, "Who is it?"

"Tish."

"Tish!" I opened the door wide, welcoming her in, so delighted to have a visitor that I forgot I had no good news for her.

She stepped into my room, saw my sketches strewn across the coconut-fiber matting at my feet, and exclaimed "You drew these? They are wonderful! Don't step on them!" She crouched and started picking them up, taking a close look at each one. "I see that your opinion of Lord Cadogan agrees with mine . . . Oh! You drew *me*!"

"That's not you," I said, trying to tease a smile out of her. "That's Flossie dressed like you."

"Of course. That's why you made me pretty."

Hearing a shadow in her whimsy, I protested, "Tish, you *are* pretty." Sitting down on the floor beside her, I picked up another drawing, the one in which I had memorialized the wine-red evening gown, and joked, "This is you dressed up as Flossie."

But as I spoke, as I heard my own words, something splashed and bubbled deep in my mind. I sat with my mouth open.

Nor had Tish smiled, only reached for a sketch of a barefoot woman in rags. In a pained tone she said, "This may be what Flossie looks like now."

"Oh," I whispered, my eyes widening like the ripples of my thoughts. "Oh, my blessed stars."

Chapter the Fifteenth

Tish and I talked for hours that night. I gave her a full report of all the efforts made by Sherlock, and by me, to find out exactly what had happened to Flossie. I told her about conversing with Sherlock on the train that afternoon, and his questioning whether we had exhausted all avenues of inquiry. And then I confided in her that there was a plan beginning to sketch itself in my mind, only a few lines of which were at this point plain to me, but she could help me work it out if she would be so kind. Taking my time, I explained as best I could.

She was at first incredulous. Later, as I convinced her that I earnestly believed in the scheme I had begun to form, Tish was terrified, dreadfully frightened, yet at the same time courageously willing to try.

By the time midnight neared, it had become obvious that neither of us would sleep that night, so I persuaded Tish to let me do her hair in an elaborate coif, after which I crowned her with one of my most elegant hats, applied a hint of rouge to her lips and cheeks, and covered her mannish costume with a flowing, fur-trimmed polonaise. I loaned her my best kid gloves, then gave her a dainty, lace-edged handkerchief and instructed her how to dangle it between thumb and forefinger by its middle, for a lady must always carry something in one hand. Then off we went, as all the clocks of London were striking the witching hour, to call on Sherlock.

According to Dr. Watson's accounts, the great Sherlock Holmes hardly ever slept, being wont to research, ponder, or do chemical experiments all night. However, that night no light showed in his windows or Mrs. Hudson's, either. For several reasons, including the effort Tish and I had expended to dress her up for the occasion, I felt unwilling to retreat. I both pounded on the door and rang the bell, knocking up Mrs. Hudson and, in due course, my brother.

Yawning, he came out of his bedroom in a dressing gown and carpet slippers, blinked at Tish, arched his brows and inquired, "Lady Felicity?"

"You see, Tish?" I told her, trying not to gloat. "You can carry it off."

Sherlock said, "Tish?" then corrected himself, "Miss Glover, please be seated," then said to me, "She can carry off what?"

"Impersonating her sister."

"Evidently. But why is it necessary to demonstrate this in the middle of the night?"

"Because I do not think she will allow me to dress her up like a doll ever again."

"Quite right," said Tish from her chair. "Nor will it be necessary. I'll gladly exchange this monstrous hat for bare feet and a ragged dress."

Sherlock's eyebrows levitated yet higher, and he pleated his long personage to sit upon his settee. Then his brows descended as he eyed me, hawklike. "Enola, are you concocting one of your bizarre schemes?"

"The most bizarre ever," I acknowledged. Then I sat down and told him about it.

"Risky," Sherlock said half an hour later, puffing on his pipe as I had seldom seen him puff before. "Very risky, and it will all be up to you, Miss Glover."

She raised doubtful eyes to him. "Do you really think I can do it?"

"You must, for this harebrained venture may be our only hope of finding your sister. I admit I have no better option to offer."

"You think we should try, then."

"Yes, and we must plan the exploit down to the last detail. We will need beeswax, soap, vinegar, petroleum jelly, rice powder, greasepaint—and what about your hair? Is it exactly the same colour as your sister's?"

"No. She, um, enhances hers with lemon juice," said Tish, blushing at her own candor. After hesitating, she added, "Nor do I think any amount of tangling will achieve the proper effect. I think—I think it would be best if we cut it all off."

"My dear young lady!" Sherlock protested, aghast.

"Tish can borrow my wigs until it grows out again," I told him in my most soothing tone. *Men*, I thought, *so excitable about trifles.*

Tish added, "The effect will be so horrifying that he will scarcely notice what I say or do, in case I lose my nerve."

"A good point. But you fairly make my head spin, you two." Sherlock glanced at the Persian slipper on his mantelpiece as if he were thinking of refilling his pipe, shook his head, then turned to us with a decided gesture. "It is very late. Let us convene again tomorrow morning. I have several affairs of moment in hand," added Sherlock, "including quite a delicate matter involving a gold mine in the Andes and a recent chupacabra attack on the British ambassador to Chile, but I admit that even that little puzzle does not exhibit the features of novelty and ingenuity promised by the singular adventure of Dunhench Hall. Young ladies, you can count on my presence and support."

By morning, I had slept a little, my excitement of mind had calmed somewhat, and I realized more soberly the danger into which I proposed to send Tish for Flossie's sake. In order to protect Tish, we would have to plan as if organizing a military sally into enemy territory.

Sherlock, I am sure, realized the same, for when I arrived at his lodging I found him setting up a large chalkboard and arranging chairs to face it. Then, to my pleasant surprise, in came Dr. Watson. As I greeted him and gave him a cup of tea, I remarked to Sherlock, "You have called in reinforcements."

"Indeed, and I wish we had more. Ah, good morning, Miss Glover," he said as she entered. He introduced her. "Miss Letitia Glover, my friend and associate Dr. Watson."

"We met once before, briefly." Just the same, always the gentleman, Watson stood up and bowed, very nearly spilling his tea.

Tish asked Sherlock, "Does he know?"

"He knows only that we need to free your sister, who happens to be your twin, from a lunatic asylum, the location of which is yet to be determined."

"And," said Watson, "I appreciate the chance for revenge upon the man who forged my signature on an official document."

"Hear, hear," said Sherlock.

I told Dr. Watson, "Simply put, the plan is that Miss Glover, disguised as her sister with a torn dress, bare feet, and harrowed face, should confront her brother-in-law so as to make him believe his wife has escaped. Our hope is that he will then reveal the location of the lunatic asylum by ordering her to be taken back there."

Dr. Watson commented only with lifted eyebrows and a low whistle.

"Exactly," said Sherlock. "We must organize every stage of this rather risky undertaking." He began to write on the blackboard, and like obedient schoolchildren we all took our seats. In blocky chalk letters Sherlock wrote:

ESTABLISH HEADQUARTERS NEAR DUNHENCH

GET MISS LETITIA GLOVER INTO DUNHENCH HALL
UNDER OUR SECRET GUARD

WHEN SHE IS FORCED INTO CARRIAGE, ACCOMPANY
AND/OR FOLLOW

IF NAME OF ASYLUM KNOWN, STOP CARRIAGE. IF
DESTINATION UNKNOWN, FOLLOW WITHOUT FAIL

IN EITHER CASE, WATSON MUST USE HIS M.D.
AUTHORITY TO FREE LADY FELICITY

Dense but docile, as always, Watson inquired, "Lady Felicity?"

"Felicity Glover Rudcliff, Countess of Dunhench, our client's twin sister and the unhappy wife of Cadogan Burr Rudcliff the Second, Earl of Dunhench in Surrey."

"Oh."

"Now, how are we all to get there? We cannot approach by way of Threefinches. Enola and I would be recognized there, and excite too much talk."

"We could travel by train to Woking, then rent a drag to approach from the opposite direction, across country," Watson said. "Perhaps we should hire a vacant cottage near Dunhench Hall, if one is to be found."

Sherlock concurred. "An excellent idea. As I am known in those parts, would you kindly go there at your earliest convenience, Watson, and call upon land agents?"

"I will go today."

"And Tish and I will visit used clothing stores in order to costume her," I volunteered.

Sherlock said, "Once we arrive at our mutual destination, I will help you render her quite ghastly, Enola, with a few tricks from the world of the theatre."

Tish asked in a small voice, "But how am I to get into Dunhench Hall?"

"Ah. There, indeed, is the rub. We must go after dark, on an evening when the charming earl is either dining or sitting alone, and I suppose we must either bribe the lodge-keeper or cosh him. I dare say you can handle things once we get you past the gates?"

"I think I can fool the butler and Caddie." Her small voice enlarged slightly. "I look like Flossie and I can act like Flossie when she is angry and I can say what she would say. Heaven knows I have seen her in tempers enough."

"Good." Sherlock's mouth twitched at the corners.

"And the worst Caddie is likely to do to me is slap

me." She did not sound as if she much looked forward to Caddie or to being slapped.

"One or more of us will be right outside to defend you. But assuming there is no need for us to intervene, after you are thrown out of Dunhench Hall, what then? We must assume they will put you in an enclosed carriage. I hope Enola will be able to slip in and hide under the seat when they bring it around for you. Watson and I must follow. But how? We need to have a gig or something of the sort hidden and waiting just outside the gate, which means we need another man, someone to hold the horse and keep an eye on the lodge-keeper. Someone we can trust."

Silence.

"Miss Glover, are you sure you have no suitable male relatives?"

"I'm quite sure."

"Watson? Have you anyone to suggest?"

He did not look as if he did. But with the vibrant sensation of a brilliant idea warming my mind, I spoke; indeed, I nearly shouted. "I know who would love to help. Tewky!"

Chapter the Sixteenth

That was on Monday, but it took us until Friday to put everything together.

We each had tasks. I posted a preliminary letter to Tewky. Watson took three days to find and secure the best possible vacant cottage for our purposes. Tish and I drew and reviewed floor plans for Dunhench Hall. Sherlock planned everything on paper, made numerous lists, and procured detailed maps of Surrey and the surrounding areas. Tish and I ventured into the slums of London's East End to search used clothing shops for a suitably appalling dress, plus a complete mourning out-fit (my idea) to hide her from curious eyes whilst travel-ing. And on a day when Tish had to work, Sherlock and I took the train to Belvidere to see Viscount Tewkes-bury, Marquess of Basilwether. I protested that I could go by myself, but Sherlock said he needed to witness this transaction if he were to believe it. "A nobleman's son and heir, driving a gig at midnight for the sake of one of your mad schemes, Enola?" he grumbled as we walked up the drive to Basilwether Hall. "Ludicrous."

I retorted, "Can you name me any other able-bodied, intelligent young man within our circle of ac-quaintance who is so blithely unemployed and free to assist us?"

He replied only with a snort before a youthful voice shouted, "Halloo!" and Tewky appeared hatless but otherwise impeccable in a shooting jacket and fawn-coloured breeches, vaulting over a balustrade to greet us. "Hello, Mr. Holmes who brought me home!" Heartily he shook Sherlock's hand. "It is wonderful to see you again. Hello, Enola!" Arms flung wide open, he threatened to give me a brotherly bear hug.

I stepped back, smiling, but spoke seriously. "Tewky,

do please settle down and pay attention. It turns out that 'black barouche' symbolizes the sort of vehicle body snatchers employ when they carry people off to a lunatic asylum. We need your help."

He sobered at once. "Anything I can do for either of you—"

"It's both of us," Sherlock interrupted, "and you'd better hear about it before you make any promises. Let us take a walk, shall we?"

Tewky had been raised in a house full of servants who, of course, eavesdropped; he understood at once. He took us for a ramble between the gardens and the woods while Sherlock and I explained the circumstances to him. His response could not have been more satisfactory. "All you want me to do is take the train to Dorking, hire a fast horse and a wagonette, meet you near Dunhench Hall, and assist you as necessary? Of course I will do it. Might I be allowed to punch Lord Cadogan in the nose?"

"Only if I punch him first," said Sherlock, sounding as dry as a gourmand's oldest wine. "And depending, of course, whether the duke and duchess will assent to your taking part in this harebrained enterprise."

"It's not harebrained at all. It's brilliant," said Tewky, very much to my gratification. "And of course my parents will be honoured to let me help you, in preparation for my career as a coachman, as driving is the only thing I'm the least bit good at."

He meant to make us laugh, and he did. But a few moments later, inside Basilwether Hall, speaking with his parents in our presence, he was quite serious. "This is a chance for me to repay, in some small measure, my debt to Miss Holmes."

"And of course, it is also a chance to have an adventure," added the duchess with a wry look on her distinguished face. Nevertheless, she and the duke assented to their son's participation in the scheme, I think largely because of the grave authority of Sherlock Holmes.

"We will all be depending on you," Sherlock admonished as he handed handwritten instructions and a hand-drawn map to Marquess Tewkesbury Viscount of Basilwether.

I think Tish ate very little during that week of preparation. Indeed, she had eaten little since receiving news of the "passing away" of her sister, and she had slept badly, so she had grown gaunt and pallid. From Sherlock's point of view, this boded well for her success in passing herself off as the unfortunate Flossie. I, however, worried about her. On the morning of The Appointed Day I took it upon myself to invite her to breakfast with me in a private room at my club—an excellent breakfast, including ham, fish, *and* tongue along with hot rolls and sweet biscuits—and I exhorted her to eat well, but to no avail. She swallowed only a few mouthfuls.

"Tish, you must bolster your strength! What will happen to Flossie if you become too weak to play your role?"

Her smile looked tired. "Stop fussing, Enola. You're not my mother."

The shock of such a notion, that I could resemble anyone's mother, hushed me for the time being, until we adjourned to my room to prepare for travel. Because we desired to attract no attention, regretfully I made myself as inconspicuous as possible in a tan serge suit and my plainest hat over hair knotted into a severe bun. As for Tish, her widow's weeds completely concealed her from head to toe, even her face being hidden by the thick black veil fastened to the brim of her stiff black hat. "Heavens, I can barely see where I'm going," she murmured, clinging to my arm as we made our way downstairs and out to our awaiting cab, into which our bags, along with a picnic hamper, had already been loaded.

Sherlock and Watson met us at the train station, and for once, my brother wore neither his deerstalker nor his top hat. Although not exactly in disguise, he did manage to blend into the populace in brown trousers bagged at the knee from wear, a slightly frayed jacket, and an old homburg. As for Watson, there was no need for him to modify his appearance in any way; he was, and always had been, deceptively undistinguished.

Meeting on the platform, seeing to our luggage, boarding the train, and even in the privacy of our compartment, we took care to speak quietly, seldom, and only of commonplaces, such as what a nice warm day it was, summery in September, and, as the train progressed out of London, how lovely was the countryside. Tish kept her veil down and barely spoke; the conductor might have thought she was a young widow sunken in grief. Sherlock read the newspapers. Watson and I, seated diagonally across from each other, chitchatted on occasion for appearance's sake.

We traveled to Woking, and got off at a station unfamiliar to me but not, evidently, to Sherlock. Hailing a porter to help with our luggage, he led us to where our transportation awaited us. The "drag" turned out to be a capacious vehicle drawn by no less than four horses, basically a large vehicle too plain to be called a carriage, a vehicle with no cloaked and cockaded coachman; a plain country fellow drove us. No shining harness or bearing reins on the decidedly commonplace horses. No filigree and no very plush upholstery, either. Once we were rumbling along and the driver could not hear us, I felt free to say, "We are roughing it."

"To simulate being a party of small means and no consequence," said Holmes.

"Wait until you see the cottage," added Watson with a smile as mischievous as a boy's.

From behind her veil, Tish spoke up suddenly, her tone distressed. "What if, after all this, Caddie isn't *home*?"

Asperity tightened Sherlock's face, but before he could say anything too cutting, Watson spoke. "I am sure Mr. Holmes has his sources of information, Miss Glover."

"Quite true," Sherlock affirmed with a reasonable degree of patience. "Lord Rudcliff remains in residence in Dunhench Hall, and he has no houseguests."

Our conveyance bucked and slewed along the rutted country roads. Evidently it lacked any sort of springs or suspension. To talk was to risk involuntarily biting the end of one's tongue off. We were silent.

The train trip from London seemed a mere whisk compared to the interminable journey in the drag along unimproved byways, and all four horses were evidently quite necessary to "drag" such a load across such terrain. Several times, I reminded myself rather sternly that this method of approaching Dunhench Hall was necessary in order to keep our arrival secret.

Finally, Watson got to his feet, stuck his head out a window and shouted to the driver, who bellowed back. Then, after several moments of such back-and-forthing as we found our way between tall hedges lining twisty lanes, we halted in front of our "headquarters."

The cottage was everything Watson had promised it to be, which is to say it was not much. Patches of plaster had fallen from the outer walls, baring the fieldstone beneath. Its low roof made its two windows and door-for-a-nose resemble a glowering Neanderthal. The two-room interior, furnished with nothing but a stove, a table, and a few chairs, looked not much more attractive—but I did not care, for I was hungry. At once I unpacked our cold and rather late luncheon from its hamper. To my surprise and annoyance, no one else except me seemed very interested in the deviled eggs, baked bean sandwiches, crackers and sardines, et cetera.

Staring out of the cottage's back window, Sherlock waved away my offer of cold Welsh rarebit. "Unless I am much mistaken, one can actually see Dunhench Hall from here."

"Correct. We are situated directly behind its grounds." Coming indoors after having seen to the luggage and dismissed the drag, Watson also gestured refusal when I thrust a sandwich towards him. "Holmes, I have a thought. If we can find or make a way to walk in from here, then we shall not have to deal with the lodge-keeper."

"Splendid!" exclaimed my brother, and the pair of

them seized sticks and sallied forth, to be seen no more before dark.

Sighing, I laid aside the Swiss cheese I was devouring, stood up, and went over to Tish, who remained standing in the middle of the room like a black-draped lamppost. I lifted the heavy veil and peered under it as if discovering her face in a cave. She looked ghastly pale amidst all that black. "Come out, come out, wherever you are," I quipped, pulling hatpins so that I could lift away the shroud of black that enveloped her head. After it was gone she stood blinking, as if the dim light of the cottage dazzled her. I took her by the hand and led her to the table. "Come and sit with me and eat something, Tish."

She sat, but she said, "I can't eat."

"Truly? Try a few crackers, at least." I opened the can of sardines.

"I can't. I'll be sick."

Munching sardines and crackers, I asked, "Why? What frightens you? His caddish Lordship?"

"Yes. But even more . . ." She gulped, looked down, looked up at me, and I could see she spoke with great difficulty. "Even more, the prospect of the lunatic asylum itself. Being taken there and—and put away."

"Tish, Dr. Watson and my brother will not let you be locked up! You will only lead the way so that we can rescue your sister. Will it not be wonderful to free Flossie?"

"If she is all right. But if—if she has become like the others . . ."

Beginning to comprehend the breadth and depth of her fears, I lost my own appetite, setting sardines and crackers aside. "I must admit I've given very little thought to the aftermath," I said softly. Where would Flossie go, where would she stay, if not with her sister? And what if Flossie had become a bit mad in the madhouse? How was Tish to take care of her and make a living at the same time?

I took a deep breath. "Tish, let me say two things. One: I will always help you. And two: sometimes it is best to deal with one problem at a time." Resolutely I stood up to take her into the other room. "Right now, you and I have a great deal of work to do."

Chapter the Seventeenth

"Let's cut my hair first," Tish said.

Get the worst thing over with, I thought. I said nothing, but neither did I begin to hack heartlessly at her hair. Freeing her long locks from where they had been pinned up behind her ears, I combed them down over her back, then braided them into a tight, thick plait perhaps half a metre long, tying it not only at the bottom, but at the top as well. Then I took scissors to her hair above the plait and cut it off. I laid it in her lap. She placed one hand atop it, accepting it, but did not speak or look up.

Cropping off what remained of her hair close to her head, I watched for tears, but saw none. Finally I asked, "How are you?"

"I feel quite literally light-headed. And it's cold. I believe my scalp is getting goose bumps."

I laughed in relief that she had some spirit back, fastened a shawl into a sort of turban around her head for warmth, and prepared to work on the rest of her. Because he knew she would not welcome his personal assistance, Sherlock had given me detailed instructions. "Change your clothes," I told her, "and we shall uglify the skin of your limbs and shoulders."

"How exciting."

"Call me when you are ready." I went into the other room, where the stove was.

During my solitary luncheon I had managed to light the stove using kindling and sticks we had brought with us in the drag. My brother had foreseen and provided for every contingency, including water, which we had carried in kegs, and basins and such. Testing the pot of water I had put on the stove, I found it to be passably warm. While I waited, I leaned my arms on the sill of the rear window and stared at the grim peaked towers of Dunhench Hall silhouetted against the sky.

"Ready!" called Tish.

I hauled the pot of water into the other room where Tish was, then set it down while I admired her. In the stained and grimy secondhand unmentionables we had bought for her, and a faded, tattered dress that failed to quite conceal them, she looked quite shocking already.

"You deserve a medal," I told her. "An investiture from the queen."

"Why?"

"You're brave, Tish." I hugged her, had her sit down, then took a bar of homemade brown lye soap, dipped it in the water and began to lather her exposed limbs with it.

"The Most Honourable Order of the Bath?" Tish joked.

"If only it were that simple. You must let that soap scum dry upon you. Meanwhile, we must see to your hands."

"What about them?"

"Did Flossie clip her fingernails the way you do?"

"No, not being a typist, she grew them longer . . . oh, dear."

"Not to worry. I have the solution right here." I set to work with a goodly supply of dried pistachio shells Sherlock had provided, fitting them exactly upon her nail beds, fixing them there with rubber cement and then snipping the ends a bit raggedly. As Tish watched, her eyes opened wide. "How remarkable!"

If by "remarkable" she meant that her fingernails now looked overgrown, splitting and dirty, she was quite correct.

"Now your toes, as you must go barefoot."

First, however, I collected an interesting selection of grime from the stove, the window ledges, and the doorstep. Down on my knees, I rubbed this mixture of soot, dust, and dirt upon her feet to make them appear as if they had gone days without washing.

"Didn't people do something like this in the Bible?" asked Tish with exaggerated innocence.

"Quite the opposite, I think."

"So you are not going to wipe my feet with your hair?"

Her tone was so droll it made me laugh. "Tish, you are being outrageous!"

"Exactly. Did you say you are going to glue pistachio nut shells onto my toenails?"

"Yes." And by the time I had done so, the soap scum had completely dried upon her limbs, making her skin look rough, neglected, and singularly repulsive, almost as if she might be a leper. For a moment I stood arms akimbo, looking her over much as a cook might survey a successful soufflé.

"I feel crusty," Tish said, not complaining at all; in fact, she sounded wryly amused.

"Yes, but I think you are not terribly durable. You must be careful not to brush against anything and spoil your delicate patina." I cocked my head in admiration. "I almost hate to tamper with near perfection," I murmured.

"But you will."

"Of course."

"What comes next?"

"Vinegar." I brought the bottle from the other room and poured a small amount of the pungent white liquid into a dish, then wet my fingers in it and flicked a few drops of it onto Tish. "I mustn't use too much, or Caddie might notice you smell like a pickle factory—oh, look!"

Where the drops of vinegar had landed on Tish, her "skin" had blistered to resemble boils or running sores. Tish looked, gasped, and said, "Jolly good! Sprinkle me some more!"

I did so, reminding myself of what Mum had taught me: a true artist must know when to stop. Then, leaving Tish to dry, immobile in her chair as if she were a watercolour on an easel, I went into the other room to melt some beeswax on the stove. Now that my assigned work was mostly done, suddenly the day seemed to be darkening and the bare little cottage felt lonesome. I wished Sherlock and Watson would come back from their walk, or Tewky would drive in.

Where *was* His Tewkiness? He should have been here by now.

"Don't fuss," I muttered to myself.

But winds of worry and conjecture began to blow in my mind, setting it to skirling like a bagpipe. Had Tewky somehow gotten lost? Sherlock had given him excellent directions and a detailed map, but still, had he somehow missed his way? Had he overslept, taken a later train, missed his stop? No, I knew better; he was not so stupid, and my droning, discordant thoughts rose to wail: Some accident must have befallen him, some calamity! What if he were lying, bloody and broken, in a ditch?

I heard someone at the front door, my heart seized upon hope, and I turned so quickly that my skirt whirled. But it was only Sherlock and Watson returning from their explorations.

"We found a way in through the back!" Watson told me with his characteristic boyish excitement.

"Where is Marquess Tewkesbury?" demanded Sherlock.

"Hello to you, too," I said.

"Enola," Sherlock insisted, "what has become of your young friend? This venture cannot go forward without him."

"Why did he not travel with us by way of Woking?" Watson asked.

"Because a drag and a wagonette caravanning in tandem would have been far too noticeable. Or so I thought. Hang everything, Enola, where *is* he?"

"What makes you think I am clairvoyant, brother mine?" I tried not to sound nearly as concerned as I was. "I hope he will be here by the time you finish rendering Tish a horror to behold."

"How are we doing with Miss Glover?"

"Go look."

He did so, walking into the other room. Following, I heard him utter "Aha!" with satisfactory fervor. "You look ravishing, Miss Glover, by the most literal definition of the word." He went over to her and removed the shawl I had wrapped around her head, lifting it off with a flourish as if unveiling a work of art, then stepping back to admire. "Miss Glover, the sacrifice of your hair . . . I salute you. The sepulchral effect could not be more salubrious for our purposes. Would you permit me a few finishing touches in the vicinity of your face?"

With a wan smile she nodded.

I watched with such fascination as to send chills down my spine as he traced most carefully around her eyes with a stick of charcoal, then applied rice powder to whiten her pallor, then rubbed a variety of grey grease-paints under her cheekbones and jaw, along the sides of her nose, and gently across her eyelids and around her eyes until their orbits filled with shadow like the sockets of a skull. With another stick of greasepaint, he whitened her already pale lips. He smoothed a ghastly sheen of petroleum jelly across her brow and down her nose. Then he rubbed both grease and charcoal into what little was left of her hair until it lost any appearance of freshness or life; it either bristled like a scrub brush or else clung to her scalp. Finally, he applied under her nose, along her lower eyelids, and around her mouth the beeswax I had melted and cooled, shaping it with his fingertips until it assumed a most unsightly appearance of dried mucus.

As he stood up and back to study his handiwork, spontaneously I applauded. "Bravo! Sherlock, I salute you. Tish, you look mad enough to frighten *me*. Would you like to see?" I flourished a hand mirror.

She hesitated before whispering, "Very well."

Approaching, I held up the mirror so that she could see her face in it. She gasped, flinching away from her own reflection.

"Tish?"

"Do . . . do we . . ." She seemed shocked almost beyond speech. ". . . we really think . . . Flossie . . ."

"No! Oh, no, not at all!" I stumbled over myself in my eagerness to reassure her, plopping down to sit on the floor by her feet. "Surely Flossie has neither lost her hair nor grown so ghastly. You do not represent her *really*, Tish, although you must pretend to *be* her."

"But . . . you think . . . Caddie will believe?"

From behind me spoke the wise yet uncomplicated voice of Dr. Watson. "If Lord Cadogan retains any soul at all, he will see in you the spectre of his guilt."

I told Tish, "You will be his worst nightmare come to life. He will feel such qualms as to obviate rational thought."

And Sherlock said, "Confound everything, where is young Tewkesbury?"

Chapter the Eighteenth

Sunlight lanced through the cottage windows at a low and canted angle. Watson settled down at the table and ate. Sherlock paced. Tish sat like a rather freakish alabaster statuette.

"If Tewkesbury doesn't arrive soon, we shall have to alter our plans!" Sherlock said loudly to no one in particular.

The sun began to set.

"If His Addlepated Lordship doesn't arrive soon, we may not be able to proceed whatsoever!"

The sun sank below the distant hills, leaving behind only twilight the hue of old ivory.

Sherlock said, "We should never have trusted him."

"Don't blame Tewky!" I cried. "Something must have gone wrong!"

And then, just as I was ready to start wringing my hands like an old woman, I heard furious clip-clopping sounds approaching. Running outside, I took one look at the impending cloud of dust and wailed, "Oh, no!" understanding exactly what had gone wrong. I dashed forward and seized the yellow horse by her bridle, helping Tewky wrestle her to a halt; otherwise, she would have shot right on past the cottage, despite the fact that she had sweated herself into a lather. "You hired Jezebel!"

"Is *that* the confounded beast's name?" Sagging on the driver's seat of the wagonette as if he were utterly wrung out, Tewky gave me a look most expressive of the epithets he would like to have uttered regarding Jezebel.

"What happened?" demanded Sherlock, who now had hold of Jezzie by the other side of her bridle as she tossed her head, pranced, tucked her hind legs underneath her, and otherwise showed every sign of wanting to bolt.

"I requested a fast horse, and she's fast, there's no denying it. But I should also have asked for an accurate horse. Direction of travel makes no difference to her, nor does staying on the road."

"Nor does discretion, evidently. She seems unlikely to fall in with our plan to wait in silence." Sherlock gave the mare a glare that would have been droll were circumstances not so dire. "Well, at least you are here, Lord Tewkesbury, along with transportation of a sort, in regard to which we need to convene in a council of war."

And so we did, once Jezzie was firmly tethered to a stout hitching post and pacified with a nosebag of oats. Tish, also, needed to be pacified a bit when told we all needed to talk, but after I draped a shawl over her head and assured her that Tewky was too preoccupied with food to look at her closely, she came out of the other room and joined the rest of us.

Sherlock took a professorial pose, arms folded, posterior propped against the table, one leg cocked rather like that of a flamingo. "Watson's very sensible plan for Miss Glover to enter Dunhench Park stealthily, through a poacher's hole in the back fence, is, alas, impractical now that darkness has fallen," he said as if ruminating aloud. "One needs daylight to pick one's way through rough woodlands. So we must enter by the front. But given the rambunctious proclivities of our horse, it now seems unlikely that any portion of our party can wait outside the gates without being noticed by the lodge-keeper."

"Therefore we need to cosh the lodge-keeper," Watson said.

"Which is risky and distasteful," Sherlock said, and then he turned suddenly to Tish. "Miss Glover, you have not eaten all day, have you? Do you feel shaky?"

She nodded, but said in a barely audible voice, "It doesn't matter."

"You are quite right that it doesn't matter once you have confronted our cad of an earl, but do you feel strong enough to walk across the lawn to Dunhench Hall? Or would it be better if we were to drop you off at the door?"

"Drop her off at the door?" I exclaimed.

"Yes. We can hide her in the wagonette. Watson

can drive. Lord Tewkesbury is dressed well enough to represent exactly what he is, an upper-class visitor. There will be no necessity to cosh the lodge-keeper if he simply lets us in. As for the element of surprise . . . Enola, Miss Glover, please think: in your experience of the place, is there any way for the lodge-keeper to forewarn Dunhench Hall of visitors?"

"Such as a telephone?" I joked.

"Such as sending a child running ahead with a message."

"Surely not at night," I objected.

"During the wedding," Tish said as if it pained her to think about her sister's wedding, "carriages simply drove in, and guests were announced at the door. But we don't want Caddie knowing how I got to his door, do we?"

"No. We want him to think you have run across country barefoot from only he knows where. Therefore, I have another question: could we drive towards Dunhench Hall across the grass, to muffle the sound of hooves and wheels?"

Tish and I exchanged questioning looks, then nodded. I answered, "The grounds in front of the hall are quite open."

"For complete stealth, could we manage without lanterns?"

I thought of the well-lighted portico. "Perhaps."

With an old soldier's fortitude and optimism, Watson said, "I think we should go find out."

Tish hid under a seat of the wagonette, on which I sat with my skirt spread protectively, regretting for the first time that dresses with fifteen yards of flounces had gone out of fashion. Sherlock sat beside me in a dark corner because of his rather seedy clothes, and Tewkesbury sat across from us, ready to deal aristocratically with the lodge-keeper. Watson, the driver, had given a bucket of water to Jezzie before we departed, and now was probably wishing he could retract such kindness.

"Whoa! I say whoa, there!" I had never heard Watson sound so ill-tempered as when he struggled to halt Jezzie at Dunhench Hall's wrought-iron gate. His angry voice brought the lodge-keeper out at once.

Viscount Tewkesbury, Marquess of Basilwether, stuck his top-hatted head out of the wagonette's window on his side. "A surprise visit to an old friend, my good man," he drawled at the gatekeeper, his bored tone achieving the perfect acme of aristocratic condescension.

"Yes, my lord. Of course, my lord." The man opened the gate forthwith, and we rattled through. As soon as the gate closed behind us, Watson chided Jezzie again, "Whoa, there! Stay on the lane!" as he steered her onto the grass. "Confounded beast, what is the matter with you?" He actually did have a rather difficult time halting her in the deepest shadows between the gate and Dunhench Hall. Instantly, Sherlock and Tewky slipped out to extinguish the wagonette's lanterns, after which one of them, I think, walked at Jezzie's head to help Watson keep control of her as we rolled across the lawn in the dark. I cannot report exactly because I did not see. Still inside the wagonette, I was helping Tish get out from underneath the bench, careful not to knock any caked soap or beeswax off of her. I knew that we must be approaching the portico because the light through the wagonette windows increased sufficiently so that I could see her standing beside me, looking like a ghost.

She was going to need to be more durable than most ghosts. "Tish," I told her softly, "remember with your whole heart what our darling Caddie has done."

She nodded.

"And think what you would say to him if you were Flossie."

Nodding again, she lifted her head as the wagonette halted.

"And sink your dagger to the hilt."

She gave me just a flashing glance as she got out, helped by Sherlock; as I got out, helped by no one. Tewky was busy at Jezzie's head; he and Watson took the mare and wagonette away into the shadows at the side of the lawn. I ran to crouch between arbor vitae bushes next to the wall of Dunhench Hall, huddling beneath a lighted window I knew to be that of the dining room. Sherlock disappeared somewhere. And Tish, barefoot and bare-headed, ghastly and nearly indecent in her tattered dress, pattered up to the front door and knocked. Only then did I realize that the funeral wreaths were gone already, after a very brief length of time.

Tish knocked, stood waiting, then thought better of it and knocked again, loudly and at discourteous length, also pounding the door with her other hand. The instant it finally opened, she dashed into the house, brushing past the butler, who uttered an exclamation most uncharacteristic of those who buttle. Indeed, what he said was too naughty to repeat.

At the same time, Tish yelled with force and ferocity far superior to any I had expected of her, "Caddie, you treacherous silver-plated blackguard, where are you!"

Reasoning that no one was likely to notice me, as all attention was on Tish, I scrooched upward against the wall, making a long neck to peek into the bottom corner of the window.

I saw, in profile, the Earl of Dunhench sitting at his end of the candlelit dining table with his after-dinner cigar motionless in front of his wide-open mouth. In the same moment, as the dining room door burst open and Tish lunged in, the cigar fell unheeded from his fingers—for, in the shadows, her shorn head looked almost like a bleached and bony skull that spoke.

"You! My Judas husband!" Tish shrieked, her shockingly naked white arms flailing upwards as she hurtled towards him. "How could you *do* this to me?"

Caddie upset his chair as he scrambled to get to his feet, albeit not as if a lady had just entered the room. "Brindle!" he shouted for the butler. "Summon help!"

Already lights were coming on, and there was a considerable hubbub of voices sounding from the corridors of Dunhench Hall, but Tish's wild soprano cries trumped them all. "You married me!" she screamed. "You vowed to cherish me! Womanizing snake, how could you stoop so low as to send me off in a black barouche?" Running up one side of the long dining table, she rushed at Caddie as if she would lay hands on him.

Caddie dodged back behind the other side of the table, his manner most undignified in retreat, although his voice attempted a lordly tone. "Flossie, please, do calm down. Remember yourself."

"*Remember* myself? The lady who used to have *hair*?" She laughed in a way that actually gave me a chill as she climbed onto a chair, then onto the table, sending china and crystal flying as she scuttled towards her "husband."

"Brilliant!" whispered Sherlock's voice near my ear. "What an actress she would have made!" He positioned himself at the corner of the window opposite mine.

Caddie gawked, his eyes dilated in horror and fixated on her filthy, unkempt feet as she swung them over the edge of the table towards him. He backed away from her in such disorder that he stumbled and nearly fell. "Brindle! Send for the carriage!" he yelled, fairly screaming.

"You disgust me! Like something stuck to the bottom of my shoe!" Tish shrilled. "When I used to have shoes!"

His Cadship turned tail and bolted out of the room. With a wordless shriek, Tish ran after him. I could no longer see her, but I could hear her yelling from the passageway, "No! Get your troglodyte hands off of me!" Evidently footmen were attempting to subdue her, for *troglodyte* would have been too kindly a designation for her to assign to Earl Cadogan.

"By all means, act like a madwoman, Flossie." Caddie sounded angry and brutal now that he was not facing her alone. "You're going back where you belong."

"But where did she come from, Your Lordship?" asked Brindle's sepulchral voice. "How did she get here?"

My heart froze as I thought that someone might be sent to question the lodge-keeper.

But Tish flared, "On my broom! In my magic slippers, can't you all see them?"

And Caddie exploded, "Keep your filthy feet on the floor. Just get her out of here, Brindle!"

"You're no man, let alone an earl. You're a coward!" Tish cried.

"Muzzle her, somebody."

There were sounds of a struggle. "The brute," Sherlock muttered. "But she has every ability to deal with him. It's time for me to be going." One moment he was there talking, whether to me or to himself, and the next moment he had disappeared into the night.

Feeling not nearly as confident as he had sounded, I stayed where I was, worrying about Tish, unable to do anything to help her. Yet.

Chapter the Nineteenth

Time is a peculiar phenomenon, pretending to be regulated by clocks and watches, yet speeding or lagging just as it chooses. Those few moments of waiting and darkness before anything else happened were the most dilatory I had ever experienced. It seemed like ages before I heard sounds coming from the direction of the stable, eons before I saw Rudcliff's carriage come rolling up towards the hall. I felt as if I had grown a beard before it was time for me, like Sherlock, to be going.

The carriage, drawn by a sturdy pair of Cleveland Bays, rolled directly past me. I hid from the light of its lanterns, shrinking into the arbor vitae. But the instant its rear wheels spun by me, I darted out, dashed to its far side, and trotted along with it, hiding behind it and in its shadow as it pulled into the portico and halted at the hall door.

Crouching on my side of the carriage, I tried to listen, barely able to hear beyond the pounding of my own heart. For perhaps ten minutes now I had not been able to see or hear what was happening to Tish. I tried to tell myself that she had done wonderfully and would emerge undamaged. My heart wouldn't listen. She had been through rigours and would go through more. The black barouche awaited her.

I heard the door of Dunhench Hall opening. A babble ensued, including, to my relief, Tish's voice raised in undiminished fervor: "You're nothing but a pack of mongrels, the whole spineless lot of you!" And I heard scuffling sounds; she was struggling, as arranged, to divert attention from any sounds I might make.

Hoping the coachman's eyes and ears were all for

the commotion surrounding Tish, I reached up to open the door on my side of the carriage as silently as I could, slipped inside, then shut the door just as stealthily behind me.

Jonah in the whale's belly could not have felt more in the dark than I did. I stretched my arms but felt nothing, and I needed to find a seat under which to hide! The voices all too quickly drew closer, among them a matronly one I had heard before. "Now dearie, do please settle down like the sweet darling Flossie I know you are. Dear lady, you'll always be my angel lamb, no matter what they done to your precious hair . . ." Dawson choked, and her voice trailed away. Mentally I blessed her, for her loquacity gained me time to feel my way to one of the lavishly upholstered carriage seats and crawl underneath it to hide in its shadow.

"Go away, you mealymouthed, simpering sheep! Let me alone!" retorted Tish. I heard more sounds of struggle, and then someone opened the carriage door. From where I lay in hiding I could see only feet, and it alarmed me that they wore sturdy brogues; none of them were bare. Where was Tish?

"Where is Caddie?" she flared, her voice directly

above me; she perched on the seat under which I hid. "Is he too much of a coward to show me his face?"

"Now, now, my lady," said Dawson from the seat opposite. I heard what sounded like the scrape of a match, then saw a light blaze—or seem to blaze, however slight, in the darkness. It steadied; Dawson must have lit a candle. Odd, to bring a candle into a carriage, but perhaps she did not want a madwoman coming at her in the dark.

The carriage door shut and its wheels began to roll as I pondered two unexpected developments: Someone had put shoes on Tish, and Dawson was with us. Sooner or later, I would have to do something about Dawson.

But for the time being, as the carriage bore us away from Dunhench Hall, stopping only long enough for the lodge-keeper to open the gates, I stayed where I was, wishing there were some way of knowing whether Sherlock, Tewky, and Dr. Watson were following as planned. Of course the lodge-keeper would see them as their wagonette dashed out directly behind our carriage, and of course the lodge-keeper would run up to the hall and express suspicions that something peculiar was going on, but by the time that happened, if any alarum was raised, it need not concern us. Pursuit would be too late to overtake us.

I listened hard, but my ears told me little. Only the motion of the carriage informed me that we had passed the gate. Once on the high road, we swayed along at a rapid clip. Time had come for me to act, but I found myself in a bit of a quandary. While I felt no doubt that I was more than a match for Dawson, my initial position—crawling out from under a seat—would put me at a disadvantage. What if she were to scream, alerting the coachman? I most certainly did not want to deal with two adversaries at once.

Suddenly Dawson spoke; indeed, she blurted, as if driven by emotion. "Lady Dunhench, you must know that none of this at all is the least bit due to nothing you did. It's the earl; he is the way he is, and it's nobody's fault—"

Tish reacted like a viper striking. Screeching something inarticulate, she coiled, snatched off her shoe, and flung it at Dawson's face. Thereafter it is hard to describe with authority the exact sequence of events. Dawson gasped, ducking so clumsily that she nearly fell. Seizing my opportunity, I slithered out from under the carriage seat and saw her discomfiture. Tish yelled, "Cow!" and threw her other shoe at Dawson, who fell to the floor whilst ducking it—or perhaps in surprise at seeing me, or more probably because the carriage came to a crossroads and turned sharply—not for the first time.

Flat on the floor, with eyes both wild and wider than I would have thought possible considering her bovine qualities, Dawson opened her mouth to scream, but I pounced, clamping my hand over her mouth before she got past her initial squeak. Kneeling on her bosom, with one hand silencing her and the other flourishing my dagger, I warned her, "Don't make a sound."

Tish got up to retrieve her shoes, and her face was a study, but that was not what first caught my attention regarding her. At some point, I saw with surprise and relief, someone had put clothing on her, a dimity frock awkwardly tugged over the tattered dress she already wore, and sagging cotton stockings, and a shawl wrapped around her head and shoulders.

I asked, "Are you all right, Tish?"

As I remained physically atop Dawson, I felt her startle when she heard the name.

"I'm exhausted," Tish said, sitting down in a way that vouched for the veracity of this statement.

"You were marvelous, you know. Brilliant."

"Is it all going as planned?"

"There is no way of our knowing for sure, but I expect so."

"Then I may get rid of these pistachio shells?"

"And beeswax and so forth? Certainly."

With my hand still muffling her mouth, Dawson made a squeak conveying astonishment and inquiry. I turned to her and spoke most sincerely, gazing down into her eyes. "Dawson, what you are seeing is sisterly love such as you are never likely to experience again. Tish has shorn her hair, starved herself, worn a pauper's dress, and undergone the utmost rigours for the sake of her twin, all in an attempt to trick the Earl of Dunhench into mistaking her for her sister. We mean no harm to you." This while my dagger still hovered over her. "Our sole purpose is to find and free Lady Felicity. Dawson, I know you have a good heart." Although not much backbone—but I kept that thought to myself. "If I sheathe my dagger, will you promise not to interfere?"

I wanted to sound like an angel of justice with sword in hand, but I found myself wheedling.

Dawson nodded so vigorously she dislodged my hand. Standing up, I returned my dagger to its sheath in the busk of my corset, then helped her to her feet and saw her re-seated, keeping a strict watch on her the whole time lest she attempt some kind of subterfuge.

"Dawson," I demanded, "*why,* pray tell, did your master see fit to rid himself of Lady Felicity in such a disgraceful and underhanded fashion?"

She stared at me, blinking and blank, before she answered. "Why, Miss Basilwether, it's just his way. He can't stand one woman for long. Her smilin' and singin' like a lark wore him out. The wonder is that he married her in the first place. I truly believe he thought he loved her."

From across the carriage, Tish called Caddie an unrepeatable name. Unsurprised and without taking offense, Dawson turned her attention to Tish, who had already peeled or rubbed most of the pseudo-ghastliness off of her skin.

"Miss Glover," said Dawson in awed and obsequious tones, "I never would have guessed it was you."

Tish replied only with a grimace. Vestiges of rage still clung about her like incorporeal rags.

But Dawson persevered. "How on earth did you know to come looking for your lady sister?"

"You truly expected me to be so stupid as to believe Flossie was dead?"

"Most people did," said Dawson humbly.

"Most people are not twins. Flossie could not have left this life without me, or I would have felt it." Her tone changed. "I feel it now, my sister's being. She is not far away!"

"That's true." Dawson looked more than ever impressed. "We should be getting close."

"Close to *where*?" I demanded.

Quite docile, Dawson responded, "The Lesser Smythnuncle Sanatorium for Imbeciles and Mental Defectives."

As I was attempting to memorize this cognomen (in case, by any mischance, it might be needed later), the carriage slowed to navigate a curving drive, then drew to a halt. We all stiffened as we heard the driver climb down from the box—I in particular, for I froze, unable to decide whether to draw my dagger to control

Dawson or hide under the seat in case the driver opened the carriage door.

Fortunately, he did not. "Dawson," he bawled, "stay with 'er a bit until I knocks somebody up."

And to my most pleasant astonishment, Dawson called back, "All right."

The sound of his boots crunching on gravel proceeded away from us. As soon as I deemed it safe to do so, I opened the carriage door—the one opposite the direction the coachman had gone—and poked my head out.

Beyond the wan light of the carriage lamps I saw only darkness.

Trying not to let my heartbeat hasten in consternation—not quite yet—I got straight out of the carriage and walked back behind it.

Nothing.

I listened but heard no reassuring sound of clopping hooves.

We had reached the insane asylum, but I neither saw nor heard any sign of Watson or Tewky or Holmes or their wagonette or their thrice-accursed yellow horse.

Chapter the Twentieth

"Tish," I said, opening the carriage door that faced away from the asylum, "the others are not here. They must have gotten lost. We must retreat."

"I'll do nothing of the kind!" It seemed as if Tish, in playing the part of her angry twin, had seriously taken on a shoe-throwing sort of personality. "I'm going in there. I'm going to see my sister."

"But Tish, you can't!" Trying to decide on a plan of action, I was reasoning backwards from the worst thing that could happen: Tish herself being committed as a lunatic. "They won't let Flossie go on just your say-so!"

"They know Lady Felicity as Nora," volunteered Dawson, observing us eagerly yet placidly, as if seated in a theatre. "Mrs. Nora Helmer."

"She's lost her *name*?" Tish sounded dazed.

"Nora Helmer!" I exclaimed. Evidently Caddie had been to see the latest controversial play, *A Doll's House*, and had chosen a unique way to mock its heroine. "How fiendish! Tish, how can you possibly expect—"

Heatedly she cut me off. "I have not come this close to finding my sister in order to hesitate! You know where she is; go for help!"

"Afoot, in this isolated place, with no idea which way to turn?" If being committed was the worst that could happen to Tish, being stranded was the worst that could happen to me—yet I could hardly ride along in the carriage back to Dunhench Hall, could I? Nor could Tish, for that matter. Somehow I must keep both her and myself out of harm's way. "Tish—"

"Hush!" she ordered, urgently gesturing for me to leave; she must have seen, as I did, the swaying light of a lantern moving towards us. I backed away, closing the carriage door as quietly as I could, but I knew I would not do what Tish wanted of me. I could not simply abandon her in the asylum.

Only one other option occurred to me, involving swift action and surprise. But luckily, the coachman had no reason to beware of me. Indeed, he had no idea I existed.

Reaching the carriage, he opened the door and spoke to Dawson. Edging around the back of the carriage towards him, I heard his bewildered voice. "They say Missus Nora Helmer ain't run off at all. She's right there in her ward where she belong."

"That's right." Dawson sounded ever so smug. "This one here is her twin sister."

Peeking out of my hiding place, I saw the man gawking like a fish. I also surveyed his surroundings and made a useful observation.

"So what am I supposed to do?" the coachman appealed.

"The earl wants her committed just the same," said Dawson, to my scowling disapproval. Evidently Dawson was a weathervane of a woman, taking sides as the wind blew.

"But—but that's awful serious, especially as she ain't the right one."

"What other choice do you have? Adopt her, you and your wife?"

Tish said impatiently, "Just call me Mrs. Linde and take me in there." Tish had not yet ceased to surprise me; Mrs. Linde was the name of Nora Helmer's friend and confidante in *A Doll's House.*

The coachman coughed in the hesitating manner known as "hem and haw." "Well . . ."

Tish put one foot on the step to get out of the carriage. He reached out a hand to assist her.

I charged. Gentle reader, please bear in mind that, while not weighty, I *am* tall and strong, and I lanced into them like a battering ram. In less time than it takes for me to tell it, I knocked them both sprawling, Tish back into the carriage on her posterior, and the coachman similarly into a formidable rosebush.

"Enola!" Tish cried, "I will never forgive you, never!"

That hurt enough to make me bite my lip as I shut the carriage door on her and darted onward, swarming up the carriage as if it were a tree, seizing the reins from where the coachman had secured them, grabbing the whip and lashing the horses. They sprang forward, and at the same time, not at all coincidentally, I sat down hard on the coachman's bench. I kept the presence of mind to ply the reins so that the plunging horses stayed on the drive, the carriage slewed and swayed its way around the turning, and we sped back in the direction from which we had come. I heard the coachman swearing and snapping thorny branches as he struggled to get up from the rosebush, and to my satisfaction, his curses faded away, left behind.

I started tugging on the reins and addressing the horses in soothing tones, telling them they could cease galloping now. My lucky fates be praised that the Cleveland Bays, scions of a fine old breed, proved to be far more civilized than Jezebel. By the time we reached the end of the drive, I had slowed them to a trot, and I reined them in even more to accomplish the turn onto the road at a walk. Otherwise, I might have upset the carriage, especially as I could see only by the light of its lanterns. But I very much feared Tish might jump out when we slowed down. As soon as I could, I clicked my tongue and snapped the whip to send the horses once more into a smart trot.

We whirled along for a few miles, when our road ended at a thoroughfare. I had no idea which way to turn, but in this case she who hesitated might have had a mutiny on her hands; slowing the horses to a walk, I took a quick glance to the left—at darkness—then to the right, where I saw a hint of a light. Peering through trees, I thought it could have been sizable but quite distant, or closer but quite small. Indeed I had no idea what was its source, but it hardly mattered. Lost in the night, like a moth I turned towards the light, urging the horses into a trot again.

As we rounded a gentle curve in the highway, I saw it more clearly, not so far away from us; I saw it move—then felt a bolt of fear straighten my spine, for I now perceived the light to be a lantern held by a man blocking our road! A robber? I could not turn such a large, clumsy thing as a carriage to flee him, I saw no way past him, and the only other choice seemed to be to run over him.

"Halloo there!" he called, swinging the lantern.

At the sound of his voice, recognition took my

breath away. I could not muster speech to answer him as I reined in the horses.

Not knowing who I was, he strode forward, lifting his lantern to have a look at me. Voice pitched about an octave above his normal tone, he exclaimed, "Enola?"

"Hello, Sherlock. What happened?" Foolish question, for, stopping the carriage, I could see what had happened. The wagonette swooned in the ditch beside the road with its wheels spinning awry while Tewky and Watson surveyed it forlornly. As for Jezebel, she was notable only by her absence and by the damage she had wrought.

"What happened?" Sherlock mimicked. "I should ask *you* what happened. Why are you driving this carriage when we both know you cannot drive?"

I had no chance to retort, for the carriage doors opened. Tish and Dawson stepped out, Dawson carrying her now nearly spent candle.

"Enola Holmes," cried Tish, her words choked by wrath and tears, "I shall hate you forever unless we go back there and get my sister straightaway."

"Well," said Sherlock, "we can't have her hating you forever, can we?"

A short time later, when we once more drove into The Lesser Smythnuncle Sanatorium for Imbeciles and Mental Defectives, our carriage lamps were not the only illumination. Several persons, both male and female, clustered out front holding lanterns, their interest centred upon a rampantly gesticulating individual.

"That's the coachman," I explained to Sherlock, who was riding up on the box with me, having helped me get the carriage turned around. "I had to shove him into the clutches of a big rosebush, or he would have taken Tish inside."

I thought I heard Sherlock chuckle, but could not be sure, because the coachman came running towards us, shouting, "You! Thief! I'll have the law on you! Robbery, assault and battery!"

"Poppycock. Do please calm down, my good man." Alighting from the carriage with his usual energy and air of command, Sherlock offhandedly gave the coachman a folded note, specifically, a Bank of England note.

Its denomination I can only surmise, but it was sufficient to calm the coachman instantly. "And you, my
good lad," my brother addressed a stable boy who was
prepared to mount a cob, presumably to go summon the
local constabulary, "all will soon be settled. Put your
nag away." The youngster did so without question, and
Sherlock turned to the others, who were staring not
only at him but at me securing the reins and descending, shockingly and unmistakably female, from the box,
and at the odd assortment of people emerging from the
carriage: Watson with the black bag of a doctor, Tewky
all dressed up like a dandy, Dawson stout and humble
and enjoying herself, and Tish with various colours of
greasepaint smeared all over her face from her efforts
to remove it.

But all eyes turned to Sherlock when he spoke.
"Who is the proprietor of this establishment?"

"I, sir, Roland Mizzlethorpe, M.D., most humbly at
your service." A peculiar sort of concave man stepped
forward, long of face, hollow of chest, obsequious of
manner. "And you are?"

"It does not matter. You will be dealing with Dr.
Watson."

The man's eyes fairly bugged out, flashing white like those of a frightened horse, as he slewed them towards Watson. Evidently he recognized the name, I assumed from Watson's fame as my brother's chronicler. But I was mistaken.

Watson told him, "I am here on behalf of a patient you call Nora Helmer, although I am sure you know quite well that is not her real name. Her sister has intervened for her, and we wish her to be released immediately."

Dawson, I noticed tangentially, had somehow obtained a wet handkerchief and was helping Tish scrub her face with it.

Mizzlethorpe visibly tottered between surrender and resistance for a moment, during which he delayed response by violently motioning his people to go back inside the sanatorium. Once the onlookers were gone, he stiffened. "On what grounds?"

"Come, come, my man, you know as well as I do that she does not belong here, " scoffed Watson.

But Sherlock had reached a more shrewd assessment of Mizzlethorpe. "We wish to see her commitment papers."

"No!" Again the man spooked like a horse.

"Ah. They are irregular?" Then Sherlock remarked to Watson, "Old chap, I will bet you a dinner at Simpson's that yours is the name signed to them. Lord Caddie seems to have got it off a list. He must not be much of a reader."

Dr. Mizzlethorpe entreated, "Gentlemen, please! I am sure we all wish to prevent scandal of any sort."

An imperious voice spoke. "Then I want my sister. *Now.*"

Tish stood, a lone, lance-straight figure in the shadowy light of lanterns, and all three men turned to stare at her as if a pilaster had spoken. Then they put their heads together and muttered. Off to one side, Tewky was conferring with the coachman as Dawson picked thorns out of him. With no one else near, I went to stand by Tish and take her hand. She welcomed me with a wan smile; evidently she had forgotten that she hated me and was never going to forgive me. The grip of her hand on mine tightened as the men began to move.

Sherlock, Watson, and the Pecksniffian asylum doctor walked off and went inside, but as the front door of the asylum closed behind them, Tish made no attempt to follow them. Perhaps she understood that she had done all she could, or perhaps she could not bear to see where her sister had been kept. Perhaps she felt weak—and no wonder, as she had not eaten all day. She did not speak; she stood like a pillar of the Parthenon, but I could feel her trembling.

We stood hand in hand for what seemed like a long time before, at last, the door opened again.

Tish gave a low, wordless cry, dropped my hand, and ran, or stumbled, into her sister's arms. They hugged, they wept, and she, Tish, looked far more pitiful than Flossie did. Beautiful Flossie, her long hair untended but only a little bit unkempt, her lovely face, mirror image of her sister's, pale but not thin, her dress dark and plain but whole. Embracing, the sisters gazed at each other's faces, then each sobbed upon the other's shoulder, then they gazed again. "Tish, your hair!" Flossie exclaimed.

"It'll grow back," said Tish with a smile—the warmest, widest smile I had ever seen on her, now that her troubles were over.

Coming out of the asylum directly after Flossie, my

brother and Watson stood smiling as I dare say I was smiling myself, looking on. Flossie was telling Tish, "It was not so bad, only that I could not sleep at night for all the screaming going on, and I saw the most awful things, and I could not cease brooding over Caddie, his infidelities, how he had doomed me for not being complaisant, and how dare he summon the black barouche for me."

I noticed Tewky had come over to speak with Sherlock, who nodded, then said to everyone in general, "The coachman has agreed to drive. Come, we must be going."

Flossie flung up her head in alarum. "Where are you taking me?"

"To the Dorking train station," Sherlock said.

"To live with me," Tish told her.

"Oh, Tish! Truly?"

"Of course."

"But—I'm frightened. Can we keep Caddie away from me?"

"Leave that to me and my brother," I said.

Flossie turned her lovely, shadowed eyes on me, their question unspoken: Who are you?

"This is my cherished friend Enola Holmes," said Tish with a fervor that warmed my heart.

"And my brother is Sherlock Holmes," I told Flossie. "It is incumbent upon us to visit the Earl of Dunhench on your behalf. If, in his obstinacy, His Cadship should wish to reclaim you, we will threaten him with scandal. He has falsely represented you as deceased, so we can hold the fear of the law over his head. I feel quite hopeful that we can persuade him to provide you with a handsome monetary settlement—is that not so, Sherlock?"

"It might perhaps be possible," he replied.

His tone was annoyingly that of a more cautious older brother, but I didn't mind. I knew very well what I could do; indeed, what I quite intended to do. "So you need not feel in any way apprehensive," I assured Lady Felicity. "We will take care of everything."

Epilogue

by Sherlock Holmes

Undeniably, "The Case of the Black Barouche," as Enola insists on calling it, presented unique points of interest, and I would not have missed it for the world. But just as undeniable was my strong sentiment of relief when we got back to London and my fearless sister once again went her own feckless way. From the moment we rescued Lady Felicity until several weeks afterwards, Enola remained mostly preoccupied with fussing over Tish and Flossie, blessedly aiming her interfering proboscis in their direction rather than mine. She ordered quantities of flowers and baskets of food delivered to Tish's lodging. She hired a maid of all work and a cook for them. She commissioned a seamstress to outfit Flossie in "necessaries." She not only loaned Tish a wig but purchased a new, blond one for her. And the moment the Glover sisters felt strong enough, she began to take them shopping. And again shopping, almost every day. And more and further shopping: for frocks, suits, coats and cloaks, boots, slippers, parasols, reticules, gloves, and hats with all the trinkets and trimmings. I have no very clear idea what "furbelows" are, but I am quite sure the three of them obtained some. As I decidedly declined to exhibit any interest in their purchases, they invited Tewkesbury to London for a day to admire their new wardrobes. Thus was I left largely in peace, for I saw Enola only in regard to business.

This being the unpleasant business of obtaining funds for Lady Felicity from Lord Cadogan Burr Rudcliff II, Earl of Dunhench.

I took this matter upon myself, intending to keep my sister innocent of it. In her youthful, swashbuckling way, Enola was determined to blackmail Lord Cadogan Burr Rudcliff II to the utmost, but even though that

Cad of all cads quite deserved punishment, I would not be a party to extortion. I had explained this to Enola, and she vehemently disagreed, but one can hardly expect a woman, even a most intelligent one, to comprehend a gentleman's code of honour.

Therefore, I made sure to act promptly, before Enola might make mischief. Accompanied by my faithful Watson and his trusty service revolver, I traveled back to Dunhench Hall only a day and a half after we had quitted it, and there we arrived to find His Cadship having the howling fantods. Even as his mournful butler blocked our entry, I could hear the earl within, ranting, "Take them down and burn them, every one of them! Burn them, I say!"

Most interesting. I quite wanted to see what, exactly, was being cremated this time. Telling the butler, "We are here on the business of Her Majesty Queen Victoria!" I shoved past him with Watson by my side, and making our way towards the hubbub the misfortunate earl was creating, we found that amoral aristocrat in the parlour, stamping to death something on the carpet as if it were a deadly viper. However, I saw as we walked in, it was just a framed picture, a dainty watercolour of flowers. Rudcliff actually smashed the glass and splintered the frame before he seized the painting itself and cast it into the hearth fire.

"Ah," I said, comprehending. "You destroy the artwork of Lady Felicity when you can no longer destroy Lady Felicity herself."

Swinging around, his head menacing like that of a bull about to charge, he bellowed, "Who the hell might you be?"

"I might be, and am, Sherlock Holmes, retained on your wife's behalf."

He let out an oath that scattered the nearby servants—they dropped their sacrificial paintings as they ran. Watson kindly bolted the doors behind them, so that the ignoble nobleman and I might not be troubled by their return. Then my good Watson stationed himself at the main entry and stood guard with his pistol in hand.

"Might we sit down?" I asked Lord Cadogan politely. "We need to arrange for your continued financial support of your wife, in the form of a settlement you will pay her."

"The hell I will!"

"Oh, you will," I told him earnestly, "or else stand in the dock on charges of falsifying medical signatures on admittance papers."

The conversation rather deteriorated thereafter. Indeed, so threatening did he become that I pulled out my life preserver—a handy pocket truncheon made of rope and weighted wood—and showed it to him. Phlegmatically Watson remained at his post by the door; he knew, as I did, that most bullies are cowards. And sure enough, His Cadship quickly resorted to bluster.

"You can't prove it about the signatures!"

"He most certainly can," retorted my good Watson from across the room. "Or at least one of them. I am Dr. Watson."

The earl recoiled as if from a physical blow, eyes darting in search of escape. "Brindle!" he howled for his butler. "Bring footmen!"

I rather lost patience. "Sit down," I ordered Cadogan, directing him with uplifted truncheon towards a chair at the parlour table. "If you attempt to eject us, we will simply return with legal authorities. Do you want that?"

The earl did not answer, but he sat. Behind me, I

heard a murmur of voices as Watson directed Brindle to fetch his master's stationery, pen, ink, blotting paper, et cetera.

I told Cadogan Burr Rudcliff II, "You will now write a complete confession. Start with the fate of your first wife, Myzella Haskell."

He balked, of course, and I had to prompt him each step of the way: he had falsified commitment papers, locked up his wife in a lunatic asylum, told her family she was dead, faked her cremation. He penned his account so bold and large that I could read it from where I stood. I had him continue to pen much the same shameful account of his treatment of Felicity Glover. Finally, I had him sign and date this document and turn it over to me. Watson then read it and witnessed it.

I seated myself at the parlour table opposite the glowering earl. "Now," I told him, "we need to arrange payment—"

"Blackmailer!" he exploded at me.

"I am a gentleman," I told him severely. "Never would I stoop to blackmail! And you have proved that you are not a gentleman whatsoever at all. Only for that reason do I require this surety." I patted the pocket wherein I held his confession. "If you *were* a gentleman, this would be merely a gentleman's agreement, not extortion in any way. As it is, think what you like; nevertheless, you are to place into a bank account for your wife each month the same amount of money that you were paying to have her put away. No less, no more." I had inquired regarding the sum, which was quite enough for Flossie to support herself in a modest way; it was probably more than Tish made with her typewriter.

His Cadship brightened, reaching almost eagerly for pen and paper, as he had expected me to insist on far worse.

Behind me, a heightened female voice proclaimed, "Great parlous piles of pig dung!"

I stiffened. No, it couldn't be.

But, I saw plainly as I rose and turned, it was. Enola stood there, imperiously hatted and dressed in her city-of-London best. Next to her, just as formidably arrayed, stood an older woman I did not know. Behind them, near the door, I glimpsed Watson, sheep-faced, not looking at me.

And Enola glared straight past me, skewering the Earl of Dunhench with her stare. "Balderdash!

Poppycock!" she expanded. "You cad!" She ordered Caddie, "Give Flossie at least three times that amount per month, or Dame Haskell and I will tell the whole world what you did to your wives. Not only Felicity, but also Myzella."

Much as I was taken aback by Enola's appearance on the scene, I retained sufficient presence of mind to pull my attention away from her, turn, and check on the earl lest he throw something. But I need not have concerned myself. All the fight seemed to have gone out of him. He sat like a great gawking gudgeon, fixated on the two females as if he saw an invading army. But his apprehension seemed focused mainly upon Dame Haskell, who had not said a word. Having given her my usual quick assessment, I saw only a short and rather shapeless old woman with quite a countrified face resembling a withered apple. Yet somehow, in their redoubtable hats, she and Enola seemed to loom like veritable Erinyes, Fates, Furies. Up until that moment I had regarded women's elaborate headgear as merely silly at best and ridiculous at worst. But in that shadowy moment at Dunhench Hall, I began to perceive it differently.

Dame Haskell tilted her head—and her imposing hat—just a threatening trifle towards the Earl of Dunhench and ordered, "Do it."

Instantly he took up his pen, and within a few minutes, with surprising celerity, the necessary papers were signed and the first deposit of Felicity's much-increased stipend turned over to me.

"Now," I told him, "I require a written promise that you will make no attempt ever to contact, or interfere in any way with, your wife or her sister, Letitia Glover."

"Now see here—" he began to bluster.

Enola silenced him. "Remember how Tish had you screaming and on the run in your own dining room?" she told him with unholy glee. "I would think you'd be glad to stay as far away as possible from both of the Glover sisters."

He glowered and sulked, but he wrote the necessary document. With our business finally concluded—although no handshakes were exchanged—Watson and I saw ourselves out, each of us escorting one of the ladies.

Enola took my arm, but once the doors of Dunhench Hall had closed behind us, I had no idea what to say to her. Descending the steps, I remained silent, displeased by her being there, by her interference—I admit it. However, the first moving object that caught my eye drove all such thoughts from my mind. It was an all too familiar prancing yellow horse hitched to Dame Haskell's awaiting brougham.

"Please tell me that is not Jezebel!" I exclaimed.

"It's not. It's Jezebel's twin sister, Jasmine." Parting from me with a grin I could not begin to decipher, Enola rode away with Dame Haskell, their mild-mannered mare trotting sweetly and sedately out of sight.

Watson stood by my side. "Definitely not Jezebel," he remarked. "It is the merest coincidence, surely, that two mares should look so much alike." He gave me his most guileless smile, and although I lifted my eyebrows in return, I no longer felt any inclination to reproach him for letting Enola into Dunhench Hall; I knew quite well how persuasive she could be when she wanted her own way.

"Indeed. I find myself quite weary of anything having to do with twins," I remarked. "Let us go, shall we?"

Once back to London, I took him out to dine, and we drank a toast to a job well done.

Flossie very sensibly used some of her funds to buy tinware and japan it—that is to say, paint flowers and such on it with lacquer, decoratively coating the metal so that it would not corrode—and with her artistic flair she rendered her wares markedly superior to most. Eventually she took a stall in Covent Garden where she sells the tins and trays and candle shades and so forth at a goodly profit, with great success, as I am frequently reminded by Enola, who at least once a week purchases from her a very pretty flowerpot, match holder, or equally useless item, then brings it to my flat and, if she finds me at home, gives it to me. Indeed, on one pretext or another, my sister finds her way often to my flat, where she is quite welcome. However, she has not yet managed to involve herself in another case of mine. Nor do I intend that she should—although, undoubtedly, somehow she will.

...s lived for fourteen ye... ...ussia, he speaks the language fluently and knows the country and the people intimately. He has also spent long periods of time in most of the countries of Europe, as well as in India, Palestine, and Egypt. For almost thirty years he has covered the world as correspondent for outstanding magazines and newspapers in America and other countries, and he is well known as a lecturer. His most recent books are *Gandhi and Stalin, Men and Politics* and *The Great Challenge*.

Louis Fischer, *editor*

Boris Alexandrovich Yakovlev was born and raised in a peasant family in a village of the Volga region. He graduated from a university as an engineer-architect and during the last period of his life in the USSR he was a leading member of one of the Soviet scientific academies. He was never a member of the Communist Party, and like many others was arrested without cause and brought to trial for alleged counterrevolutionary activities. He was captured by the Germans in 1941 and survived life in a prison camp.

Boris Alexandrovich Yakovlev,

Thirteen

Who ...

(Con...

an engineer, a ...
ment officia...
ask whe...
lieved...
manity, su...
them is to kn...
is really like.

The stories were c...
edited by Louis Fischer, note...
of such books as *Gandhi and Sta...
Men and Politics, The Great Challenge.* Recently Mr. Fischer, who lived
fourteen years in Soviet Russia and
who speaks Russian fluently, went to
Germany where thousands of these
fugitives from the Soviet Union now
live. With the help of Boris A. Yakovlev, a Russian-born architectural engineer, he interviewed several hundred
of the political exiles. He then chose
thirteen whose experiences seemed
most typical and most interesting,
whose accounts seemed least embit-
tered and most objective. The thirteen
authors got only one instruction: Tell
the truth.

Here it is.

Edited by LOUIS FISCHER

Thirteen Who Fled is the first book
published since the Bolshevik revolution of November, 1917, in which a
representative cross-section of the Russian people tell their own true story.
Many have spoken for Russia, many
have spoken against Russia. Here the
Russians speak for themselves.

These are not Soviet diplomats who
have deserted the service; these are
not exceptional persons, save in the
remarkable vividness of their stories
and the importance of their decision
to leave their native land. They are a
cross-section of the Russian people—
a teacher, a farmer, a worker, a Red
Army officer, a housewife, a student,

(Continued on back flap)

THIRTEEN
WHO FLED

Books by LOUIS FISCHER

GANDHI AND STALIN

THE GREAT CHALLENGE

EMPIRE

A WEEK WITH GANDHI

DAWN OF VICTORY

MEN AND POLITICS (an Autobiography)

THE WAR IN SPAIN

SOVIET JOURNEY

MACHINES AND MEN IN RUSSIA

WHY RECOGNIZE RUSSIA?

THE SOVIETS IN WORLD AFFAIRS (Two Vols.)

OIL IMPERIALISM

THIRTEEN WHO FLED

EDITOR
LOUIS FISCHER 1896-

SUBEDITOR
BORIS A. YAKOVLEV

TRANSLATORS
GLORIA AND VICTOR FISCHER

HARPER & BROTHERS
PUBLISHERS : NEW YORK

CONTENTS

INTRODUCTION:
THE RUSSIAN PROBLEM

by Louis Fischer

The Soviet Union will long remain a major concern of the United States. This arises from the fact that without American support most nations in Europe and Asia could easily be conquered by Russia. The Soviet Union's geographic position and military supremacy would doom any Eurasian area the Bolsheviks coveted unless it had the protection of the United States.

A similar statement might be made about the United States: America too has the arms and men to overrun Spain or Italy or France or Indonesia or Australia, for instance. But most persons are more apprehensive about Soviet aggression than American aggression because Russia has, since 1939, actually annexed Finnish, Esthonian, Latvian, Lithuanian, Polish, German, Czechoslovak, Rumanian, and Japanese territories. All these annexations violate the Atlantic Charter which the Soviet government signed and most of them violate treaties which Moscow had with the victims. In addition, the Kremlin has obtained extraterritorial rights in China and openly tried hard, but failed, to achieve direct control over Iran and Turkey. Russia also helped Yugo-

1

slavia get a foothold in the Trieste region and endeavored, by diplomatic means, to win Greek, Italian, and Austrian land for Yugoslavia when that country was completely within the Soviet orbit.

Fear of Russia is fed, further, by the existence in all countries of Communist parties whose friendship for, undeviating approval of, and ideological kinship with the Soviet government make them at least potential "Fifth Column" vanguards of new Russian expansionist thrusts. Thus it was the Czechoslovak overturn early in 1948, accompanied by the death of Foreign Minister Jan Masaryk, which produced the worst war scare of the year because it showed that a Communist party with minority electoral support could, by force and without a new election, seize full control of a country.

American foreign policy aims to prevent such internal aggressions by strengthening the nations that lie in the path of a possible Soviet expansionist move. The United States lacks the means and sometimes the wisdom to pursue this purpose with equal success in all parts of the world, but where it could it has reinforced the economic and on occasions the military might of countries which were threatened or seemed to be threatened by Soviet imperialism or Communism.

However, even a perfectly democratic, highly prosperous, and well-armed Greece or Turkey or Iran or Italy could no more resist a Russian invasion than Norway and Denmark did the Nazi blows of 1940. Peace lovers therefore hope to see a world union of democracies, or multinational regional federations or, as a minimum program, a reformed, vitalized United Nations, whose pooled resources could safeguard weak countries against foreign attack from any quarter—for, alas, Russia is merely the biggest but not the only postwar aggressor.

The United States has a special interest in preventive measures against Soviet expansion because American national security would be imperiled if one nation threatened to dominate all of Europe or all of Asia or all of both. The United States went into

2

the First World War and into the Second World War, indeed Great Britain went into the First World War, the Second World War, and the Napoleonic wars, for one and the same reason: to keep Europe out of the grip of a single great power. If, at any time, Russian control of Europe or Asia appears imminent, there will be war or, if there is no war, there will be Russian subjugation of the nations that do not go to war. Steps which prevent Soviet expansion are, accordingly, stepping stones to peace and national freedom.

This is the essence of American foreign policy and, in particular, of America's attitude toward the Soviet Union. Some try to chocolate-coat American policy as anti-Communist, but its primary motivation is not, in fact, ideological. It never occurred to President Roosevelt or any American in authority to combine with Hitler in 1941 to crush the Soviet state. Instead, the United States combined with Communist Russia to destroy anti-Communist Nazi Germany. This was wise, but if America's transcendent motive had been the extirpation of Communism another and opposite view would have prevailed.

Moreover, the American and British governments facilitated Soviet expansion into eastern and Central Europe and into Asia during and after the war although they of course knew that Russia was an anticapitalist, communistic dictatorship. It was only when the appetite and drive of Soviet imperialism belatedly alarmed the Western nations that they decided to call a halt and adopt the policy of containment. The United States helped Communist Russia defend itself against foreign attack and changed its policy when that same Communist nation undertook foreign assaults which imperiled world peace.

The issue is not Communism but imperialist aggression.

Today, the United States is supporting reactionary regimes, democratic regimes, and socialist regimes abroad and would logically support the Communist regime of Marshal Tito were it altogether certain that he is not a Muscovite puppet. Clearly, therefore, American policy is not ideological, not based on eco-

3

nomic dogma or sociological doctrine. It stems rather from the thesis, amply demonstrated in the 1930's, that unless totalitarian aggression is nipped in time it will lead to war just as Hitler's, Mussolini's, and Japanese aggression led to war.

The desire of Americans, and of most others, not to have a war with Russia guarantees a continued high intensity of interest in Soviet affairs. What a country does abroad is determined, in considerable measure, by what it is at home. Hence the eager and universal wish to know the Soviet system and Soviet conditions.

Russia is a puzzle, and the puzzle is double: What about the Soviet government? and, what about the Soviet people?

When we discuss a democracy the central question is the people, because they make the government. But in a dictatorship the government makes the people. The dictator who is deified until he seems to be more like a god than a man, tries to re-create the people in his own image.

A dictatorship could conceivably be—but usually isn't—for the people and of the people, but if it were by the people it would not be a dictatorship. Stalin became supreme Leader in 1927; the population of the Soviet Union did not elect him, could not recall him, cannot control him, and does not instruct him. Thus the essential fact of the Russian dictatorship, as of all dictatorships, is the gulf between dictator and people.

This manifests itself in endless ways. It has been many years since Stalin or any top Soviet leader mingled freely and at close range with persons not known and screened by the secret police. The Soviet public is not informed where Stalin lives; spectators are barred from the route of his automobile and train. When he goes to a theater or opera performance every cubic inch of the building is examined in advance; no previous announcement is made of his intention to attend; he generally sits where he cannot be seen. Fear of assassination surrounds him with a moat. He has as little contact with the people as they have with him.

This same mistrust of the people characterizes every action of

4

the Soviet government. Elections are held, but there is only one list of candidates; the citizen is given no choice because he is not trusted to make the right choice. Each inhabitant of the Soviet Union must hold a passport when he is inside the country and he cannot change residence or travel or change jobs without showing that passport; no one must ever leave the ken of the police. Few Soviet men and women go abroad; few foreigners enter Russia. The Soviet people read what the government wants them to read and, with the exception of the "Voice of America" and similar foreign programs recently inaugurated, hear what the government wants them to hear.

The arrangements of the Soviet government could not and do not inspire its subjects with love, loyalty, or faith. The government is usually referred to as "they."

The dictator's highest ideal is an obedient citizenry. Terror to instill obedience and prizes to reward the most obedient are the Soviet regime's favorite political weapons. The individual's only road to safety and comfort is through complete suppression of his own will and abject submission to the will of the omnipotent, omnipresent state. Years of such living make the Soviet people automatically conformist and blindly compliant. Their instinct of self-preservation is highly developed because it is always active; it breeds sycophancy, insincerity, indifference to all but material things, and moral supineness. The effect of Soviet education and Soviet life is to weaken inner discipline and put a premium on cynical resignation to outer compulsion. "Theirs not to reason why, theirs but to do or die."

Soviet psychology has been a war psychology for twenty years. Every Soviet citizen is expected to be a peacetime soldier.

Russia, consequently, needed only minimal psychological adjustment when she went to war. The regimentation was not new, neither was the killing or the atmosphere of violence. The political tension was the same, indeed for fighting men there was some relaxation because at the front the military were often able to shield soldiers and officers from the constant surveillance of

5

the secret police. (The Red Army and the secret police are not on the friendliest terms.)

Reared to strict obedience, the Red Army fought badly in that phase of the Finnish war when it had to operate in small groups against the Finns who were defending their soil in small groups or even singly. The Russian army did better in large masses against the Germans. But history records that it retreated precipitously during the first six months of the war; hundreds of thousands were taken prisoner by the Nazis and vast arsenals abandoned to the Germans. The first stand of the Russians was in front of Moscow in December 1941, when the Wehrmacht, its lines of communication and supply overextended, and suffering from the severe, unaccustomed cold, succumbed to unending assaults of new units hastily transported from Siberia. Flesh won.

All objective evidence, and a correct reading of Soviet sources, indicates that the combat spirit of the Red Army was not aroused until the middle of 1942 when the soldiers had seen with their own eyes the atrocities committed by the Nazis in occupied Russian territory. The Kremlin fed the sentiment of the army. One impressive Soviet poster, widely distributed at the front, showed a Nazi killing a Russian boy, and the child screaming, "Papa, Strike the German." Ilya Ehrenburg, a skillful Soviet journalist, shook the army and the country with bloodcurdling descriptions of Nazi horrors and bloodthirsty summonses to hate Germans. Enraged, the Red Army commenced to fight in earnest and did so until the triumphant end. No longer did it surrender in complete regiments as in 1941. But there is documentary evidence to prove that as late as 1944 and even in 1945 when the Wehrmacht was in headlong retreat before the Russians, whole Soviet units went over to the enemy.

Stalin's conduct of the war won it but could scarcely have won the heart of the Russian soldier. Russia is rich in manpower and it is not in the Russian or Bolshevik tradition to spare it. General Dwight D. Eisenhower writes in his *Crusade in Europe* of a conversation he had in 1945 with Marshal Zhukov, the Soviet commander who captured Berlin.

Marshal Zhukov [Eisenhower reports] gave me a matter-of-fact statement of his practice which was, roughly, "There are two kinds of mines; one is the personnel mine and the other is the vehicular mine. When we come to a mine field our infantry attacks exactly as if it were not there. The losses we get from personnel mines we consider only equal to those we would have gotten from machine guns and artillery if the Germans had chosen to defend that particular area with strong bodies of troops instead of with mine fields. The attacking infantry does not set off the vehicular mines, so after they have penetrated to the far side of the field they form a bridgehead, after which the engineers come up and dig out channels through which our vehicles can go."

I had a vivid picture of what would happen to any American or British commander if he pursued such tactics, and I had an even more vivid picture of what the men in any one of our divisions would have had to say about the matter had we attempted to make such a practice a part of our tactical doctrine. Americans assess the cost of war in terms of human lives, the Russians in the over-all drain on the nation.

Here, graphically, is the distinction between a dictatorship and a democracy at war.

But human beings are human beings even if the dictator is inhuman, and they don't like to be killed or maimed because in the government's price list life is cheap and limbs are cheaper.

The war showed every Russian soldier how little he counted, how little "they" cared. He was patriotic but he was also bitter. In the army they talked more than they dared at home. Each man heard his own experience with the regime's cruelty and inefficiency repeated, sometimes exactly, by comrades from all corners and social classes of the Soviet Union. Each person discovered that his experiences were not a matter of chance or bad luck but of ineluctable fate under Communism.

How helpless the individual feels when he sees that everybody is in the same boat and nobody can do anything about it.

7

The war laid bare to the Soviet citizen the true nature of the dictatorship and thus created many postwar problems for the Soviet leadership. To outsiders, the Nazi-Soviet war was a revelation of unsuspected Soviet power. To Soviet participants the war was a revelation, or confirmation, of the regime's abiding moral rottenness.

The bravery or effectiveness of soldiers does not always reflect their condition of life or their devotion to their government. A Russian army consisting chiefly of serfs defeated Napoleon. In the Spanish Civil War the best warriors, next to the International Brigade volunteers who understood the issues in the struggle, were Franco's Moors who didn't know what it was all about. The Moors were brought up to fight and die.

Love of country inspired the Red Army in its valiant contest with Nazi Germany, not love of Stalin or of Sovietism. The British resisted Hitler longer and better than any other nation, and they did it under the talented leadership of Winston Churchill. But the moment Hitler was defeated, and even before the war in Asia was over, the British people voted Churchill out of office and put Attlee's Labor government in power. The Soviet electorate might have done a similar thing if Russia were a free country.

Victory under Stalin constituted no vote of confidence for Stalin.

The war was the first occasion on which some Russians could decide how they felt about their government and act on the decision. In America, England, France, India, and elsewhere, one met anti-Nazi refugees who had left Germany, legally and illegally, after Hitler's advent in 1933. There were tens of thousands of them. But from 1925, when the rigors of Soviet peacetime terrorism commenced, until 1941, probably not more than a few hundred anti-Soviet persons contrived to get out of Russia. The Soviet Union was a sealed country. Then the Nazis invaded Russia and transported millions of prisoners and slave laborers to the Nazi fatherland. It is an irony and tragedy of history that

8

this barbarous act of a brutal fascist dictator offered Soviet citizens their first opportunity to vote against Bolshevism. Lenin once said that the Czar's soldiers voted for peace with their legs; they walked out of First World War trenches and went home. In the same way, a considerable fraction of Hitler's Russian prisoners and slaves voted against Stalin by choosing not to go home.

This is the most significant thing I know about the Soviet Union.

Ordinarily, a soldier surrenders to the enemy for a military reason: it is impossible to fight or flee. But the Nazis captured millions of Soviet prisoners whose reason was often purely military, sometimes purely political, and sometimes military as well as political. In addition, the Germans carried off as slave laborers large numbers of Soviet men and women. Not even Nazi-captured documents disclose the total number of Soviet prisoners and slaves; estimates run as high as ten million.

How did these prisoners and slaves behave when Soviet restraint was withdrawn? While the war lasted, they had merely exchanged Nazi restraint for Soviet restraint. Yet an irresistible impulse drove them to seek maximum freedom despite the confinement.

Perhaps the Nazis sensed this. Perhaps too the Nazis meted out worse treatment to their Soviet prisoners of war than to others. The fact is that Germany is not known to have found more than a handful of military recruits among their Polish or French or British or American war prisoners. The Nazis did, however, find large numbers of soldiers among the Russians, Ukrainians, and Moslems they had taken captive in the Soviet Union.

In 1942, the Nazis captured Red Army General Andrei Andreievitch Vlassov. Born in 1900, he had been a Communist party member of long and good standing. In January 1942, the Moscow daily *Pravda* had announced a special decoration in appreciation of his defense of Moscow.

Shortly after his capture, General Vlassov volunteered to raise a Russian army among Germany's war prisoners. His slogan was "For Russia, Against Stalin." He argued that if he were allowed to organize and lead some Russian military units into battle the Red Army would refuse to fight, and the ultimate result would be the overthrow of the Stalin regime. Vlassov contended further that the Nazis were already making military use, at various fronts, of Ukrainian, Circassian, and other Soviet prisoners of war, and that if he could unite these prisoners into a single Russian army under an anti-Bolshevik flag, the effect inside the Soviet Union would be disastrous to Stalin.

The Nazis never quite trusted Vlassov. Ribbentrop, Rosenberg, and other top fascist leaders sabotaged his plan; Hitler refused to see him; and only Gestapo boss Himmler lent a helpful hand. Although masses of Soviet war prisoners and slave laborers volunteered to serve under Vlassov, he was allowed to recruit only two divisions, and only one of these ever received full equipment.

Two battalions of this unit were sent by the Wehrmacht into a fatally exposed triangle of the front on the Oder River opposite the advancing Red Army. It was 1945; the Nazis were on the verge of collapse. The Vlassovites lost heavily and then, in defiance of German orders, left the front, marched cross-country to Czechoslovakia where they became involved with Soviet regiments in the assault on Prague and disintegrated. Somewhere in Czechoslovakia in 1945, Vlassov himself was captured (whether by the Czechs or General Patton of the US Army is not established) and delivered to the Soviets. The Soviet press subsequently announced that he had been hanged as a traitor.

This Vlassov episode was pitiful yet remarkable. It is difficult to imagine a general from a democratic country fighting for Hitler; none did. Vlassov found it possible. Vlassov and Stalin belonged to the same totalitarian school. They (and the reactionary Western appeasers) had no instinctive abhorrence of collaboration with Hitler. Stalin and Hitler called one another black until it suited their purpose to sign a pact in August 1939, partition eastern Europe, and co-operate economically. But for happy circumstances, this might have resulted in Hitler's victory over the West. Similarly, Vlassov would have taken Russia out of the war (as Lenin did in 1917) had his fantastic scheme succeeded. That would have been Hitler's great gain.

In self-defense the Vlassov-movement remnants now living in western Europe declare that they did not believe the terrible things the Soviet press used to write about Hitler because the Kremlin was anti-Hitler until the 1939 pact, pro-Hitler after the pact, and anti-Hitler again after the Nazi invasion. They therefore discounted what the Soviet propaganda machine said about him. It would be more accurate to say that the total materialism and cruel practices of the Soviet regime did not equip them to recoil automatically from the Hitler regime. Vlassov and his followers were opponents of Bolshevism. Yet they were the children of Bolshevism; they could not help that. Soviet citizens under forty (and they constitute the bulk of the nation) have no mature recollection of anything but Communist dictatorship. The vast majority of the Vlassovites and of the much larger number of Soviet prisoners and slave laborers who did not join Vlassov had never had any contact with democracy or with the outside world. Their first non-Soviet experiences must have been strange indeed. The Nazis employed them in Poland, Germany, Holland, Belgium, France, and some even in Italy. Wherever they went they encountered a standard of living which was far higher, despite the destruction and strain of war, than anything they had known at home. Soviet newspapers and the Soviet radio had not prepared them for this: on the contrary, Soviet information created the impression that Russian conditions were wonderful and compared very favorably with the poverty and slavery of capitalism. Whether the prisoners and laborers had or had not been skeptical readers of the Soviet press, they now could not escape the conclusion that the Kremlin, their government, lied. This was a psychological preparation for flight.

Toward the end of the war, Nazi power crumbled and the

11

Red Army erupted into eastern Europe and then into Germany. Wherever the Bolsheviks arrived unexpectedly they took over the Russian prisoners of war and slave laborers and sent them back into Russia. But where there was an interval between the disintegration of German authority and the appearance of Soviet forces, the prisoners and slaves were confronted with a life-and-death decision: Wait for the Red Army or move westward out of its reach?

In Germany during the summer of 1948 I had long private talks with at least a hundred of those who decided to move westward. I asked each one individually why he or she (there were women among the slaves) refused to go home to Russia.

Their replies of course varied. Usually, several considerations operated, and what was the most important factor with one person might scarcely influence another at all. They were generally agreed, however, that the known hostility of the Soviet government to returned prisoners had worried them. They told me that the Russian war prisoners taken by Finland and repatriated after Finland's defeat never reached their homes and were presumed to have been banished to Siberia.

The Soviet suspicion of war prisoners came to the official attention of the United States government in this way: In the latter part of the war, the USA, with Soviet permission, established an American shuttle air base at Poltava, in the Ukraine, where airplanes might land after bombing missions from Italy and England to the Rumanian oil fields, Germany, etc. When the advancing Russian army liberated American airmen held captive by the Nazis in Poland and eastern Germany, Americans from the shuttle air base went to receive the liberated fliers and bring them to Poltava. It is not difficult to imagine how those former prisoners were treated; they were shaved, bathed, given new clothing, the best food, and every possibility of recuperating and having a good time before going home to America. But the Soviet military who had over-all charge at Poltava remonstrated with American officials of the shuttle base: "How can you know why these men were taken prisoner; maybe they gave themselves up out of sympathy for Germany or because they didn't want to fight. Maybe the Nazis propagandized them in the prison camps and converted them to fascism. These ex-prisoners should not stay here at all, but be rushed instead, via Odessa, to an American screening point for interrogation."

The Soviet government adopted the same suspicious attitude toward Russians who had been taken prisoner and, in the case of the Vlassovites, it would have been justified. But the Soviet prisoners and slaves had no taste for a screening by the Kremlin's secret police whether it was called GPU, or NKVD, or some other initials. This was a very prevalent reason for attempting to escape to the West rather than falling into Stalin's hands again.

Nevertheless, it is a momentous matter to cut yourself off from the country where you were born and lived all your life and where your family, relatives, and friends live, and to face a new world without its language, without citizenship, without a job, without contacts of any kind, and, frequently, in bad health and low spirits.

Great numbers of Soviet citizens took this bold, desperate step into the dark out of a feeling that the unknown possibility was better than the dread certainty. For all except a thin upper class of high officials, army and secret police officers, artists and writers, technical experts, engineers, and workers who excelled in making speed-up records (perhaps ten to fifteen million persons altogether), Soviet life has been very hard these last thirty-two years. It has been very hard to achieve the three freedoms: Freedom from Starvation, Freedom from Privation, and Freedom from Arrest. The physical, mental, and moral strain of Soviet existence is tremendous, and only a fresh, unspoiled, fundamentally healthy nation like the Russians could have borne up under it at all. The promise of future benefits does not sustain one for three decades unless there is more performance than the Soviet population has witnessed to date.

Even the ruined, rubbled, ragged, hungry Europe of 1945

13

seemed to offer a brighter prospect of liberties and groceries than Soviet Russia. So masses of Russian prisoners and slaves rushed away from the advancing Red Army and in the direction of the American, British, and other Western armies that were also pushing into Germany. In the territories they themselves occupied these armies likewise found many giant Nazi camps filled with Russian prisoners and slaves.

At Yalta, in the Soviet Crimea, in February 1945, President Roosevelt and Prime Minister Churchill had promised Stalin to return to him all Soviet citizens they encountered in western Europe. Pursuant to this agreement Soviet officials presently appeared in the western zones of Germany and asked for possession of all Russian prisoners of war and slave laborers. The Americans and British complied although they could not have been ignorant of the fact that they were thus, in effect, sentencing people to death or concentration camp.

According to official American figures given me in Munich, Germany, in July 1948, the total number of Soviet citizens repatriated to Russia from the United States zone in Germany was, until September 1945, 1,060,000. According to this source, 2,031,000 Soviet citizens were repatriated in the same period from the American, British, and French zones combined. No one is in a position to assert how many of these repatriations were voluntary, how many forcible. But it is important to note that the Soviet authorities were permitted by the Western powers to use force in repatriations and the force was often employed. Moreover, the Russians rounded up many prisoners who had broken out of the camps and were roaming the German countryside. In fact, Soviet armed commissions ranged far and wide throughout Europe in this greatest of postwar manhunts. Aided by French Communists who then honeycombed the French police, GPU agents carried concealed prisoners from private apartments in Paris and other cities. There are records of these incidents in the archives of the French police. Similar Soviet abductions of

14

Russian prisoners seeking to elude Soviet power occurred elsewhere in western Europe, not to speak of western Germany.

The repatriations, forcible and otherwise, of Soviet citizens from western Germany continued, though on a smaller scale, until the beginning of 1947, when General McNarney, the US military governor, announced that no more compulsory deportations would be tolerated. His British and French colleagues made equivalent statements. The Western powers were no longer in a mood to serve as GPU (NKVD) accomplices in this ugly business.

Several hundred thousand, probably at least half a million, Soviet prisoners of war and slave laborers have, however, managed to this very day to avoid returning to Russia. The reason the exact number cannot be ascertained is in itself instructive. The Western powers have prohibited forced repatriations of Russians, but under the Yalta charter, Soviet representatives were still being permitted to visit displaced-persons camps in the American zone in the summer of 1948 when I was there. The American military showed me records and photographs of such visits. The Soviet agents hoped to convince some former prisoners to change their minds and go home. In a number of instances, also officially recorded, these agents were attacked by the Russian displaced persons and only saved from serious bodily harm by the intervention of American constabulary. Now one of the most noticeable, and depressing, characteristics of these ex-citizens of Soviet Russia is their lack of faith in almost anybody. "Do you think the American government will reinstitute compulsory deportations?" they asked me. "Do you think Truman might come to a new arrangement with Stalin which would include our involuntary return?" To avoid such a horrible contingency, most Russian prisoners and slaves deny they were ever Soviet citizens.

There are numerous camps for Russian displaced persons in the three western zones of Germany. In one of them, at Schleissheim, a few miles outside Munich, where over four thousand

Russian-speaking individuals are "housed" by the International Refugee Organization, I addressed a Kalmuck. The Kalmucks are Asiatics from the Volga River region near the Caspian Sea. Most of them are Buddhists and they have large, flat faces, yellow skin, narrow slit eyes, and short, straight black hair.

I said to the Kalmuck, "Where are you from?" expecting him to say, from Astrakhan, or Stalingrad perhaps.

"I'm from Yugoslavia," he replied. If an Iowa farmer said he was from Tibet it would be no more palpably untrue and funny. The Kalmuck wanted to deny his Soviet origin.

I was sitting in my room in the Munich Press Center when I heard a knock at my door. I opened it and a man of about twenty-five addressed me in German. Because of his accent I asked whether he spoke Russian. He said he did. I inquired after his nationality. He said, "Ukrainian." I said, "From where?" He said, "From Poland." His Russian was too pure for that, so I said, "Look, if you don't tell me the truth I cannot talk to you." Thereupon he admitted that he was not from Poland but from the Soviet Ukraine. (He had come to enlist me in the publication, in America, of his two novels.)

These Soviet deserters pose as Poles, Yugoslavs, Balts, etc., anything but former Soviet citizens; they are still afraid of the long arm of the Kremlin. This confounds the statisticians.

If, at the end of the war, several million American soldiers had preferred to stay in Germany, Italy, and Japan instead of going home to their families one would have been justified in saying that there was something wrong with the United States. Invariably, the Soviet exiles assert their love of Russia and their repugnance for the Stalin dictatorship. They vow not to return until it is overthrown but to come back from the furthest corner of the earth when it *is* overthrown. They are beginning to emigrate from Germany to Canada, Australia, New Zealand, Latin America, and the United States.

Among the men and women who have chosen exile from Russia are former high government officials, army officers, secret

16

police agents, university professors, prominent scientists, poets and writers, doctors, journalists, workingmen, peasants, schoolteachers, factory directors, engineers, economists, etc. They hail from every rank and stratum of the Soviet Union.

It is interesting and revealing that these former prisoners and slaves are not the only Russians who have escaped. After Hitler's collapse, the Soviet government sent armies of occupation into various European countries. Officers and soldiers of these armies have been and are deserting. The Kremlin has tried to stem the flow by relieving the troops as often as possible and sending them back to the Soviet Union before they get the chance to figure out a way of escape. Of late, the Soviet authorities have refrained from advance announcements of impending shipments home; such announcements had precipitated a spate of flights. Moreover, the Soviets have used many Asiatic units for occupation duty on the assumption that Europe would be too unfamiliar to lure them.

Despite these measures, Soviet citizens continue to escape into western Germany and western Europe. By the beginning of 1949, the flow had become a considerable stream. The Western nations do not encourage it. It needs little encouragement. The prison door is slightly ajar; light streams in from the West; the inmates follow the beam—if they can.

The ex-Soviet emigrants in Germany and other places in Europe possess a gold mine of information on Soviet conditions and Soviet methods.

Between 1922 and 1936 when I worked in the Soviet Union as an American correspondent, foreign journalists and diplomats could travel rather freely through the country to collect impressions and data. On short trips to Moscow in 1937 and 1938 I found this privilege drastically curtailed, and today it is practically nonexistent, for though the few foreigners now resident in Russia can receive occasional permits to travel along prescribed routes, only persons authorized to do so will engage in conversation with them and then only in *Pravda* phraseology. Some-

17

times, on a train or in an isolated spot, a foreigner can have a chance meeting with a Soviet citizen; the relationship will be cordial, for the Russian people like foreign visitors, but fear will limit the value of the interchange.

Even in the somewhat safer period, before the savage purges which began in 1936, Soviet citizens hesitated to associate freely or speak freely and honestly with foreigners. While in Moscow I had several intimate Soviet friends who would, when conditions became too terrible for silence, come to me and pour out their bitterness. They had to talk to someone and it was safer to talk to me because as a foreigner I could not be forced to inform against them. Yet even they did not tell the whole story; I suspect they were afraid to hear their own voices say that all hope was gone. One needs some faith in order to live.

Now, all friendly and unofficial contacts with Soviet people are dried up. Official Soviet utterances are designed to conceal, sometimes to distort; at best, they are quarter-truths. No leader in the Soviet Union has published his memoirs or a diary. This is the Iron Curtain. Apparently, the Kremlin has much to hide, much to be ashamed of—else why its increasingly arduous, assiduous efforts in the last dozen years to keep the world from knowing the truth about Russia?

To be sure, the texts and omissions of Soviet newspapers, magazines, books, and speeches still give a clue to the policies of the Soviet government; so do its acts abroad. Nevertheless, experts and laymen who wish to understand the Soviet Union are painfully aware of the inadequacy of their information.

Fortunately, more and more anti-Soviet refugees are appearing this side of the Iron Curtain who know Soviet life because they have lived it and who will tell because they intend to live it no longer. Some of the books of these ex-Russians have shed considerable light. A few are sensational and cut to fit the emotional pattern of prospective readers. In all cases, the authors were not average Soviet citizens; they had held high posts, usually abroad, or had been married to foreigners. Their status was exceptional and privileged.

I believe *Thirteen Who Fled* is the first book published since the Bolshevik Revolution of November 1917, in which a representative cross section of the Russian people tell their own true story. Many have spoken for Russia, many have spoken about Russia; here the Russians speak for themselves.

The history of this book is of general interest.

We have never had—from any source—a picture of Soviet life as the people themselves live it. Foreigners cannot know this and persons inside Russia are not free to describe it. But the displaced Russians in Europe know Soviet life and are free from Soviet restraint. It occurred to me that a group of them might write a valuable book about the Soviet Union.

As soon as this idea came to my mind I wrote to my wife, Markoosha, herself a Soviet citizen until 1939, who had been working for several months in the American zone in Germany as representative of the International Rescue and Relief Committee, an American organization which aids refugees of all nationalities. I asked her whether she thought the project practicable and whether she would co-operate. The plan fascinated her, but she mentioned a number of difficulties which boiled down to the reluctance of most Russian DP's to disclose their identities; they were still afraid the NKVD would get them or wreak vengeance on their relatives in Russia.

However, Markoosha enlisted Boris Alexandrovich Yakovlev, former vice-president of the Soviet Academy of Architecture, a man of forty-nine, highly cultured and very courageous. He agreed to canvass the Russians in the camps and also those thousands of Russians who, like himself, no longer reside in the camps.

Yakovlev undertook to line up a dozen or more former Soviet citizens to write brief autobiographies. My only instructions to him were, "Let them tell the truth about things that happened to them." The stress was to be on Soviet conditions so that the

19

whole, coming from persons of different professions, ages, classes, and background, would constitute a rounded description of Soviet Russia. Yakovlev told each contributor more than once that those who had been pro-Soviet must do full justice to that phase of their experience.

I arrived in Munich in July 1948, expecting to collect the manuscripts. But I had underestimated the hurdles. The refugees knew Markoosha or knew about her, and they knew Boris Alexandrovich, so the question of trust did not arise directly. However, they wondered whether their names would be used. Well, I said, they could employ pseudonyms. But couldn't they be traced from their stories and wouldn't their families in Russia suffer? This difficulty eliminated quite a number of prospective authors; we had only two stories.

With Yakovlev, I commenced interviewing Russians. Some still hesitated to talk or, when they did recite the tale of their lives, they hesitated to write. Others accepted the assignment but never carried it out. They would promise the work for a certain day, give an excuse for not delivering, and make a second promise which again was not kept.

We were having some success, however. A few more manuscripts were added to the folder. Here and there I noticed a special kind of reluctance, and when I probed, I discovered they did not believe anything would ever happen with their stories. They had no confidence that the book would appear or, if it did, that they would receive compensation. Their faith in their fellowmen had been "liquidated"; their faith in promises were near nil. So we gave them an advance in food purchased with dollars. This was a real incentive, first, because they needed the nourishment and, second, because it convinced them that the undertaking, as Russians say, was "serious."

Nevertheless, plenty of troubles remained. The peasant told his story beautifully but couldn't write a word. We got him a Russian stenographer. Ugryumov, formerly a prominent Communist, was worried about harming a friend in Russia who fig-

20

ured in his autobiography; we helped him over this hump. One woman became too emotional when she rehearsed her past in her mind. An Armenian factory director, whose life story was a gem, never did reduce it to paper; I think he didn't believe we were "serious."

Finally, months after I left Germany, all the thirteen chapters arrived in New York. Harper's sent several copies of the contract to Yakovlev in Munich. Later a report came on what happened. The contract showed how the royalties would be divided, percentage-wise, between the thirteen authors and Yakovlev who was subeditor. This impressed them no end. They were very moved by the fact that their associates in this enterprise were solicitous about them and were protecting their interests. Somebody had been good to them. And this too: the contract gave them a new sense of dignity. They were displaced persons who had found a little place. Only a displaced person knows how important that is.

I think this is a most valuable book, giving a new insight into Soviet conditions and Soviet policies. It covers not only the present but also the past, back to 1917. It is authentic. No fairminded reader will ask, "Is this really true or is it a bit exaggerated and invented?" Each story has all the marks of honesty, validity, and simplicity. The authors did not write for a market: They do not know America or England or France: they had no ghosts. They wrote from their hearts. They are plain people who echo the voice, otherwise stilled, of the Russian nation.

Thirteen Who Fled is human and personal and therefore politically illuminating. The book should create love for the Russian people and understanding of the Soviet dictatorship.

THIRTEEN
WHO FLED

I

THE LIFE OF A SOVIET SOLDIER

by Peter Gornev

My father, Ivan Petrovich Gornev, was a peasant in a village of the Tula region. I was the youngest in a family of six. All my childhood and youth were spent in my native village and from my youngest years I learned to work and to love peasant life.

At the end of 1915 my age group came up for the draft. In the town of Kungur (Siberia) I was inducted as a private in the 53rd Infantry Reserve Regiment. By 1916 I was already in combat on the northwestern front and after eight months of fighting I was decorated with two Georgian Crosses, third and fourth class.

In 1917 the front began to disintegrate. The discipline among the troops deteriorated from day to day. Self-demobilization began. In March 1918, hungry and exhausted, I made my way home.

At home there was nothing to eat. I joined the masses of people who traveled to places where bread was more plentiful. After two months of fighting hunger and need, I was called into

25

the Red Army. I didn't want to be conscripted; for twelve days I dodged it. In the end I was forced to go.

I began my career in the Red Army as an assistant squad leader. The intensive military training of the troops and, more important, the political education began immediately. Meetings and discussions were a daily affair. The talk was of socialism and communism, of the bright future, provided we smash our class enemies. The world bourgeoisie was condemned.

During the years of the Civil War, 1918-1920, I fought from front to front—against Denikin, Wrangel, Makhno, and the Poles. For military merit, I was decorated with the Order of the Red Banner.

Demobilization began in 1921; I remained in the army. In 1924 I was told to join the Communist party.

I stayed in the Red Army and served it with devotion. In the Red Army I traveled the long road from noncom to colonel.

The Red Army is not only an instrument of war but also of politics. From the first days of its existence it mirrored all the political storms and stresses of the country and rivalries among the Party leaders.

The army always took an active part in the political life of the country. Since the army was a cross section of the people it was often used in various political campaigns for the purpose of influencing the broad masses of the people. This activity was directed by the political workers of the army: the commissars, the Party and Komsomol* organizations, and the army officers. In 1921, thousands of army propagandists were used to popularize the NER† in the villages. During the period of collectivization, the twenties and early thirties, the army again sent tens of thousands to conduct a propaganda campaign. Often whole units were detached to "facilitate" collectivization.

* All Union Communist Youth League.
† New Economic Policy. Introduced by Lenin in 1921 to spur economic reconstruction through a partial return of private enterprise. It lasted till 1928.—tr

26

I remember one episode.

When collectivization began I was a battalion commander. One Saturday the regimental commissar called me and the secretary of the battalion's Party organization to him. We were given the following order:

"Comrade Gornev, today you and the secretary of the Party organization must form a special company under Company Commander Alferyev. Choose the best men, especially those who have worked in the Komsomol. Tomorrow send them to "X" region for the purpose of collectivizing. Report back when mission is completed."

"Yes, Comrade Commissar."

Sunday morning I sent the commissar the following report:

Acting upon your orders, a special company of 120 men, including 75 Komsomol members, was formed under the command of Company Commander Alferyev and at 7:00 of this date proceeded to the "X" region to conduct collectivization.

(signed) Commander of the First Battalion,
P. Gornev.

Two days later the company returned from the collectivized region with a complete victory. Company Commander Alferyev reported:

"Comrade Battalion Commander, the order of the Party and the personal order of Comrade Stalin has been fulfilled. The region has been 80 per cent collectivized. Three collectives were organized: the Comrade Stalin, the Comrade Voroshilov, and the Fourteenth Party Congress. The majority of the peasants gave their consent and signatures to the closing of churches and the removal of church bells. A list of kulaks* of the village is enclosed."

The commissar, in a regimental order of the day, issued a statement of gratitude to the special company.

Several days later one of the participants of the campaign told me:

* Well-to-do peasant.

"We went around to the peasants and suggested their entering the collective and closing the churches. As you know, when a military man speaks it is regarded as an order, so they all signed."

Collectivization provoked dissatisfaction in the higher circles of the government and the Party as well as among the broad peasant masses. This mood also appeared in the army, and an internal fight was waged to suppress anticollectivization elements. This fight was waged along two lines: political and punitive. The political method took these forms:

In all military units, special meetings were called. After a lecture extolling collectives, the commissar dictated letters which the soldiers were to send to their families in the villages. The soldier would ask and then insist that they enter the collectives.

Letters from home received by individual soldiers were read aloud to the whole company. Obviously, the letters chosen had also been written upon dictation at the other end. They told of the wonderful life in the collective, how easy the work was, how much more food each received, etc.

Punitive measures consisted of pointing out soldiers whose families were kulaks. An attempt was made to surround them with an atmosphere of hate and distrust. After a short while they were dismissed from the army as "a foreign element."

Once during this period I was called up by the director of the Special Section (NKVD) of the army who lectured me in a loud voice:

"Comrade Battalion Commander, what the hell is going on in your unit! Every company swarms with kulak sons. These people cannot be entrusted with arms, and yet yesterday you issued an official statement of gratitude to one of them."

I tried to explain that the statement of gratitude was issued to a soldier of the Red Army for military performance, irrespective of whether he was a kulak or a collective member. Kulaks are the concern of political commissars.

My retort provoked a storm. I was immediately accused of class blindness, of political spinelessness, and all sorts of other sins. Two days later I received an official reprimand from the Party for lack of class vigilance. In addition, the reprimand made the point that the woman who for two years had been bringing milk to my personal quarters was the wife of a kulak.

Upon returning home after this I told my wife:

"Listen, Katyenka, you must get rid of our milk woman. Find yourself another one who unquestionably comes from a collective. Nowadays the milk of a kulak cow is sour."

After the great famine of 1932-1933, the army was used for harvesting crops in those regions where the population had been reduced by starvation. Many questions arose in the minds of the Red Army men, but seldom were they expressed.

In 1928 the country entered the First Five-Year Plan. The feverish tempo, the whole meaning of the slogan, "Five-Year Plan in four years," naturally affected the army. Although the length of the military training period was cut in half, the qualitative demand remained the same. Every field of army activity was confronted with a similar situation. Like individuals and groups all over the country, the army too pulled its belt tighter —food, clothing, everything was sacrificed to the needs of the Plan.

To finance the First Five-Year Plan, the government borrowed from the people. Everyone had to subscribe at least one month's salary, and everyone had to sign up within three days. The wall newspaper* portrayed my battalion as a turtle in this connection. Next to it was my name as commanding officer and a note saying: "This battalion is spoiling the record of our regiment." And, further, "Take an example from the communications platoon," which was depicted on the diagram as an airplane.

That's bad, I thought, I'll really catch it now.

It depressed me for a long time.

Once when I came home to dinner my wife said:

* Typewritten and illustrated news bulletin displayed in most Soviet factories, schools, offices, etc.

29

"Petya, I wasn't able to get anything decent for dinner; I prepared a dish but you probably won't like it. You subscribed to the loan more than anyone else, but we also need something at home. There is nothing in the stores, and the black market is very expensive."

"That's all right, darling, just wait. When we finish the Five-Year Plan everything will be available. Can't you just see our future although you must now do without a piece of soap or a yard of material? What if supplies are short at the moment? Tighten your belt, let's wait."

I believed this. I was hypnotized by figures—progress in construction, promises for the future. I was encouraged by the appearance of new factories and construction projects all over the country.

In the factories there developed the Stakhanovite movement for raising the industrial output. This was duplicated in the army. The commanders of the Red Army had to assume the burden of unnecessary, thankless work.

For example, the battalion was scheduled to make a long march out to the firing range and there engage in target practice. The competitions usually occurred between squads of a company and between companies. The company commander conducted a preliminary meeting at which the points of the competition were worked out. He supervised the signing of the competition agreements. In the evenings the results were computed and individual scores determined. There was always a final meeting where the victors and the losers were announced.

Units were rewarded with points for the excellent conduct of the march, the fewest stragglers owing to foot trouble, the best political work during the march, the best score during target practice, and a whole list of minor determinants according to the particular problem. The company commander had to check every squad and mark the results. He observed the progress of the march, and at its conclusion received and noted the reports of the squad leaders. He also had to register the results of the target

30

practice. All this data had to be assembled and the results weighed and arranged on a general scale.

This is socialist competition.

The majority of officers understood that all this was just tawdry showmanship, harmful to the preparedness of the army. In the race for percentage fulfillment of norms it was forgotten that the main thing in the army was its military training. But I, like all the others, had to do this kind of work and keep silent.

The commissar in the Red Army represents the Communist party. He is its eyes and ears. His rights and privileges exceed those of the line commander. As the ideological-political overlord, the commissar exercises complete control. He can judge and pardon; he can decorate and rescind decorations. A military career depends on the commissar. Even when there has been no breach of military regulations he can discharge individuals from the army on the grounds of "not conforming with the spirit of the time."

Commissars were introduced into the Red Army shortly after it was activated in 1918. Their primary function was to supervise former czarist officers who were employed to make up for the lack of trained Red commanders. In addition, they were used to spread the principles and philosophy of the new regime. During the Civil War the commissars justified themselves in this capacity.

In succeeding years, the dual control of commissar and commander gave rise to many difficulties. The hidden frictions and hostilities were reflected in major and minor situations, often to the detriment of the soldiers. I remember receiving a request for a new pair of socks. I approved it and sent an issue order to the quartermaster. There it was stopped because it lacked the signature of the commissar, absent that day on private business.

In another instance a soldier was prevented from attending his mother's funeral. He had received a telegram notifying him of her death and I granted him a five-day leave. Because the commissar was attending a conference in a neighboring town, neither the furlough nor the necessary travel permits could be authorized. The papers lacked his signature and the unit stamp which was always in his possession.

Once a week, usually on Sunday, I had a day off. One Sunday I was out walking with my wife when I saw our unit commissar riding toward us. Before I had a chance to greet him he began shouting at me.

"You, Comrade Commander, are obviously enjoying yourself, but do you know what is going on in your unit? Two of your men were drunk when they came back from their furloughs. Report to the company immediately and conduct political discussions. Your laxity will not go unpunished!"

Not only was my day interrupted, but the next day I was the object of an official reprimand.

Double supervision might have resulted in strict discipline. But because there was never any actual co-operation between commanders and commissars, this was never so.

The Red Army emerged from the Civil War with the discipline of guerilla fighters, a discipline determined in each instance by the quality of the individual commander. Conversion to a peacetime army necessitated the introduction of "army discipline." Regulations were issued. However, the aim of the top command was for "conscious discipline," and was to be achieved through political education and understanding. In their propaganda, discussions, and lectures, the commissars tried to promote "conscious discipline" by ridiculing the discipline of the czarist army and capitalist countries. As a result, the men often complained to the commissar about "strict commanders" in order to escape punishment or hard work.

I was against any kind of iron-clad discipline, but at the same time I believed that an army could not function efficiently on "conscious discipline" alone.

Once I arrested a soldier for disobedience and had him put in the guardhouse for seven days. At the end of that period I received the following insolent note from him:

Comrade Commander, I have enjoyed my seven days in the guardhouse. I rested well and found that my health improved. Can you arrange to prolong my stay here?

I arrested him for fifteen more days and was going to court-martial him for insubordination. My commissar objected.

"You can't do that. We must talk to him. He will understand his mistake."

Nothing ever came of the affair and my authority suffered greatly.

On the other hand, any conduct unsatisfactory from a political standpoint was not trifled with. The Special Section, the arm of the NKVD in the army, immediately took over and subjected the individual involved to the heaviest punishment conceivable. Whatever discipline there was among the men stemmed from fear of the Special Section which could always ascribe a political basis to a nonpolitical act.

This situation existed until the Finnish campaign in 1939. Only after the Finnish war proved the shortcomings of "conscious discipline," did Timoshenko introduce new disciplinary regulations. Saluting was reinstated, as were disciplinary battalions and severe arrests. Internment was made an unpleasant experience. New guardhouses were built in damp dark cellars. Those sentenced to solitary confinement found themselves in a three-by-six-foot cell without a chair during the day. In some cases, such as direct refusal to obey orders, the commander had the right to resort to the use of arms. Many tragic and unnecessary incidents resulted from misuse of this right, particularly when the new regulations were first put into effect.

On a long march during tactical maneuvers, one of the men suffered from a blistered foot and fell behind. The commissar, noticing the straggler, ordered him to catch up to his company.

"Comrade Commissar," replied the soldier, "I can't. My foot is terribly sore."

"No back talk! Get back in your position!"

The soldier stood still and looked beseechingly at his superior.

33

Without another word the commissar fired. The soldier fell dead upon the road.

When "conscious discipline" was the fashion of the times, the commissars had been its chief advocates. Now that "iron discipline" had been introduced into the army, the primary advocates were these same men. As before, they enforced the will of the Party. Most officers, including myself, had been against "conscious discipline" and now opposed Timoshenko's inhuman regulations. The kind of discipline that I wanted—fair, strict, and human—I never saw in the Red Army.

In 1937, Stalin introduced the policy of criticism and self-criticism. It was designed to ferret out internal enemies of the Soviet regime. Nikolai Yezhov became the head of the NKVD.

Criticism and self-criticism became obligatory in the army. One could criticize anyone and anything. At one of our unit meetings I, as regimental commander, gave a report on the past month's progress and posed problems for the future. Men and officers were given the opportunity to criticize the report and me. One soldier, a Komsomol member, attacked me for having placed him under arrest. Then he launched into a denunciation of the regiment's method of conducting target practice. He wound up his speech thus:

". . . We must investigate this matter thoroughly. An enemy hand may be involved. Incidentally, the wife of our commander does not stem from a proletarian family."

As a result of such proceedings the morale and discipline of the unit was measurably reduced. Officers had to close their eyes to many things if they wished to avoid constant criticism.

In June 1937, Tukhachevsky, Uborevich, Yakir, and several others were shot as "enemies of the people." I did not believe in their guilt. I knew several of them personally and could not conceive that men who possessed such authority in the Red Army, and who had devoted their lives to building it up, could be enemies and spies.

Following Tukhachevsky's execution, the wave of persecution

34

rolled with increasing momentum. Everything was peered into; everyone was investigated. My chief of staff was arrested and sentenced to six years' imprisonment. He had once told an anti-collectivization joke, and had also attended a party of Uborevich, now an "enemy of the people."

In June 1937, I was called before the division commissar. It was not a warm reception.

"Comrade Gornev, answer us frankly, it will be better for you. How long have you been a spy for a foreign power?" asked the commissar glowering at me.

"Comrade Commissar, I don't understand what you are talking about."

At this he yelled and slammed his fist on the table.

"We have this much information on you," he said holding his hand shoulder high. "Piles of papers! Why did Uborevich, a spy and an enemy of the people, give you money and other valuable gifts? Why was your wife friendly with the wife of former Division Commander T., who was shot as an enemy of the people? Why don't you put the proper emphasis on political work in your regiment? Think this over! Dismissed!"

The next day no one would greet me. Even friends looked away when we met.

Three days later I was arrested. After a month, a high military official with whom I had become friendly during the Civil War intervened on my behalf. But only at the end of fourteen months was I reinstated. Everyone concerned apologized; I received my back pay; my entire family was sent to a resort.

The whole affair ended well enough for me. The fate of many was far worse. At least twenty-five thousand Red Army officers were persecuted during the years of Yezhov's reign of terror. Most of these perished. Some became invalids physically, the rest spiritually.

As a result of the Five-Year Plans, the military techniques of the Red Army were improved. The internal policies of the Soviet

35

Union switched from defense to offense. The country was preparing for war.

As early as September 1938, the Red Army stood at the eastern frontier of Poland, ready to fight its way through to help Czechoslovakia. The western and Ukrainian military sectors were mobilized. Only the Munich Agreement prevented the Soviet government from taking the decisive step.

In 1939 the policy of the Soviet Union changed sharply in favor of Germany. It was obvious that this was only a trick designed to weaken Germany and the West for the decisive blow at both. This was not even concealed. At a large meeting of high-ranking officers of the army, Manuilski said: "We married the Germans out of expediency, not love." Nevertheless, antifascist posters disappeared, and the anti-German film *Alexander Nevsky* was taken off the screens. Trainloads of gasoline and supplies constantly moved westward to Germany.

At 5:00 A.M., September 17, 1939, the Red Army crossed the Polish border. We moved ahead almost without resistance. Could Poland possibly resist Germany and the USSR at the same time?

By the twenty-first, the Red Army had occupied all previously agreed upon areas. This was not war. It was a poorly organized triumphal march. In Poland, all of us, officers and men, saw the riches and prosperity of a capitalist country and couldn't believe our eyes. We had never believed there could be such an abundance of goods and at such low prices—especially not in "backward" Poland. Our propaganda had described her as a backward nation.

Upon entering a town, our troops descended upon the stores and bought up everything in sight, particularly dress material. The buying spree was understandable, but the local population couldn't figure it out.

"Tell me, sir," a Polish salesman once asked, "why do your men buy all sorts of trash, not even bothering to ask the price? If you tell me that you don't have such things I couldn't believe it. You have such big tanks, and so many of them!"

I did not answer his query.

This first meeting with the capitalist world had come too unexpectedly and was too stunning. It gave many of us a shock and directed us toward new thoughts and understanding. Those who had at first honestly believed we were going to free our class brothers found themselves overcome by doubt.

"Comrade Colonel," I was asked by my chauffeur, "didn't we come to Poland to liberate our brothers, oppressed by landowners and capitalists? We have traveled far together. We have been in towns and villages, but I have seen no class brothers of mine. To me they all look like kulaks and bourgeois. A peasant has three or four horses, five or six cows; there is a bicycle in front of every house. Workers wear suits, hats—the same as a big Soviet director. There is something here that I don't understand."

Shortly after our arrival, the goods in the stores disappeared. The Sovietization of Poland took place rapidly. All types of business and industry were taken over by the state. Life in Poland gradually developed the same characteristics as in the Soviet Union.

Six months after the occupation of Poland, there was an election for regional and district officers and for the Supreme Soviet. Thousands of officers and men were assigned to the propaganda campaign preceding the elections. I was among them. We were briefed on topics for formal and informal discussions. They fell into seven major categories:

1. The world situation.
   a. The pact and friendship with Germany.
   b. England's provocation of war between Poland and Germany. Her deceit in promising aid to Poland and then remaining on the sidelines.
2. The reasons for Poland's defeat.
   a. The government's senseless foreign policy and not the Polish people should be blamed.
   b. Contrast the Polish government's lack of foresight with the Soviet Union's preparedness program.

3. The life of peasants and workers in landowner-capitalist Poland: exploitation, poverty, unemployment, lawlessness and the persecution of national minorities (White Russians and Ukrainians).
4. The Soviet government's concern for all its people.
5. The role of the Communist party and Comrade Stalin in building socialism.
6. Democratic rule in the Soviet Union.
7. Discussion of candidates, including their biographies.

By means of these discussions we were supposed to convince the population to vote for the approved slate. In addition, each propagandist had to keep track of attendance at meetings, notice the moods of the people, and make a list of the less trustworthy. Finally we had to see to a 100 per cent turnout at the polls.

The success of the elections was also insured by the NKVD, which used its regular, standard methods of taking care of recalcitrant citizens. For instance, the night before the elections, ten thousand people were removed from Bialystok. Five hundred trucks were delegated for this project. The NKVD also saw to it that church services were cut short that day. The same last words were spoken by every priest in Poland: "You fulfilled your religious duty. Now I call upon you to carry out your civic duty—take part in the elections."

Just to make sure there were no slip-ups, fully armed military units held street "maneuvers" on election day.

June 22, 1941—war began with Germany. Our frontier armies met quick defeat. I fought on the central front at the approaches to Moscow, where I was later wounded and taken prisoner.

As we battled against the invader—against those same Germans whom we'd fought in '16 and '17—I could see that many of our people did not want to fight. Hundreds of thousands surrendered to the enemy almost at once. Many plans of the command were shattered by this lack of fighting spirit, and to me it

38

seemed the people's way of rebuking their government and leaders.

I was a member of the Communist party. I was an officer in the Red Army. In the course of years I came to believe less and less in the Soviet regime, in its promises and its potentialities. Still, believing that I served my people and my homeland, I faithfully carried on my work.

The war brought me to my senses. As a prisoner of war, I had a chance to review my whole life and make a decision. I decided that Soviet citizens give too much and get too little. In Finland, Poland, and Germany, I saw that most people were better off than we were. Soviet propaganda had told us just the reverse. The Soviet government had always lied to us. Now I had a chance to escape from the lies.

2

SECRET FLIGHT

by Irina Karsavina

1933—Hunger

I didn't notice anything around me as I rushed down the crowded Kiev street on my way to school. I might have saved my energy and gone by trolley, but I didn't trust it to get me there on time. They were all crowded with people hanging onto the sides, and it was a miracle when one did come along with enough room for a person to squeeze inside.

The walking, as such, didn't bother me. All my thoughts were concerned with eating. I was hungry that day, as I had been the previous days and the previous weeks—since I had felt the first pain in the pit of my stomach months ago. At times it grew stronger, at other times it ebbed. It almost disappeared on days when my mother went down to the store and, after standing in line for hours, brought back a pound of heavy, dark bread. Both my mother and I existed on her meager ration of four ounces per day, which wasn't enough to keep even one person satisfied when there was nothing else to eat. And I was eighteen, with a big, healthy appetite. . . .

In the school yard I was met by a pale and excited group of students.

40

"What happened?" I asked them.

"Look. There by the fence, under the bushes. An old woman. . . . She must have strayed in during the night. . . ." one of the girls said, pointing with a shaky hand.

Automatically I moved in the indicated direction. I jumped back as I beheld those two blank eyes staring at nothing. The dead woman's gray face made me ill. For a few moments I even forgot my own hunger.

The bell called us, and silently we repaired to the classroom. Looking at the teacher, I was overcome by the thought that he too probably wished for a crust of bread.

A surprise awaited me when I got home—the mail had brought a money order for 150 rubles from my uncle.

"Mama, do you think the market is still open?" I quickly asked.

"Of course."

"Then let's cash the money in a hurry, and I'll run down and buy a pound of bread and some sausage."

At the market one could buy all the bread one wanted. It was sold by speculators and women whose husbands received large bread rations and wanted to buy other things with the money they could realize from the sale of the extra bread. Under ordinary circumstances, we were never able to buy anything there. Mother's monthly salary of ninety rubles compared very unfavorably with the market price of bread—five rubles a pound.

In the market the bread was laid out on plain tables in booths. There were whole loaves, small pieces, and bags with crumbs. The women guarded the bread like hawks, for gangs of hungry boys prowled around the market in search of an unguarded piece of bread. I clutched my loaf with one arm while I was getting the money out and paying the woman. Suddenly a dirty hand reached from behind and grabbed onto my bread. I pressed it as hard as I could against me, holding on with all my strength. The saleswoman ran from behind the counter, and the bedraggled sixteen-year-old retreated under blows from a club which the woman kept on hand for just such occasions.

The closer it came to spring, the more peasants from the surrounding villages congregated in Kiev. They roamed the streets, unsuccessfully begging food from the hungry and therefore easily angered pedestrians. Peasant mothers proclaimed their sorrow in loud voices, appealing to people to save their children who were dying in front of their eyes. The children, with their bloated stomachs, sat along the curbs in hopeless resignation, gazing with half-dead looks as people passed by without noticing them.

Early every morning carts went around the city picking up the corpses of those who had died during the night. I often saw these carts on my way to school. Everyone gradually built up an immunity to such sights. The instinct of self-preservation didn't permit us to react to things in the usual human way. People tried to avoid meeting the eyes of dying women and walked, unseeing, past people going through the terrible agonies of a hungry death. I was just like everyone else. I was battling desperately for my own survival, and knew nothing but this battle.

The horror reached terrible proportions. And then suddenly the first ray of light appeared—the government opened several stores selling unrationed bread. For 3.50 rubles anyone could buy a whole pound of bread. Kiev came to life again. People congregated at bread stores during the night, and when the doors opened in the morning a terrible noise and crush began. The police had to come in to restore order. Unsuccessful people were just pushed out of the lines onto the street.

I stood in these bread lines many times. One instance particularly is preserved in my memory. It was the height of summer, the sun was beating down. I stood on the sidewalk from 7:00 A.M. to almost 5:00 P.M. Just before I reached the door of the store, I was pushed out of the line. The terrible words: "She wasn't in line! Throw her out!" were hurled at me. A policeman

42

approached, and under his threatening glance I was forced to withdraw.

I came home completely crushed. My only reply to my mother's questions was:

"They threw me out. Just before the door, they threw me out."

In vain did she try to tell me that a pound of bread wasn't worth my tears. That only made me cry more. It was then that I was first overcome by a feeling of resentment again those who were doing this to us, those who made hungry animals out of people.

A year later, when I was attending the university, I spent the summer with a group of students working in a kolkhoz (collective farm). The people in the village still weren't well fed, but the period of starvation was over. The only sign of the hard times that had been lived through was the empty peasant huts.

I looked at the endless fields of wheat. I knew that the crop in 1932 had been just as heavy. Why then these terrible statistics that people quoted to each other: "Eight million dead from starvation in the south of the Soviet Union"? The answer could be given in terms of an official slogan: "Nothing is impossible in the land of Bolshevism!"

I knew that the hunger of 1932-1933 was created artificially when the government confiscated all wheat and other food products from the peasants. It was done to break down the peasants' resistance to collectivization. I also knew that while whole villages and regions were being depopulated by hunger, the government was selling wheat to foreign countries below cost.

University life

In the fall of 1933, I passed my entrance examinations for Kiev University. A new page of life opened before me.

I had always been interested in the social sciences and wanted to take up the study of history. But that was impossible. Even though I was only eighteen, I understood perfectly well that history was a highly dangerous subject in the Soviet Union.

Marxist and Leninist theory governed the study of history. Even historical research had to comply with the policies set by the Party. Woe to him who accidentally, or out of ignorance, slightly overstepped the bounds.

I had no desire to let my thoughts become completely enslaved. I rejected the work I had dreamed of since childhood, and enrolled in the biology department. In this field one could at least work without worrying too much about ideology and the zigzagging Party line.

Youth is wonderful under any regime. I felt inexhaustible energy within me. I studied well, attended school meetings and lectures on scientific subjects. Outside of school I played the piano, took singing lessons, didn't miss a single symphony concert, read poetry, and attended the theater. I was happy and full of vitality and tried to close my eyes to many things. Involuntarily I shied away from all the unpleasant aspects of university life.

And there were many unpleasant things about the university. It had, as everything else in Soviet life, its Party Organization, which penetrated into every aspect of university life. Every course had to have its own Party representative. If no Party member was enrolled in the course, a Komsomol member was appointed. Besides, a class chairman and a union representative were elected. The latter took care of all affairs that had to do with the trade or professional union corresponding to the course. Chemistry students, for instance, were associated with the Chemist's Union. The Party and union representatives, and the class chairman made up what was called the "course triangle."

A joke resulted from this designation. New students were asked:

"In what triangle are all angles obtuse?"

Answer: "In the 'course triangle.' "

One of the "triangle's" duties was to organize political-education and extracurricular work on social projects. We had one

44

political-instruction class every week; under the leadership of the Party representative, we studied speeches delivered before Party congresses, government decrees, and important editorials in *Pravda* and *Izvestia*. The class was inconceivably boring, a complete make-believe. Everyone spoke in memorized phrases. Usually we had to read pertinent sections from Lenin's and Stalin's writings on the topic of the day.

The majority of students looked on the political hour as an unavoidable evil and tried to spend as little of their valuable time on it as possible. This was easy for those who were used to reading a lot and could grasp the basic idea immediately. Our mainstays in these classes, however, were those students who had mastered the art of "slinging the bull." A student who was well versed in this "art" had nothing to be afraid of. Whenever called upon by the instructor, he could start a speech composed of stock newspaper phrases, general praise for the wisdom of government policies, discussions of Marxism, etc. The orator could spout on like that until the instructor, tired of listening, stopped him. We had several experts in this "art," who could get up on the spur of the moment and talk for a whole hour on any subject. They were held in great esteem by their classmates, who could dream a bit or finish their studying while the speaker raved on. Students like this often saved the day for us when the whole class was unprepared.

Another duty which poisoned the students' lives was extra-curricular work. Every student had to have at least one or two social activities. One person was an agitator among housewives and talked to them about the necessity of industrializing the country and the importance of collectivization; another belonged to the "League of the Godless" and had to lecture the workers of a confectionary plant on the bankruptcy and evils of religion; a third issued the wall newspaper, usually having to write all stories himself since no one else wanted to bother.

Anyone who shirked such social obligations was looked upon as an "anti-Soviet element" and "rugged individualist," and was subjected to endless attacks and persecutions. Such a person was castigated before general meetings and accused of not having the proper Bolshevik consciousness.

Unnoticed, a new factor crept into my life—fear.

1937—Terror

Four years of school were behind me and only one remained. This was the only thought that gave me any happiness.

Terror was in the air. Yezhov was reigning in the NKVD. His name was pronounced with trepidation.

In 1933, carts went around Kiev picking up the dead. In 1937, "black marias" were the fashion. In the dead of night they stopped before buildings and took away their marked victims. There was no discrimination in arrests: old and young, professors and janitors, men and women were taken. And then. . . . We didn't talk about what came after arrest. All knew that the world hadn't seen anything like it since the Spanish Inquisition.

Arriving at the university one morning, I was met by one of my close friends. He drew me away from the students streaming into the auditorium.

"Professor D. was arrested last night," he said in a low, depressed tone. "I guess that's the end of him. . . . How terrible!"

D. was our favorite professor. His daughter, a close friend, who also studied with us, was in school as usual. The iron discipline of school attendance would permit nothing else.

We were just closing our notebooks and getting up after the last lecture on that day, when the Party representative mounted the rostrum.

"Comrades! Remain in the auditorium! There will be a meeting," he shouted above the din in the hall.

A deep silence settled over the auditorium. Everyone guessed what was up.

"Comrades, we all know that lately the traitors to our country,

46

the foul hangers-on of fascism, have been conducting their under-mining activities with increased insolence. The filthy tentacles of the enemies of the people have penetrated into the midst of the proletarian student body. We have to improve our vigilance, Comrades, we have to destroy the dastardly agents of imperi-alism. . . ."

We listened in silence. This phraseology wasn't new to us. The papers were full of it. But then the speaker went from the general to the particular.

". . . Comrades, everything is not well in our university. The glorious organs of our NKVD have uncovered an enemy of the people—Fascist D."

In fear, the students lowered their eyes and sat rigid in their seats. The Party representative proceeded to hurl invectives at the professor.

"Traitor to his country D.! Foul spy D.! Villain D.!" the Party's voice thundered through the auditorium.

Many of us cast worried glances at Olga, professor D.'s daugh-ter. She was sitting, pale and shaky, with her eyes cast down.

". . . and can we permit the daughter of an enemy of the people to remain amongst us and with her breath poison the proletarian atmosphere of our university? I hereby propose to expel Olga D. from the university! Any other suggestions? No? Then we'll vote —all those in favor raise their right hand."

Olga looked around in alarm and quickly whispered to us:

"Please, please, raise your hands. Don't suffer for me, it won't help me anyway. For God's sake, do it. Look he is counting already. . . ."

All of us—her friends—slowly raised our hands. What else was there to do?

"Unanimous!" the Party representative announced.

The above was but the first of many arrests of professors and students that occurred at our university. And whenever any question came up to a vote we raised our hands . . .

An unconquerable fear of the heartless power of the Stalin regime, in whose power I was and which could destroy me any minute, made me pretend and lie. I loudly praised that which I hated and despised; I applauded the leaders at meetings, and mine were among the loudest yells during demonstrations and celebrations.

I felt the watchful stare of Bolshevism on me always and everywhere. And all the time it was as if I were trying to justify myself, to prove that I was not a criminal.

This fear oppressed me the more because I was not faint-hearted by nature. My whole internal "I" rebelled against the heavy pressure on my personality. Sometimes I consoled myself with the thought that it is better to be a slave under such obvious coercion, than be a slave of one's own free will.

Aftermath of war

June 22, 1941, marked the beginning of the war. It also marked the return of hunger and cold. Again constant fear of death. Again endless insults and humiliation.

We knew much, but when the Germans came, they taught us still more. We saw the monstrous, completely open ruthlessness of the conquerors; the murder of hundreds of thousands of Russian prisoners of war; mass execution of Jews; and gallows in the streets of Kiev!

In weather below zero we were chased out on the streets. They called us *Untermenschen* to our faces. By thousands we were sent into slavery, taken to Germany for forced labor.

Germany's surrender found me in Württemberg, where I was working in a small textile factory. The area was occupied by the French. Joy and exultation reigned. Frenchmen, Belgians, Dutch, Czechs were happily getting ready to go home. They were going to free countries and none of them were afraid of their governments. They weren't threatened by accusations and persecution on their native soil.

Only we Russians looked with alarm into the future.

"What should I do?" I wondered.

I knew the Soviet system with its far-reaching, insidious system of force and coercion. I had long before comprehended and condemned its crimes against my people. The thought alone of returning to the USSR made me shiver. I had been in Europe, had seen a different life, had talked and thought freely. I had come out from under the grasp of the Soviet propaganda machine and from their viewpoint had undoubtedly become "infected with harmful anti-Soviet ideas." That in itself would have been enough to seal my fate.

I knew that I could not go back to the Soviet Union. But how could one escape repatriation? Soviet officers were all over Württemberg. They could grab me and put me behind bars without asking the French authorities. The French were of no help either. They arrested at least one Russian, an engineer who lived across the street from us, and handed him over to the Soviet Repatriation Mission.

Summer came to an end. The last contingents of Russian repatriates were going East. The Soviet Repatriation Mission sent order after order instructing me to report to the nearest camp. Poles, Serbs, Rumanians, and other nationals were entitled to refuge. For me there was nothing. Everyone turned away from me. The French just shrugged their shoulders in answer to my appeals for help; the Germans threatened me with arrest.

What could I do? Should I claim that I was Polish or Serbian? But I couldn't speak those languages, had never been in those countries, and didn't have a single document to prove such a statement.

Or should I set out on foot for the American zone? But I had no money, no food, and anyway, I would have been apprehended along the road. Above all, the Yalta Agreement was in force everywhere.

In desperation I jumped from one futile idea to another, until

49

one day the burgomaster called me in and announced that if I didn't leave for camp the next day, he would call the police.

Rather than be arrested and be sent back as an imprisoned traitor to the country, I decided to join the last train of repatriates leaving the area. I figured that I would get lost in the mass of returning people, and somehow find a way to escape.

A breath of the Soviet fatherland

In the Soviet zone of Germany the train stopped at a tremendous repatriation camp surrounded on all sides with barbed wire. Men were ordered to unload on one side of the tracks, the women on the other. Under armed guard the men were marched to another camp ten miles away.

Before we had a chance to settle ourselves in the barracks, we were called to the local section of the NKVD. I had never had any direct contact with this all-powerful department, and the fear of it which I had harbored in my younger years returned in full force.

I tried to appear calm and independent as I entered the examiner's office. But despite all my attempts at self-control, my hands shook and my voice broke repeatedly.

The interrogation began with the question: "How did you get to Germany?" I began the story of my sufferings and the forceful deportation to Germany for slave labor.

The examiner tapped his pencil on the table, and looked somewhere behind my ear.

"What you are trying to say is that you voluntarily went to Germany," he said, putting strong emphasis on "voluntarily."

"Just the reverse! I have told you what actually happened. . . ."

And I retold my story, showing him the documents supporting my statements:

"Here is the Gestapo summons, and here is the 'Ost-Arbeiter' (slave labor) certificate."

He listened, but was obviously thinking of something else. When I finished, he halfheartedly asked me again:

"Then you admit that you voluntarily went to Germany?"

He picked up his pen and was ready to enter that statement into my file.

"But I've shown you documents which prove that wasn't so! Here—look over these papers. . . ." and for the third time I went through my whole story. But at the end I heard the same illogical question, asked in the deadliest monotone.

I went over the story once again—with the same result.

I began to get panicky.

"Why do you insult me?" I screamed. "Why these unfounded accusations? I don't want to listen to your insulting questions! You have no right to question me in this manner!"

For a moment the inquisitor was taken aback, but he recovered immediately.

"So I have no right! Do you know what you are saying?"

"But you are trying not to recognize what I tell you, you don't even consider my documents. You have no idea about the actual events!"

"We know everything much better than you think!" he retorted.

After arguing like this for a long time, he finally certified that I had been forcefully removed to Germany. In place of my documents which were taken away, I received a paper certifying that I had been OK'd by the filtering commission and was being sent to my old place of residence. On arrival I was to report to the local NKVD to be issued a resident's permit.

The barracks were filled to capacity. I climbed into an upper bunk and tried to think. People were exchanging impressions of the day. The consensus seemed to be that the filtering commission was but a prelude to the future. Everyone talked guardedly, but the fear and hopelessness was obvious.

I could hear a seventeen-year-old girl sobbing near me. The examiner had written in her file that she had come to Germany voluntarily. The inexperienced girl was overcome by fear. Not daring to contradict the NKVD man, she signed the statement.

Many of the young people were particularly disillusioned,

their deepest feelings insulted. They had been taken to Germany in their teens, directly from their parents' homes. They were still unacquainted with Soviet life, all they knew was the propaganda they were fed in school. After having experienced all the horror of slavery in Germany, they craved with all the fervor of true patriots, to return to the Soviet Union. And they were met like traitors. . . .

Several days went by, taken up by camp details. I gathered my remaining fortitude and determined not to give up my idea to escape. By listening to conversations, I discovered that officers came to the camp every day and recruited people they could use outside. I managed to make myself known to them, but despite my knowledge of German I was never taken.

Then a new opportunity opened—an entertainment troop was being organized among the repatriates. I applied and was accepted the same day. I was an actress, singer, pianist—depending on what the occasion demanded. The threat of immediate departure for the Soviet Union was deferred.

Our troop serviced near-by camps and army units. Whenever we gave a show outside our own camp, we were accompanied by several soldiers. There was no chance to get away.

Letters began to arrive from home. The majority guardedly advised us to remain in Germany as long as possible. There were hints of returning repatriates being persecuted and exiled by the NKVD.

Many people didn't want to correspond with repatriates, fearing for their own safety. One of the men in our troop received the following note from his brother:

I am very glad that you are alive and well, but I ask you not to write to me and don't come to see us. My wife can't even stand hearing your name mentioned. Even though your quarrel with her was a long time ago, she still hasn't gotten over it.

The quarrel alluded to was fictitious. It was just a hint to the brother not to return.

52

The camps were gradually emptied by continuous shipments home, and our troop became smaller and smaller. Fear again returned. Any day I might get a notice saying that I was to report for shipment in two hours.

But fortune smiled again.

Our troop happened to be in a neighboring camp when a major arrived to recruit people for a chemical factory in Germany. With permission of the new NKVD chief, Beria, it had been decided to organize a course there to study certain chemical processes unknown in the Soviet Union. I was among the thousands who applied for the course. Thanks to my biology training I was one of the few who was accepted.

A week later I was in our new place. There was no barbed wire, no armed guards. We lived freely in a factory village. The instructors were recruited among the repatriates. I gave lectures on inorganic and organic chemistry.

We worked and studied through the whole winter and spring. Our happiness was only dimmed by the knowledge that in the fall we were to be returned to the USSR.

With the coming of warmer weather the first "flights" or escapes began. The director of the factory closed his eyes and obviously sympathized with us, giving passes on the most fantastic pretenses. There was complete solidarity among the participants in the special course. During the whole time there was not a single case of denunciation.

I was able to receive a special assignment for a week's trip to the Zeis factory in Jena. Everything that followed was like a dream. I never went to Jena, instead I proceeded immediately to the southwestern border of the Soviet zone.

The border towns swarmed with military men. Shaking with fright at the thought of someone asking me for my identifications, I walked from tavern to tavern, striking up conversations with Germans, buying drinks and handing out cigarettes freely. Thus I was able to obtain the address of someone who could help me. I went to the home of the guide and arranged for crossing the border. Then I returned to the factory to get several other people who were escaping with me.

Finally, on a dark, rainy June night we set out. At one point we had to pass through a brilliantly illuminated strip near a checking station. If one of the Soviet guards had looked out the window it would have been the end. We had no documents whatsoever, and we knew exactly what would happen if we were apprehended. But we passed this danger successfully.

Not much later we stopped suddenly. The German guide whispered excitedly as we heard the roar of approaching motorcycles:

"Patrol! Into the woods, quick!"

We rushed into the dark woods, and the motorcycles raced by.

We walked more than ten miles. At first along a road, then over trails through forests and over hills.

Finally we saw the blinking lights of a small house. The relative of our guide awaited us in the American zone.

3

THE LONG ROAD

by Alexei Gorchakov

"What is your name?"

"Alyesha," I replied pertly.

"And your last name?"

"Gorchakov."

"How old are you?"

"Seven."

"And do you want to study in our school?"

"I do," I answered.

"All right then. You'll be in the first grade," said the old and genial school principal, affectionately stroking my head.

It was in the middle of the class hour. In a large and sunny classroom neat students sat primly behind desks. I was put next to a snub-nosed girl. After a short while she threw me an inquisitive glance and in a half-whisper said:

"And do you know—people also live on the moon!"

"Sure I know," I replied confidently.

"Olya!" the teacher called her sternly, "don't talk, you will have a chance to talk with the new student between classes."

Thus I was called a student for the first time. This was in the fall of 1928. Our school was in exemplary order. All lessons went according to plan, and normally we received no political instruction. Only on holidays the walls sprouted red flags and posters; then the school had the Soviet look. This happened only twice a year: in May and November.

Life at school proceeded smoothly, but one morning when I entered the class several kids ran excitedly toward me:

"Have you heard? Leonid Ivanovich has been arrested!"

This was a shock. I, like all the others in the school, had a deep love for the kind principal.

". . . they came at night in a car, tore pillows, were looking for something. They also tore the floor up. Borka and his mother were kept in the kitchen by men with rifles."

Borka, the son of our principal, was just as fat and genial as his father. Now he stood near the wall and sniveled.

"And I am glad that he was arrested," freckled Kolya announced. "He told my father that I broke the window. It serves the fatso right."

The next day a new principal arrived. Our whole way of life was turned upside down. For some unknown reason we were continually shifted from one classroom to another. Students often did not know where their classroom was. They spent a lot of time roaming around the school and looking into all doors. Some came late to classes, others cut two or three periods, justifying themselves by saying that they were unable to find their group.

For weeks, instead of studying, we went to various dumps, factories, and private apartments, collecting broken glass, used paper, rusty iron and other scrap needed for the Five-Year Plan. All this was taken to our school playground, which soon took on the appearance of a junk yard.

"Children, today again we won't study. . . ."

"I won't go collect rusty iron! Last time I cut my hand and now it is festering," I interrupted the teacher.

"Calm yourself, Alyesha. Today we will sort the school library." The glass doors of the massive closets containing the

56

books were wide open. The director himself walked up and down with a sheet of paper in his hand and gave orders all around.

"Take this into the yard. Have Uncle Roman burn it. Here is another book out of tune with the times—to Uncle Roman into the fire."

"Hey, you," the principal yelled at me roughly, "here is a book by Dostoyevsky, take it down too."

In the yard the books were fed into an enormous bonfire. The tongues of flame ate up the gold and embroidered bindings of the volumes. Uncle Roman, our janitor, sadly stirred the fire with an iron poker.

"Here, Uncle Roman, here is a book by Dostoyevsky. He said to throw it into the fire."

"Dostoyevsky?" he asked. "Sad, our poor Leonid Ivanovich loved these books, and now they must be burned. Look at these covers! You can't find them like this now."

"Can't we tear them off?"

"No. I already asked the principal. He said that there is no use for them, that soon we will have our own Soviet books in red bindings."

Of "sticks" and pioneer leaders' vigilance

In the winter of 1931-1932 I struck up a great friendship with Valya, a tall skinny boy, and Borka, the son of our former principal who had never been released after his arrest.

One day the three of us were at my house, stuffing ourselves with bread and sausage and making plans for the future. We argued extensively over the relative advantages of being professional pilots or sailors. I defended flying, Borka the sea. Valya couldn't swim and therefore supported me. Finally, we agreed to become pilots. We were only eleven years old, so could not even begin to dream about flying. Therefore, we went to a children's technical center and enrolled in the model-airplane section.

On our first visit to the model-airplane section we found the kids sitting on tables, waving their hands and singing:

Comrade Voroshilov, war is almost here,
But Budyenny's cavalry went out to get some beer. . . .

No one was making airplane models, but that didn't dim our enthusiasm a bit. There was a poster on the wall: FROM MODELS TO GLIDERS, FROM GLIDERS TO AIRPLANES. This was what we were looking for.

The leader of the section, Georgi Vasilyevich, was a friendly and likable individual. He wore a semimilitary uniform with blue lapels. This evening he was giving a talk on the history of aviation. He spoke evenly and in a low voice, but somehow it was fascinating—so simple and clear.

The kids listened wide-eyed and held their breath. When he was through, it was late and we went home. It was cold out, but that didn't bother us. We walked through the heavy snow, quoting whole sections of Georgi Vasilyevich's talk. From this evening on, flying became our religion. All our previous interests and games were completely forgotten, and we spent our free time at the model-plane section. In the beginning we made balloons out of uncut cigarette paper, and then we built kites. The kites didn't work at first, but we put all our energy and resources into them and were finally able to make them fly. Freezing our ears and noses, we flew the kites for several days. When this began to bore us, we threw ourselves with increased fervor into the construction of airplane models with rubberband motors. There never seemed to be enough time for our work, and we often cut school. Since Borka's mother was a teacher and was never home during school hours, we would meet in his apartment and build models. Often we competed with each other.

"Alyesha, I challenge you to a socialist competition and pledge myself to finish my model in two days."

"I accept your challenge, and pledge that I will finish mine tomorrow."

"You lie, you can't finish that quick!"

"I bet I will finish!"

58

"Go ahead and show us!"

We worked hurriedly. Our hands were scratched, our clothes covered with glue, oil and lacquer. For several days, sometimes weeks, each of us worked on his model, and then the whole section would go to an open field out of town and send up the models. After a short while in the air the models came down and were smashed. Within a few days they would be fixed and flown again. The process of fixing and breaking continued till the models were beyond repair. Then the calculations and drawings began again. Aerodynamic books were consulted, newer and better forms were selected. All this was accompanied by constant arguments about details.

Over the winter we became so proficient in aviation terminology and knew so much about flying that we received a new name in school—the pilots. Naturally we were very proud of that.

Before May 1st there was a Pioneer* meeting to discuss preparations for the holiday celebration. Unexpectedly I was put on a crew assigned to decorate the school. I protested, saying I had enough model-airplane work to keep me busy twenty-four hours a day.

"What do you mean? You think that your sticks are more important than Pioneer work?" Grinko, our Pioneer leader, asked me.

I was angered by such a condescending approach to airplane modeling.

"Yes! I do think that my 'sticks' are more important than all your Pioneer bother," I replied viciously.

"All right, Gorchakov, we'll talk about this after the meeting."

Grinko's eyes shone with a mean light. He was an old member of the Komsomol. He worked in different places, conducting Komsomol and Pioneer organizations.

"Listen, Gorchakov," Grinko turned to me after the meeting, "where do you do your plane-model work?"

* The "Pioneers" is a Communist party youth organization to which practically all children of school age belong.

59

"At the children's technical center."

"How are the kids there?"

"Very fine."

"And how is your instructor?"

"Oh, he is wonderful."

"Is it he who told you that model work is more important than Pioneer activities?"

Grinko was talking in a wheedling tone. I suddenly felt some alarm and began to change my attitude.

"Oh no, just the opposite, our instructor feels that Pioneer work comes before anything else."

"Then why did you talk at the meeting the way you did?"

"Because I was hurt by what you said. I work night and day on my models, and then you call them 'sticks.' I was just speaking rashly. . . ."

"Just rashly, hah?"

"That's right."

"Well, watch out. Don't be too rash in the future or we might do something about it."

Through the Donbas mines

During the summer of 1932 my father took me along on a trip through twenty mines in the Donbas region in southern Russia. He was sent there by his trade union to give a series of lectures.

The poverty and conditions under which the miners lived made a deep impression on me. Houses were leaning over, almost in a state of collapse. The faces of the miners, blackened by coal dust, were thin and emaciated. Near many a mine was a shining, new building—the miners' "Palace of Culture."

They were real palaces: parquet floors, tremendous meeting halls, and everywhere portraits of the leaders. But the miners sat in their tiny hovels, too tired and hungry to visit the palace.

"They build us palaces, but we don't even have a decent bathhouse, can't even wash the coal dust out of our skin," they said.

60

I have seldom since met such anger. I remember my father's very first lecture. Almost in a chorus the miners began yelling:

"Why tell us about Shakespeare? Is that all we need, fat . . ."

The lecture was interrupted. Later the director of the Palace of Culture, an old Communist and hero of the Civil War, told us:

"You didn't get off so badly, we've had much worse."

I also saw a different kind of life in the Donbas. Near one mine, apart from the regular miners' huts, there stood neat rows of white houses with tile roofs. Not far off, a herd of fat cows grazed in the pasture. These were the homes of German Communist miners who had come to work in the USSR. Each of them received a private home, his own cow. They even had a separate store where they could buy practically everything. The prices were amazingly low and the quality of the goods far better than in a Soviet store. In their dining rooms caviar, oranges, and wonderful wines were served. They worked on the easiest and least dangerous jobs. They were paid in gold currency.

Besides their work, the German Communist miners were enrolled in Communist schools in which they were taught the principles of Marxism and Leninism, and schooled in methods of propaganda and agitation. After a while the majority returned to Germany where they carried on Communist subversive activities.

"And higher, and higher, and higher . . ."

When I returned to Kiev in the fall, a great shock awaited me. Valya and Borka had entered the glider school. Not as students —but to work there, carrying glider parts, scrubbing and cleaning gliders, and doing similar unimportant tasks. But they had the opportunity to sit in the pilot seat and work the controls. I had never in my life even touched a real glider, and was terribly envious.

My friends understood this and arranged to have me join them. Soon I was monkeying around the gliders, happy and satisfied.

61

The anniversary of the Revolution was approaching. The glider pilots were to be graduated and it was announced that during the parade on November 7th they would march in full uniform. When the uniforms were being handed out, the director of the glider school called us.

"Come here kids," he said. "Because you have been a great help to us, I am giving you these uniforms. Don't forget, I procured them for you myself. No one has the right to take them from you. Wear them happily in payment for those trousers which you tore climbing around under the gliders."

Then he told us that we were to march at the head of the column of glider pilots.

"Hurray!" we yelled, running across the airfield holding our old clothes in our arms. We were already wearing our brand new green uniforms with blue lapels. Beyond the gate we fell into step—the uniform demanded that.

I rose early on November 7th and put on my uniform. Then I noticed my torn shoes. I plugged the holes with cotton to keep my socks from showing. When I got out into the street, I saw the cotton creeping out through the holes. I had to sacrifice my good handkerchief. I climbed under a truck, smeared it with grease, and blackened the bulging cotton so it wouldn't show. It looked pretty good.

The glider pilots marched behind the civilian fliers. At an intersection, our column and another one met head-on. Everything became entangled and disorganized, but the pilots kept pushing through.

"Stop! Let the others go through first!" screamed Grinko, who was running around with the red arm band of a traffic director. He ran to the head of our column and spreading his arms attempted to stop us.

"Out of the way, louse," a six-foot-four pilot thundered at him, and with one hand he pushed Grinko aside.

Grinko stood there at a loss. Going by, I couldn't resist the urge and stuck out my tongue at him.

As we entered the big square, the band struck up the "Aviators' March":

And higher, and higher, and higher . . .

My heart beat at a terrific speed and a lump came into my throat. Soon we were marching past the reviewing stand. As we went by, I looked closely at the men assembled there. Instead of joyful and happy expressions, I saw the sleepy and indifferent faces of the Party leaders. It made a disappointing picture. Could they be unfamiliar with the notes of our cheerful march? Didn't the valiant fliers bring out their enthusiasm? Weren't they glad to see the blue lapels on the pilots' uniforms? I wondered.

I was not the only one who had been so poorly impressed by the men on the stand. When our column was halted and the fliers broke formation, they also had something to say:

"Did you see those guys?" a young fellow nodded in the direction of the square. "Probably were getting drunk all night long, and now they're working off their hang-overs."

"Yes, they live well, not like us sinners," the tall pilot, who had shoved Grinko out of the way, assented.

"How old are you, lad?" he slapped me on the shoulder.

"Thirteen," I lied; I wasn't even twelve.

"Long live our future relief! Hurray!"

They began to throw us into the air, as high as the trees.

This was my first flight.

A small piece of butter

A terrible hunger fell upon us in the winter. Skinny and bedraggled kids walked to and from school like shadows. During our lessons we were often told of starvation in Europe and America. We learned how the capitalists, while the unemployed died of hunger, poured milk into rivers, sank ships loaded with wheat, and burned coffee in steamship boilers. This was explained by saying that an economic crisis existed in the West, and though people were starving, the capitalists destroyed food

63

to keep prices up. One day, after a similar story, I asked the teacher a question.

"Isn't it right, Vera Ivanovna, that a crisis exists not only when there is too much of everything, but also when there is a shortage of things?"

The teacher agreed to that.

"Then," I said, "a crisis exists in the Soviet Union. Because here we don't have anything."

Vera Ivanovna blushed and did not know what to answer. The whole class supported my conclusion.

"Yes, yes, that's right, we also have a crisis."

Vera Ivanovna rose and replied:

"Remember, children, that we can never have a crisis, because we have a Soviet regime. The rest you will understand when you grow up. Let's not talk about this any more—that would be better for me and for your parents."

The teacher's tone was excited and frank, and we asked no more such questions.

Our inseparable group starved like everyone else. But we did not give up. As before, we spent whole days in the shop working on our models. We were dizzy from exhaustion, but our enthusiasm for aviation was not diminished.

In the spring, when the buds began opening on the Kiev chestnut trees, Valya suddenly became ill. He started bleeding from the mouth. It was diagnosed as tuberculosis.

"He needs wholesome food," the doctor said.

"But where can one get it?" Valya's mother asked, wiping away her tears.

From this day on, Borka's and my life changed. We spent most of our evenings sitting at the bedside of the pale, thin, deathlike Valya. During the day we cut classes and stood in line for bread. The bread which we were able to obtain was stone, but as soon as it was in our hands, we ran to Valya. We ran for two reasons: first, because we didn't want to waste time getting the food to him, and secondly, because it was torture to walk with a pound of bread in your arms. The temptation to break off just a tiny crust was terrific and we well knew that after the first piece a second and a third would follow, and nothing would be left. But bread didn't help Valya much. His condition became worse and worse.

"Well," Borka said once, "I heard that pigs were being fattened for export. If we could only get a small pig or some chocolate for Valya!"

"Oh, he doesn't need all that. If he could only get a small piece of butter," Valya's mother sadly replied.

"We'll get it then. Won't we Borka?" I insisted.

"We sure will," he supported me.

Apparently we overestimated the possibilities. Days of continuous search began. We were defeated in all attempts. I even took my best model and spent a whole day with Borka on the market, but no one would give anything for it. People were dying from hunger, and nobody had any use for a small graceful plane.

About two weeks later, when I came home from school, I smelled pancakes. Mother, pale and exhausted, was lying on the bed. I found out that she had her gold teeth taken out and had exchanged them for food.

Suddenly I noticed a small piece of butter wrapped in wax paper. Butter! Without hesitation, I put it in my pocket and ran to Valya.

I walked home in a depressed mood.

"Alyesha, did you notice where the butter went to?" father asked.

"I don't know," I answered embarrassedly, "the cat probably took it."

"That's what I thought," mother said, grabbing the innocent cat.

"Stop!" I yelled, and told them everything.

Father and mother listened to me in silence. Then father said:
"Good boy, Alyesha!"

Five minutes later I was again running to Valya, carrying the pancakes wrapped up for him by my mother.

"Life is better, life is happier!" (*Stalin*)

Borka and I never stopped our model work. Valya began to improve. Food began to appear in stores. One could buy everything, though at high prices. It was 1935. Everywhere posters carried the message:

LIFE IS BETTER, LIFE IS HAPPIER!

The three of us made friends with a gray-haired old man with a young face—Uncle Vanya. He was an amazing person, Uncle Vanya. He was over fifty, held no job; he earned his living chopping wood in the summer and shoveling snow during the winter. His daily food consisted of two pounds of bread and a pound of onions; once in a while potatoes. He lived in an unheated room and slept on boards, but he knew so many wonderful stories! He could read easily in German, English and French, all of which he had learned without outside help.

We often met in his room. Uncle Vanya would bite into his onion as though it were an apple and read German or French books to us. He translated as he went along. Sometimes he told us stories about his life or about the sea. He had been a sailor in the Baltic Fleet, had taken part in the Revolution, and had been a Party member. For his services he had been decorated with the "Order of the Red Banner." Later he left the Party and lived in solitude.

"Uncle Vanya, why don't you have a job?"

"To do that, one has to adjust oneself. But I can't, nor do I want to."

"Uncle Vanya, how was life under the Czar?"

"Bad."

"And now it's better, isn't it?"

"No, it's even worse."

"What can be done to make it better?"

"Grow up—you'll find out, you're still too young. You have an

66

idea—that's good. A person without an idea—is not a person. Serve your idea, but remember that besides aviation you have a people, a great and unhappy people. Love them. For them, if necessary, give your life—spare nothing for them."

In 1936 people were being arrested all around us.

Father prepared a small suitcase with underwear, socks, a blanket, and some dry food—just in case. If they did come to arrest him, he would have something to take along. Father was not the only one who had a suitcase packed—many were ready.

If mother heard steps on the stairs during the night, she would nervously wake father:

"Nikolai, Nikolai, don't sleep. . . ."

Mother was not frightened without cause: in my father's office many had already been taken away and the rest awaited their turn. Besides, father had written some articles for magazines and newspapers. To write in the Soviet Union is a dangerous thing. The following "proverb" was making the rounds at the time:

"A Soviet citizen shouldn't think. If he thinks, in no case should he talk. If he talks, he shouldn't write. But if he writes, he must immediately run to the NKVD and repent."

In addition to all this, a relative of ours, Vasili Kuzmich, a high-ranking commander in the Red Army, had been arrested in connection with the Tukhachevsky case. Because we had been very close and had often visited each other, mother was afraid of repercussions against our family.

I particularly enjoyed the visits to Vasili Kuzmich. I was attracted by great and well-known people of the military world. At his apartment, I saw commanders like Yakir, Dubovoi, and Schmidt. The "Red Generals," as they facetiously called themselves—for at that time the term "general" had not been introduced into the Red Army—met there to play chess and hold discussions. They were well acquainted with everything that went on in the country and often, even in the presence of outsiders, criticized policies of the government.

About a week after the arrest of Tukhachevsky and the other military leaders, father and I dropped in on Vasili Kuzmich. He was all alone, having sent his wife to relatives. At first he met us with open arms. Apparently he was looked upon as doomed, and people no longer visited him. But suddenly Vasili Kuzmich became excited.

"You shouldn't have stopped by here," he said to my father. "This might have unpleasant consequences for you."

"What are you talking about?" father wondered. "You don't think that you might also be considered an 'enemy of the people'?"

"They never were enemies of the people!" Vasili Kuzmich replied angrily. "They were better friends of the people than anyone!"

He quieted down, and for a long time sat tapping his fingers on the table.

"Go, Nikolai," he finally roused himself, "go. I am not fooling. There is no sense in uselessly inviting trouble."

Father warmly embraced Vasili Kuzmich.

"Don't worry, Vasili, it will all go well," he said as he left.

I stayed on. After father's exit, Vasili silently paced the room for a long time. Then he sat down and hastily scribbled a letter. It was a note to his wife, and he asked me to deliver it.

"Don't worry," he remarked handing me the envelope, "there is nothing dangerous inside. I just wrote about my health."

Several days later both he and his wife were arrested. In fact, during a two-month period his apartment building, where the families of high-ranking commanders lived, was completely cleared of its occupants. They say even the janitor was arrested. The wave of arrests reached a climax. My father fled from Kiev to a city where he would be less known and the chances for survival better. After a while mother and I followed.

New town, new people

In the new town, I enrolled in the model section of the Flying Club. At the club we had a most friendly group of fellows. The spirit of the group was set by "the professor," a twenty-year-old fellow who just happened to stray into the club one day. He was tall, wore glasses, and was extremely funny. About every five minutes he made some clever remark. All of us would laugh uproariously, but "the professor" never cracked a smile.

Before the October holidays a crowd of us was noisily ambling along the main street. Suddenly "the professor" stopped and with a grand gesture pointed to a tank made of electric bulbs. The light bulbs representing the tank's tracks were madly blinking on and off. It seemed that the tracks were moving rapidly, but the tank stood still.

"Comrades," said "the professor," mimicking the voice of a guide, "here you see how our Soviet tank is irresistibly moving toward socialism."

A nimble fellow in a leather jacket, breeches, and boots pushed his way to "the professor." His "civilian uniform" identified him as an NKVD agent.

"What do you mean by that?" he asked.

"I said that our tank is moving toward socialism," "the professor" replied quietly. "Maybe that doesn't suit you?"

"It suits me," the agent said in a chagrined voice.

"But I don't like it," "the professor" remarked thoughtfully.

The agent came to life again:

"And why not?"

"Because our tank should be moving toward capitalism!"

The crowd was silent. The agent opened his mouth in amazement, not finding anything he could say. "The professor" remained composed.

"Toward capitalism," he repeated, "in order to smash it so that all workers can live as happily as you and I."

The agent smiled stupidly. He couldn't criticize "the professor" —he was repeating official Soviet language.

I didn't break my connection with Borka and Valya, we corresponded constantly. During the winter I received sad news: Uncle Vanya had been arrested. The reason for his arrest was his refusal to vote for the official candidates in the elections. No matter how his friends and his neighbors argued with him, he would not go to the polls. Afterward his room was searched. Under the torn-up floor an "Order of the Red Banner" and an old rusty revolver, a Civil War relic, were found.

At the beginning of the summer I received a second piece of bad news: Borka wrote that Valya had died of tuberculosis. Borka had been with him constantly until his death, but had never mentioned our friend's poor health in letters to me. He was afraid that I, hearing of Valya's illness, would abandon school and examinations and rush to Kiev.

A flying school was attached to our club. Theory was taught in the winter, flying during the summer. I was too young to be enrolled as a student, but I was a member of the club and could fly as a passenger all I wanted. I exploited this opportunity. At five in the morning I was at the airfield and left only when it became dark. All day long I would climb from one plane into another. Sitting in the cockpit I would lightly, so as not to disturb the pilot, hold the dual controls and follow the pilot's actions.

Once I flew with an instructor who was a close friend of mine. When we landed he extended his hand.

"Congratulations, you can pilot a plane."

I was astonished. Unknowingly, I had been the pilot during almost all of the flight!

After that I began to prepare systematically for entrance into the club's flying school.

For one thing, I decided to enter the Komsomol. Two of my friends were already members and they gave me the necessary recommendation for entering the organization. Komsomol membership was the key to entrance in the flying school.

But I was not destined to become a pilot—a heart murmur prevented me from passing the physical examination.

Get up! Sit down!

In the beginning of September 1939, Voroshilov issued an order requiring everyone nineteen or older to go through a period of military duty. There were no exemptions for heads of families or those attending institutions of higher learning. I was sent to a military academy.

Conditions at the academy were gloomy. From morning till night every independent thought was being knocked out of our heads. We marched in goose step. The form was copied from the Germans, but whereas they used this step only during parades, and then only when passing a reviewing stand, we had to use it constantly.

The political-instruction periods were the only relief: while the political instructor read in a dull monotone, our bodies, exhausted by constant rushing around, had a chance to relax. We sat in a half-dreamy state, sometimes napping two or three minutes.

Then the order:

"Get up! Sit down!"

For a minute this interrupted dreams and sleep, but until the next "up-down" one could again relax.

I finished the course at the academy early in the summer, 1941. Resplendent in my new uniform, with creaking belt and straps, I reported to a unit on the Rumanian border.

"Graduate of the N Military Academy, Lieutenant Gorchakov, reporting!" With these words, heels clicked together, and every muscle in the body stiffened in accordance with military regulations.

At dawn, on June 22, 1941, shells began falling on our positions.

It was the beginning of war.

Fire and death

I was wounded and hospitalized. After several months I rejoined my unit. We fought our way beyond the Dnieper. Behind us the air was shattered by the demolition of the Dnieper Dam and we, protected by the flooded river, looked forward to a well-deserved rest. But we were not fated to rest. Somewhere in the region of Kiev the Germans were able to cross to Dnieper, forcing our unit to move out quickly in the direction of Poltava.

Large houses and stacks of wheat were burning all around us. Grain flamed in the elevators, throwing out cascades of sparks; oil burned in barrels and cisterns. The night was as bright as day. Smoke engulfed us; soot settled on our faces, our clothes, our horses. Bedraggled kolkhozniks—old men, women, and children—looked in terror at the flames which spread as far as the eye could see.

"The grain is burning, the grain is burning," they said with fear and despair. "We will all die of hunger."

Desertions increased from the Red Army. It became almost a rule that the day following the announcement that a town had surrendered to the Germans, most men from that area would disappear. Many towns were surrendered, and the men were running away in broad daylight.

The war loosened tongues, and the local people often said to us:

"What are you fighting for? Drop everything and go home. It won't be worse than under the Soviet regime."

In a village near the town of Lebedin we were attacked by tanks. There were many of them—around fifty. Our single armored car went forward to meet them, but was knocked out in short order. The tanks were shooting point-blank from cannons and machine guns—defense was senseless. Those who could, ran.

I led my unit out with only a few losses. We were being chased by five tanks, when we came upon a cut forest. By taking our horses at full speed between the stumps we were able to elude the enemy.

72

We hit a road and headed toward Lebedin. Several men who had become separated from their units joined us, and after a while we grew into a large column.

A car approached us.

"Halt! Where are you going?" the unknown major general yelled as he climbed out.

Two captains followed him, submachine guns ready.

I told the general what had happened.

"Back!" he ordered. "Meet the tanks and don't yield a yard!"

"Comrade General, we have only one light machine gun for the whole troop. What can that do against tanks?" I protested.

"Don't try to reason! Go at the tanks with bayonets and grenades!"

I turned the column around, and the general drove off toward Lebedin—to the rear. The soldiers cursed the general openly and freely, and with all their might.

"That coward, he flees to the rear, while he sends us to stop tanks with our bare hands."

To go after the tanks with our equipment would result only in a senseless loss of men. No matter how many of us died, we couldn't possibly stop them. I turned the column into the forest.

"Dismount! We will defend here."

About twenty of the men stayed on their horses and began talking among themselves.

"You speak for us, Yermin, go ahead," they coaxed one of the older men.

Yermin didn't say anything for a while; then he turned to me:

"Comrade Commander, we have decided to go over to the Germans. The Soviet power won't hold out and we don't want to sacrifice ourselves in vain."

"You are not of my unit, and I hereby release you to look for your own detachment. There you can do as you wish," I answered.

The men dropped the rifles they had been pointing at me, turned their mounts and rode off in the direction of the Germans.

In the beginning of November 1941, our troop was rushed into the Moscow sector. Hurriedly reinforced by new men from Siberia, we took up defensive positions.

Heavy, bloody battles ensued. Sometimes more than half of the men were lost in one engagement.

Every day our ranks were filled with reinforcements, and every day only sad remnants of the troop survived. Those who had been in our unit since the start of the war could be counted on one's fingers.

The soldiers were sent into battle without any regard for the cost in lives. There were cases where hundreds of men perished due to inefficiency on the part of the high command.

For three days we fought for the possession of the village Katerinovka. For three days the Germans inflicted heavy losses on us because we were not supported by artillery and "katyushas" (rocket launchers). Finally we took the village, but half an hour later a cloud of shells and rockets descended on us from our own lines. Our unit, severely depleted during the savage fighting, was almost completely annihilated. The Germans counterattacked and again forced us to withdraw.

In December we began to advance from Moscow. The liberated population met us with mixed feelings.

"What will happen to us now?" an old woman asked. "Is it possible that we will be punished by the Soviet regime for having been under the Germans?"

"Don't be afraid, nothing will happen," she was comforted by our commissar. "If there were ten of you, or even a hundred, some action might be taken. But there are sixty million of you. All of you can't be repressed. Of course, it won't go too well for everyone, but that isn't our business. When the authorities come back they will check you."

74

I asked an old man: "Well, pop, are you happy to be liberated from the Germans?"

"Sonny, my heart is glad, but my skin shivers."

All were dissatisfied with the Germans, but they also expected something new from the Soviets.

"We used to think that the Germans were an educated people, but they are worse than pigs. I'm glad you chased them away, or they would have tortured us to death," an old woman said to me. "Do you think the Soviets will do away with kolkhozes now?" she asked hopefully.

At the end of December 1941, the Germans were no longer retreating—they were running away. Previously, when withdrawing, they abandoned a truck or tank here or there. Now all roads, sometimes for miles, were cluttered with abandoned trucks, tanks, and guns.

The winter was unusually severe. Those who strayed from the roads often got stuck in snow up to their necks. The Germans, lightly clothed and unused to the cold, perished by the hundreds. Sometimes we found whole companies frozen in their defensive positions. One day we came across a German battery. The guns stood ready for battle, and next to them or leaning on them were the bodies of German soldiers frozen to death. Our troops also suffered from the freezing weather, but we were accustomed to cold winters. Above all, we had large quantities of warm clothing.

In January 1942, the Germans began to burn everything they abandoned. Whole villages were burned to the ground. To protect themselves from the cold, the peasants excavated pits in the frozen earth.

Having advanced over three hundred miles, we fought our way into the German rear in the region of Vyazma-Dorogobush.

In the enemy rear
Roaming behind the German lines, we organized guerilla squads. Escaped prisoners, persons in hiding, and the local pop-

ulation were enlisted. At first we took only volunteers, but then we began to conscript. The guerilla squads were very unreliable —they ran away at the first serious engagement. They were also terribly afraid of being captured. At that time capture meant death. The Germans mercilessly destroyed all who fell into their hands. In the small town of Dorogobush we found that the Germans had buried fifty thousand prisoners of war. Often the Germans also destroyed every man, woman, and child in villages which had been defended by Soviet guerillas.

The Soviet forces in our area controlled around fifteen hundred villages. In May 1942, we were attacked by the Germans with planes, tanks, artillery, and large infantry units.

Just before abandoning Dorogobush, members of the Special Section of the NKVD shot all German prisoners. This caused great dissatisfaction among our ranks.

"Here we are with one foot in the grave, and they kill the prisoners. What can we expect from the Germans now?"

During the attempt to fight our way back to our own lines, we were completely smashed. German planes hung over our heads, releasing a constant rain of bombs. Enemy tanks and infantry followed on our heels, cutting one group off from the other, and annihilating each pocket.

The agony of the last resistance arrived. My unit was able to hold off a large number of SS soldiers for over six hours. In the end, with one eye gone and shrapnel wounds in one shoulder, I crawled away. Exhausted and hardly alive I made my way into the forest.

For twenty days I existed on grass and wild berries. Finally, I encountered a guerilla unit.

The reception was not friendly. I was immediately taken before the Special Section representative.

"Why do you bother me now?" I asked him. "I have not been bandaged yet, I have a fever. I can hardly stand on my feet."

"That's all very well, but first tell us for what purpose the Gestapo sent you here!" the NKVD man replied.

I don't remember what I told him then. It seems to me that

I tried to grab him by the throat with my good arm. He pushed me and I fell. As I went down, my wounded shoulder hit against a tree and I lost consciousness.

I woke in the field hospital where I was operated on. For eighteen days I lay with my eyes bandaged. I was fed hot water with herbs, a cupful in the morning and one in the evening. I had the feeling that death was slowly engulfing me.

On the nineteenth day the guerilla hospital was attacked by the Germans. Machine guns were firing near by and bullets whistled through the tent. I tore the bandage from my eyes, was temporarily blinded by the sudden daylight, and then crawled toward the woods.

In the morning I was picked up by guerillas and taken to Lieutenant Colonel Vasilyev's unit. He promised to send me by plane to our own lines.

However, the next day he came to me and said:

"I'm sorry, but you won't be able to fly back. An order has just been received to evacuate only officers who are in a condition to fight. Heavily wounded such as you can't be taken."

I remained in Vasilyev's guerilla band. I was fed horse meat and after a while I began to walk around pretty well. Then Vasilyev flew back to our own lines and left me in command.

"Well, men," I told them, "we have the following military operation to perform: find potatoes, bread, and if possible a pig or two."

We got by like that. Sometimes a German supply truck was captured or a couple of cars were stopped—this always meant a sure piece of bread.

We had one jolly guerilla—Fedyunchik.

"An abnormal situation exists," he would say. "All through the war they have been telling me that I have to fight for Stalin, but no one ever proposed that I eat for Stalin. So now I have decided to let Stalin fight for himself, and I'll take care of myself. What does Fedyunchik need? First, to eat a bit; second, to see that he isn't taken prisoner."

77

We all felt like that, but our comparatively easy existence ended soon.

Our forest was blockaded on all sides by the Germans. No planes, of course, brought us anything. We stubbornly held on, repulsing all enemy attempts to smoke us out.

Gradually men began to die from lack of food. To fight our way out as a unit was impossible. I told the men to try to make it in groups of two or three.

I succeeded in sneaking through the brockade. Having gone about twenty miles, I stopped at a village for food, and was suddenly confronted by a German patrol. I had no strength to run, not that that would have helped—a submachine gun is accurate at five yards.

This was the end.

Did I act right?

I went through much as a German prisoner: hunger, typhus, and beatings. Several times I was on the verge of death. When the last shot was fired and the war was over, fate brought me to the shores of the Danube. On the eastern side stood a Soviet guard, and beyond him my country—father, mother, friends. All was native, known, close. . . . A powerful force pulled me to the East. But when I remembered all I had been through, all I had seen, I turned West to go into the unknown.

4

A YOUNG COMMUNIST

by Peter Kruzhin

I remember a June morning. Alexei, the local Komsomol leader, brought me a stack of pamphlets.

"Here is some material on the Tenth Congress of the Komsomol. Report to the Regional Committee in two days. Your political literacy will be tested, and if all goes well you will be accepted in the Komsomol. Don't fail me!"

Early on the specified day, five of us, led by Alexei, set out on the ten-mile hike to town. We were all dressed in our holiday clothes, and except for me everyone wore shoes. My father had offered me his leather boots, but fearing that they would make me look too peasant-like and give me an un-Komsomol appearance, I refused them.

We arrived in the city and went directly to the Komsomol Regional Committee building. Alexei went through a doorway marked "Secretary of the Regional Committee." After a short while he returned and invited us to follow him.

The secretary's office was spacious and light. A tremendous full-length portrait of Stalin, pipe in hand, was opposite the door. The Regional Committee members were seated around a table, and among them I noticed Misha Korovin, an acquaintance of mine. The secretary of the committee, Comrade Podgayetz, a dark-complexioned man of thirty-three, was dressed in a new light suit. From time to time he would get up from his place and pace up and down the room. His pants were tucked into his boots, his steps unhurried. He had a pipe with which he never parted although he seldom put it in his mouth.

A malicious thought raced through my mind: He's copying Stalin.

We joined another group of applicants who were seated along the wall and watched the proceedings.

"Comrade Gulin, tell us your biography."

A youth, who looked like a worker, arose and began to go over his family tree.

"Be brief, Comrade! Do you have any relatives in foreign countries? Are there any members of your family who have been repressed by organs of the Soviet government?"

After acquainting themselves with the important elements of the biography, the investigators fired questions of cultural and political significance at him:

"Have you read the proposed Stalin Constitution?"

"Is it possible to build socialism in one country?"

"Enumerate the members of the Politburo?"

"What do you think of dancing?"

"Have you read Avdeyenko's *I Love*?"

Any displeasing answer brought a sour look to the secretary's face.

My heart pounded: "I will fail, I will certainly fail. . . ."

Already three of those who had come with me had been rejected. The fourth was accepted as a candidate. My turn arrived.

"What important event recently took place in the Komsomol?"

"The Tenth Congress of the Komsomol which adopted a new program and new regulations."

The secretary nodded his head in assent.

"I feel that you are working on yourself. What are you reading now?"

"I recently finished Sinclair's *Jimmy Higgins,* now I am reading Ostrovsky."

Misha Korovin smiled and turning to the other members of the committee said:

"I have known Kruzhin for a long time. He was one of the active Pioneers in the area—one of that hardy group who helped with collectivization. You may be interested in his opinion on private property: there is not a single garden in his village where he hasn't stolen apples. His spirit is ours, that of a good Komsomol member."

The secretary winked at me and in an official tone announced:

"There is a motion to confirm Comrade Kruzhin as a member of the Komsomol."

I was accepted!

Two weeks later the Regional Committee called me in again. It was raining. Barefooted I splashed through the puddles to the familiar building. A crowd was in the secretary's office. Many obviously were from villages. One after another went before the secretary, Podgayetz.

Seeing me, he stretched out his hand in a friendly greeting.

"Well, how are things, 'Komsa'? You didn't freeze, did you? Sit down."

"Komsa" was the highest compliment. It was the name used for Komsomol members of the Civil War and the early period.

Podgayetz dismissed the village fellows, sending them to work on the construction of a new airplane factory. Then turning to me: "You are to work with Pioneers. Organize a squad in your village."

I stopped by to see Korovin, who gave me the necessary instructions and some magazines.

A few days later my Pioneer squad received its first big assignment. Our collective was ordered to harvest several extra fields. If we failed to mow them within three or four days they would be reallocated and we would be left without hay for the winter. Since there was not enough manpower for the task, we faced a difficult situation.

The Komsomol met in order to figure a way out.

"A crisis has arisen in our collective," the Komsomol leader began, "something must be done. . . ."

Someone suggested using the wall newspaper to stimulate increased production. Through the paper, the members of the collective would be urged to cut down rest periods and prolong the workday.

My brother, who was on leave from an NKVD school, rose and reproachfully said:

"Well, well, and you—members of the Komsomol! Do you really think the newspaper will help? Prolong their working hours! Shorten their rest periods! Bah! They'll work one day and then have to stay in bed. How is socialism to be built? By those who don't really care? We have enough of these in the country without you.

"Here is how help can be given: tomorrow morning all of you, everyone without exception, go into the fields. Petka," nodding toward me, "will collect his Pioneers. The kids can relieve the grownups by spreading the hay to dry. Komsomol members, bookkeepers, foremen, tractor drivers—all will mow. I myself will go with you."

The fields were six miles away. The collective members had already spent several weeks out there—sleeping under blankets and returning to the village only on Sundays. When we arrived, a group of them were standing near the temporary field kitchen.

Seeing our pitchforks and scythes, they smiled:

"Oho! Some help! Now we'll go places!"

For several days we worked without rest. Our dinner was brought to us wherever we were. At night we slept fully clothed on the spread-out hay. But the job was finished in time.

In the fall my brother no longer needed civilian clothes and I was presented with his made-over jacket. I bought a pair of cheap trousers, and my father managed to fix a pair of worn-out shoes for me.

When school opened I enrolled as a second-year student in the high school of a near-by town. The first day of school we were lined up according to height, and I found myself next to a skinny fellow.

"Let's be friends," he proposed. "My name is Igor Snezhinsky."

The second day of school, an upper-class student named Gordeyev came into our room.

"Attention! Will all members and candidates for membership in the Komsomol remain after school," he announced. Besides myself, another sixteen-year-old student remained behind.

"Sokolov," he introduced himself. He had wise, calm eyes and blond hair that fell stubbornly over his forehead.

In all, four members and one candidate were at the meeting. Our history teacher, Dubov, an old member, was elected Komsomol leader.

In our class a closely knit group gradually developed: Igor, Gromov, Lyusya Balina, Isayev, Sorokin, Sokolov, and myself. Soon all of them were accepted into the Komsomol.

We spent all of our afterclass hours in school—at lectures, meetings, in clubs, or discussing the political education of youth. Gromov edited the wall newspaper and Igor and I usually helped him. Lyusya Balina worked with the Pioneers in the lower grades. Sokolov was the head of a political literacy club. We often sat until late in the evening in the room set aside for extracurricular work. Here we did our homework. Sometimes Lyusya would suggest:

"Come on, kids, let's go to a movie."

"That's all right, if you buy the tickets," I would reply.

We didn't have much money. I received enough from home for my daily ration of two pounds of bread and four ounces of sugar. The other kids who came from out of town were no better off.

After the movie we all walked home together. Often I held Lyusya's hand when we said good-by, and sometimes I would take her glove home with me. We considered it bourgeois to show one's feelings more openly.

Once I received a note from Lyusya:

You and Igor come to X. for a New Year's party. My friends and some kids from another school will be there. We should have a very good time if you are willing to enter into the spirit.

Ah, probably one of those bourgeois parties that one hears about, I thought.

For a long time Igor and I debated whether or not to go. He shared my opinion that a member of the Komsomol should have nothing to do with middle-class ways of life, but we were very curious to know what was wrong with that life. Besides, we couldn't believe that Lyusya, our sweet and good Lyusya, could have another side to her, a side which was bad. We considered her a good member of the Komsomol, with nothing to mar her record.

Finally we decided to go and take a look. If we didn't like what we saw we were determined to take Lyusya out of those surroundings.

As Lyusya had promised, there were many young people at the party, and the parents of the hostess considerately left us alone. There was plenty of food, but the evening games were more popular than eating. Everyone except Igor and I joined in playing post office and other kissing games. We two sat stubbornly in a corner and made wry faces. Obviously our presence disturbed the well-prepared coziness of the party and annoyed our hosts. Nevertheless we stayed on till the party broke up at 4:00 A.M.

Discussing it on the way home, we decided that only the absence of liquor made us reluctant to share the "bourgeois" pleasures of the evening. Certainly there was nothing unpleasant about such ways.

That whole winter I wore my summer jacket. I was able to exchange my thin trousers for a woolen pair which my father

84

had bought during the NEP. These I amateurishly darned every day, for they insisted upon tearing in one place after another. I replaced my completely worn shoes with a pair of high rubber boots and turned down the tops until they resembled those worn by the old musketeers. But my clumsy dress didn't bother me. Neither did it amaze people on the street—they were quite used to such apparel.

With deep Komsomol conviction I believed that in no country in the world could I be so free and happy. The regional paper printed a poem of mine which included the lines:

> There is no land where one could live as happily,
> No other land where heroes all could be.
> What other land can one love like a bride?
> Where else would one wish to live, to be alive?

A girl in our class suggested that I change the word "live" to "love." Measuring her contemptuously from head to foot, and using the most condescending tone I could assume, I told her:

"We mustn't fall in love. We must only prepare our lessons conscientiously. . . ."

I lied shamelessly. I had long been in love with Lyusya. However, I carefully hid that fact, for according to my convictions love was a thing of the past. Between people of the present day only a warm, close friendship could exist.

The news of the trials of the opposition within the Communist party suddenly exploded in our midst in 1936. Meetings were held everywhere to demand the death sentence for the "enemies of the people." Reports of these meetings filled the newspapers.

Once Igor secretively called me aside.

"I don't believe all these lies about 'enemies of the people,'" he told me. "Just take a look—the accused are all members of Lenin's Old Guard. Apparently, Stalin decided to take over the leadership of the Party and is getting rid of his competitors."

After class Igor invited me to his home. Among his father's

papers he had found some reports of the old Party congresses. He showed them to me to support his statements. Until 1930 Stalin was seldom even mentioned in the reports.

I saw that Igor's arguments were irrefutable and knew that he was probably right. But I didn't want to believe that the Party of the Bolsheviks had degenerated into a tool of Stalin's dictatorship.

Arrests continued and one in particular stands out. Lyusya's mother was arrested; her father was ousted from the Party for "moral decay." Lyusya was thrown out of the Komsomol and moved to another city.

Toward the end of the same school year we heard that Gamarnik, the political chief of the Red Army, had become involved with foreign agents and had committed suicide. News of the execution of Tukhachevsky and other army leaders came soon afterward.

I could not help but think of Igor's words.

The Komsomol Regional Committee sent Sokolov, Gordeyev, Gromov, and me to work as Pioneer leaders in a summer camp.

Hard days began. The work with the children was tiring and nerve racking. The chief difficulty grew out of the conflict between the interests of the children and the plans of the Regional Committee—plans which included mass cultural education, political education, and various other group activities. We leaders were expected to hold regular discussions with the children concerning the Party leaders, the Stalin Constitution, the lucky, happy life in the land of socialism, and the subversive activities of "enemies of the people." The kids, however, were interested primarily in bathing, fishing, field trips, and in picking berries and mushrooms. But according to camp regulations all this could be done only according to schedule and in appropriate clubs. The kids ran away from us and from our discussions and group amusements. All we received were reprimands for not organizing the Pioneers.

86

While we were still at camp, we heard that a purge had begun in the Komsomol. Kosarev, the secretary of the Central Committee, one of the Komsomol's early organizers, was accused of "moral decay" and removed. Feinberg and other well-known members of the Central Committee were arrested.

"These things are no good," Sokolov said shaking his head. "They began with the Party, went over into the army, and are finishing up with the Komsomol. Someone seems to want a different spirit."

Not so long afterward, Korovin, who was in charge of all Pioneer activities in the region, arrived in our camp. He called a meeting of the group leaders and when we were all assembled read us some new pamphlets describing the wily methods of the "enemies of the people." Then, taking care that there were no Pioneers within earshot, he said:

"Now we must decide the question of Komsomol member Sokolov."

We looked at each other in bewilderment.

"Comrade Sokolov," continued Korovin, "has long been a Trotskyite. One of our members noticed Tomsky's pamphlet on Trotskyism on Sokolov's table. Saying that the pamphlet was very valuable and interesting, Sokolov proposed to read it to this member. He does not have enough facts to prove that Comrade Sokolov carried on subversive activities in this camp, but it is interesting to note that severe infractions of camp rules occurred in Sokolov's squad."

"Any questions?" asked Gordeyev, the chairman of the meeting.

"Which member discovered this pamphlet in Sokolov's possession?" I queried.

Gordeyev looked at Korovin questioningly.

Then Gromov arose from his seat. His face was flushed and his voice strained as he announced:

"The duty of a member demands that I be open and frank. I am the one who said that Sokolov is taken in by Trotskyism.

It was to me that he proposed to read Tomsky's pamphlet. Comrades, there is no room for Trotskyism in our midst, and I propose that Comrade Sokolov be excluded from the Komsomol!"

After Gromov, the camp athletic director spent about a half hour berating Trotskyites, Bukharinites, and all supporters of the old order.

This deeply shocked me. I knew Sokolov very well. I knew his honesty, his sincerity, his deep belief in Komsomol principles and in the glory of Communism. But it was clear that ordinary logic could not help Sokolov.

"Comrades," I began, "this question is so serious that we cannot make a decision in haste. We must find out whether Sokolov is actually a Trotskyite, or whether he had simply decided to acquaint himself with Trotsky's ideology in order to compare it with our own ideology, and thus see its baseness. It seems to me that it would be far wiser to place the matter in the hands of the NKVD. If they prove him guilty, there will be no need to be sentimental about Sokolov."

I made the suggestion feeling certain that the NKVD would just laugh off this accusation of a sixteen-year-old student and reprimand all who started the affair.

I went on to tell of Sokolov's brilliant character, of his many fine activities and of his devotion to our cause. I am sure he deserved all my praise.

The result, however, was quite the reverse of what I had expected. Sokolov was expelled from the Komsomol; I was accused of defending an "enemy of the people." The question of my membership was deferred until the next meeting.

A week later Korovin came to the camp again. He called me into a private room and tried to convince me to acknowledge that my political vigilance had not been very acute.

That really aroused me.

"What are you talking about? Whom do you consider an example of political awareness? Gromov?—this opportunist, who

88

criticized the Party at the time of the bread shortages and now tries to win confidence by drowning his comrades?"

Korovin smiled just a little and, locking the door, became suddenly very friendly.

"You're OK. We were evidently somewhat hasty in accusing you at the last meeting. Now tell me in detail everything you know about Gromov's conduct during the bread shortages."

Only now did I understand my mistake and I tried to evade his question.

"I am not used to gossiping, Misha."

"We aren't talking about gossiping, Comrade Kruzhin. Perhaps Gromov is a masked 'enemy of the people.' If so, it is your duty as a member to help us uncover him. . . ."

And so I was forced to disclose everything I knew about Gromov.

That evening I was reprimanded for my dulled political vigilance, but Gromov was thrown out of the Komsomol as "an enemy of the people."

Shortly before school reopened, I met my classmate Isayev. I told him about the events of the summer in camp and hinted that one couldn't be too careful these days.

Suddenly Isayev struck himself on the forehead:

"Do you know—I actually saw that pamphlet once, but it never even occurred to me that Sokolov could be a Trotskyite."

I bit my lip hard. After all my hints about being careful it was difficult to understand what made Isayev disclose his secret. It was obvious to me that Isayev would pay dearly.

To become an informer was loathsome and repugnant. But to lose my membership was unthinkable.

"You will have to forgive me," I told Isayev after his indiscretion, "but unless you report this to the secretary of the organization, I will be forced to."

Early in September, Isayev's case was reviewed at a school

meeting of the Komsomol. He was expelled from the organization for failing to report Sokolov's Trotskyite leanings in time.

Isayev asked for the last word.

"I agree with the decision of the Komsomol. I deserve to be expelled. Because of people like me enemies still hide in our midst. I am handing in my membership card, but I want everyone to know that I remain true to the cause and will help the Komsomol to the limit of my abilities. That is why I consider it my duty to declare there are still unreliable members among you. . . ."

Isayev stopped for a moment to let the full meaning of his words sink into each of us.

Then he continued: "Once Kruzhin made this statement to me: 'It would be much better if the NKVD would reinstate Lyusya Balina's mother.' Now, Comrades, what does this mean? It means that Kruzhin thinks 'enemies of the people' should not be destroyed, that they should be left to continue their subversive work. I have had my say. The rest is up to the meeting."

All eyes turned toward me. "He who lives by the sword, dies by the sword" flashed through my mind.

I can't remember everything that followed, but I do know this: The Regional Committee representative proposed my exclusion and the upperclassmen intervened on my behalf. After long arguments, I was removed from membership in the local executive committee of the Komsomol. I was issued an official declaration of political nonconfidence and was forbidden to engage in any organizational work among school youth.

This was the beginning of bitter days. All around me there was constant activity, but I was set apart like a leper. Among all my friends, Igor alone was not afraid to associate with me.

"Why the hell should you want the confidence of this riffraff?" he asked. "You aren't missing anything by not engaging in activities. You aren't out to get a medal, are you?"

Nevertheless, I couldn't sleep nights wondering how it could

90

be that I, who had so completely identified myself with the Komsomol, could be given a vote of political nonconfidence!

In December, preparations for the national elections to the Supreme Soviet began. All Komsomol members were mobilized for agitation work. Because there were not enough experienced agitators in our school, the Regional Committee gave me special permission to take part in the pre-election activities.

On our free days we went into the villages and called upon the collective members to fulfill their civic duty and vote for the Communist-approved slate (the one and only slate on the ballot).

I remember the perplexed looks of the women:

"You mean that the names of candidates will be printed on sheets of paper? Well, what am I to do with them?"

"You drop these sheets into the box without any changes if you are in agreement with the selection. If you don't like a proposed candidate, you make a change on the sheet."

"That's all?"

"Yes, that's all."

"And they chased you all the way out here to tell me that!"

It became uncomfortable with such simple remarks. There was nothing to answer. Like these plain women, I also understood that I was engaged in some clumsy, unnecessary business. It is true that I was supposed to do more than explain the mechanics of voting—I was supposed to show the people that it was their duty to take part in the elections, and that, even though he didn't help choose the candidates, a person was voting for something he wanted when he dropped the ballot in the box. But how could I do that? On the very first day I engaged an old man in a discussion on Soviet democracy. Cunningly narrowing his eyes, he asked me:

"Well, and if I write my brother-in-law's name on the paper— he is awfully clever at solving all sorts of puzzles—would the paper be valid?"

"No, it wouldn't."

"So that's how it is," he said winking at me, "and you call it 'democracy.'"

I remember a group of women standing near a well. After listening to me, one of them, as if in jest, called out:

"I don't know about everyone, but we women will support Nikolayeva! Being a woman, she might even help eliminate collectives!"

In another place an aggressive little woman looked over my light clothes and reproachfully shook her head:

"Why do your bosses clothe you so poorly? They send you out in pants that are almost transparent and expect us to believe what you say about the good life. At least they should give you a coat to make you look more impressive."

In embarrassment I lied that I had left my coat in the first house because it was too hot.

It is no wonder that we returned from such agitation in silence and with heavy hearts.

On election day we rose early and went to our assigned district. The polls were in the school. Curtained plywood voting booths lined the corridors; rugs were spread on the floor. One of the classrooms was used as a lounge. Here the people who had fulfilled their civic duty could relax, read, play chess and checkers. Another room was equipped as a nursery and, while they voted, mothers could bring in their children and leave them with one of our Komsomol girls. A special car had been assigned to the election officials by the Regional Committee. It was constantly flashing in and out bringing old people and invalids.

Igor and I went around to those who hadn't voted yet, and appealed to their conscience. Once we escorted an old woman to the polls. She looked at the voting booth curtains and shook her head violently:

"So this is what they mean by a cultured life! Once upon a time they made dresses out of such material. Weren't we uneducated then! It never occurred to us that elections could be conducted with such joy and happiness for all!"

By 2:00 P.M. all ballots were cast. The next day the newspapers carried the announcement that our district, No. 256, had voted unanimously for the proposed slate of candidates. Later one of our Komsomol members, who was on the ballot committee, told us in confidence that dozens of ballots had been crossed out. Some, in obviously disguised handwriting, carried words that are usually found only on latrine walls.

In February, the Central Committee of the Communist party issued a statement about the excesses which had been committed during the cleansing of Party ranks.

Immediately our committee met and, in view of the new regulations, absolved me of all my "crimes." Taking advantage of the moment, I insisted that the committee enter a statement on its records to the effect that it had "treated me rashly and heartlessly, not having restudied my case at the time."

In the fall of 1939 I was sent to a Red Army officers' training school. Days of strict schedules and order began. Reveille at seven, eight hours of class instruction, one hour of training in modern military techniques, two hours of preparation for the next day's classes. During the whole day we were allotted forty-five minutes of free time. It could be spent either in the clubroom or in the library. Retreat was at eleven.

On Saturday and Sunday a number of passes were issued. According to regulations, only 10 per cent of the personnel could be off at one time. In our class there were twenty-three men, and each week six received passes: two on Saturday, two before dinner on Sunday, and two after dinner. No order was followed in allocating passes. They were given to outstanding students and to those who were active politically.

On June 17, 1941, after two hard and long years, I finished my course and left the academy—new officer's uniform, shiny leather belt, two neat lieutenant's insignia. In my pocket was an order sending me to the Baltic region.

I stopped off at home for a few hours. Before leaving, my father called me into his room.

"Mother," he said in a nervous voice, "while no one is here—bring out the icon. Let's bless our son."

Mother lifted the image. And I, for the first time in my life feeling the solemn necessity for the rite, bowed my head. . . .

The railroad station in Moscow was packed with young officers. Because there was not enough room on the trains, it was two days before I was able to leave.

On the twenty-second we reached the border town of Sebezh. The train was scheduled for a half-hour stop, so I stepped out with a few other officers. Suddenly an excited railroad employee came running toward us.

"Comrades, hurry to the station! Documents are being checked."

"What's going on?" we demanded.

"Didn't you hear? Molotov just made a speech over the radio. German planes bombed Sevastopol, Kiev, Kharkov. . . . War!"

The next day we arrived in Riga. A reserve officer met us at the station and drove us to the barracks. It was a frightening feeling to pass through the quiet streets and have the city look out at us through windows crossed with strips of paper.

At the barracks the commandant of the post addressed us.

"Comrades—officers," he began, "never forget that you are Red officers. Here in the Baltic region the people of the newly annexed countries are against us and only the bayonets of the Red Army support the Soviet regime. . . ."

There was something horrible in these quietly spoken words. We had long forgotten how to call things by their right names, and the frankness of the speaker blew on us like an icy wind.

Events unmercifully defeated us with their inexorable logic.

The Baltic region was abandoned. The old borders couldn't stand either. We weren't even able to hold the historic border of Pskov-Novgorod. While the papers shouted untiringly of the smashing victories over Nazi SS divisions and devoted whole pages to the heroism of Soviet sergeants, cities were abandoned one after another.

We retreated to Novgorod. Crying women met us and gazed eagerly at the dusty hollow faces of the soldiers, trying to find their own. We were tired, oblivious to the surroundings. We walked without words, without smiles, without life. A vicious, black cloud rose behind us. Ruins of cities were smoldering, fields were on fire.

There were posters on the fences in Novgorod: FATHER, KILL THE GERMAN! Alexei Tolstoy and Ilya Ehrenburg called for holy revenge. A pamphlet—*The Science of Hatred*—was being circulated.

I had no time to read it. I was busy suppressing the stubbornly recurring thought of the lies and deceit on which we had fed for years. I was beginning to hate Stalin and all those around him. But at the same time another fact was even clearer to me: foreigners had descended on the country. They trampled my native soil with their boots. They were bringing us slavery. I could not bear the thought of my mother washing the feet of a German corporal, of Lyusya undressing before a wild mob of drunken SS men—and I rushed into the heat of battle.

In a hospital on the outskirts of Novgorod I received a letter from my brother.

By the tone of your note I understood that you were somewhat scratched. Keep up your spirits. I was at the Pan-Slav Congress in Moscow. What organization! Don't give in, believe that victory will be ours.

Shells were exploding over the city. An excited doctor ran into our ward:

"Comrades! We have no means to evacuate you. Those lightly wounded will have to proceed on their own. . . ."

Overcoming terrible pain (I was wounded in the back by shrapnel), I went out into the hot, dusty street. A young nurse helped me along. Trucks and cars filled with people carrying fat briefcases rumbled over the torn-up streets. From all sides women carrying great sacks and accompanied by children streamed onto the road. I remembered my brother's phrase: "What organization!" What mockery!

I lifted my hand to stop a passing vehicle. The fancy car carrying NKVD personnel whizzed by without paying any attention to us. I shot after it. The nurse cried quietly . . .

We turned off onto a forest road. In the evening we arrived at a small village.

"Why did you come? What are you fighting for? If you'd give yourself up—there'd be no war, no collectives."

I couldn't believe my ears: who are these—these peasants—are they enemies, or honest, frank, Russian people?

They were our Russian people. Enemies wouldn't have given me milk, hidden me under hay in the barn, and told the Germans who came through on motorcycles: "No commissars."

When I was partly recovered from my wound, I began a trek through miles of swampland in order to cross over to our lines. Finally I reached a division headquarters.

"Lieutenant Kruzhin, just out of encirclement," I reported. "Please direct me to my unit."

"Cut out the lying! The Gestapo sent you over. Tell us, how long have you been collaborating?"

"Are you crazy?" I asked indignantly. "You better find out when I last ate. Isn't it enough that I, a severely wounded man, was abandoned to my fate when the troops withdrew from Novgorod?"

A commissar arose from his seat:

"You are engaging in enemy propaganda. When was anyone ever left without help? Stop this vicious talk! And where are your insignia? According to Stalin's latest order, any soldier who is not in full uniform when he returns from encirclement will be regarded as a coward and a traitor. . . ."

By chance I was saved from further insults. Just then a general's aide, a friend from my military academy, entered the room. He identified me and vouched for my loyalty.

On the way out I asked him:

"What kind of birds have you got here?"

"Quiet," he interrupted, "say thanks that I turned up. They would have given it to you, and no one would have been the wiser . . . you aren't the first to arrive here."

I was assigned to the 60th Regiment, guarding the Front headquarters.

One night, long after dark, we arrived at a village where we intended to remain until morning. Stopping at the first hut, I knocked on the door. We could hear whispering inside, but it was only after repeated, insistent knocking that someone answered.

"Who's there?"

"Open! Ours, Red Army men."

"Who? Red Army men? We have no room for you! Get out of here!"

The morning of the next day we were awakened by cries:

"Germans! The Germans are coming!"

On the street, men and women in holiday clothes were rapidly assembling. Someone brought an icon. An elder carried a cloth-covered tray containing the traditional bread and salt.

I could hardly believe my eyes.

"Meeting the Germans . . . with bread and salt?" I muttered half to myself.

Then, without another word and with purposely slow movements, I set up the machine gun. The barrel was pointed in the direction of the approaching Germans. Those who had gathered for the welcoming party now hurriedly dispersed, glancing sidewise at the gun.

My heart was empty. Russian people, in whose defense I fought, were afraid of me—scared of their own soldier. It was obvious that for them I was less a Russian soldier than a defender of a regime for which they had long awaited the end.

The Germans fortified themselves on a high bank of the river. We were given additional tank support which guaranteed the

97

success of a break-through. The defense of the Germans in the Kokoshkino region was smashed. Tanks and infantry of three armies tore through a three-mile-wide corridor. One army went in the direction of Vyazma. Another turned west. Ours, the 39th Army, under General Maslennikov, led the advance on Rzhev.

But the corridor was left undefended, and within a week, on the fifteenth and sixteenth of January, 1942, the Germans closed the point of the break-through, cutting the armies off from their rear and leaving them without food and ammunition.

We went through difficult days. The Germans threw planes at the remnants of our army. There was no place where a shell didn't hit, shrapnel penetrate, or that wasn't hit by a bullet. Our "small earth" was gradually compressed until its radius was less than a mile. There was no one to take the place of men who fell every day. The only food was the meat of dead horses. Only two or three shells per gun remained. Every day the Germans attacked, and every day they were thrown back. Evenings, all was quiet, except for single Soviet planes which buzzed the plowed-up earth and dropped newspapers and mail.

I remember my father's last letter:

See to it, son, that you don't disgrace my gray hair. I know the front, but I also know what life is. . . . Among our kin there are no traitors.

I guessed what my father wanted to write. I knew what he meant by the word "life." Yes, I well understood that he was warning me about the fate of the family should I be taken prisoner.

No, I answered my father in my thoughts, I am not thinking of traitors. I am thinking that once the last German is thrown off our native soil, a terrible reckoning will come to those who have mutilated our lives.

We lost track of time. And still the political commissars went around the trenches signing up men for membership in the Party!

A friend of mine, who had recently taken the place of a fallen commissar, approached me.

"And why aren't you in the Party yet?" he asked. "You've been in the Komsomol since 1936."

I tried to laugh it off.

"I still feel unworthy of the honor of being called a member of the Party of Lenin and Stalin."

Then I added quietly:

"There is no sense to it . . . or is it necessary so that you can place a nice little notice in the division paper: 'Twice decorated member of the guard, Senior Lieutenant Kruzhin, held his pistol to his head and exclaimed "I want to die a Communist!"'"

I thought he understood, but then he asked,

"Don't you believe in victory?"

"I believe in victory, but I don't believe in all this bunk."

The division political department issued a statement:

"Yesterday the army commander talked by radio with Comrade Stalin. Hearing of our situation, Comrade Stalin asked if we could hold out another two days. In two days he promises to have a shock brigade here to secure our exit from encirclement. Comrades, only two days!"

For two days we lay half dead under terrific attack. For two days our trenches were constantly raked by machine-gun fire. The third day came. In the evening we were called into the staff dugout.

"Comrades Commanders! Load your supplies in packs. Anything you can't take, destroy. Tonight we will fight our way out —alone."

The light went out of the commanders' eyes. It wasn't fear, we were used to the idea of death. But there are things worse than death. With the last word of the order many commanders lost their last belief—their belief in Stalin.

In the middle of the night the endless band of people moved out. We went silently, weaving from exhaustion and hunger.

99

Horses fell in the deep snow and didn't have the strength to extricate themselves. In the carts the wounded moaned:

"Brothers . . . how can you . . . don't leave us."

The nurses huddled in their coats. With death in their eyes they looked after the receding column. True to their duty, they were remaining with the wounded.

The rest of us went forward silently, and with bowed heads so as not to view these terrible scenes.

Gradually the column disintegrated, breaking up into groups which went separate ways. I headed about fifteen men of our regiment.

At dawn we were surrounded in a thick forest. We lay there, seldom firing at the dark green shapes that appeared among the trees. I remember someone from the German side calling to us in pure Russian tones:

"Comrades, Red Army men! Finish off your commissar and give yourselves up! The Germans won't bother you!"

"How could it be? A Russian . . . with the Germans!"

"Choke, you traitor!" I cried as I sent a long burst in the direction of the voice.

For a long time we wandered around the forest repeatedly meeting enemy patrols. Five of us remained. Two were wounded.

There was nothing to eat. Our heads were giddy. The wounded greedily lapped up the snow and gritted their teeth.

We could do nothing in the forest. The blizzard threatened to bury us alive. Supporting our wounded, we slowly proceeded toward a snow-covered village. I was nauseated. A sweet, lulling fatigue encompassed my whole body and I longed only for sleep. But my mind kept saying: "Forward, or there is only death."

Constantly falling, and rising only with difficulty, we somehow reached the village. I was dazed. As through a dream I remember men in dark green uniforms approaching us. My weakened hand instinctively pulled out the pistol. Using all my strength, I raised it, intending to shoot at the approaching Germans. Suddenly my legs gave way and darkness fell on me.

I awoke in a hospital. Comrades, racked with typhus, tossed deliriously near by. A German soldier, carrying a carbine on his shoulders, passed by the window.

"A prisoner!" I groaned.

5

A WOMAN'S HEART
by Valentina Kamyshina

The story of my life is not unusual. Many Soviet women have had similar experiences.

When I was four years old, World War I began. The October Revolution in 1917 (the Bolshevik Revolution occurred on November 7, 1917, by the new calendar, but on October 25 by the old calendar. The Bolshevik Revolution is therefore always referred to by the Bolsheviks as the "October Revolution") and subsequent events made very little impression on me.

So far as I know, the Bolshevik Revolution brought no significant hardship to my family. A lot on which my parents had hoped to build a summer cabin was taken from them. It is true, they had been dreaming about having the cabin for a long time, but the loss was not very great. The family was small—father, mother, grandmother, a sister, and myself. My father, a railroad employee, held no important posts under the czarist regime. He belonged to no party. Because of heart disease he had been exempted from military service. Consequently, neither the war nor the Revolution greatly affected us. Of course, many people were killed in those years, but that made little impression on my childish mind. Sometimes during evening prayers my mother would tell me: "Pray for so-and-so, my dear, he died recently." But these deaths caused me no sorrow. Materially the family began to live less well, but even during the famine of 1920-1921 my mother always saw to it that we didn't go hungry.

It was through literature and stories told by eyewitnesses that I became acquainted with the events that occurred during my childhood. I accepted the Revolution and with it the Bolshevik regime as part of history—perhaps inevitable. Although my parents often tried to prove to me that life was considerably better under the czarist regime, I argued endlessly that the opposite was true.

When I was eighteen, I married a talented engineer. Still comparatively young, he had the degree of master of technical sciences and was preparing a thesis for a doctorate of technical sciences. He was a leading instructor in his institute. Serious and very honest, he was a person who kept to himself. He was in love with science and gave it his whole life. Although my husband taught at three institutions of higher learning, he spent many hours working at home. Here he wrote a textbook, as well as many articles for technical journals.

Today it seems remarkable to me that he was able to do any work at all at home. Our "apartment" consisted of one small room in an eight-room house. A family lived in each room. There was a single kitchen which we were all supposed to use, but I preferred to prepare our food in the room. My husband had to work through the noise of my cooking and my conversations with friends.

Politics did not interest my husband. He accepted the Revolution although some of the policies of the Bolsheviks were not clear to him. However, being a conscientious person, he worked honestly. During all of our ten years together I never heard him tell a political joke—something very unusual in our time.

My husband had friends, but he also had enemies. Most of his enemies were unsuccessful students. It was not those who could not learn who were unfriendly to him, but those who didn't want

103

to study. This latter category consisted almost exclusively of Party or government people sent for special training to universities. They were people who had no preparation for this kind of work.

My husband lost his father when he was fourteen years old. From then on, while attending high school and universities, he had to support his whole family, including two small children. His youth was spent running between classroom and work—usually hungry. Despite this, his work in high school and at the university was excellent.

That is why he couldn't reconcile himself to students who didn't want to study. He often commented on how well students lived under the Soviets. They received a stipend and living quarters; therefore, they should be able to study well. Comparing this with his own school years, he was convinced that his attitude was justified. He could never close his eyes to those student-Party members who regarded the university as a factory whose sole function was to dispense diplomas. The fancy official titles of such students didn't scare him. His scrupulous honesty would not allow him to compromise. It was obvious that his actions would bring him much unpleasantness. Possibly they brought him death.

On March 1, 1938, my husband was arrested and by decision of a "troika"* was convicted to ten years' imprisonment under strict isolation and without correspondence privileges. Under what article of the statutes he was accused, I was never able to learn, despite many appeals to magistrates and governmental officials.

When I received the announcement that my husband had been sentenced and was being sent to the far north, I began to watch the prison trains going out.

The nights were cold; it was raining. Maybe it didn't always

* A secret tribunal of three judges operating under the orders of the Soviet secret police.

rain, but when I think of those nights the rain is always there. The trolleys had stopped running. One had to walk far out of town to the stations. Every night prisoners were shipped out from freight stations at different ends of the city.

Since it was impossible for one individual to cover all stations, several wives in the same position as I joined together. Every evening we would meet and decide who would go to what station and there call out the names of all the husbands. Officially this was forbidden. We were cursed in the vilest language by the guards. Police dogs were sent at us. We were chased with bayonets, sometimes even shot at. But still we would go every night, like reporting to work. You go, and inside you are cold, empty—no feeling in the heart, and the most horrible, the most frightful thing is that I, for one, passionately prayed to God that I wouldn't see my husband. I was afraid with every fiber of my body to see him among these sad, bent figures with hands behind their backs. I loved him, I was proud of him, that is why I didn't want to see him in this degradation. It seemed to me that if I should see him something horrible would happen; what, I could never imagine. Every night I went through this fright. Every night I went to see the prisoners leave. And it never happened—I never saw my husband. Thus he went out of my life, forever. Others met theirs, fainted, went into hysterics. The soldiers cursed violently, chasing the prisoners ever faster with their bayonets.

Morning brought another torture. On my job I hid the fact that my husband had been arrested. I was listed as a divorced woman. It seems that I was never so gay and witty as at that time. I never had so many admirers as then.

I had to keep silent. I would have been fired immediately had the news of my husband's internment reached the office. And I had a sick mother and my sister's little daughter on my hands. Being the wife of a prisoner, it was practically impossible to find another job.

Days and nights passed, then everything ended.

My office found out that my husband was an "enemy of the people." I was fired, and soon thereafter sent out of the city. In the beginning, with great effort and the help of friends, I was able to obtain various unskilled jobs—as a scrub woman in theaters, or as a laundress. Later I took up embroidery. I earned little at this work, but it kept me occupied.

Not being able to obtain real work in the town where I was sent, I decided to return secretly to my mother, and lived with her without police registration. To live without police registration in Soviet cities was risky. If discovered, one might be sentenced for as much as two years. For people like myself the end might even be worse. Therefore, fearing afterdark checkups by the police, I tried to keep awake during the night. I think that if I had had nothing to keep me occupied and had been left alone with my thoughts, I would have gone mad with fright. However, embroidery, like most other methodical work, calmed me.

Except for the fact that he had been sentenced to ten years' imprisonment, I was never able to learn anything of my husband's fate. In the beginning I visited various administrative and judicial offices with the hope of getting some details. Finally I decided to call upon the prosecutor of the Republic himself. In my naïveté it seemed to me that he would be able to give me the information I sought.

I arose early one morning, and with a feeling of great excitement, set out for the prosecutor's office. I arrived there at eight, although work didn't begin until an hour later. When the office opened, I was escorted into a corridor-like small room. It was completely bare and very cold. Right next to it was the official reception room, and occasionally, when the connecting door was opened, I caught glimpses of a light, warm room with wonderful soft furniture. But such as I were not admitted there.

Hours went by. The prosecutor went out to lunch. I was afraid to remind anyone of my presence, fearing that I would not see him at all if I seemed overanxious. My legs were numb from standing for so long, my head ached.

Finally, at about seven o'clock in the evening, I was called to the prosecutor's office. Three or four other people were in the room, talking and laughing. Naturally, I was not invited to sit down. Confusedly, I began to relate my request to the prosecutor: to go over my husband's case and to give me permission to remain in the city.

From his first words, I knew that this interview would bring me nothing, that I would learn nothing about my husband. Half-heartedly he asked me questions.

"How long have you been married?"

"Ten years."

"And having lived with him for ten years, you did not know of his traitorous activities against the Soviet authorities?"

I was tired. Nervous tension gave way completely to a continuous fatigue. Almost not understanding, I answered:

"He engaged in no traitorous activities, he was very busy," and for some reason I added: "He was always very secretive."

The prosecutor came to life, smiled.

"There, you see! A secretive character—therefore he was a spy!"

This didn't sink in immediately. But then a feeling of bitterness overcame me. I didn't want to plead any more, I couldn't. Looking straight at him, I said:

"And, Comrade Prosecutor, if my husband had had a sociable character—then he would have been a counterrevolutionary?"

The other people in the room broke out into laughter. The prosecutor became angry. He rose abruptly from his chair.

"I don't know the affair of your husband, we didn't handle it. But I can tell you one thing—if your husband is accused of espionage, then nothing can help him."

And then in complete irritation he added:

"And why are you trying so hard to find out what your husband's crime was? What does it matter? Maybe he did nothing. The action taken might have been completely prophylactic."

The interview was over, I went out of the room. On the street, snow was falling softly, the evening was beautiful.

Oh, my God! Oh, my God! Ten years under strict isolation—a prophylactic measure! "Maybe he did nothing" . . . But the life is smashed. Why is it smashed? "Maybe he did nothing" . . . PROPHYLAXIS—my whole attention centered on this word.

I saw this terrible word everywhere: with bloody letters it burned in the sky, over the street, on houses. I saw the word in the falling snowflakes. In every evening sound of the city I heard this word. Prophylaxis, prophylaxis!—it was in the hum of automobiles. Prophylaxis!—I heard it in the trolley bells. It seemed to me that all the other people on the street kept repeating that word.

My mother came to meet me at the door.

"Mother do you know what prophylaxis means?"

She didn't answer and asked nothing.

"Come on, dear, come inside," she said, gently taking my hand.

That night I broke out in a nervous, burning fever.

Gradually I lost the desire to find out anything about my husband. All my attempts, visits to Moscow, constant trips to the NKVD had come to nothing. I understood that I could do nothing. Now my only desire was to obtain permission to live in my native city with my mother. She was seriously ill and needed my constant attention and support. It helped her just to have me live with her. But I couldn't earn enough to support two separate households in different cities. Dragging her into the unknown was likewise impossible.

At the NKVD and prosecutors' offices I was often told:

"Why don't you get married? You are still young, beautiful; you must build yourself a new life. But if you want to wait for your husband, stubbornly holding on to his name, you might as well wait where you were sent. We are sick of mobs of women crowding our reception rooms. If you get married—that would be a different matter. We wouldn't break up a family. You could live wherever you wish."

I was also given this advice by my friends. Even my mother, who had deeply loved my husband, told me:

"Marry again. It would be easier for you, and your husband Misha wouldn't resent it. He is a good man, he will understand."

At first I didn't even listen to such advice. I was frightened by the idea of marrying again. Then my hard, wearisome life forced me to think about it, especially since my last visit to a high NKVD official. I had based great hopes on this visit, but the official told me openly:

"I have always turned down your written requests to change your residence. Now you are here in person, and I'll tell you directly: until you marry again you will not receive permission to live where you want. There is no reason why you should wait for your husband. Even if you did wait that long, and I don't believe you would, you would probably receive him as an invalid. You are a young woman . . ." etc, etc, all the things I had heard so often.

I didn't fear the thought of my husband's returning an invalid. No. Only to get him back! But in order to help him, to be useful to him then, I had to survive, to save some of my strength. This had gone on for two years, and I had become very tired. Maybe I only wanted one thing—to spend my nights in peace. It sounds odd, but that's the way it was. I couldn't even think of taking my mother to a different town and start life all over again. I just didn't have the energy. There was just one thing left to do, take the step everyone advised.

With great difficulty I forced myself to apply for a divorce. I felt like a traitor. I was even ashamed to look at my husband's picture. It seemed that there was reproach in his eyes.

Finally, I received the divorce. Now I had to get married. It was a difficult action to take.

The same day that we were married, my new husband and I applied to the NKVD for permission to live in my native city. This time an affidavit was attached, certifying that my husband was a resident of that city and had a job there.

Several months went by—and then I received a refusal. I was stunned. Why a refusal, I was no longer the wife of an "enemy of the people"? With great difficulty I managed to get an appointment with the high NKVD official on whom my fate depended and who had so insistently advised me to get married. He smiled, and looked at me condescendingly.

"You are queer! Why, that was just a simple joke—my advice. You don't seem to understand jokes."

For the first time in all my visits to the many offices, I burst out crying. What a joke! What an expensive joke it was for me. . . .

I was dazed when I came out of the NKVD building. I walked a block, maybe two, then I sat down on a doorstep. I remained there for a long time, several hours. . . . My last hopes were smashed and I saw all the tortures I had gone through.

It was all just a joke. . . .

Several months passed. The war began. My situation became even more difficult. The spy mania and the desertions produced frequent searches. I spent the days in the corner of the room, not daring to go near the window, and nights in a secret cellar. My husband was at the front from the first day of the war. Soon the city I had been assigned to was occupied by the Germans.

When the Germans came I was not happy, but still I breathed more freely. My secret existence ended with their coming. A year later I heard that my husband had been taken prisoner, and a year and a half after that I met him again in Germany.

When the Germans withdrew from the city, I went with them. It was not easy—leaving your friends, your native town, your homeland—to go into the unknown. But there was no other way.

6

A SOVIET GIRL'S DIARY

by Tatyana Senkevich

I can still remember our room. In it were three beds, one child's crib, a wardrobe, a small closet for dishes and food, a bookshelf, and a few chairs. There was a table in the middle; the stove in the corner was used for heating and sometimes for cooking.

There was no space in which to run around. I could meekly sit on a chair and spread toys on the table, or play on the floor between a bed and the closet.

A summer morning. . . . Mama is preparing breakfast in the corridor which served as a kitchen for us and two other families. Brother Oleg and I are dressed by Lida, our older sister.

Mama would run into the room, grab whatever she needed and run out again. As she rushed around, she set the table and made the beds.

At eight everybody left the house. We attended a playground operated by the public-health department. There were nine in Novomoskovskoye. Mama was a bookkeeper for all the playgrounds. She was so busy that we seldom saw her until she came for us around five or six in the evening. Sometimes, having waited for her till seven, we would go home by ourselves. When

111

Mama arrived much later, she would be completely worn out. But the round of work began again: cooking, washing, cleaning, sewing and mending. I never saw Mama idle.

Mama was a teacher, and the beginning of the school year changed our routine. My brother and I went to kindergarten. Sister Lida took us there at eight-thirty. Then she returned home and prepared her lessons. At twelve-thirty she went to her school. After five Lida came for us and we three went home together. At home Lida heated our supper, prepared by Mama the evening before. At nine she put us to bed and waited for Mama to return around ten or eleven. Mama ate hurriedly and began to prepare our breakfast, dinner and supper for the next day. We almost never saw Mama except on holidays. We children were completely cared for by Lida—she was ten years old. I was six.

At the end of March 1934, we moved to Nikopol. I cried. I didn't want to part with school, with my new friends.

Because there were no Russian schools close to our house, Mama put me in a Ukrainian school. I couldn't read Ukrainian and was laughed at for my accent. This made me miserable and I pleaded with Mama to send me to a Russian school. Even my teacher advised that I be transferred, but Mama insisted on having her way, and I remained.

During the second term I suddenly began to read and speak correctly. Everything went so well that at the end of the year I was rewarded as one of the better students.

On October 11th I learned that I was to become a Pioneer. That day I started keeping a diary.

11 OCTOBER 1934

We are preparing to celebrate the anniversary of the October Revolution. I am learning the poem "Pioneer." On the holiday we will become Pioneers. We'll put on the red ties.

28 OCTOBER 1934

Got A in writing. Vova got C. He beat me up. I won't let him copy any more.

112

Laugh! Laugh!

5 NOVEMBER 1934

Mama gave me three rubles for a tie. Lyuda was teaching us to march. I couldn't do it, kept getting mixed up. Vova was punished for teasing me

7 NOVEMBER 1934

Our class was accepted into the Pioneers today.

On the seventh I rose at six, though we didn't have to be at school before ten. Mama dressed me in my holiday clothes; Oleg wore a sailor suit. He was in the first class of the same school and was to accompany me. I couldn't eat or sit still at the table and at eight-thirty I tore out of the house, dragging Oleg behind me.

It was a solemn ceremony. The students were called to the stage in alphabetical order. There the red ties were ceremoniously put on. Finally I was called. Someone pushed me forward. I was so excited that my legs almost wouldn't carry me. Before I knew it, the red tie was around my throat and I was being greeted:

"Be ready!"

"Always ready!" I answered the Pioneer challenge, raising my right arm in the Pioneer salute.

Our whole class joined the Pioneers, and from that day we had to wear our ties at all times. A special clip—five logs, enveloped by three tongues of flame—fastened our ties. The logs represented the five continents; the fire symbolized revolution spreading over the world; and the three tongues of flame—Pioneers, Komsomol, and Party.

Every class constituted a Pioneer detachment and each detachment was headed by an upperclassman of the same school. The detachment was broken up into squads of five to eight members, one of whom was elected squad leader. Each squad had a name such as "Red Star," "Hammer and Sickle," or "Stalin."

The Komsomol Regional Committee directed the work of the Pioneer leaders who mapped our activities. Special emphasis was put on political education.

Lyuda, the leader of our detachment, was in the eighth class of our school. She was a beautiful girl, with sparkling blue eyes and long blond braids. We never tired of listening to the stories which she read or told to us, and unquestioningly believed everything that we heard at Pioneer meetings. Regardless of the statement, anything that Lyuda said was "true," and no amount of reasoning by Mama or Grandmother could convince me otherwise. Even my sister Lida, whose authority I always recognized, was helpless with me.

Lyuda loved us. She was with us during the recesses between classes. She played, ran, and jumped around with us. Sometimes she collected us in a group around her and told us about the lives of Party leaders, of their devotion and love for the people, and of their aspirations to bring happiness to all mankind. As we listened, we thought it would be wonderful to be like our leaders. She also told us of the Soviet Union's many enemies, how they sabotage our work and make it difficult to build a happy life.

Lyuda read us stories from the Pioneer papers. I remember one in particular. It was called *Pavlik Morozov* and concerned Pavlik, the son of a kulak. One night kulaks assembled at his father's house to plot insurrection against the Soviet regime. Pavlik, lying in bed, heard them. In the morning he denounced his father to the local authorities. His father and the plotters were arrested, but other kulaks killed Pavlik.

My diary tells how I felt about this story.

10 DECEMBER 1935
I cried today. How sorry I am for Pavlik. Why did the kulaks kill him? When I grow up I will kill all kulaks. Vasya Bykov wants to be like Pavlik, I too.

13 DECEMBER 1935
Today Lyuda taught us a new song about Pavlik. What a hero he is.

Lyuda knew how to make us children feel that our leaders and their deeds were right.

114

At one meeting she said: "I have told you how difficult it is for our leaders to carry on their work when there are so many enemies. I have told you how selflessly they devote their lives to the welfare of the people. You, little Pioneers, can and must help them. The government needs paper and rags for books and notebooks. There are many old books which no one needs, bring them. Iron is also needed. Grownups have no time to gather iron rusting behind sheds and in cellars. Collect it and bring it in. That way you can help. Each of you must fulfill this quota: ten pounds of iron, four pounds of paper, and two pounds of rags. Those who collect the most will be mentioned in the papers. The whole country will know of the little heroes."

Lyuda inspired me. I came home when no one was there and immediately went to work collecting paper. In a matter of a few minutes I had amassed quite a pile of Mama's and Lida's books. But Mama checked them when she came home and eliminated one volume after another. My collection decreased considerably. She tried to explain that it had taken many years to collect those books and they meant a great deal to her. But I couldn't understand why Mama wouldn't give up her art books, which seemed completely unnecessary to her happiness.

Iron was more difficult to obtain. All I could find was four pounds and this was not enough. Someone said there was much iron in the cemetery—crosses and fences. Like a cloud of grasshoppers we Pioneers descended on the cemetery. Then, loaded with crosses and the remains of iron fences, we moved through town on our way back to school. Seeing us, people turned away. But we did not feel any sin in our action. Our conscience was clear. We sang our favorite songs and walked with heads held high in the knowledge that we had done our duty.

We surpassed our quota two or three times, but we never got into the papers.

My third year in school was notable because for the first time we had a New Year's tree, both in school and at home. I had seen

115

such trees before, but only at Grandmother's. Mama never gave in to our pleadings to have a tree at home and always brushed us off saying she had no money for one.

Where did Mama get money for a tree this year? I wondered. Even Grandmother never had such a tree as ours.

Later I found out that 1935 was the first year the government permitted New Year's trees. Had Mama given in to us before this, someone might have reported it and she could easily have lost her job.

Our tree stood from January 1st to the 19th.

8 SEPTEMBER 1936

I am studying in Russian school No. 2 now. I don't see why I had to transfer. Lida is in the same school too. She is in the eighth class, I am in the fifth. I am proud of my sister and want to be like her. I have no friends. I am ten and a half and am the smallest and youngest in the class. I am constantly laughed at and teased.

25 SEPTEMBER 1936

Lida is true to her diary, but I don't write much. I love Lida, but not Oleg—he teases and beats me. I am now receiving the *Pioneer Pravda*. I read it every day, and even Mama reads our paper. How many enemies the Soviet government has! They all try to hurt us. Do we bother them?

10 OCTOBER 1936

I am so happy that the holidays are coming. I am memorizing the poem *Na Strazhe* [On Guard] and am painting a large poster in school.

5 NOVEMBER 1936

For whole days we have been preparing for the great celebration of the October Revolution. We went out of town for greens. Yasha almost drown. We were all scared, even the Pioneer leader. How many flowers and green branches we brought back! We will decorate our classroom better than all the others. Everything, portraits and flags, will be decorated with flowers. The sky looks grim, I hope it doesn't rain! What joy! I will be marching with all the grownups, but Oleg can't go. I am sorry for him.

The school year raced by—holidays and celebrations, the New Year's tree again, the Lenin days of mourning, anniversary of the

1905 Revolution, all sorts of meetings and congresses highlighted by speeches about the "enemies of the people." I drew, studied, recited. My drawings were on exhibit, making me proud and happy. Again May 1st passed with its alarms, worries, speeches, and demonstrations.

21 MAY 1937

I forgot that I have a diary to which I can bring my great sorrow: Lyuda, my dear Lyuda, was excluded from the Komsomol. Why? We were told that her father is an enemy of the people. I wonder where she lives? I want to visit her. She couldn't be an enemy.

29 MAY 1937

I saw Lyuda. How she has changed, the poor one. When I was leaving she said: "Don't come here again. There might be unpleasant consequences for you and your mama." I don't understand. . . . Why? I will ask Lida, she will know.

3 JUNE 1937

Our geography teacher is also an enemy of the people. How odd that there are so many enemies.

12 JUNE 1937

Lida Degtyar's father was arrested. She cried. Her mother worked in Mama's school. The students say that Lida D. can't remain a Pioneer. Why don't the enemies give us peace? All is so wonderful here! In other countries people live so much worse. What do the enemies want?

At the end of the school year I successfully completed all exams. But my happiness was limited. Neither from Lida nor Mama, nor my schoolteacher, did I receive an answer to all my questions about "enemies of the people." I didn't understand and it bothered me.

11 SEPTEMBER 1937

Now we are in the village. Marya Dmitrevna, my history teacher, lives with us. She is a better instructor than the history teacher in Nikopol. It is easy to work from her class notes. Marya Dmitrevna advises Lida to join the Komsomol, but Mama tells her not to. I will definitely join.

117

This year I did a lot of Pioneer work. I was attached to a group of students in the pre-Pioneer stage and spent all my free time with the little ones. I played with them, read to them and told them stories. Even though I was no bigger than they, they listened to me well. Maybe the glasses I had just started wearing impressed them. I remembered how Lyuda worked with us and I tried to imitate her techniques.

I also had much to do during the pre-election campaign. I made posters and prepared our classrooms for voting. Everything had to be decorated with greens and flowers—the many portraits of the leaders, placards, windows, doors, etc. I also went around with Komsomol members, carrying on a pre-election educational campaign.

In 1938, my sister, Lida, was accepted in the Komsomol. I was terribly jealous of her and often cried or picked arguments with her. I prepared a calendar for myself and crossed off each day as it passed. Thus I planned to keep track of the passage of time until I, like Lida, would enter the Komsomol.

In September of that year I was transferred to a high school. All three of us were in different schools. When we came home in the evening, we compared notes and sometimes Mama checked over our school diaries. This was a record that every student had to keep. It included grades received during the week and conduct in school. If necessary, the teacher made special notes concerning the progress and behavior of the student.

In high school I continued to participate in extracurricular activities. One of my jobs was to help prepare the bimonthly wall newspaper and the endless posters needed for the many holidays and celebrations.

In the summer of 1939, my brother and I went to Pioneer camps; he went to one, I to another. The cost was 160 rubles and though it was a large sum for Mama to pay, she consented, knowing how much it meant to us.

118

Camp was wonderful. We rose at seven to the call of a bugle. I always ran to the river to bathe quickly and soon many others followed my example. Usually we spent only five minutes in the water, but sometimes we got back too late for roll call. Then we were punished by not being taken along on hikes.

During the summer we had two big campfires. I especially remember the second one—on our farewell night. Representatives of the National Commissariat of Education, the Komsomol Regional Committee, and of the Party attended.

A large pile of logs and branches had been prepared in the middle of a clearing. The Pioneers and camp leaders sat in a circle around it. When darkness fell the fire was lit, and as we watched the bright flames shoot skyward, we listened to our guests. They told us how the Party and the government cared for us and that we must be grateful for this care. We were told to be especially grateful to the wisest of the wise, Comrade Stalin, as he was responsible for our happy childhood. . . .

Every word found response in our young hearts. So grateful did I feel that I ran up to the Komsomol representative and kissed her when she had finished talking, trying to tell her how happy I was and how good I felt.

The evening ended with singing, dancing, and poetry recitations. By midnight it was all over, and we Pioneers, tired, satisfied, and happy, went off to bed.

13 SEPTEMBER 1940

I just can't keep my Pioneer word of honor—to be serious. If I behave for one period, I am naughty during the next. I was practicing something new today: throwing spitballs. I even hit my dear Slava—now he walks around with a sore eye. Poor, poor Slava!

29 DECEMBER 1940

Oh, what a relief! Mama finally gave me permission to meet the New Year with all the others in school. I had been so afraid that she wouldn't. Lida is celebrating at her institute; Mama and Oleg are staying home.

I decided not to do any work for the New Year's celebration. Let someone else do it this time. Slava and I are writing New Year's wishes for everyone.

1 JANUARY 1941

The official part of the evening was boring: endless speeches about Stalin and the Party. There were appeals to us, the youth, to be merciless with our enemy. It gets so tiring! To hear it once or twice is good, but to hear it constantly for nine years is something else.

The second part of the evening was wonderful. Much singing and reciting. Slava sang. How wonderful it sounded! I never suspected that he had such a voice. Our New Year's wishes and caricatures brought laughter all around. Lida Soboleva was quite hurt, however. I had no intention of hurting her feelings when I drew her tall, thin figure as a fishing rod. Fedya liked his drawing so much that he showed it to everyone. Our math teacher was very offended because of Slava's poem about him. I was drawn as a tiny figure stretching to join the Komsomol, but never quite reaching it.

Winter vacation flew by, and soon we were back in school. At numerous meetings we were told the same things over and over again: that there is no God, that church and religion are the opiate of the people. These meetings always ended with appeals to fight religion.

Grandmother was the first person I attempted to enlighten. I told her not to go to church, insisting that there was no God, that all this was thought up by the czars to keep the people subjugated. I sat with her for hours and read articles from the magazine *Godless*.

Grandmother always listened attentively, but she never accepted the truth of my words. Having been defeated in my first attempt, I did not try to convince anyone else. I felt that if I could not convince my grandmother, then I could convince no one. From then on my efforts were concentrated in spreading antireligious pamphlets.

30 APRIL 1941

Tomorrow is May 1st. Oh, how I wish I could stay home. I would sleep late, read, take a walk along the river, or view the demonstration as a spectator and not a participant. I remember with what impatience I had awaited the day on which I could march in a demonstration with the grownups. That was so long ago! The first time I went I was so proud and happy. Lida's attitude toward the demonstration had already changed, and she complained, saying: "Ah, I don't want to go, but I have to. . . ." I didn't understand then and scolded her.

What I wouldn't give to stay home, but the whole class must be there. Punishment would await those absent. We'll march around the main streets of town and then take our position near the reviewing stand decorated with pictures of the leaders, flowers, and flags. And there we will stand. We'll listen to the speeches, or rather seem to listen—the loudspeakers are always so weak that one can't hear anything anyway. Besides, we've heard everything dozens of times before. We'll stand there for hours and hours, applauding at the proper time and if we try to steal away, our teacher will drag us back in shame.

Yes, tomorrow is May 1st. I will have to go.

24 JUNE 1941

War! But Mama isn't with us. She is in Minsk looking for work. We received a letter in which she told Lida to look out for us. What will happen to us without Mama? In case it becomes too difficult for us we are to go to our father: let him worry about us for a change! Since I was five he never cared for us; all the weight lay on Mama's shoulders.

The Germans are advancing . . . almost the whole male population has been taken into the army. Harvest-time is approaching. The Party and government appealed to all Komsomol members and Pioneers for help. With joy and readiness all students volunteered to work in kolkhozes.

Twenty of us were to go to a village together. We had been told to report at the school at 10:00 A.M. in order to arrive at our destination in time for lunch. We came and waited—one hour, two, four. Finally after 2:00 P.M., hungry and worn out by the long wait, we left for the kolkhoz.

When we arrived, the kolkhoz members showed no joy at seeing us:

"The spongers have arrived, they'll eat our last crumbs."

Without a moment's rest we were sent to work. Our job was

121

to pick sunflower roots out of the plowed earth. Basically the work was not hard, but the constant bending and pulling was very tiring.

The next morning we ate breakfast with the others in the kolkhoz dining hall. Bread and gruel was served. . . . We were given wooden spoons: round, large, unwieldy. Eating with them was punishment. I spilled more food than I got in my mouth.

This day we were to weed a field of sunflowers. We were given sickles, but the majority of us had no idea how to use them. But we had to keep up with the kolkhoz members in order to prove that we were earnest about this work. The sunflowers caught in our clothing. To keep our dresses from tearing, we took them off and worked in our underclothes. As a result the skin on our backs and shoulders became badly burned.

At twelve o'clock we went to lunch. We were given lentil soup and gruel, and though it was tasteless, after our work it didn't seem such a bad meal. Then we rested and went back in the fields at four. Some kind of soup was served for supper at eight.

After three days our ranks began to thin out; already ten had quietly gone home. I also had the desire to leave, but as long as some of my friends remained, I would have felt too ashamed to go.

The weeding was over and it was time to harvest the wheat. This had to be done before rains came. The work went on feverishly from morning till late into the night. There was one combine in the kolkhoz, but most of the time it was in repair. Our job was carrying the wheat sheaves to the waiting trucks.

Even though the work was tiring, we never felt as badly as we did after the first day of work. Sometimes we even had enough energy to spend part of our midday rest period in one of the gardens, filling up on raspberries, apples, plums, or cherries. We badly wanted fruit, and since no one gave it to us we helped ourselves.

The first week we were fed the same food as the kolkhoz

122

members, but after that the students were given much more filling, varied and better meals.

During the harvesting campaign our workday was divided into three periods: work from eight to twelve, rest from twelve to three (members of the kolkhoz worked during this period), then work again till eleven or twelve at night, taking advantage of the moonlight.

Three miles from us, in another kolkhoz, were some other students from our school. Their situation was much worse than ours so far as quarters and food were concerned: all twenty to thirty of them lived in one classroom of the local school and slept on straw spread on the floor. We, however, were quartered with individual families.

After twenty-four days on the collective farm we left for home. The kolkhoz members had grown used to us and were sorry when we had to leave. They even gave us bread and honey for the trip. None of us received any remuneration for our work.

25 JULY 1941
War. . . . Our troops are retreating. Everyone is feeling uneasy. Endless trains of refugees passed through from the western provinces. Will we also have to go through that?

30 JULY 1941
Another obligation—go from house to house explaining how to fight incendiary bombs. The population must be prepared for anything. Mama is out of work, and the savings banks won't permit any withdrawals. Mama is in quite a low mood.

3 AUGUST 1941
We have night watches in our block. Today is Mama's turn, but I will take her place. Let her rest a bit, she is so worn out.

Why did Popov, our neighbor, tell me yesterday: "With the coming of the Germans a new life will begin. You, Tanya, don't understand much yet. Live a while—you'll see. Then you will see that I am right. I am glad that the Germans are coming."

Why is he happy that the enemy is coming? How despicable! I had never imagined that he could be so traitorous. Yes, there

123

are many enemies. The Party is right when it says every third person is a traitor or informer and we have to watch out. I see for myself now.

5 AUGUST 1941

There was a general mobilization. Those taken are leaving today. It's good that Oleg is still little; it is hard to see one's relatives go. Lida wants to become a nurse and Mama is terribly worried. But Mama could also be a nurse, and I feel that I too could be useful in a hospital. What would happen to Oleg and Grandmother then? It's good for those who have a father to take care of everything.

Popov is very silent, worried; his son George may be taken into the army.

13 AUGUST 1941

Evacuation was announced today. That means that our soldiers are on the run. We also made ready to leave, but can't: no money; it's all in the bank which won't hand it out. We'll stay or leave on foot with the army the first minute.

And Popov is exulting! His happiness is shining in his eyes. Oh, how I hate him! Traitor! Why doesn't anyone report him? I told Lida about Popov, but she told me that ". . . he will find his own fate. Don't interfere. Let no one accuse you of a low act: informing is not heroic, it's very base. Remember that." What's wrong with Lida? And a Komsomol member too! Don't tell me she is changing? I am afraid to even mention anything to Mama.

14 AUGUST 1941

Our town has been bombed. Demolition and incendiary bombs were dropped. Many people were hurt. Mama wasn't home. So frightful! Confusion everywhere . . . and Oleg is running back and forth bringing news, one item worse than the other. "All will be chased out and the houses blown up; those who remain will be shot." And what about the sick, will they be shot? "All males over fourteen will be taken along when the army pulls back. . . ." Could they take Oleg? How could Mama part with him? Almost all my friends are staying. There are no means of transportation, and they won't let anyone on the trains.

124

15 August 1941

Hurray! The evacuation has been stopped! How wonderful it is to be with your friends and not shiver awaiting the enemy. . . . If everyone would hate the Germans as I do, they would never get here.

Popov looks crushed. Serves him right! I am so happy. I visited my friends and they are all glad. Mama asked me not to go out while she went to exchange some embroidered handkerchiefs for potatoes. But I used the opportunity to go out alone.

Lida is worried, doesn't believe there is a real improvement in the situation and insists: "If they reached Krivoi Rog, they will get here. The Dnieper River will never hold them."

16 August 1941

The town is being looted. The population is looting everything, especially the food warehouses. They say the flour mill will be blown up. We also went there and took two sacks of flour. Why destroy it? Long before the enemy would go hungry, our own people, deprived of supplies, would starve to death. It seems better to distribute the flour than to destroy it. But now that this stage has been reached it means that our soldiers are definitely retreating. . . .

The mill was not blown up as rumored, but fire was set to it. Now it's burning like a torch. What a horrible fire; it's hot a block and a half away. The people near by are trying to save their homes by pouring water on the walls. I went to help them. . . .

Ours are retreating. . . . We dug a trench to hide in during the bombings, but I don't want to be there alone; it's better in the house with Mama. Mama isn't scared and cooks our dinners.

17 August 1941

The damn Germans have come! What will happen to us? I don't expect anything good. Mama won't let me out of the trench: a fortuneteller once told her that she would lose her second-born, and right now she is so superstitious that I sit in the trench all day to please her. Even my food is brought out to me and I have to sleep in the trench.

The Germans stopped by. Pfooey, I gritted my teeth. How I hate them! George Popov is trying to pay attention to me, sometimes to Lida. It seems to me that he looks at me more often, and

125

his father called me "bride" today. How stupid! Who would think of love at such a time?

23 AUGUST 1941

Nina R. and her sister visited me. They are excited and gay. No trace of any hate for the enemy; I can't even look at them! They stopped to talk to the Germans who are stationed with an antiaircraft gun near our house. They called to me to join them, but I swore at them and called them traitors.

Lida is studying German; to me it is repulsive. I can't even say those words which I learned in school. Hatred locks my tongue.

Everything is quiet, they haven't touched anything. Even schools have been reopened, but only the Ukrainian, not the Russian schools. Poor Lida, the institute remains closed. Mama found work in a village and walks five miles each way. It's not so bad now, but how will she be able to walk that far in the winter?

18 FEBRUARY 1942

A week ago the conscription of laborers for Germany began. Through friends, Mama arranged for me to study bookkeeping. Will this save me from Germany? I don't think that they will take Lida because of her lungs.

20 APRIL 1942

The school which Oleg is attending has been exempted from shipment to Germany. Anyway, we don't have to worry about him because of his age. Mama is unrecognizable: she has lost weight, looks terribly old. These conscriptions have taken everything out of her—she is so afraid of losing us. A new one will take place in May. I have almost lost all my control. I would hate to go!

22 APRIL 1942

Mama has found a way out: she arranged a leave for me from the bookkeeping course on the pretense that she received a letter from my father saying that he is very ill and wants to see me, maybe for the last time. It will all turn out well—no one will say that I am running away; I have leave papers and official permission to go. Only how did Mama arrange all this in such a hurry?

126

6 JUNE 1942

Another recruitment. When will these tortures cease? Those cursed enslavers! Tomorrow Lida and I have to go before the commission. What will happen to Mama? She couldn't stand it if we were taken. I try to comfort her as well as I can. But how can I comfort her, when I myself am deeply upset?

I wonder what Popov thinks of them now? For his son will surely be taken this time. Oh, why didn't we go away on foot when ours were retreating? Why did we remain? When will we be saved? Or is it permanent slavery? Now they can do anything they want with us.

7 JUNE 1942

Well, this time the storm blew over. For how long? Lida wasn't taken because of her tuberculosis; I was rejected for my poor eyesight. When we left the commission all those who were being sent away cried and said to us: "How lucky you are, why don't I have bad lungs or a bad heart or something wrong with me?". . .

Everything affects poor Mama, she can hardly stand on her feet. There is no money for food. She sits and embroiders kerchiefs, for which she is paid in potatoes. Once Mama even received some butter in return.

It's good that Oleg went to a village to work: at least he is well fed.

11 NOVEMBER 1942

I am working as a bookkeeper. But apparently even the job won't save me from Germany. They cooked up something new —each department must make a list of those whom they can get along without. It was announced that three from our office can be spared and I am one of them. How can I tell Mama? I have to go as a slave! Will I ever see my home again? I have a feeling that this time I won't be able to escape conscription, and that I will have to leave everything dear behind. Poor, dear Mama, what will happen to you? How will you get over this?

I couldn't work, so I came home. Why should I work, anyway? The three of us were of no use to the office—we would just sit there and cry.

Damn that Hitler! No, we won't be slaves forever, he will break his neck someday! They can't make an obedient slave out of me! Oh, how I hate them!

12 NOVEMBER 1942

Tomorrow I have to go before the commission. I tried the last thing that might have saved me. It's November, very cold out, and many are wearing their winter clothes. Despite the freezing weather I decided to go swimming in the Dnieper. I thought maybe I would catch cold and not have to go.

I put on a light dress and sandals. I carried two buckets so Mama would think I was going to get water. I shivered with the cold. Leaving the buckets on shore, I climbed into one of the boats and slowly started undressing. The freezing wind chilled me to the bone. People working along the shore looked at me in amazement.

"Are you getting ready to drown yourself?" they asked.

"No, I'm just going to swim around a bit."

"You kids are all crazy! The water is like ice."

I jumped in. The water was so cold that my body became numb all over. I felt that if I stayed in I would surely drown. With great effort I managed to climb out of the river. I sat in the chilling wind for about ten minutes. Then I began to get dressed. My hands hardly moved. My teeth chattered from the cold. Filling the buckets, I made my way home.

I told Mama everything. She almost died from fear! But I tried to comfort her by saying that this might save me from going to Germany.

13 NOVEMBER 1942

No cold, no signs of one, no fever. . . . That means I will go. I have to report to the commission now. I know that I will pass this time. . . .

There were many luckless ones like me—about four hundred were at the station. Our families had come to see us off, but at the gate we were separated, and they were told to go home. I tried to get away from Mama as fast as I could. I couldn't look at her tears, and didn't want to let her see mine.

We were separated into groups of thirty to forty and put into freight cars. The cars were filthy and foul smelling. We were chased into them like cattle and locked in. To them we were cattle!

Time passed slowly. Every hour carried us further and further from home. I wondered whether I would ever see it again. The train rolled on . . . where to? No one knew.

Finally, after two weeks we arrived at a distribution camp. I was sent to work in Salzburg, Austria.

The work was hard, dirty . . . all around were strangers.

But the continuous working day left no time for contemplation. After finishing work I would go to the room I shared with eleven Russian girls and immediately lie down to sleep. Sunday afternoon was our only time off. Then, wearing an arm band that identified us as slaves, we would go into town and look at the strange people, see their world.

A strange thing happened. Gradually our hate began to disappear. I saw women like Mama, girls just like Lida, kids like my brother Oleg. They also lived in a war-weary world, but here it somehow seemed better, quieter, simpler.

With my friend Katya, I observed the life, ways, clothes of the citizens of Salzburg. We became acquainted with some of the local women, and then I saw the full difference, the whole contrast between our former life and the life of Europeans.

This didn't come about at once, it was a gradual awakening.

I wrote long and detailed letters to Mama in Nikopol, describing everything with which I had become acquainted for the first time in my life. Mama answered me and asked more and more questions. She didn't know this new land either.

Thus a year passed.

At the end of 1943 the letters from Mama ceased coming. I went through terrible days and weeks. I wanted to run away, look for Mama, my sister, brother. . . . But I stayed.

Toward the end of 1944 I was called out to the gate of the camp. I went out wondering what awaited me . . . there was Mama.

During the long winter evenings, Mama and I sat with our remembrances. We talked about everything, every little detail. After one of our early conversations, Mama cried bitterly.

129

When I asked her why she was crying she said she was crying for joy. "This is the first honest talk I have ever had with you," she explained. "In fact, this is the first frank conversation I have had for several decades."

Then she cried some more and when I asked her why she was crying, for I felt there was now a difference in her crying, she said she was crying because in Russia, the country she loved, one could no longer have a real conversation even with one's closest relative or friend. Fear filled every heart; you became a hypocrite. One expressed false feelings and concealed one's true feelings.

Then the Americans came. Mama and I noticed how well cared for they were. They behaved so differently from our Red Army soldiers. They behaved like free people. Something about them showed they were not afraid.

I saw Katya off. She was repatriating voluntarily. I know what a weight was on her heart. She didn't believe in her future under the Soviets. But her family was there. I was not in the same situation. Lida had died, and we knew nothing of Oleg.

Mama and I remained with the Americans. There was nothing else to do. Mama did not have the energy to face life again in Russia; it was too hard. And I had nothing to go back to. I was a stranger here and I had no roots. But I could see light and I felt that a day would come when I would laugh and smile and relax.

7

THE TRIALS OF A SOVIET WORKINGMAN

by Nikolai Markov

To make up for the shortage of workers in the logging industry in the late 1920's, an appeal for volunteers was issued by the Komsomol organizations. Workers were recruited from the leather shoe, tool and die, brick, and other industries. All the men were between the ages of seventeen and twenty. Before we left, a meeting was called and it was announced that our pay was to be two hundred rubles a month plus free quarters. This was guaranteed. An official farewell was organized, we were accompanied to the station with banners, flags, and music. The mood during the trip was very good. We spent much of the time on the train singing.

We arrived in Archangel, and immediately local political workers began a series of meetings and discussions. We were told not to associate with the kulaks exiled to this area for hard labor. We were to have nothing to do with the crews of foreign ships and by our looks and our bearing we were to show that we lived in plenty. We were to accept no offering of any kind.

We were quartered in a log barracks. Forty-five of us from

131

Kursk were placed in one room. It was much too small for our numbers. The cots stood one against the other, leaving only a four-foot aisle down the middle of the room.

Our work, loading lumber, was to begin at seven the next morning. With great enthusiasm all of us threw ourselves at the task. We were loading the logs aboard the ships manually. The lumber was to go to foreign textile and paper mills.

In the harbor where we worked there were about eighty ships belonging to different countries: England, Denmark, France, Norway, etc. Many of them flew small red pennants. We were wondering about this, and were told that foreign companies, coming to Archangel for lumber, made contracts with the Soviet government which specified the time in which the ships were to be loaded. If the job was not completed on time the Soviet government had to pay a specified sum of 420 rubles in pure gold for each excessive day. According to the number of pennants, we judged that about 80 per cent were being loaded behind schedule.

We were divided into groups, and socialist competitions were arranged. In order to increase production and whip up our enthusiasm, a special band was hired to play in time with our work. For the first three or four days we were well fed, then we went on a cod diet. It came to us in all forms: fried, baked, boiled; soup with cod, borscht with cod, gruel with cod. Our barracks, our rooms, our clothes were stenched through and through with cod odor. Meat and potatoes we never saw. Once in a great while we received plain wheat gruel on which we could spread some sugar.

Working all day long in snow and rain is tiring. Without proper food our efficiency was lowered and production fell. This called for a meeting. "You must work," we were told. The dissatisfaction of the youth answered the leaders. Some said openly that when there isn't enough food people can't work. There were shouts of: "What are we—exiles? Only exiles would be fed thus! We are Komsomol members. We were told that all efforts would

132

be made to situate us well, but we were deceived. Now we are in the same fix as the exiles."

Such talk lasted for a week. Payday arrived and we went to collect. We were met by Director Movsh, who announced: "We are having financial difficulties and cannot give you any money now. For having fulfilled your norms I will give twenty rubles out of my own pocket to your group—go buy something for yourself." Our brigade leader, Paul Sorokin, took the money. When we got back to our barracks we did not know how to apply the money. Finally we decided to buy some tobacco, which was distributed among all.

The next day we appointed three men to go to the director and demand our pay. They were given specific instructions not to accept any alms. But Movsh had his answers ready. "You have free food," he told them, "and you can work and live. When the year is over your contract will expire. By that time you will have saved a large sum of money and will be able to buy anything you want."

"Comrade Movsh, we want to eat and drink normally every day. What will happen in a year we don't know," said one of the delegates.

"You will have to endure, just as the whole country endures. If you ask for, or demand anything, you will be considered 'enemies of the people.'"

The idea that any repressive measures could be taken against us did not enter our minds. We were sure that our pay was there and thought that if we did not appear for work it would be given to us. The idea seemed so good that we decided not to go to work the next day. But to be successful we had to have the support of all the others. Sorokin got a red banner from the clubroom, and forty of us fell into a column and marched around the camp singing. We first went to the Leningrad group, talked to them, and they also decided not to go to work. They joined us and we all went to the Tula contingent—they joined us; then the Tambov group, then Smolensk, Moscow, and others had finally joined us.

133

We proceeded to the office and demanded to see Movsh. He came out, smiling with self-assurance, and said: "Take it easy and don't organize any antigovernment strikes; go home and all will be taken care of." We believed him and broke up. As soon as it got dark we heard cars stopping at the barracks. GPU soldiers came in and called fifteen names. These fifteen went outside, were put in cars and whisked away. Hearing what was happening the rest of us ran out to the cars. We were threatened with rifles and told: "Don't be foolish, otherwise we will shoot you down like rabbits."

The next day Party leaders came down from Archangel and announced that "if any of you act as your comrades did you will meet the same fate." We never saw or heard from those who were arrested.

Under these conditions our work continued. We started thinking of means to escape this penal servitude. Some began to smoke tea leaves, others rubbed onions under their armpits in order to cause fever; I remember one who injured his hand with an ax and was sent to a hospital. But all our attempts were fruitless, we still had to work as before. Infirmary attendants were given orders that anyone with fever or similar complaints be sent back, not accepted in the infirmary, and none was to be given an excuse from work.

I was still inexperienced and didn't know what to do. But I met an old acquaintance, who was in exile there, and he advised me to write a letter asking my family to send a telegram to the effect that either my father or my mother was dying. I did what he said. In two months I received a telegram which I took to Movsh announcing that I had to go home as my father was near death. Movsh smiled and said that didn't mean anything. "By the time you get there he will be dead anyway, and the work is much more important." But I was able to convince him to give me the necessary documents and travel permits. Only when I was on the train did I let myself realize that I was finally leaving this hell. In my joy to be home again, I even forgot my suitcase on the train.

In September 1933, I went to Moscow to escape the famine in our region. I went to a friend who was in the "Mozherez" factory working as a Komsomol organizer in the mechanical shop. He knew many people there and helped me get a job as a locksmith. I knew this craft well and after six months became head of the locksmith brigade. In another half-year I was made a foreman in the mechanical shop. I worked honestly, fulfilling all my duties, all orders and norms which were given every day. My shift was first in fulfilling the program of the factory.

Our factory had only recently been built and was just beginning to achieve full production. There was still much defective output, sometimes as high as 70 per cent.

The next fall a large number of young workers arrived in the factory—machinists, lathe operators and others who had just finished a special course at a factory school. The young people were assigned to older, experienced men—two to a man. The Komsomol organizations gave orders to the shop committee and to the shop administration to encourage them and give them a chance to work independently. Before two weeks were up, the new men were working at the machines.

At this time I was transferred to the lathe section of the shop. The lathes were all from Germany and had cost a tremendous amount of money.

I was on the shift which worked from midnight to 8:00 A.M. All night long I went through the shop checking on the workers and giving them directions. I especially watched the new men, warning them to work carefully. I told them to be extremely cautious with the machinery and reminded them of the high cost of the units. I made no excessive demands on them, only tried to make them aware of their responsibility and the need for constant caution.

Going through the shop around two o'clock one morning I

135

suddenly heard a terrible crash and noise. Fearing the worst I jumped to the main switch and disconnected all machines. Then I ran to where the noise had come from. Indeed, one of the lathes was wrecked. The side supports were smashed, bent out of shape. I rushed to the young fellow who had worked at the machine. "What have you done! How did this happen?" He didn't answer. Pale and trembling he started to cry. Seeing there was nothing to be gained by remaining here I ran to the manager on duty. Five minutes later the NKVD (GPU) arrived. All details were recorded and my name was taken as foreman of the section. An hour later a messenger came to tell me that the director wanted to see me.

The director of the factory was sitting behind a large table. "Fine job you did!" He hit the table with his fist and shouted that such wreckers, such scoundrels, should be hanged.

"Comrade Director," I protested, "I warned the shop committee and administration not to put new workers on the night shift. They aren't used to night labor. They tire easily and fall asleep. That's what happened this time—the worker had fallen asleep without shutting off his machine. The piece he had been working on was finished, that's why there was an accident."

My words meant nothing to the director. "Go home and stay there. The proper authorities will handle your case."

I went out crushed. There were 150 workers in the shop and I couldn't watch out for everyone at the same time.

I returned home. I could neither eat nor drink. All day long I paced nervously about my room. Late in the evening I went to bed but I could not fall asleep. At 2:30 A.M. I heard a car stop at my door. There was a knock on the door . . . I opened . . .

"Markov?"

"Right here," I answered.

"You are arrested. Follow me."

I was taken to the Lyublyanka, the NKVD prison in Moscow. In the morning I was processed. My head was shaved, the buttons on my clothes were cut off, my belt, shoestrings were taken,

136

and my pockets turned inside out. I was put in a cell, fifteen feet square. There were sixty-three people in it—I was the sixty-fourth. People not only did not have room to lie down, but they could not even sit. They had to stand all the time, scarcely able to shuffle their feet.

I stayed there four days. The fourth night I was called to the NKVD investigator.

"Tell me to what subversive organization you belong and who gave you orders to produce the damage at the factory?"

I told him I belonged to no organization and that I did not understand what this was all about. I explained that it was not I who was responsible for the accident but the administration whom I had warned repeatedly not to put new workers on the night shift.

"Let's not lose any time," he said with irritation in his voice. "Just sign this statement." The paper included my name, birthplace, present address, etc., and said I was a member of a Trotskyite organization, upon whose orders I caused the wreck.

I refused to sign.

"Think it over, or it will be worse for you," the examiner said.

I was taken back to the cell.

The next night I was called out again and presented with the same demand. This time the "confession" was written in a different form, but the content was the same. Again I said I was not guilty and would not sign. Again I was returned to my cell. This went on for six nights.

The seventh night I was called in and given a clean sheet of paper. The examiner said that I could put down everything as it had happened. I began to write. When I had written all the details of the event, he took the paper and put it into a folder. He handed me another prepared form and said:

"Will you sign?"

"No, not for the world."

"Will you sign?"

"Never."

"Read it!"

I began to read, crossing out whatever was not in agreement with fact. I crossed out the first line and began to delete the second. The examiner rose, picked up a steel straight-edge and began to wave it. When I continued to cross out whole sentences, he cursed me with the foulest words in the Russian vocabulary and hit my hand with the steel ruler. The blood burst out, splashing the paper and I was returned to my cell.

For three days I was not touched; then I was called out and faced with the same accusation. Again I was asked to sign the statement. I categorically refused and hysterically cried:

"I am a young specialist, I worked honestly, I was never connected with any subversive organizations, I don't even know what the Trotskyites stand for, I only have one desire—to serve my country."

"Shut up and forget about such junk," the examiner shouted. "We know everything." He cursed me again as he swung with his fist and hit me on the ear.

When the examiner began stomping on me I rolled over and lost consciousness. I awoke in the cell. My cellmates questioned me about what had happened. After I told them, an old man advised me to sign nothing; otherwise, he said, I would perish.

This torture continued for forty-eight days. I was questioned evening after evening. Then, one day I was called out in the morning and, as usual, the examiner said: "Sign!" I was so used to this demand that the answer came automatically: "No!"

"Read it, you fool!" I began to read and tears came into my eyes. I could not believe what I saw:

I, Nikolai Markov, entertain no grievances against the examiner. I was treated well, am satisfied with everything and promise not to disclose anything I saw or heard here.

I quickly signed the paper and the examiner told me I was free.

I was led out of the NKVD building. After five steps I collapsed. My legs were swollen and I was completely exhausted. A woman ran to me and helped me up. She put me in a cab and I went home. My good fortune in being released was due to a change in the highest offices of the secret police. Others, just as falsely accused as I, were liberated simultaneously.

Six days after I was freed, I received a notice from the police ordering me to report. When I appeared at the station I was told to leave Moscow within forty-eight hours.

I went back to Kursk where my parents still lived. My mother took care of me. I could not get used to regular food immediately, as anything fat nauseated me. Gradually, my health returned. In a month I was sufficiently recovered to start looking for a job.

I found work in a motor-repair factory. After three and a half months the Party organizer of the factory called me and announced: "We cannot keep you at your job because you have been arrested by the NKVD and accused of sabotage." In order not to complicate matters I was offered the opportunity to leave my job "voluntarily." I signed the necessary papers and received my pay. My financial situation was bad—my father was out of work and the pay my mother received sewing ladies' underwear could not support three people.

Shortly after midnight on November 4, 1937, NKVD men came to us with a search warrant and a warrant for my father's arrest.

They found nothing in the apartment, but my father was arrested.

Mother went to the NKVD to inquire about his fate—she was told nothing.

Knowing that many prisoners were sent to Siberia or the north, Mother and I began a nightly vigil at the stations. We, like the hundreds of other people who watched for their relations, hoped for at least a glimpse of father.

We kept this up until the twenty-sixth of February when we received notice that my father had been accused of "counter-revolution" and on the decision of a three-man NKVD tribunal had been shot.

I know that my father never participated in any counterrevolutionary movements. He was by nature a timid character. He had been a trade union member since 1919, had always done his work properly, and had never occupied any important posts. He had gone through four or more purges, always being approved. But the wave of the Yezhov period engulfed him and he became a completely innocent victim.

A month after father's execution the building superintendent, accompanied by the police, came to us with orders for immediate eviction. It was still winter, cold and damp; the ground was covered with snow. Nevertheless, as we stood aghast, they began to carry our things out to the street.

There were no apartments available in Kursk, but thanks to acquaintances we were able to find a narrow corridor where my mother and I stayed.

In 1939 I got a job in a tractor factory. I had been working for two months when I was called before the Party representative. He told me that I had to quit work in the factory because my father had been shot as an "enemy of the people." I moved to a small town, Shebekino, not far from Kursk. There I worked in a machine and tractor service station. I became technical supervisor in one of the workshops. The Finnish campaign was going on at this time. I worked hard to earn confidence, and the management was very well satisfied with me. But in view of the fact that there was an arrest on my record and that my father had been executed by the NKVD I was not taken into the army. I worked in Shebekino quite a while, saved money and returned to my mother in Kursk. I took a job in a streetcar depot. Here I managed to cover all traces of my past and became foreman of the repair shop.

Yes, I was unhappy when I was sent by the Nazi army as a slave laborer to Germany. But now, even in the unsettled position of a DP, I am happier than millions living in the Soviet Union. Having experienced the Soviet "paradise" and German bondage, I came to an unalterable decision: to return to Russia only when the totalitarian regime no longer exists.

140

8

TWO EVILS

by Lidia Obukhova

In September 1929, at the age of nine, I went to school for the first time. Poor health prevented me from starting earlier, but because I had studied at home I was put directly into the fifth grade.

Our class was divided into brigades headed by the oldest member. He had the right to appoint the student who would answer for the whole brigade during question periods and examinations. All members of the brigade received grades based on the answer of the selected student.

"You go, Lida," I was often told, "you must know, your father is a professor."

It was in vain that I attempted to convince the others that my father never had anything to do with my work.

Father was quick tempered and many of the changes wrought by the Soviets annoyed him. Sometimes he expressed his dissatisfaction, but a reproachful glance from mother would quiet him. One night I overheard my mother talking to father:

"I know what you are going through but you must restrain yourself in front of the child. Lida is going to school. She is

141

studying the economics of the Soviet system. She will have to live and work under this system. Why upset her? Life will be easier for the child if what she hears at home is not in conflict with what she learns in school."

In 1932, my parents took me on a boat trip down the Volga. Our ship, the *Spartak*, was one of the best afloat. The first- and second-class cabins were excellently equipped. The dining room served wine, sturgeon, caviar, etc.

Once we docked at a small village. A crowd of peasants stood on the pier trying to get near the gangplank of the ship. The ship's crew rudely pushed them away but the people desperately surged forward. I learned that these were former kulaks who had been chased out of their homes and were now trying to get away to escape starvation. Similar incidents took place at other stops. The sailors always shouted crude oaths and most of the kulaks were left despairing on shore as the ship sailed.

One day my mother sent me for the steward to order a bath for the evening. In order to reach the crew's quarters in the bow I had to go through the hold of the ship. There I stopped horrified. Before me, lying on the filthy metal floor of the lower hold, among barrels of stinking fish were that same kind of people whom we had watched struggle onto the ship. The air was stifling, there was no room to breathe. The people lay almost on top of each other; a crew member passing through stepped over and on them uttering curses as he went. I looked down at my own white dress and shoes with a feeling of guilt when I turned and ran quickly up the stairs to our clean cabin.

At the town of Gorki a group of Americans came aboard. They were high school and university teachers on an excursion in the USSR. Soon we were all well acquainted, and one of the teachers proposed that he and my mother exchange children for a year so that his son and I might learn the language and the customs of the other's country. The prospect of giving me a brief chance of living in the United States was very tempting,

142

but after some deliberation mother decided that it would be impossible. First of all, even in the homes of well-to-do specialists, living conditions were poor by American standards. But the trouble that could result from such an exchange of children was by far the most important consideration. In the Soviet Union it would have been viewed with great suspicion, and even if no immediate repercussions were to follow, upon my return there would be no telling what might happen. Even though there was no one else present during my mother's discussions with the American, she was afraid to admit her real reason for refusing. Consequently the American could not comprehend how my parents could refuse what to him seemed such a generous offer.

In the last year of high school we began to plan where we could continue our studies and in what field. All of us wanted to go on with our education in order to help our country and our people and accomplish something great in our lifetime. Therefore we worked hard to prepare for the final examinations before graduation. In all there were seventeen: Russian, Ukrainian, and French languages and literature; mathematics, physics, chemistry, history of the revolutionary movement, history of the Communist party, political economy, and other subjects. In the end, all of us passed.

The graduating class held a farewell party. Toward morning when we tired of merrymaking we sat around and shared our plans for the future. I had still not decided what field I would enter. There seemed so much to choose from. The school poet in a farewell song, dedicated to our future activities, had this to say about me: "Will excel in physics, chemistry, mathematics, literature, history, astronomy, and a variety of other subjects." After long considerations and sleepless nights I decided on chemistry. At the moment it seemed to be a more needed field for our country.

Immediately following graduation we started to prepare for college entrance examinations.

At this time I was given the job of preparing two thirty-five-year-old Party members for entrance in the Technological Institute. One of them was a commissar in the Red Army, the other an army officer.

"We will accept them regardless," the chairman of the committee on admissions told me, "but it's better that they know something."

By the first of November the entrance examinations were over. Eight graduates of our school, including myself, were accepted by the institute.

The second semester at the institute began with the promise that at the end of the term the outstanding students in studies and extracurricular activities would be taken on a tour of the battlefields of the 1918-1921 Civil War. The final issue of the institute newspaper listed the lucky participants. They included all the members of the Komsomol, about twenty of the best athletes and marksmen of the institute and the ten best students. I was in the latter group. On this "campaign" through the south of the USSR we were accompanied by several old veterans of the Civil War.

Early on a sunny July day we assembled on the campus. After long meetings we loaded the rifles, ammunition, boxes of hand grenades, books, and supplies onto the trucks. Toward sundown, accompanied by the sound of martial music, our column left in the direction of Poltava.

For one month we traveled around the south of the USSR, visiting many cities, towns, and villages. Sometimes we slept in hotels or empty school buildings, but usually we spent the nights under the open sky on haystacks. As we went from one historic spot to another, the Civil War veterans told us of the events that had occurred fifteen years before. This was one of the methods of educating us, the youth, and at the same time carrying on propaganda among the population. We distributed literature in the villages, organized athletic and shooting competitions with the local inhabitants, and discussed current events with the people.

The "campaign" ended in Kiev with a reception by the heads of the Ukrainian Communist party and the staff of the Ukrainian Military District. There we were also acquainted with the technical achievements and military preparedness of the modern sections of the Red Army. Light tanks leaped, swam, and destroyed apparently indestructible targets. At the end of the maneuvers, the students thanked the commander of the tank detachment. Coming to attention smartly, he answered:

"I serve the working people."

The rest of the summer was spent at a resort. The members of the group made plans to write a book about the tour, shared impressions, and reconstructed the stories about individual heroes and episodes of the Civil War.

Winter passed in schoolwork and the preparation of separate chapters of the book. The members of the summer group studied different courses and seldom saw each other, but all were united by our experiences during the preceding summer.

One day in the summer of 1937 I had just completed an exam and was sitting with a group of students in front of the main school building.

Suddenly a voice came over the loudspeaker that was mounted above the entrance:

"Attention, attention! Here is a special announcement. The NKVD has uncovered a group of Red Army commanders who sold out to foreign capitalists and delivered military secrets of the Soviet Union. The group includes: the assistant commissar of defense, Marshal of the Soviet Union, Tukhachevsky; the commander of the Ukrainian Military District, Yakir; the commander of the White Russian Military District, Uborevich, and others. The traitors to the fatherland were condemned to death by shooting. The sentence has been carried out."

The students stood around in shocked silence, not knowing

145

what to think. When unknown people are accused of horrible crimes one can accept it. But we who had participated in the previous summer's tour had met Yakir and talked to him. It did not seem possible that a man who had spoken with such a devotion to duty and was so beloved and respected by the soldiers could be guilty of such an offense. We remembered the stories told by the Civil War veterans—they all spoke of the unequaled courage and military talent of Tukhachevsky. They spoke in reverent tones of Yakir, who had liberated their villages during the Civil War. What could make these people who had tied their fate to the Soviet system in those years when it was weak, betray and sell it now in the years of the "victorious building of socialism"?

Clearly, we could no longer mention Yakir or Tukhachevsky in our proposed book about the Civil War; the book never was written.

During the winter of 1937-1938 many professors and students were arrested and expelled from the institute. Friends stopped recognizing each other. One did not greet his acquaintances. One looked at strangers wondering if they too were not "enemies of the people."

In those days I withdrew into myself. I felt the deepest hostility toward the men responsible for these unpleasant conditions. I definitely decided that in order to keep my self-respect I would have to remain outside the Communist party.

The May 1st celebration, 1939, was approaching. We made posters and garlands and painted portraits of the leaders.

The morning of the holiday all students assembled on the institute campus. After a long wait, the columns were formed. The posters and portraits were distributed, and we began to move toward the square. We were halted for many hours on a side street but when the parade really got started it did not take long to reach the tribune on which Party and government leaders stood. We passed with yells of "hurray" and almost immediately

146

broke up. Those who were carrying placards had to return them to the institute.

Two days later a general meeting of the student body was called. When everyone was assembled, the Komsomol secretary, Boris Kirilenko mounted the rostrum and announced that the Komsomol had received a report that one of the students had spit upon the portrait of Lazar Kaganovich.

"Comrade Kotov has the floor," he added.

"Here is the situation, comrades," Kotov began. He was an elderly student and a Party member. "Last night as I walked down the corridor to the men's room I saw placards and portraits standing along the wall. Nearest to the men's room was the portrait of the great member of the Politburo—Lazar Moiseyevich Kaganovich. I met Ilya Rottstein coming out of the lavatory just as I was going in. A few minutes later when I came out there was spittle on the portrait of Lazar Kaganovich. Who had done it? Naturally Ilya Rottstein! No wonder he ties his black tie neatly and wears a brown suit—he surreptitiously sympathizes with the German fascists! Comrades, I propose that this counter-revolutionist be expelled from our proletarian midst."

The meeting passed a resolution excluding Rottstein from the Komsomol and the institute. All his attempts to acquit himself, all his assurances that he had never spit at anything, all his protests that this was just a figment of Kotov's imagination came to nothing.

This was the last time anyone at the institute was accused of being a "fascist." The word was mentioned less and less, and finally this label completely disappeared. In August 1939, when the *Pravda* carried a front-page photo of Molotov and von Ribbentrop smiling at each other, I remembered the "fascist" Ilya Rottstein.

On June 22, 1941, I awoke to the sound of march music on the radio. Molotov's speech was broadcast at noon. Announcing the war, he called on all Soviet citizens to defend the fatherland and repulse the invasion of fascist barbarians.

Now began the uneasy nights spent in the expectation of air raids; nightly rooftop watches; practice alerts; and the fight against the "vicious violators of blackout regulations." If any window showed even the tiniest speck of light, the occupants of that particular room were arrested and put in jail. The people of Kharkov were mobilized to dig trenches around the city. Gas masks were issued to "important" people. To buy groceries, people stood in lines for hours. Refugees passing through the city told of disorder and panic among our retreating armies. They were senselessly destroying everything that was necessary to the survival of the remaining population. Children and adults, overcome by an espionage mania, took to the police anyone who looked the least bit suspicious. At the institute, inflammable materials were prepared in bottles for the destruction of German tanks. Everywhere there were collections for wounded soldiers. During alerts the man on duty in the institute bomb shelters read aloud the reissued antifascist pamphlets and books.

I visited a hospital and was amazed at the almost complete absence of heavily wounded soldiers. I asked one of the soldiers the reason for this.

"There are many wounded, my dear girl," he replied, "and there are many who are badly wounded. But no one carries them off the battlefield. They say that the Germans finish them off. Here you will find only those who had enough strength to crawl away on their own, or who were helped by their friends."

The army units passing through town appeared more and more disorganized. Officers went around in open coats, with vodka bottles showing from their pockets. People whispered stories that there were not enough bullets at the front, that wrong caliber ammunition was delivered to the cannons and sometimes none at all was delivered, that teen-agers were sent to the fronts —so-called "volunteer inductees," who had just been taken into the army and were still without any training.

148

How could all this be? each of us wondered. "For twenty-five years we prepared for foreign attack, twenty-five years we economized, worked day and night, got almost nothing in return, suffered privations, went around in poor clothes and torn shoes—and believed that everything we earned went for defense. Now it seems that we had been living on lies."

Two or three times daily air alarms were sounded. Antiaircraft artillery fired vigorously and many air-raid wardens were injured by falling shrapnel. But German planes did not appear until a month before the city was occupied. Then a rain of bombs descended on the city before the alert was even sounded. More and more raids came every day. Finally, evacuation of the city was announced, but there were very few trains and only a small portion of the population could leave.

Before leaving, the director and the secretary of the Party organization spent several days destroying the equipment at the institute. Expensive glassware, the finest analytical scales, valuable precision machines, of which all members of our institute, one of the oldest and best equipped in the Ukraine, were so proud—all this was thrown on the floor, shattered and destroyed beyond usefulness. In front of the library a fire burned for twenty-four hours. It was fed by textbooks, scientific monographs, dictionaries, and other scientific literature. Members of the institute who were remaining behind pleaded in vain to be given the books for safekeeping, promising to return them as soon as the Red Army returned. The books continued to fly into the fire.

For three days before occupation the city was continuously shaken by explosions—bridges, electric generating plants, the water supply system, and railroads were being blown up. For three nights the sky was illuminated by fires set to all public buildings, hotels, hospitals, etc.

On Sunday morning we looked out of the window. Across the street, carrying submachine guns, Germans were carefully advancing, hugging the buildings along the street.

"Lida," my aunt turned to me, "remember forever what I tell you: I have seen much during my life, I know Russian history and world history well. Believe me, no matter how victorious the Germans may seem as they enter, they will inevitably go back. There has never been an army that could take Russia by force."

With the coming of the Germans a terrible winter began. Kharkov, a city of almost a million inhabitants, was left without light, without water, without fuel, and without bread. The corpses of those who died of starvation were taken to the cemetery and stacked like wood.

The healthier and stronger of the people went out of the city to find food in the more distant villages. Once, returning with a rucksack of frozen potatoes and beets, I stopped to spend the night with our former maid Marusya. It was late when the men returned from the fields.

We sat down for dinner.

"No bread today," said the old peasant woman who had prepared the food. She quietly added: "The Germans were taking prisoners through here, so we gave them all we could. Maybe someone will give my sons something one day."

"We have no luck at all," said one of the peasants. "The Soviets were here—things were bad, the Germans came—things are even worse. Where is our fate?"

Having become acquainted with the German "liberation," the weary people greedily listened to the words of Soviet propaganda coming over the radio.

"Dear brothers and sisters, toiling under the hated yoke of the fascist usurpers . . ." thus the announcers now addressed the people.

Rumors flew thick and fast: the Soviet regime has changed, people are not taken to court any more for being late to work, the NKVD is subdued, religion is not persecuted, etc. Rumors of German reverses at Stalingrad passed from person to person

150

with the hope of imminent liberation and the coming of the new, free, and democratic Soviet regime.

Once again the city burned, this time ignited by the Nazi SS. Day and night along the main roads leading east and south, German artillery, tanks, and infantry were withdrawing. At dawn one cold February morning in 1943 Soviet troops re-entered the city. They came on foot and by horse-drawn sled. They came in worn-out coats and patched felt boots.

From the stories of the soldiers, we knew that no change had taken place within the Soviet Union. Soon after the front-line troops, the Party organization and the NKVD also came. Denunciations and interrogations commenced. The regular soldiers behaved very well and sympathetically toward the populace, but the representatives of the government seemed to act on the assumption that people who had survived under the German occupation were not full-fledged Soviet citizens any more.

March 8th is "Women's Day." At a triumphal celebration in the miraculously preserved opera house, the writers Vanda Vassilevska and Korneychuk, as well as Khrushchev, the secretary of the Communist party of the Ukraine, appeared. All of them assured the people that the city would remain in Soviet hands.

But on the next day the Red Army suddenly abandoned the town. The wounded in hospitals were left without food and medical supplies. Only a few soldiers remained—those who were to engage the Germans in street skirmishes.

Mother and I were returning from my aunt's house. We were terrified by the constant whine and thunder of artillery shells. An old Russian soldier, with a tired, emaciated face, approached us.

"Why are you women out here?" he asked. "It is dangerous. You may be hit. Go, hide in a basement."

"And why don't you hide? You are also a human being and you could also be killed."

"Then it would be my fate to die," he calmly answered my

mother. "But why should you die, since you can live. Go, go to a basement." And with a slow, tired gait, limping a little, he went down the street, holding the rifle like a thing that was of no use to him.

A little farther on, we heard the roar of approaching bombers and ran into the nearest shelter. There were many people in it, including some high Party officials who had not left yet.

"Comrade Nazarenko," a voice asked in the darkness, "why is it that only two days ago we were celebrating our victory, and today the situation is hopeless?"

"The situation was hopeless eight days ago, but you didn't know about it."

"Then why didn't you tell us? So many thousands of people would have had a chance to leave the city. Now you will go away, and when you return again you will accuse us of remaining a second time to help the Germans."

"We don't care what you do," the Party leader announced. "All the advice we had we gave in 1941. Now do what you wish."

After a while things quieted down outside and we went home.

Again SS troops entered the city. Enraged by the savage street fights, they burned down hospitals, shooting at the windows so the wounded couldn't escape. They tore into homes, killing any man on sight.

Another week passed. Soviet troops again approached Kharkov.

A dilemma faced me: to remain under the Soviets or to go with the Germans.

All night long I debated the question. I did not want to abandon my home and tear myself away from my people. I feared the prospect of going out alone, without friends, into the large, cold, and strange world. I remembered the stories I had heard of the hopelessness of an emigrant's life.

No. I won't go, I decided.

But then I imagined what would happen if I did stay: the quaking at every stop of the trolley, the constant fear of coming late to work; seeing around me the unhappy, scared, hungry people and not being able to help them; primarily, the constant lying, the necessity of showing tremendous enthusiasm at the "wisdom and big-heartedness" of the leaders and the laws issued by the government. Many such thoughts went through my mind, and I decided:

No. I shall go.

When I saw the empty streets of the city the next morning, when I found that most of my friends had already left or were in the process of leaving, I felt that my decision to leave the Soviet Union could not be wrong.

"Fräulein Lidia," the German living next door to us called to me, "I must congratulate you: we are withdrawing, and you will soon be rid of us and will see your friends again."

"I am not staying," I told him, quickly turning away so he would not see the tears in my eyes. He was perplexed. But how could anyone understand the tragedy of people who are forced to flee "their own" with the hated enemy!

The next day I stood at the window of the train carrying me away from Kharkov. Through tearful eyes, I looked out at the endless fields of sunflowers as we passed by. The day was bright, not a cloud in the sky. Everything breathed of quiet and peace. It seemed as if nature was not concerned with the tears and moaning of millions of people suffering and dying this minute.

"Do you think you will ever return?" someone interrupted my thoughts.

"Yes," I firmly replied, "the day will come."

Yes, I will return, I said to myself, turning again to the window in order to imprint on my memory, for years if necessary, the picture of the country which is my home.

9

A CLOSE-UP OF THE SOVIET SYSTEM

by Paul Seversky

In the beginning of 1934, before I had completed my studies at the Veterinary Institute in Kiev, I was called into the army. After brief training my unit was shipped to the Far East. At that time Soviet diplomatic relations with Japan were strained. All of us thought we were being sent to reinforce regular garrisons of the Red Army.

After two months of travel by rail and steamer, we reached our destination. Our job was the construction of fortifications in one of the militarized sectors of the Far Eastern shore, opposite Sakhalin Island.

The population in this area was scattered through the wilderness. A few Russians, some Chinese and Koreans, and various mixed tribes inhabited the area. All of them were either hunters or fishermen.

We were quartered in barracks that had been occupied by workers recruited for military construction. Although they had worked only nine months of the year they had signed up for, they were scheduled to leave on the ship that had brought us.

154

The men whom we saw when we docked were walking skeletons. Fifty per cent looked to be in an advanced stage of scurvy. Some could no longer move. They lay in pain, with joints swollen, and blue spots on their chests, arms, and legs; blood ran from their mouths; their teeth had fallen out and the gums were rotting. Men in this condition were quickly put on stretchers and carried aboard ship to prevent our Red Army soldiers from seeing them.

I was able to talk with one of them.

"Have you been sick long?"

"Two months." ..

"Were you being treated?"

"Some treatment! They told us to eat more onions, but wouldn't give us any. It's lucky for us that you came so we can get out of here!"

"What were you fed?"

"Three times a day we were given soup with dried vegetables and bread. Once a week canned meat."

"Did you have a dispensary?"

"Sure, but there was no medicine for scurvy, and there was no doctor, just a medical attendant."

I asked if anyone had died from scruvy.

"Oh, yes. In eight months there were thirty-one deaths."

After two months the first signs of scurvy appeared in our unit. Thanks to prompt measures we were able to control its spread. Nature supplied us with remedies—the wild onion and ramson which grew in the forest.

Our main assignment was to establish coast artillery batteries. This involved dangerous demolition and concrete work. There were many casualties.

One day a friend, the commander of the 4th Company, came into the newly built dispensary where I worked. He looked worried and I asked him what the trouble was.

155

"Just now two of my men working on the demolition squad were blown to bits," he said. "I reported the accident to the commissar and proposed that a full military funeral be given them. I also suggested taking up a collection for their families."

"Good idea," I commented.

"It was," he said bitterly. "But the commissar forbade any kind of public funeral. Furthermore, to avoid any unpleasantness, their deaths are to be announced by the hospital: 'one died from appendicitis, the other from cancer.'"

"Why, that's foul!"

"Worse, it's inhuman . . . but I have to follow orders," came the reply.

During the fifteen months that I spent in the region many other families received similar notifications: "drowned in the sea while bathing" or "lost in the forest while skiing."

I clearly remember one of the accidents that necessitated such a notice:

In order to cement in the guns, a tremendous wooden platform with about fifty hatches was built. Concrete was poured into the openings from wheelbarrows carrying concrete from twenty-five cement mixers. At the bottom of a seventy-five-foot pit, under the platform, soldiers distributed the steady flow of concrete.

During the three or four days on which concrete was being poured, all military units were called in to help. Two bands played. But the music didn't help, everyone was tense. Furthermore, because of the noise of the cement mixers, the wheelbarrows, and the pouring of concrete, not a note could be heard.

On the morning of the second day, we noticed some confusion near several hatches. I heard a shout:

"Five men! Down . . . hurry! Spread the concrete! Hurry or you'll be shot!" It was a commissar thundering at the reserve concrete men. At that moment two engineers ran up.

"What happened, Comrade Commissar?"

"Nothing, it's all right now. Those bastards down below were asleep. . . . Well, sleep! . . . Over here! Pour it in here—hatch ten, twelve! More . . ."

Afterward we found out what had happened.

In one place concrete was poured down on a worker. He didn't have time to pull the rope, to close the trap door. . . . He was crushed. . . . The concrete kept pouring down. . . . Two neighbors crawled over. They wanted at least to drag out their comrade's corpse. In the excitement they forgot to close their trap doors. . . . They were also covered with concrete. The commissar saw all this, but did not halt the work for a minute.

After several days, notices went out to the families: "they were out riding in a boat and capsized—all drowned." According to Soviet law, under such circumstances of death the families are not entitled to any monetary assistance. Above all—the military secret was preserved!

During the summer several high-ranking Red Army leaders unexpectedly flew in from Moscow and Vladivostok. Among them were Marshal Tukhachevsky, Marshal Yegorov, Marshal Gamarnik, and Marshal Blucher. The purpose of their visit was to review the garrison's artillery practice and examine the fortification of the district.

They went into every barracks, visited the officers' quarters, the hospital, kitchens, shops, etc. All of them were sympathetic and friendly, but Tukhachevsky and Blucher were the most popular among the men.

Once Tukhachevsky came upon a group of us who were taking a break from work. As he approached, everyone snapped to attention.

"That's all right, I am here just as an old comrade," Tukhachevsky said. Then he shook hands all around and asked: "Where are you fellows from?"

We were all from the Ukraine, and in a chorus named the major cities of the Ukraine.

"How's the work, pretty hard?" he asked.

"Oh, we work all right, but it's not so bad," one of the engineers replied. "Only occasionally we'd like a day's rest, maybe a couple of drinks, but we don't have any vodka."

Tukhachevsky smiled.

"I like your frankness. It's a justifiable complaint. But you know as well as I that vodka is prohibited here. I promise to send you some wine though."

(In a month we actually received forty caskets of wine from Vladivostok.)

On another occasion I rode in the same truck with Gamarnik. He sat in the cab with the driver. On the road we overtook two soldiers. Gamarnik stopped the vehicle.

"Where are you going? Can we give you a ride?" he called out.

The men just stood there overcome by such an easy approach.

"Yes . . . we . . . well, yes, we are going this way."

"Climb up then!" Gamarnik laughed.

When we reached our destination and Gamarnik had left us, I asked the driver: "What did you two talk about?"

"What a man! What a heart!" the driver exclaimed. "He asked about my home—whether I had a wife, children. I told him I was from Varvarovka in the Ukraine, was married and had three children. 'Do you belong to a collective?' he asked. I hesitated and then told him the truth—'no.' He asked what they wrote from home. It's neither good nor bad, I told him. My wife writes that if I don't send her one hundred rubles for the tax they'll take our cow, but I only have fifty. 'Here, take fifty rubles as a present from me and send them to your wife,' Garmarnik said. What a man!"

In April 1935, I was discharged from the army and went home to finish my veterinary course. Upon graduation, I worked as a veterinary, a sanitation expert, and as bacteriologist in laboratories and veterinary centers in different parts of the Ukraine.

In 1936, with a group of other veterinaries and bacteriologists, I was appointed to work in a brigade attempting to control "infectious anemia," a dangerous contagious disease that had appeared among horses in the Ukraine. "Infectious anemia" is a disease of the blood. The afflicted horse breaks out in a fever that recurs every few weeks. There is a weight loss and, afterward, a breakdown of heart functioning. Finally emaciation and death. No method of curing the disease has been found. The more seriously affected horses are destroyed; the others are isolated. That was the procedure in all countries.

Our brigade used these methods. Over a three-month period between two and three hundred horses were shot in the district where we operated. Finally the disease was almost completely wiped out, and we returned to our homes.

Suddenly, a month later, nearly all members of the brigade were arrested. Only three escaped arrest; I was one of them. To this day I cannot explain why I was spared.

Sometime later the local paper carried the headline: SUBVERSIVE ACTIVITIES OF VETERINARY WORKERS. Below were these words:

The doctors of the people, veterinaries and their assistants, by order of the counterespionage of a foreign power, infected horses with "infectious anemia" in order to undermine agriculture and weaken the power of the Red Army. The investigation has been completed. The trial will begin in a few days.

The trial, when it started, was secret, but the daily results were carried by the press and radio. The newspapers, naturally, demanded the highest punishment—"death to the enemies of the people." The questioning of veterinarian K., the head of the brigade and a Party member, was transmitted over the radio:

"Accused K., do you admit your guilt?"

"Yes." The reply came without hesitation.

"Did you infect the horses on your own or by order of a foreign power?"

Again he replied quickly: "We infected the horses by order of

159

a foreign agent in order to damage agriculture and the Red Army in the Ukraine."

"Were you recruited by this agent or by someone else?"

"I was recruited by the agent."

"By what means did you bring the other accused into your subversive activities?"

"I gave them large sums of money . . . and assured them that it was necessary for the liberation of the Ukraine from the Bolsheviks."

My wife and I wondered what torture must have forced these innocent people to utter such lies and repeat self-incriminating statements.

The sentences were severe: execution for all seventeen.

Two days after they were announced, I read in the paper:

The sentence against the subversive organization of veterinarians has been carried out.

Three years later, however, we discovered that no one had been shot. Instead they were taken to an isolated region in Central Asia. A shortage of veterinaries existed in that area, and nobody would go there voluntarily. The families were permitted to carry on a limited correspondence (one letter a year) with the prisoners.

In 1938 I was sent to a large collective in the Ananyevsky district to investigate the alarming death rate among calves and pigs.

Arriving in the district, I presented myself to the local "authority," the director of the agricultural department, who took me to the chairman of the District Executive Committee.

"Comrade Kuzin, here is the regional veterinary who is to investigate the 'Zarya Kommunisma' collective*."

"Ah, that's good. You'll be able to help. Our veterinary is a funny one . . . maybe even a saboteur."

* 'Dawn of Communism'—tr.

160

On the way out to the collective I was able to question the district veterinarian.

"Colleague, how many calves and pigs died this year?"

He shrugged his shoulders hopelessly.

"The situation is very bad. Out of 150 calves, ninety-five died. Out of three hundred pigs born, only sixty remain. Why? You will see for yourself. The quarters are crowded, damp. The care is poor. It is natural that intestinal disorders and dysentery appeared, and under the existing conditions it is impossible to eliminate them."

"Have you written to the government representatives?"

"I will show you my letters. . . . I used up stacks of paper."

"What kind of replies did you receive?"

"They said that I should exercise more 'vigilance.' They've put off constructing new quarters for two years—always waiting for lumber. The old piggery was meant for ten pigs, but forty are kept there. The same is true with the calves. And everywhere, even in the pigsty, there are posters: CATCH UP TO AND SURPASS THE CAPITALIST COUNTRIES IN LIVESTOCK RAISING."

We approached the collective. At the entrance was a freshly painted sign: ZARYA KOMMUNISMA. In the center of the village was a new building with a tile roof. The sign over the door read: ADMINISTRATION.

Two men came out of the building and turned toward us. They were the collective chairman and a member of the management committee. I explained the purpose of my visit. I desperately wanted to rid myself of the representatives of the collective, otherwise the people wouldn't talk openly. I turned to the chairman.

"Do you wish to accompany us?"

"Yes . . . yes."

"All right, we will meet you at 2:00 P.M. at the calfhouse. In the meantime I must go to the veterinary dispensary."

Alone now, we drove immediately to the piggery. As my colleague had told me, the building was old, crowded, dark, low, and damp. The troughs were dirty, the aisles wet. Flies covered everything. There was a penetrating odor of urine. The pigs were thin, some coughed.

We approached one of the women at work.

"Auntie Motrya, don't be afraid of him, he is our regional veterinary," my colleague told her.

"Oh, how can doctors help!" she blurted out. "If they'd only finish the new pigsty. . . . Come into the orderly room, doctor. Over here. . . ."

I began questioning the woman.

"Why do you think so many animals die?"

"Can't you see for yourself? We need a decent building before we can raise pigs. But there is something else. . . ."

"What do you mean?" I prompted.

"Well, you work and work, but there is no order. Sometimes I feel like throwing up my hands and walking out. You just don't get anywhere. I suggested selling half of the litters to the collective members, to let them raise the pigs. But no—that's 'robbing the government.' What happens? The pigs die and no one benefits. Take another case . . . the cucumbers, watermelons, cantaloupes, and tomatoes ripened. For a whole month they wouldn't turn the stuff over to the collective peasants—they were 'waiting for an order from the district—the government has first choice.' The produce overripened, began to rot. Finally an order came through. Everything was taken down to the station, but the food inspectors wouldn't pass it, not that I can blame them. Then we were given the rotten leftovers. . . . That's the kind of organization we have."

In May 1941, I was ordered to Moscow for a three-month requalification course at the military academy. Our group included about one hundred doctors.

A Comintern* representative addressed one of our meetings.

* Communist International or Third International, now called the Cominform. Its purpose is to foster world revolution under Moscow's orders.

He discussed the world situation and the diplomatic relations between the Soviet and other governments. However, his talk was concerned principally with our main enemy—Germany. I remember a few of his statements very well.

"Don't let it seem to you that we signed a treaty with Germany in order to help her. This was a marriage of convenience and not love."

His conclusion was especially impressive:

"Enough of peace policies, enough waiting! The hour has come when we must stand up and free the workers of the world from the chains of capitalism. That is our historic role. . . . We have finished singing 'our armored train stands on a siding.' No! The train is ready and under steam! The engineer is only waiting the signal!"

The same day I wrote my wife: "Darling, I will probably not return home after finishing at the academy. There are large-scale maneuvers ahead. . . ."

On June 22nd war broke out; the Nazis attacked Russia.

There was a general mobilization and all doctors had to report to previously assigned military units. Since my veterinary hospital was being activated in my home town, I got another chance to see my family.

Arrival at home, getting ready, farewells—in three days we were moving out again. I had been designated assistant commander of the hospital.

Our unit was sent directly to the front; there it was quickly smashed.

I was taken prisoner. . . . The German soldiers helped themselves to everything we had—watches, Soviet money, and other 'souvenirs.' They treated the prisoners abominably. While the NKVD tortured and shot people secretly, the Germans bragged about it. Their arrogant behavior provoked our fiercest hatred. After a few months only five thousand out of forty thousand prisoners survived.

Due to the great shortage of medical men in German-occupied Ukraine, several of us doctors were miraculously freed.

I worked as a veterinary until the fall of 1943, when the German troops began retreating. As they retreated, they took people for forced labor in Germany. I was caught in one of the conscription raids.

I was sent to work in a bacteriological institute in Berlin. There I washed laboratory apparatus. During an Allied raid the building burned down, and I was transferred to a small town in Bavaria. There I spent the rest of the war, and there I still live.

I decided to stay after I had tasted life abroad. I feel a stranger here. But material conditions are better, and there is much less tension. I did not want to go back into the tension and strain of Soviet life.

10

IN THE NAZI RING

by Alexander Pokrovsky

I was born and raised under the Soviet regime, and before the Second World War knew nothing about any other way of life. Both my father and grandfather were scientists and both were outstanding men. My father was a person completely divorced from life, giving everything he had to scientific labors. Politics had no meaning for him.

When I was born, my father was still a student. We lived in Leningrad, in the home of a former "bourgeois" family. There were carpets on the stairs. The former owner, a woman, occupied two of the five well-furnished rooms. We lived in the other three. We paid no rent for the first years after the 1917 Revolution, and lived on a government stipend which my father received as a student.

Upon finishing his course in 1924, my father took a job near Moscow.

This was during the period of the NEP, when the government permitted private initiative with limited private ownership of property. The Soviets also began to attract foreign participation in our industries. The results were amazing. In a short period normal life returned to the country, stores were literally filled with goods, and people began to live fairly well.

Father, as a young engineer, received a salary of 280 rubles a month, seventy-five of which were deducted for rent, electricity, and heating. On the remaining amount we could live quite decently. My mother tells me that at that time a cow cost around fifty rubles, a good man's suit was about the same price, and a loaf of white bread was half a ruble.

In the fall of 1927 father received a position in Leningrad and we moved there, renting two furnished rooms.

Nineteen hundred twenty-eight marked the end of the NEP and the beginning of the attack on private trade, as well as a fight against foreign capital. The favorite method used to rid the country of foreigners and their investments was to accuse them of espionage. To increase the plausibility of such accusations, scapegoats were selected among Soviet specialists and these were accused of collaboration with the foreign agents. By this method a number of foreign firms were closed. Among them were Faber, manufacturers of office supplies, and Chlorodont, which produced toothpaste and tooth powder.

My father became a victim in one of these anti-foreign campaigns.

Late one night in May 1928, our bell rang and a GPU agent appeared on the doorstep. He showed my father a warrant for his arrest and a search warrant. However, he did not search our apartment, and in general was very courteous.

"Tell me what this is all about. What am I accused of?" father asked.

"Please don't worry," the GPU man answered quickly. "You are being summoned only as a witness. But since all this may take several days, I would advise you to take along some underwear and things you might need."

Father was taken away.

I was still too young to understand what had happened, but a few days later when I saw my mother in tears, I gathered that

166

something unpleasant had occurred. Not only was Father called as a witness, but also he was charged with espionage and sabotage.

Weeks went by. Mama had no time to look after me and there was no money to pay for the apartment. She sent me to my grandmother in Moscow, and she moved in with some distant relatives.

After eighteen months of investigation, Father was brought before the court. The case was a loud one because of the well-known firm involved. The trial was not only talked and written about in the USSR, but also in other countries, and a large number of foreigners and foreign correspondents attended the trial. My father's trial lasted several days, but no guilt could be shown, and the case was postponed for further investigation. However, it never returned to a major court, and eventually my father and several others were sentenced to ten years' exile by the three-man secret tribunal of the GPU.

How the family of a political exile lives in the Soviet Union is well known. All, even the closest friends, abandon the family. Even the relative with whom Mama lived told her:

"You know, Olechka, I love you very much, but you must understand that for you to continue to stay here is out of the question. It could bring only unpleasant results to us, and would spoil my children's future."

On top of everything else, my grandmother died, and Mama had to take me back from Moscow. An accidental meeting resolved the difficulties. At this crucial time Mama met our former landlady with whom we had lived during Father's student days. Tears came to her eyes when she heard about our plight.

"I'm sorry that I can't offer you much," she said, "because I only have one room left, and they want to take even that away from me—they say it's too large for one person. If you want to come and join me there, you are very welcome."

Mama gladly accepted the invitation, and we settled with Marya Nikolayevna in one room, divided by means of a curtain.

167

A Soviet statute allowed each individual one hundred square feet of living space. Marya Nikolayevna had almost three hundred square feet; she took us in out of pity, but also because sooner or later she would have been evicted or have two strangers quartered in her room.

The change which had taken place in the apartment during the six years was amazing. Twenty-three people now lived in the five rooms, and because no decent corridor existed, two of these rooms were used as access to other rooms. The inconvenience was terrible. Nine people lived in what had been a dining room. In one corner was a homemade wooden bed on which a whole family slept—father, mother, and three children. In another corner, also in one bed, slept a father, mother, and their ten-year-old daughter. A young man had another corner of the same room. It was like a gypsy camp. Bright materials were used to curtain off all the beds. Aside from the three beds, the furniture consisted of a table, bench, and two stools. There was no wardrobe or bureau. Similar conditions existed in the other rooms. All these people were peasants who had abandoned their property in fear of collectivization, and had become workers in the city.

The kitchen was a noisy place with seven primus stoves hissing away and seven housewives running around. All had to prepare meals there. Fighting over every inch of space, quarrels, misunderstandings, pouring kerosine in someone else's soup or throwing salt in the neighbor's pudding, cursing, and sometimes even fights—these were everyday occurrences. We, as the family of a "traitor," were singled out for special persecution by the other occupants of the apartment.

Despite such difficulties, our most serious problem, the housing problem, was solved. Though we didn't have a room to ourselves, it was better than nothing. But there was still another worry—Mama had to find work. The chances were not good. In those days jobs were scarce, and the official employment office was besieged by crowds of people looking for work. But Mama also went.

"What kind of work are you looking for?" the interviewer asked.

"I would like to work as a secretary or a machinist," Mama replied.

"What is your marital status?"

"Married."

"Then your husband should work. At the present time we can't give work to two members of one family."

"But my husband is in exile."

"Under what statute?"

"Fifty-eight."

"Oh, fifty-eight. That's the counterrevolution section, and you want a job! We have nothing for such as you. We take care of honest Soviet citizens."

"Then according to you, my child and I should die of hunger and . . ."

"That doesn't concern me. This is an employment office, not a social welfare agency."

"But I want work, not a handout!"

"Enough! We have nothing to discuss. There is no place for such as you in this country. Next!"

The conversation was over. With tears in her eyes, Mama walked away from the window and came home. Further attempts to find any means of earning a living were without success. Finally an acquaintance advised her:

"You'd better get a divorce, then you could get something."

"But what will my husband think of me?" Mama retorted.

"He will understand that this is necessary."

"And his relatives?"

"Let them talk all they want. What is more important to you—someone's gossip or your child's life?"

Mama hesitated for a long time, but there was no other way out, and she applied for a divorce. As her reason she stated that

169

she "didn't want to be the wife of a traitor of the fatherland." The divorce was granted.

Afterward Mama was able to find a job as a cleaning woman. Her pay was seventy rubles a month, ten of which were withheld for taxes. But even the sixty rubles which she actually received were a godsend and we were able to exist on that amount.

On every possible occasion Mama and Father continued to correspond with each other. At first Father was in Karelia, near Finland. Then he was sent to work in the mines, and we began to receive regular monthly letters from him.

After a while Mama transferred to a job as a messenger at ninety rubles a month, and later was made secretary in an office. After work, Mama, like all other working women in the Soviet Union, spent many hours standing in lines to buy food for us. I was left to myself most of the day. After school I ran around the streets, played and fought with other boys.

In 1933 so-called "passportization" began, and every man and woman was issued a new passport. In Leningrad, officials found this law a means of ridding the city of "unreliable elements." Primarily this meant families of political exiles or those who could not give proof of their "proletarian origin." All was done without sentimentality. The victims were called to the police, where their old passports were taken away. They were given a paper stating that the individual had to leave Leningrad within ten days and could only settle outside a sixty-five-mile radius of the six major cities of the country.

If the individual did not leave within the specified time, all his possessions were confiscated and he was deported on the first train leaving the city, regardless of its destination.

Naturally, passportization overtook us. I well remember the cold January day when I returned from school and found a police notice addressed to Mama. Three or four days before that I had had a fight with a boy in the block and had knocked out one of his teeth. The boy's father was a Party member, and the

170

kid threatened to have me prosecuted. Seeing the police notice, I immediately thought of my misdemeanor and hurriedly disappeared from home. I stayed at a friend's house until nine. When I finally returned home, contrary to all expectations, Mama paid no attention to my arrival. She was sitting in a chair with her hands over her face and crying. I kissed her. She wiped off her tears, and addressed me like a grownup:

"I was at the police today. They took away my passport and gave me this paper." She handed me a small slip of paper. "It says that we have to leave Leningrad within ten days." And she explained it to me in detail.

The next days were hectic. From morning till night Mama ran from one official to another. After much pleading and on the basis of her divorce, she was granted a postponement of three months. Later we obtained permission to remain in Leningrad.

Life was incredibly difficult. My mother's salary was just sufficient to keep us from starving. The government had first issued ration coupons for food and manufactured goods in 1919. In the beginning one actually received something, but around 1932-1933 the rations became very small. It is true that no one was dying in our city, but we were in a continuous state of semi-starvation. Anything available was of the lowest quality and very expensive.

About this time, as a result of the government's desire to increase its reserves of foreign exchange, a special type of store, "Torgsin," was opened. In these stores, in exchange for foreign currency or gold, one could obtain any amount of food without ration coupons. Numerous collecting stations were established which issued tokens, called "bons," good in any Torgsin. A gold pince-nez, for instance, brought 4.50 bons, which was enough to buy eighteen pounds of butter. Subsequently the number of such stores increased, and even manufactured goods were sold there. Purchases could be made in exchange for silver and precious stones, as well as gold and foreign currency. Mama bought some things in Torgsin by selling an old piece of jewelry.

In the spring of 1934, Father returned from exile. His sentence had been reduced from ten to six years. How he had changed in those six years! He was only thirty-eight years old, but looked like an old man. His face was ashen, his hair had turned white, he had almost no teeth left, he was deaf in one ear, and had a sick heart and stomach. Still, he had returned, and that was the main thing. Two of his friends who had also been convicted to ten years had died in exile. Father never, not even in the most intimate circles, wanted to talk about the years of his internment.

Upon his return, Father immediately went back to his technical work. Despite all his labor, however, he was made to feel that he was a "former traitor."

We lived modestly in our one room, keeping to ourselves, and trying to stay out of everyone's way as much as possible. However, Father's accomplishments made this difficult. His work attracted the attention of scientific circles; soon his name began to be mentioned in technical journals. He even received several rewards for his excellent work.

In 1936, after great difficulties, we were able to obtain new living quarters. Though it still was only one room, it was somewhat larger than the old one and, what is most important, we shared the apartment with only one other family.

But this peaceful life did not last long. The terrible years, 1937 and 1938, came. A wave of arrests spread over the country. The terror surged all around us. Those arrested were not the only victims. A classmate of mine shot himself when he heard of the execution of his father, a high-ranking naval officer. Our history teacher went out of her mind after her husband's arrest and was sent to a psychiatric hospital.

Father said: "All citizens in the Soviet Union fall into three categories: those who have been imprisoned, those who are imprisoned, and those who will be imprisoned. And the first category is equivalent to the third."

Father was right.

172

At one-thirty one night our bell rang. Mama went to open the door.

"Who is it?" she asked.

"Open up!" Mama immediately understood.

Two NKVD policemen and an NKVD soldier, with rifle and bayonet, entered. Papa already was getting dressed. I was awakened and told to get my clothes on. The soldier with the rifle posted himself by the door, while the policemen, having seated us, began questioning Father.

"Name? Year born? Place born? Profession? . . ."

After this, one of them announced:

"We have to search your room."

"And arrest me?" Father asked.

"We'll see about that later," was the noncommittal reply.

The NKVD men turned all drawers and closets inside out, while we sat under the soldier's eyes. They began with Papa's desk, from which they shortly extracted a folder with sketches and diagrams.

"What is all this?" one of them asked, excited by their find.

"They are plans relating to my work," Father answered.

"Then why are they here and not in your office?"

"Because I usually work at home in the evening."

Gradually the whole content of the desk was spread on the floor. Then they turned to the bookcase. This was cleaned out. Among other things they found a photo of an uncle in Czarist uniform; a slip of paper with the phone numbers of my school friends; and my father's diploma from high school. He had finished school in 1913, the year of the three-hundredth anniversary of the reign of the Romanovs, and therefore the diploma included portraits of the first and last czars of that dynasty. The NKVD men, however, decided that they had found proof of anti-Soviet sympathies.

"Are you a monarchist?" they asked. "Why do you keep portraits of the czars?"

173

"This is just a document certifying my completion of high school."

"We know those excuses," one of them growled, "haven't you got enough Soviet documents?"

Finally the search was completed. They took the picture, the paper with the phone numbers and Father's diploma. Then Father was given a form:

"Here is a warrant for the search and your arrest. Read it. Certify that nothing unnecessary was taken, and then let's go."

Mama quickly packed a small suitcase, and Father left with the NKVD men.

"Where are you taking him?" Mama shouted after them.

"Where he belongs!" was the reply.

I ran out on the stairs to see Father once more. He turned around and said:

"Take care of Mama."

He was taken away. Where to and what for? From that day Father disappeared from our life. Neither Mama nor I ever saw him again.

It was practically impossible for anyone to find out where their relatives were held; no information was given out. But it was possible to send money three times a month. If one of the prisons accepted the money—that meant he was there. There were many prisons in Leningrad, and it took a lot of running around to find out where Father was. After four months, when as usual I brought the money to the prison office, I was told:

"He isn't here any more. He was sent to the Far East without correspondence privileges."

Six months after Father's arrest, Mama was called to the police. She was notified that she was being sent into exile to Central Asia. She was given ten days to wind up her affairs. All her attempts at getting permission to stay were unsuccessful this time. She was exiled for five years. But after two years, in 1940, she was released and returned to Leningrad.

They also wanted to send me. I tried unsuccessfully to get an interview with the NKVD official in charge of exile matters. Then I learned his phone number. After my first attempts to reach him were thwarted by his secretary, I used a ruse. I said that I was Comrade K.'s nephew and wished to speak with him on a private matter.

Finally I heard his hoarse voice on the phone:

"Hello! Is this you, Vasya?"

"No, this isn't Vasya. My name is Alexander Pokrovsky."

"And what are you bothering me for?" he asked in a highly unfriendly tone.

"My name is Pokrovsky," I repeated quickly, "my mother received an order to go to Central Asia and the local police officer wants to force me to go with her. I am seventeen years old, in my last year in high school. I plan to enter a university next year. I plead with you, Comrade K., permit me to remain in Leningrad to continue my education!"

"Who was arrested in your family?" he asked.

"My father."

"If it's your father, there is nothing to discuss, you have to go with your mother."

"Do you know what Comrade Stalin said?" I insisted, "that the son is not responsible for his father."

"You are just a little fool—trying to teach me! But if you want to quote Stalin, then you should know that he made the statement in connection with a kulak's son, not the son of a traitor."

Angrily, K. slammed down the receiver. Without losing any time, and not giving him a chance to compose himself, I called again. I told the secretary that the conversation with my uncle had been cut off. Again I heard the hoarse voice:

"Hello! Who is speaking?"

"We didn't finish our conversation," I told him.

Apparently he completely lost his temper.

"If you don't quit bothering me this minute, I will see to it that you are taken care of!" he yelled into the phone.

175

I did not dare contact him again. I tried something else—I wrote a letter to Zhdanov, a top Communist. Time was running out, but no reply came. Finally, two days before we were to leave, the police notified Mama that I could stay in Leningrad. I was never able to find out what had been responsible for my staying: the quotation from Stalin, the letter to Zhdanov, or just a lucky break.

After Mama left, I was faced with the problem of finding a place to live. However, our widowed neighbor, whose husband had died around the time of my father's arrest, took me in.

I was in my last year at high school. Everywhere I was asked why my father was arrested. What could I say? To reply that it had been without any cause was impossible: it would have been construed as an insult to Soviet "justice" and could have very sad consequences. All I could do was try to evade the question. When this was impossible, I just said: "I don't know, they didn't tell me. Ask the NKVD if you have to know."

Mother worked during her exile in Central Asia, and was able to send me small amounts of money. I also earned a little. I was a sailing instructor, fixed doorbells, laid electric wires, and did other small jobs.

I wanted to continue my education after high school. But for a son of an "enemy of the people," the son of a "traitor," this wasn't easy. My deepest desire was to study navigation and become an officer on an ocean-going vessel. I didn't even dare show myself at the naval institute. I attempted to enroll in a railroad engineering course; I was rejected. The same happened when I applied to the electro-technical institute. I found that the only institutes where I stood a chance of being accepted were the agricultural, dairy husbandry, forestry, and medical schools. I decided to become a medical student.

I was accepted, and moved into the institute dormitory. I had a cot in a room with six other freshmen.

176

Studying was difficult. There was a shortage of textbooks. We were lucky when one textbook was available for four to five people. Sometimes one had to do for more than fifteen students.

When I first entered the institute, the overwhelming majority of the students received government stipends. Those who had no other income were able to make ends meet somehow. But in 1940 the general scholarships were rescinded. Only students who obtained a grade of "excellent" in every subject were still given scholarships—the rest had to pay four hundred rubles annually to attend the university. The trouble was that besides the basic courses, everyone had to study the "Principles of Marxism-Leninism," and even the most talented student could not obtain a scholarship if he did not enjoy the favor of the Komsomol organization. Thus the granting of scholarships lay in the hands of the Party leadership.

This decree forced many students to leave the university and caused indignation among students and professors. The new law was in direct opposition to the Constitution, which says, black on white:

Citizens of the USSR have the right to education.
This right is insured by . . . a system of state stipends for the overwhelming majority of students in universities and colleges.*

The class meeting concerning the new decree was the stormiest I ever attended. The auditorium hummed like a beehive, but silence fell when the Komsomol secretary, a recent graduate of the institute, rose on the platform.

"Comrades!" he began, "the law concerning the revocation of state support and the introduction of paid tuition is a crushing blow against all idlers, for whom there is no more room within the walls of institutions of higher learning. . . ."

He called on everyone to raise the quality of his work and show the world the capabilities of Soviet students.

* Article 121, Constitution of the USSR.

177

"That's all right for you to say! You graduated! It doesn't concern you!" yells came from the audience.

". . . in it we see again the care and attention which the Party, the government, and Comrade Stalin personally give to institutions of higher learning!" The noise was increasing. The secretary stopped talking and looked around. Then he walked out, slamming the door.

A deathly silence reigned in the hall. The students began a panicky flight. We were overcome by fear because of the spontaneous outcries that might carry heavy consequences. Everyone tried to get out into the open as fast as possible. It was as though the building was enveloped in flames and the ceiling might cave in any minute.

Two days passed. Students feared to look at each other and tried not to talk about the new law. Several disappeared without trace, but no one asked about them: to show any interest in them would only attract danger. When the director of the institute called a meeting of all students and began to tell with what enthusiasm both students and faculty had greeted the decree of the Party and the government—not one voice sounded in protest. Someone made a motion that we proclaim ourselves in favor of the new decree. A telegram was also sent to "Dear Comrade Stalin" expressing our gratitude and appreciation for his fatherly concern. All motions and resolutions were accepted unanimously.

At first glance, life in the Soviet Union before the war seemed to be improving. Actually it was full of contradictions and difficulties. The price of food and consumer goods had no relationship to the pay of the majority of the people. A cleaning woman, for example, received seventy to one hundred rubles a month, but a pound of black bread cost fifty kopeks, a pound of butter —ten rubles. A young doctor earned 350 rubles a month, while a decent pair of shoes cost 130 to 140 rubles; a suit of average quality was three hundred, and a coat cost four hundred to five

178

hundred rubles. Furthermore, even if the average person had the money, he couldn't buy everything he wanted because many goods were distributed to special stores in which purchase was restricted to a few select—high Party officials or NKVD members.

Those who did not belong to the chosen few had to resort to the black market. The government, while fighting speculators, was the biggest black-marketeer itself. In the prewar years a series of special stores was opened. In them one could buy all the things never seen in regular stores—but at a cost four to five times the price in regular stores. The differential in price was reaped as profit by the government.

In 1940 a series of severe laws was introduced. The worst of these concerned absenteeism or lateness at work. To be absent without a valid excuse (and this meant only a certificate by a special doctor) or to be more than twenty minutes late for work, was considered truancy, and the guilty person immediately had court action brought against him.

The first time a person was less than twenty minutes late he received a reprimand. The second time he was taken to court. The sentence in such cases usually said: "six months at forced labor" or "three months in prison." If sentenced to forced labor, the individual remained working at his regular job, and one-third to one-half his wages were withheld. A conviction of this type also carried with it a loss in seniority. No extenuating circumstances were ever considered by the courts.

This is how we lived until the war.

On June 22, 1941, I rose early. I was twenty years old and felt quite wonderful. I was young, healthy, and in love.

We were still in the middle of our examination period, but I wasn't worried. I had already successfully passed the difficult finals in physiology and biochemistry; now I was preparing for "Principles of Marxism Leninism." The subject was not hard, just very uninteresting. It was a matter of memorizing and being able to repeat whole phrases from statements by Party and government leaders. German was the other examination we still had to take.

My mother had returned from exile. I went to her room to study that day. While I sat over my books, she was busy sewing. Around one o'clock she went out for a walk. A few minutes later I heard her hurried steps on the stairs, and she burst into the room excited and out of breath:

"War!"

I jumped up in disbelief:

"What? With whom? Where?"

She didn't seem sure about anything, but said:

"I think it's with the Germans."

We turned the radio on, but only the music of marches was coming over the air. I ran nextdoor, hoping that Mama had misunderstood something she heard on the street, but the neighbors confirmed the news.

Before 3:00 P.M., the first strict orders were issued over the radio: all radios had to be turned in to the police immediately; it was forbidden to hoard food. The penalty for violators of either provision was death.

"What are you going to do?" Mama asked. "Will I now have to lose my son, after having lost my husband?"

I calmed her as well as I could. Then I proceeded to my dormitory, promising to return later that evening. The dormitory was like a madhouse. Students who had received draft notices were packing their belongings. I found a notice to report immediately to the first-aid station where I had been working lately. I grabbed a piece of bread and went out.

The station was in complete disorder. The whole staff was on hand. By order of the chief doctor we were supposed to be quartered on or near the premises of the station, but no suitable quarters were available. In the meantime all sat around in the dining hall and the squad room. Many doctors, assistants, and drivers had come for their last farewells before leaving for the

180

front. The parting was very touching. People who scarcely knew each other embraced and kissed. Here and there the words: "God be with you" were heard—an expression which was almost never heard in the Soviet Union before this period. The Party leader of the station made a little speech about the holy duty of defending the Soviet fatherland and its leaders.

An old orderly, who had been with the first-aid station for over thirty years, interrupted the speaker:

"Quit throwing fine words around. Give us a chance to part with our comrades in human fashion. Possibly we may never see each other again."

Late in the evening, due to lack of barracks facilities, all those not on duty were permitted to go home.

On the twenty-third, I again reported to the station and was put on twenty-four-hour duty. The main job at this time was to prepare for the first influx of wounded who were expected soon. Many schools were converted for this purpose. An order was also given to clear out all the hospitals in the city. Some hospitals were to be emptied completely, while in others the number of patients was to be reduced to a minimum. All those who were not in critical condition were sent home, as were those whose condition the doctors had given up as hopeless.

Our job was to take the people to their homes. What would happen to them there? Would they have any care at all or would they be abandoned?—no one was interested in that. Patients who could not be sent home, but had to be removed from hospitals designated for complete clearing, were taken to outlying sanatoriums, most of which were not equipped to take care of the type of patients they received.

I worked all day and night without rest, and on the twenty-fourth was told that the lack of medical personnel necessitated my staying on duty another twenty-four hours. Again the whole day was spent in the ambulance, and only at night was I able to grab four hours of sleep.

The same story in the morning: another complete tour of duty.

I went to the head of the station, asking for leave. My final examination was to take place the next day, and I needed some rest before then. But the director said:

"I am sorry, the only thing I can do is let you off in time for your examination tomorrow. I will try to arrange it so that you can sleep a few hours tonight."

On the morning of the twenty-sixth I arrived at the institute. There was no time at all to prepare. Anyway, after three straight tours of duty I was completely worn out and couldn't possibly have studied. All male students in our group had been mobilized, and I was the only one left among twenty-four girls.

Somehow I got through the examination. As soon as I learned I had passed, I rushed out of the room. I had only one desire—to get to a bed and sleep.

The second week of the war was also spent at the first-aid station. There was not much to do once the job of emptying out the hospitals was complete, and since no wounded were arriving yet. But we had to be ready for action at all times.

The one frequent cause for calls was abortion. The difficult life in the Soviet Union forced many people to forego having children. To reverse the decreasing birth rate, the government, in 1936, issued a law prohibiting abortions and providing subsidies to large families. This law actually raised the birth rate of the country, but at the same time it led to innumerable secret abortions, which in turn undermined the women's health and caused many deaths. With the outbreak of war the number of abortions immediately took an upward turn. Women, left without husbands and not knowing what was ahead, used all possible means to interrupt their pregnancies. After the women were taken to a hospital, they were subjected to tough questioning to find out who had performed the abortion. Very few women ever gave this information.

One day I answered a call to a store where a saleswoman had received notice of her small son's death in an air raid. He had

182

been staying with a grandmother in White Russia. Her reaction to the news was violent. She threw herself at people, beating them and calling them traitors.

Another time I had to pick up an army colonel at the airport. His whole family—wife, two children, and mother—had been killed in a raid on their village the very first morning of the war. He was in a state of complete depression, not reacting to anything that went on around him.

Riding about the city in the ambulance every day, one was able to observe the changes. The number of refugees increased as time went on. They were primarily families of army personnel who had been stationed in the Baltic countries, or peasants who had settled on Finnish territory after the war with Finland. They were crowded into schools and other public buildings, where they slept on hay or on the bare floor. Diseases began to spread among these people, especially among the children. Cases of dysentery, measles, and scarlet fever were particularly numerous. Attempts were made to help these people, but owing to lack of organization not much was accomplished.

Stores were being mobbed by people buying all they could, sometimes things for which they had absolutely no use. It took hours of standing in line to get to a movie, and then the show was often interrupted by air-raid alarms. To raise the morale of the people, the government dragged a bunch of old czarist heroes out of the archives and tried to compare this war with the war against Napoleon in 1812, also calling it the "Fatherland War."

All reverses at the front were blamed on spies, traitors, and saboteurs. Quantities of posters, newspaper stories, and radio dispatches on this topic precipitated mass hysteria. Conductors stopped calling out the names of stops and no longer gave information to passengers, in order to make it difficult for spies to orient themselves. A question from a passer-by concerning the location of a street brought a quick "I don't know," or, if the person asked really wanted to show his vigilance, "Who are you?

183

Where are you from? Why do you want to know this?" etc. If, knowing the trend of things, you attempted to show the "watchful citizen" your documents, it made not the slightest impression. He was convinced that any agent would be fortified with all necessary papers.

On July 18th, rationing was imposed on all food and manufactured goods. The quotas under the rationing were larger than the amount we ever used before it was introduced. Now, however, we bought all we could—one never knew what would happen the next day.

On August 4th, school started again at all universities. I began my third year. Our most interesting work was beginning—we had our first contact with patients. After dull class exercises we started to work in clinics. Our studies proceeded normally and our lectures were never even interrupted during air-raid alerts. But it didn't last long. A short time after school started, we were attending a lecture on internal diseases. The professor was just approaching the end of his talk when a letter, with the inscription "urgent" was delivered to him. He gave the messenger a dirty look for interrupting the lecture, but tore the envelope open immediately. The auditorium was silent as we watched him go over the contents. Finally he looked up, his face disturbed, and began to address us:

"Comrades-students! I have just received a directive from the dean. There's to be an immediate suspension of all studies! You will remain in your seats. In five minutes the secretary of the Komsomol committee will give you further details."

A few minutes later the new secretary, himself a fourth-year student, mounted the platform.

"Comrades! Despite firm resistance by our troops, the enemy has succeeded in moving forward. Our city is in imminent danger. Leningrad, the cradle of the Revolution, is threatened! Therefore, after discussing the situation with the military author-

184

ities, the Leningrad Soviet and the Party organization in the city have issued the following orders:

"1. All studies at institutions of higher learning, with the exception of several technical courses and the last two years of medical schools, are suspended.

"2. All students, and part of the faculty, will be sent to dig trenches.

"3. Upper-class students of high schools will be sent to dig trenches.

"4. It is suggested that factory directors allot part of their workers and administrative personnel to dig trenches.

"In accordance with this order, Comrades, all first-, second-, and third-year students will report to the institute at eight tomorrow morning with the following equipment: a blanket, change of underwear, personal belongings, a plate, spoon, and a cup, as well as a two-day supply of food. I warn you now that anyone not appearing at the designated time will be expelled from the institute. The only valid excuse will be a certificate from the institute clinic. No students having outside work will be exempted from digging trenches. They must report here at eight with all the others. Any questions?"

Many people began talking at the same time, attempting to show the secretary why they couldn't go.

"Please, please, not all together—one at a time," he pleaded.

I asked for the floor.

"You said that no work will exempt anyone from going out to dig. I want to make sure of your words. I, for instance, am on first-aid duty."

"Yes, you are right," the secretary quickly replied. "First aid is almost a military organization and naturally you will not dig trenches. I simply didn't remember this exception; you are probably the only one here who falls into that category."

The next day all the others left and I continued my work at the first-aid station.

Every day the enemy came closer and closer to our city.

The trench diggers, who at first worked with tremendous zeal, gradually slowed down, becoming convinced that their work could never stop the enemy. Morale was falling. Rumors began to spread. On top of everything, the Germans, flying low over the trenches, dropped leaflets which attempted to convince the workers that they should go home, or that they should dig potatoes instead of occupying themselves with their fruitless task.

Although not a day went by without an air-raid alert (there was a record number of twelve on one day), Leningrad was not subjected to a single bombardment until September 1st. But that day the first incendiary bombs fell on the outskirts of the city. Most of the bombs fell on an electric generating plant, causing a terrible explosion. One building was wholly destroyed while the rest were severely damaged. Ten ambulances were called to evacuate the wounded. My ambulance was stopped by the head doctor of the first-aid station and an NKVD chief. The doctor pointed to four half-burned corpses and said:

"Comrade Pokrovsky, take these bodies over to the morgue. And be sure not to tell anyone where they came from."

"Just a minute doctor," I objected. "We never transport corpses. They can be taken on a truck. If I were to take them the ambulance would smell for weeks of burned flesh. Where could I put four anyway? I only have two stretchers."

"No more philosophizing!" the NKVD chief interrupted me. "You don't have to reason—just carry out your orders. And watch out! Keep your mouth shut—or else!"

The enemy approached nearer and nearer. The city was threatened with complete encirclement.

Martial law was declared, and it was forbidden to be on the streets after midnight. Orders were issued to evacuate all military academies and the majority of industrial plants. However, the organization was poor. Poorly crated, or completely uncrated machines were left out in the rain for days and weeks awaiting shipment. Anything that wasn't shipped remained rusting in the street.

186

October arrived with its shorter and colder days. The ring of the blockade around Leningrad closed completely. Hunger was making itself felt more and more every day. Nothing could be bought. When payday arrived, no one cared. The money was accepted indifferently—it was just so much paper.

Every day our work became more difficult. To the large number of wounded were added people suffering from malnutrition.

Rations were cut to a minimum. As the hunger spread, the first cases of scurvy appeared. People began to die of starvation. Men between the ages of seventeen and forty suffered especially. Women seemed to take it better.

The severe Leningrad winter came. The cold added to the miseries of the people. . . .

Around ten o'clock one evening a thirty-five-year-old man came in and, complaining of dizziness, asked for permission to lie down in the dispensary for ten or fifteen minutes. Five minutes later a doctor who came through found him dead. Cause—exhaustion. Boris K. and I were given the job of taking the corpse to the morgue.

When we arrived at the morgue, I knocked at the main entrance. An attendant came out and said:

"We don't take them through here any more. Do you have a lantern?"

"Yes," I replied.

"Then take the stretcher and follow me."

He went ahead, and we followed with our load. We went in the back way and down a narrow stairway to the basement. A few more steps—and we were in a narrow passage between two mountains of corpses.

"Here we are," the attendant announced.

"What do we do with him?" I asked, in a quandary.

"Swing the stretcher, and throw him on top of one of these piles," he suggested.

Outside again, I asked the attendant:

"What do you do with them? Do you just let them lie there?"

"Oh no," he answered, "we let them pile up there till there are

187

about three hundred, and then we take them out by truck and bury them in a mass grave."

"What about their relatives?"

"Who cares about such things now? We never give out any information, and anyway, no one ever comes around to ask about any of them."

The hardest part of my life had become the duty at the Tushinsky Hospital, to which I had been transferred in December. The absence of electricity, heat, and water made work extremely difficult. The temperature in the wards usually stood between 30 and 35 degrees Fahrenheit. The patients lay fully clothed, with coats and blankets, and sometimes even mattresses, piled on top of them. The walls were covered with frost. During the night water froze in pitchers. The hunger had the effect of causing diarrhea among the patients, many of whom from weakness were unable to use the bedpan. Sheets on the beds were filthy—no water for laundering. The only medicine available was sodium bromide, and the doctors prescribed it to the patients under various names.

The meals at the hospital were as follows: a cup of ersatz coffee, a few grains of sugar, and two slices of bread in the morning; at noon—a bowl of soup made of oatmeal or barley and a saucer of watery gruel; and in the evening—some more gruel. The same diet from day to day.

After breakfast the doctor made his rounds, wearing an overcoat, fur cap, and gloves. Coming into the ward he could see no patients—their heads were under the covers. He proceeded to lift the covers of the foot of each man's bed and pull his leg. If the patient showed no reaction, he nodded his head—meaning "take him to the morgue." If the patient objected to having his leg pulled, a conversation ensued.

"Your name?" the doctor would ask. The patient replied.

"What is your complaint?"

A long enumeration started: hunger, cold, no hot water, no heating pads, the nurse stole the bread, etc.

188

"This has nothing to do with the case," the doctor would tell the loquacious patient. "Tell me why you were brought here." At this the conversation usually came to an end.

After the doctor had gone, the corpses were loaded on a truck and carted away.

At the end of February 1942, the blockade was breached, and food began to come into Leningrad. At the same time, evacuation of the population commenced. The rations increased to almost the same level at which they had been before total encirclement. We were able to breathe easier again.

In March, I became a doctor in the dispensary of Factory No. 4. About fifty men reported to me every day, at least forty of whom were usually completely exhausted and in advanced stages of scurvy. But I was only permitted to give a maximum of ten excuses from work a day, and if I gave ten for several days in a row I was lectured by the director of the factory for "letting so many loafers get away with their sly tricks."

The factory was not in operation owing to lack of materials and power. However, an order had been issued to clean up the city, and all workers had to get shovels and get out on the streets if they wanted to remain eligible for their rations.

The men came to me, requesting to be freed from the hard labor, but all I could do was to say:

"Yes, you have scurvy. I know it is hard for you to work. But a new healing method has been discovered. First of all, don't give in and just lie in bed—you must move around and work in the fresh air. Work is the best medicine for scurvy! I will give you a few prescriptions, but I can't free you from work."

And the ill man went away cursing, knowing as well as I that he couldn't get the prescription filled.

In April, the first classes of our institute were evacuated from Leningrad. Mama was given permission to go with me, and on April 9, 1942, we left the city for the North Caucasus. We were in such poor condition, that we were immediately put in hospitals, where Mama stayed for a month and I for a month and a half.

The first evacuees from Leningrad were met with open arms and feted with honor. But we were among the last to arrive in the Caucasus, and the people there had already gotten used to the sight. Instead of looking at us with friendly curiosity and pity, they approached us with hostility. We were looked upon as the cause of their getting smaller food rations, on which they received few items besides bread.

Before I had completely recuperated, the Germans came. With thousands of others I was corraled to work in Germany.

When the war was over I ached to go back to the Soviet Union. It is my country despite all the faults of its government. But I had worked for the Nazis and I was afraid this would be held against me by the NKVD, especially since my record was stained by the fact that my father had been in a Soviet prison. Of course, I worked for the Nazis as a slave and therefore it should not be held against me. But how did I know that the NKVD would look at it that way? I though of the anecdote that circulated in Leningrad:

Once, all the rabbits of the Soviet Union started running to the Polish frontier and tried to cross over into Poland. The Polish border guards asked what was happening.

"Well," replied the rabbits, "the Soviet government has issued a decree ordering the death of all camels in Russia."

"Yes," said the guards, "but you are not camels, you are rabbits."

"That's right," answered the rabbits, "but does the NKVD know that?"

I was afraid that the NKVD would regard me, the son of an "enemy," as an enemy because I had been with the Nazis. Rather than invite repressions, rather than go into that kind of nervous existence again, I decided to gamble on building a new life in the West.

190

11

ONE OF THE MANY MILLIONS
by Nikolai Koval

In 1930, collectivization began in our village. It started with the liquidation of the well-to-do peasants, the so-called kulaks. First a special assessment, thirty-six hundred pounds of grain, was imposed on them. When the specified amount had been sent to the government there was another eighteen hundred-pound assessment. A third levy usually followed, but by this time most of the peasants had nothing left. Then a commission would arrive to inventory the property and transfer the case to the district court. The court confiscated the peasant's possessions and sentenced him to ten years of hard labor in some concentration camp. Thus a kulak was liquidated.

Peasants of average means were similarly dealt with. Those who stubbornly refused to join the kolkhoz, or who did not fulfill the government norms, likewise were taken to court. The penalty was often six or seven years' exile, confiscation of property, and eviction of the family.

Through such coercion, peasants were gradually "persuaded" to join the collectives. In 1930, about 30-40 per cent entered, but the Party demanded 100 per cent membership. Specially authorized agents were sent from regional collectivization headquarters. Through one means or another they saw to it that the peasants entered the kolkhoz.

Having been forcefully enlisted in the collective, the peasants did not want to work. Then the GPU police and regional agents arrived, attempting to find those guilty of instigating resistance. Often completely innocent people were accused of spreading anticollectivization propaganda. The "guilty" person was arrested and exiled.

Collectivization was completed in 1936. By that time 90 per cent of the remaining villagers had entered the kolkhoz. The rest lost their land, their homes, and the right to vote. For them the only escape from arrest was to flee to the city illegally.

The pay rate in the collective was computed on the basis of workdays. An individual's annual income was determined by the total number of workdays. The peasant was promised that at the end of the year he would receive ten to fifteen rubles in cash and twenty to twenty-five pounds of grain for each workday unit. In practice this was never so. The individual rate was about one ruble in money and less than a pound of grain per unit. And then, the grain which he received was not clean, but that which the government rejected as low grade. In years of especially good crops, the kolkhoznik might receive up to ten pounds per workday, but through additional compulsory buying of grain by the government, this amount was also taken from him.

The government got even more out of the peasant by issuing loans to which he had to subscribe. No one dared protest the loan, lest he land behind the bars of an NKVD prison. Though the kolkhoznik was hungry, cold, unshod, it was necessary to buy the bonds without showing dissatisfaction.

Before collectivization, the peasant worked his land diligently and with great energy. He knew what he was working for and what he would receive for his labor. After collectivization, he was less sure of his return and therefore worked only to make the day end faster. His greatest interest and devotion was to his own plot of land. According to Soviet law, each kolkhoznik was entitled to a piece of land not to exceed one-third an acre, which he could use to grow anything he desired. This plot was the saving factor for us. As long as we had it, we could keep from starving.

The work in the kolkhoz fields consumed thirteen hours a day. From the time our kolkhoz was organized I was one of those who worked the fields. I started work at 6:00 A.M. and worked until eight at night, with an hour off for supper. The work was measured according to established norms. For instance: plowing one and a half acres with two horses, or manual mowing of grass (six men per two and a half acres) equaled one workday unit.

After the village was collectivized, peasants began to treat the horses very badly. Since the horses were no longer their personal property but belonged to the kolkhoz, they figured there was no advantage in taking time to treat them well. The same was true of agricultural machinery. When a kolkhoznik was through with a machine, he usually went off without even oiling it—just to get home as soon as possible. One reason for this carelessness was that the introduction of machinery in the kolkhoz took away another part of the peasants' income, as the members had to pay for the use of the machines which were supplied by centrally located government machine-tractor stations.

Our kolkhoz was poorly supplied. There were stores in the village, but nothing was to be had. The co-operative store received practically nothing. Three or four suits would come in during the month. This was not enough to supply the thousands of members. When something did arrive, the peasants never saw it. The few suits would be taken by the chairman of the village Soviet, the chairman of the co-operative, and other Party members in the local administration.

About all the average kolkhoznik could hope for was two to

three yards of cotton material from time to time. Most peasants wore clothes made from material manufactured in the home. As far as shoes were concerned—if one was able to get hold of some leather, he could make himself a pair of boots. But the majority of shoes were no more than rags tied about the feet. In the summer most of us went barefooted.

Even necessities were scarce. Salt, matches, dishes—none of these was available in the village stores. Sometimes some peasant-made earthenware was shipped in, but there never was enough to meet the need.

In 1933 there was hunger in our village. The crops had been good in the kolkhoz fields and in our private gardens, but everything was taken from us, to the last grain. Everything was delivered to the government this year, and even the proceeds from our own plots had to be surrendered. Through the hunger period we ate dead horses, grass, and weeds. At the beginning of collectivization our village had three thousand people; after the famine eighteen hundred were left. The same was true of all the surrounding villages.

Before collectivization I owned two sheds, a barn, a lean-to, and a two-room hut. Afterwards I was left with the hut and one shed. The rest was taken for collective property.

Before the Revolution, I had twenty-seven acres of land. No one interfered with me, I lived well. Collectivization took away my land, my property, horses, and farming implements. It was just possible to stay alive. Before the Revolution I used to sell three thousand to four thousand pounds of grain on the market. I also sold pigs and calves. With the kolkhoz I didn't even have these things for myself.

The provisions which we received from the kolkhoz lasted us only for about six months, and the rest of the time we existed on grain rejected by the government because of poor quality, different seeds, weeds, and grass. This was not food—just a makeshift substitute.

Plunder and embezzlement of kolkhoz property could lead to heavy punishment. Under a law passed in 1932, the guilty individual could be imprisoned for ten years. One of my neighbors was sentenced to seven years for tearing off a handful of wheat while he was on his way from the fields.

We had a special building in the village which was used for meetings at which various communal questions were discussed. However, no one could say what he thought. We could only repeat what the kolkhoz chairman or the secretary of the Party organization said. All meetings in the kolkhoz were held under the control of secret NKVD agents or the police.

If anyone spoke in opposition to something favored by the administration, he was likely to receive a prison term of three to five years and be considered an "enemy of the people."

We had such cases. For instance, in 1934 there was a meeting of all kolkhozniks at which the tightening of discipline was discussed. One peasant objected to a proposed move, saying it was not tightening of discipline. He added: "Anyway, the whole thing is just deceit. We strengthen our discipline, but receive nothing in return." For these words he was sentenced to five years.

Before the Revolution we always had a church, and practically all attended. Under the kolkhoz system, churches were closed, desecrated; only the memory remained. Religious holidays had to be celebrated secretly.

Once a detachment arrived while the priest was in the middle of religious services. The priest continued the service and said that he would not leave the church before finishing. When it was over, they tried to arrest him. But the people intervened. Shooting began and led to a regular battle. Fifteen peasants were

195

killed and approximately fifty taken away. We never heard of them again. The priest became ill and died in three days.

After this the church was closed, the icons smashed. The gold was torn off them and the church furnishings were loaded on trucks and carried off.

A special brigade was organized which went from hut to hut collecting icons. Those who dared hid them and prayed in secret. Every peasant had to sign a statement that he had given up his icon. Those who were later discovered harboring icons were sentenced to a year at hard labor in special camps.

No steps were taken to improve the life in the village after it was collectivized. All remained as it had been before.

We didn't dream of having radios. We had no electricity. Every few years we were promised that it would be brought in within five years—but it never came. There was a movie in the district center, none in our village. We had no time to go there, as we worked on most Sundays and holidays, leaving little time for leisure. I never left the village—never went to the district center, nor any other town. If anyone had the desire to leave the hard kolkhoz life, he could not do it: no one had the right to move to any other location.

Our women had the same rights and duties as the men and worked the same as the men. In order to free them for work, village nurseries were organized. Though the nurseries were supported by the collective itself, the children did not fare well in them. The mother took her children there in the morning and got them out after work. The children in the nurseries were dirty, and the women did not want to send them there voluntarily. As a result, attendance became compulsory.

The school had only a seven-year course. It was through with the child when he was fifteen years old. The school functioned all right in the fall and spring, but in the winter things were bad. Since the children had no warm clothing, they couldn't attend classes when it was cold. Therefore, the school usually shut down during the severest winter months.

We had our own wall newspaper, which devoted most of its space to news of fulfillment of various plans. There never was any real news—never anything about events which occurred in the Soviet Union or in other countries. The only time we were told anything about foreign countries was on May 1st celebrations. Then we got speeches about the hunger beyond our borders, the lack of freedom there, and how wonderful our life was in comparison.

We were told that May 1st was freely celebrated only in our country; that in capitalist countries this celebration was repressed and police dispersed the workers with clubs. We were always told that freedom and happiness existed only in the Soviet Union. Above all we were told that Soviet kolkhozniks lived better than peasants anywhere in the world!!

But what I saw in German villages convinced me that what we heard in the Soviet Union wasn't true. I was astounded by the kind of farms I saw in Bavaria: how many pigs each farmer had, even the poorest farmer, and how healthy the pigs were; how orderly everything was, how smoothly the farms worked, without supervisors, bookkeepers, and orders from the government. This was farming as Russia hadn't known it since 1917. How quiet life was in the villages I worked in, how quiet compared to the politics of our kolkhozes. Though I was working for Germans I did not like, I enjoyed myself because I felt again the pure joy of tilling the soil, tending animals, and making things grow. I am a peasant and in Russia I had not been allowed to be a peasant. I dreamed of having a little farm of my own, my own pigs, my own cow. I knew I could never have it in the Soviet Union. I decided to have it somewhere outside of Russia. This is my ambition.

12

FAITH BETRAYED

by Gregory Ugryumov

First steps into life

I was brought up in the village by my grandparents. When I was nine years old and my "city mama" came for me, I was already an independent individual. Even though I couldn't read or write, I was a good worker in the fields and could easily handle a team of horses.

After the free life of the village, city life with the tiny yard behind the house, going to school, and the constant arguments between my mother and my drunkard father didn't appeal to me. Before I finished high school my father left us and I joyfully dropped out of school. That was in 1926.

With all the ardor of a fifteen-year-old, and fully aware of my responsibility to care for my sick mother, I became an apprentice in a bakery attached to a large lumber mill near Archangel. My career as a baker did not last long. The work there seemed too monotonous and dull to me, and after a while I was chased out for "rowdyism and conscious discrediting of the management." This was equivalent to being black-listed.

Two pranks, which gave me tremendous popularity and gained

198

great sympathy for me among the workers, were the cause for my dismissal.

My duties included taking a load of fresh rolls to the factory management office and the Party office around noon every day. One day I noticed a coffin in the yard next to the bakery. It was too short for the dead worker it had been made for and had therefore been discarded. Without a moment's hesitation, I put the coffin on my sled, put the rolls in the coffin and, sitting on top of the coffin, I approached the administration building with complete self-satisfaction. The news of the rolls in the coffin spread like wildfire, and before I even stopped my horse, officials, typists, secretaries, and everyone else came streaming out of the building.

"What the hell is this?"

"Maybe a corpse was in it?"

"The rolls have to be thrown away, so no one else eats them!"

"This is revolting! We should report him!"

"Someone must have put him up to it!"

These shouts came from one side. On the other side, a crowd of workers returning from lunch assembled, and laughter, jokes, and shouts of approval came from them.

The outcome was prosaic—I got a beating from the head baker and was sent out with another load of rolls, this time in baskets.

The other escapade came soon after the first. The chairman of the factory's trade union committee, Nifontov, criticized the work of the bakers at every union meeting: ". . . the bread is of the lowest quality . . . pieces of string have been found in the rolls . . . there are always pieces of dough that weren't properly mixed in . . . even nails have been found in it . . . in general the work is completely unsatisfactory!"

All our bakers were terribly shocked by the unfair criticism. We did the best we could with the primitive equipment that we had.

With another apprentice, I devised a plan which was shortly

199

put into effect. A silver half-ruble coin was baked into a hard roll. With the help of a cleaning woman, we were able to sneak the roll on to the union chairman's desk. How Nifontov reacted to the roll and its content—we never found out.

But at the next union meeting, during the discussion period after another typical speech by Nifontov, I got up and spoke in defense of the bakers. I told the workers about the unjust criticism that had been levied against the bakery and told them about our prank.

My last sentence: "As you could see, Nifontov mentioned nothing about the coin . . ." was buried in a burst of laughter which completely finished off Nifontov.

That was the end of my job.

I was noticed

Three years of sailing on a trawler in a fishing fleet on the Arctic Ocean stabilized my passions, strengthened me physically, and prepared me morally for the coming battles of life.

In the spring of 1930, my suggestion to organize an all-Komsomol trawler, made at a Party-Komsomol meeting, was enthusiastically taken up by Party and Komsomol leaders in Murmansk.

A month later I was triumphantly advanced from the Komsomol into Party ranks and appointed secretary of the Komsomol Committee of the all-Komsomol trawler *KIM* (Young Communist International) which at the time was being completed at Danzig.

After the captain and I assembled a crew for the new trawler, all of us left for Danzig.

I took very seriously the responsibility and trust shown me by the Party. In my case the briefing on vigilance, on the dangers lurking beyond our borders, the cunning capitalists, and in general on behavior in foreign countries, was quite unnecessary. I also understood that since an exception had been made in my case so I could be accepted into the Party at nineteen, I was obligated to exert every effort to justify this confidence by guar-

200

anteeing the success in testing and taking the new ship from Danzig to Murmansk.

I still remember the first stunning impressions after we left the Soviet Union. Everything was different from what we had known. Grass and even trees were neatly trimmed, the fields in the country were tiny, toylike; for some reason all roads were asphalted. Many people wore uniforms, even all hotel employees were dressed alike. Members of the leisure class had nothing to do and sat around in cafés drinking wine, but no drunks were visible. Everything was available in stores, and one didn't have to argue about prices with the sales clerks. When the train from Hamburg to Berlin left on time, I didn't say anything. But when the Berlin-Danzig train also left exactly as scheduled, I remarked to the fellows:

"They sure are trying! They are doing this just so we don't see their faults—they want to impress us. Just look out that you don't disgrace yourself. Always remember—we are among enemies."

Policemen especially impressed me with their amazingly grand uniforms. I couldn't reconcile myself to their lacquered leggings, gold eagles on helmets, and above all their clubs which I had previously only read about in books or seen in movies.

"Here, fellows, take a look at this club. It is for use on people. What a disgrace! That is how the capitalists support themselves in power."

The foreign mission was completed successfully, and I was rewarded with a month's vacation in the fishing industry's rest home in Yalta.

After the vacation I stopped off at Archangel to see my mother and friends. All advised me to give up the seafaring life and do something that offered greater possibilities. Also, I became acquainted with the daughter of a merchant who had been disowned and disenfranchised after the Revolution. Even though I, proletarian and a Party member, and the daughter of a dis-

201

enfranchised man, were a poor match according to Soviet standards, as they say—love has no bounds. For the first time my own view did not coincide with that of the Party and the Komsomol. I attached no significance to the whole matter, until my "case" was taken up by the Regional Committee and I received a warning.

With the help of a friend I was able to receive a release from my old job and was sent to work as recreation director among trade unions in the northwestern region of the country. In 1931, after a year of this work, I was sent to Moscow to attend the congress of the All-Union Central Council of Trade Unions.

I will never forget the meeting I had with the secretary of the Central Council, Abelin, a meeting which greatly influenced my future.

"Comrade Abelin, I would like you to meet one of our youngest athletic directors, Comrade Ugryumov," the chairman of the athletic bureau of the Central Council Kanygin, introduced me.

Abelin shook hands with me. After asking me about my work, he said:

"We have to keep educating our good men. How do you feel about studying?"

"I would like it very much, Comrade Abelin, but the local organization would not let me go, and I never completed high school."

"Well, we can take care of that," Abelin told me. "Comrade Kanygin, see to it that Ugryumov is sent to the Central School."

The happiness which I experienced at Abelin's first words left me immediately. The career of a trade union worker held no attraction for me and I had no desire to attend the Central School of the Trade Union Movement. But I did not feel that I could refuse the high honor accorded to me.

"Well, are you satisfied?" Kanygin asked me after we went out.

"Not at all. I would much rather attend a school for physical education."

"Then why did you keep your mouth shut in there? I almost

202

said myself that it would be better to send you to the physical education institute, but when you didn't say a word, I figured you were satisfied. Well, wait a minute. I'll be right back."

After two minutes, during which my heart was pounding, Kanygin returned from Abelin's office with a new paper in his hand.

"Here you are. Report to the institute in the fall. Till then wind up all your work, pick a good successor. That's all there is to it."

Promotion and love

Abelin's note worked wonders. The local organization gave me my leave. Admission requirements were waived, and I was accepted at the institute though I had not taken the last two years in high school.

I knew that I had to thank the Party, of which I was a member, as well as Abelin for the chance to resume my long-interrupted education. I was told hundreds of times that I had to justify the trust of the Party. No one had to tell me that. I was completely devoted to the Party and was ready to do anything ordered by the Party or the Komsomol.

My first two years at the university rounded out my general education. But during the third year I took only specialized courses. They gave me no trouble.

Having time at my disposal, I again threw myself into Komsomol and Party activities and soon was elected assistant secretary of the institute's Komsomol Committee. Shortly after that I was also chosen a member of the institute's Party Committee.

An excess of time and energy was not the only reason for my increased political work. By my activities I was also trying to atone for a sin I had committed—the discrediting of an instructor who was a member of the Party. It happened this way:

During a seminar on "Economic Policies," the professor was discussing the "absolute and relative impoverishment of the working class in capitalist countries." I did not quite understand the

203

essence of "absolute impoverishment" and gave the instructor the following example:

"With the growth of culture and civilization, man, even if he belongs to the lowest rank of the proletariat takes advantage of railroads, automobiles, electricity, and all other technical developments. How can one say then that 'absolute impoverishment' can exist under such conditions?"

The professor tried to convince me and the other students of the validity of the concept. He approached the matter from different angles, but after a long argument I was still unconvinced.

The next day a closed meeting of the Party Committee took up the matter of "the undermining of an instructor's authority by Party member Ugryumov."

I was saved from expulsion from the Party, and maybe the institute, by my "sincere repentance," and acknowledgement of my "gross error, bordering on the actions of a class enemy," and, above all, by the unexpected defense by the institute director who knew me as a good student. He described my action as a "thoughtless offense, resulting from a sincere and healthy desire to get to the basic truth of the concept."

The result of this meeting was an official reprimand and an order that I publicly correct my error at the next session of the class.

During the last two years in school, I completely made up for my fault and, after the institute was decorated with the Order of Lenin, the highest award in the country, the reprimand was erased from my records.

I was proud to be a member of the institute delegation which accepted the Order of Lenin at the Kremlin, and my name was among the signatures on a report sent to Stalin by the institute's Komsomol organization.

When jobs were being assigned before graduation from the institute, I was appointed athletic director of the Forestry

Academy in Leningrad. It was just the kind of job I had hoped for.

My fiancée, Olga, who with my help had also been enrolled at the institute, likewise received an assignment in Leningrad. Now, we began making plans to get married immediately upon graduation. Our happiness was complete.

But it did not last long. A few days after we were told what our work would be, I was called to the director's office. In the office I was greeted by the director, the Party secretary, and the chairman of the faculty.

I had a premonition that something bad was coming.

"Sit down, Comrade Ugryumov.

"We have decided to advance you to a highly responsible position and we hope that you will fulfill our trust and will always remember the traditions and leaders of the institute at which you were educated. . . ." The director went on like this for fifteen minutes.

When he had finished I said:

"You know, Comrade Director, that the will of the Party is my highest law."

"When we discussed you for the position, we knew that we would never get a different answer. You have been chosen to work with the School of the Central Committee. You are to report there tomorrow."

"I would like to ask whether I will be useful along the lines of work I trained for here."

"Yes, I think so . . ." the director said, but the Party secretary interrupted him:

"And if not? You wouldn't object, would you? You know very well that the Party uses its personnel where they are of greatest value."

Any further conversation was futile, and I thanked the board for the honorable assignment.

For the first time in my dealings with the Party a mutinous thought entered my mind: If they had only asked me whether

205

I wanted to! But another voice inside me insisted: You have to thank the Party for everything that you are. Therefore it has the right to use you, and you have to serve it faithfully in any chosen capacity.

To top everything off, my fiancée met me in the corridor with tears streaming down her face and unable to say a word. Her assignment had also been changed.

"Calm down, Olga," I told her, "I'll make another effort to bring us together. It won't make any difference that we will live in Moscow instead of Leningrad."

But Olga just shook her head and continued to weep. In the evening I found out that she had been called to the dean and had been reassigned to teach in the Archangel medical institute. All her arguments that she couldn't go teach in Archangel because everyone there knew her as a little girl, that that would decrease her usefulness and make her work very difficult, were dismissed.

Finally, out of desperation, Olga said that we were in love and were getting married and wanted to be in the same city. She was then told that I had been reassigned to Moscow and that she couldn't remain here, that there were enough qualified people working in Moscow already, and that the city was overcrowded and there were no apartments, etc.

Thus all my plans and dreams collapsed. I tried to convince myself that all was for the benefit of the Party and that after a year or two I would be able to bring Olga back to Moscow.

Among the chosen

The highest school for Party organizers of the Central Committee of the All-Union Communist Party had just been organized according to a personal directive from Stalin. The school was under the direction of Grigory Malenkov, the chief of the personnel division of the Central Committee.

I was given the task of selecting proper athletic quarters in the building assigned to the school and obtaining all equipment necessary for the athletic classes or individual and group exercises.

I had no financial restrictions. Anything that I thought might be of use, irrespective of price, was approved for purchase. For instance, I found a set of billiard balls that sold for seven thousand rubles. When I told my superiors that this was much too high, I was asked but one question: "Aren't they what you need?" When I replied in the affirmative, I was told to buy them.

In September 1936, the students began to arrive. They were primarily secretaries of district and regional committees, editors of the leading papers, and senior political workers of the Red Army. The daily schedule was arranged so that they had an hour of compulsory physical exercises in the morning, followed by four to six hours of lectures given by the biggest historians, economists, scientists, and other specialists in the country. On two occasions Stalin himself lectured on organizational matters within the Party.

From 5:00 P.M. until late at night I was occupied with very tiresome and highly diverse work. Sometimes I would give instructions in volley ball and then judge a game between editors and army men; or I worked on two or three rising "leaders" to decrease the size of their growing bellies which we politely called "socialist accumulation"; I taught basketball, tennis, billiards, demonstrated gymnastics on our equipment, and gave lessons in boxing, wrestling, and jiujitsu.

I spent days and weeks among the highest Party functionaries and acquired their trust and respect, and was able really to learn all about them.

In the beginning I determined their average physical condition and by the end of the course I had a good picture of their spiritual qualities.

It was obvious from the first that members of the school could be divided into two groups according to their education, culture, and abilities.

The first group included primarily newspaper workers and some of the younger district and regional leaders who had previously attended Party schools or universities. The representatives of this group were, by comparison with the others, better educated, very well read, skilled in the use of the pen as well as the tongue. Some of them spoke foreign languages, usually German. They were aware of their superiority over the other students and among themselves often laughed about the ignorant ways of the others.

The interests of the first group were very broad and they had more leisure time to develop them as they didn't have to answer a stream of telegrams and letters which the others received from their home offices. The books read by these people covered all topics. Among the more popular were Aristotle and Kant, Shchedrin and Guy de Maupassant, Marx and Engels. Most students read many newspapers and magazines, and everyone read *Pravda, Izvestia,* the *Komsomolskaya Pravda,* and the monthly Party magazine *Bolshevik.*

The second and more numerous group consisted of most secretaries of regional and district Party committees, and all representatives of the political leadership of the Red Army. The majority of this group were of worker and peasant origin, had climbed to their positions by exercising the fullest obedience to the Party and Stalin. Few had more than high school education and many didn't even have that. They were not specialists in any one line, but knew some generalities about a lot of things.

About half of this group sincerely had the interests of their district or region at heart. This was especially characteristic of representatives of national republics. But their final allegiance was always to the Party. The other half consisted of Party workers sent to their specific area by the Party, and the district or region in which they were located was of no greater importance to them than the neighboring region, where they might be sent the next day by Party order.

208

These men depended on the Kremlin, and all their efforts were directed at serving and pleasing the Kremlin. Their initiative was turned in one direction—toward the better fulfillment of plans, directives, and orders of the Politburo.

The majority of these local leaders tried to copy Stalin in everything, even their clothes. They all had two sides to them —the servile, which was shown to superiors in the Party, and the bossy one, which they assumed toward people in their own district. Only very few acted simply, without affectation, and these were primarily of the older generation of Bolsheviks.

Most of the men in the second group were secretive and reserved, and only conversed in groups of two or three with some of their previous friends. They all worked very hard at giving the appearance of hard workers and of being greatly occupied with affairs back home. One purpose of this was their desire not to give anyone a chance to destroy the reputation they had built up for themselves at home.

Often some local leader seeing me unoccupied, said:

"Hello, Gregory, I see you aren't too busy. How about inviting me to your place for a glass of tea?"

And we would go to my room, drink tea, play the guitar, listen to the radio, gossip a bit, or just sit in silence.

I had the feeling at such times that my guest was actually relaxing from the constant tension of "playing the role of a leader." Only with me, who was not a politician, could they feel free to drop their mask.

The life of an official

During the year which I spent in the Party school, my position in the Party was further strengthened, and after a series of promotions I was appointed director of the personnel department and member of the All-Union Physical Culture Committee under the Sovnarkom (Council of the People's Commissars), the Soviet Cabinet.

A monthly salary of twelve hundred rubles, a car, meals in

the Sovnarkom restaurant, a private office, secretaries, and other privileges available only to responsible officials in the forefront of Soviet life—all this again gave me a feeling of the trust and responsibility reposed in me by the Party.

I knew that many of my subordinates, even if they weren't more intelligent, were more experienced and educated than I, but naturally I never expressed such thoughts. My predecessor had been arrested. This somewhat depressed me at first when I took over the position, but I looked bravely at life, certain that no such fate was ahead for me.

1937. . . . Many of my recent acquaintances from the Party school were falling from their lofty positions and disappearing into the unknown as "enemies of the people."

I had no doubt that not a single one of them was a Japanese spy, or a German agent, or even in serious opposition or deviation from the Party line, but I was just as sure that none of them was arrested without cause. I was of the opinion that the Party was just trying to keep people from "bringing its dirty wash out into the open" and therefore ascribed other crimes to people whose real crime might be moral decay, vain bluster, neglecting to perform their duty before the Party, or causing unintentional harm to the Soviet system.

Nine people were arrested among the leading workers of the All-Union Committee before and after my arrival.

Soon after I arrived, the assistant chairman of the committee, Lapin, was arrested. He had been a high NKVD official before he had been assigned to improve the efficiency of our office.

One morning, before my own car had arrived at my home, a strange car drove up and the driver gave me a note:

Stop by to see me before reporting to work. Release your own car. I won't keep you long. Rudakov.

Fifteen minutes later I was in Rudakov's office. He was the NKVD official who supervised the work of our department.

"Hello, Ugryumov. Did you sleep well?"

210

"Why shouldn't I sleep well? Of course I did."

"Well, I slept neither well, nor much. We took Lapin away. Messed around all night long."

I didn't know Lapin any better than Rudakov, and was therefore not particularly scared, especially as it was quite obvious to me that he was arrested not for committee errors, but for some former sins. I knew that any questions about the cause for the arrest would bring only a meaningful smile, but no answer, so I just waited silently. Rudakov continued:

"His office has been sealed. Send me the key to his safe. Tomorrow the seals will be taken off and your key returned. Today after work I want you to call a meeting of all your employees and tell them that in Lapin's desk and safe we found many gold objects, cigarette cases, precious stones, watches, and similar things. Hint that we don't know exactly where he got them. Fix your story up good.

"After you leave I will phone the secretary of our Party Committee. Lapin has to be expelled from the Party before the next meeting. There is nothing to discuss, so the committee won't even have to meet. Ask all the other committee members whether they agree. That's all. Get it?"

"Sure, I understand, but . . ."

"But what?" Rudakov interrupted.

"Oh, nothing. So long."

"That's better. Good-by."

When the chairman of the All-Union Physical Culture Committee was arrested, the Sovnarkom appointed an active Komsomol worker, Knopova, to fill his place temporarily. Where the old chairman relied on his helpers and specialists and showed a love for his work, Knopova was a dull, colorless tool of the Party. Only twenty-six, she never considered anyone's thoughts or advice, and relied solely on the authority of the Party which had sent her. She obviously considered that if she hadn't come into a camp of "enemies of the people," she was amidst their followers, and that it was her task to clean out the

Augean stables of the leading sports organization of the country.

I remember one meeting at which all committee members and some outside experts were present. Knopova came up with a crazy idea for mass cross-country exercises in which millions would participate. This was against all our basic plans and, to a man, we opposed her proposal. Burning with anger and without a moment's hesitation, Knopova grabbed the telephone and said:

"Connect me with Vyacheslav Mikhailovich, please!"

The room quieted down immediately. We all knew perfectly well whom she was calling—the chairman of the Sovnarkom, Molotov. All understood that with Knopova the question was whether she would rule the committee or not.

"Vyacheslav Mikhailovich, how are you? . . . This is Knopova. Excuse me for disturbing you, but my committee is meeting and they are insisting on the same old ideas. I proposed a series of mass cross-country runs, but they are afraid of any fresh wind and insist on their old position of working singly or in small groups. As far as I am concerned that is but a reflection of bourgeois sport. Now I am in a quandary, and ask you for your advice."

None of us heard Molotov's reply.

Those present during the conversation, professors and doctors, specialists and organizers, who had devoted everything to sport, were in the position of guilty schoolboys.

Putting down the receiver, Knopova gazed around with the satisfied look of a winner and, content with the sad appearance of the others, said:

"The plan is accepted. Each of you is personally responsible for the section of the plan assigned to him. And don't think that you can oppose or sabotage the decision. The meeting is closed. All except members of the Party Committee may go."

For another hour Knopova continued her tirade before the Party Committee members, insisting over and over again that the resistance came from those bureaucrats "afraid of any fresh wind."

Not long after that meeting, I gave Knopova the manuscript of a new manual for physical education schools. The manuscript was ready for printing, and I asked Knopova to give instructions to "Physical Culture and Sports," our publishers, to have the manuals printed by the beginning of the school year.

"Leave them here, I'll look them over."

An hour later Knopova called me in, and greeted me with: "What kind of nonsense have you written here?"

"First of all, not I, but a group of authors wrote this, and secondly, their contributions have been approved by a special board of experts on athletics and sports."

"Don't pick on my words! You, a Communist! do you let these so-called experts lead you around by your nose?"

"What do you think must be changed? What are your orders?"

"You should know that better than I. You are a specialist and a Communist besides. You give the necessary instructions. Call the authors together, and make sure that every manual is saturated with political ideology."

"Just a minute," I objected. "How can you bring political ideology into this manual on boxing, for instance. This is not a political theory book, but a practical manual."

"So you don't think it can be done? Maybe you have to be taught something. How long have you been in the Party?" Knopova shouted at me, apparently completely shocked by my attitude. She proceeded to lecture me: "You must bring out in the introduction to every part of the exercises that before anything else the boxer has to be completely devoted to the fatherland, the Party, and our dear Comrade Stalin. With this thought in mind and for the glory of Stalin, the boxer can then learn boxing. Fit in these ideas throughout the books. As long as these manuals aren't re-edited in line with what I have told you, I will not have them published, even if all eleven physical culture institutes in the country have to shut down! I hope you understand now. I had never expected such lack of principle from you, Comrade Ugryumov. That is all."

I passed these instructions on to the chairman of the special board which had edited the manuals, though I did not put everything as crudely as Knopova had. I did not have the least desire to confront the authors and give them such senseless instructions.

One day in 1937, a large box was brought to my office. The sender's name, Shvarsh Narinyan, was completely unknown to me.

"Please get some men," I told the secretary, "and have the box opened."

"Oh, how wonderful. Look, Comrade Ugryumov," she shouted when the box was finally open.

The package was actually a valuable one—it consisted of Caucasian wines, first-grade tea, lemons, oranges, and many varieties of Caucasian sweets.

What the hell is this? In an hour everyone will say that I received a big bribe, I thought to myself. I asked the secretary to find out who the sender was.

"Don't you remember Narinyan? He is the Armenian who graduated from our institute recently and was assigned to work in Karaganda but had a bride in Armenia and you felt sorry for him and changed his assignment to Erivan."

"So that's who he is," I said, but I was thinking: What a fool, at least he could have sent it to my apartment. Now, I'll have to get myself out of this mess.

The affair ended by my semi-officially inviting all my co-workers, other department heads, and influential Party members to stop by my office after work for "clearing up several important questions." The "questions" were promptly cleared up, and all left my office in high spirits.

Bribe giving and taking is considered a crime in the Soviet

Union, and anyone wishing to give, or accept presents, must use the utmost caution if his actions could in any way be construed as bribery.

War

In the summer of 1939 rumors of war multiplied.

I always went gladly to the Sovnarkom restaurant, where the chiefs of all important departments and bureaus met. Besides the restful atmosphere there, one had a chance to pick up information on the latest official moves of the government, on any changes in the Red Army and Party, on troop movements, and other inside information which could give one a somewhat clearer picture of the situation.

When the Soviet troops crossed the Polish border an intense mobilization of the Red Army reserves began. I was a reserve officer but I did not expect to be called into active service because I belonged to the special defense unit of the Central Committee of the Party. However, this immunity did not help.

The Party organizations in all offices were ordered, without changing the functioning of the department too greatly, to pick as many trustworthy Communists to be attached to the Army as possible, and I decided to volunteer to go to the front.

The triumphal march through Poland, besides a feeling of satisfaction, left no special impressions on me. After overcoming the first weak resistance, the Red Army advanced for days without a shot being fired. I was amazed, though, by all the goods available in the stores and their low prices. A ruble, for which I could buy only a package of cigarettes in Moscow, could be exchanged for ten zlotys, for which one could buy a wonderful pair of boots.

The Soviet-Finnish war, which came soon after the Polish campaign, was neither a "triumphal march" nor a campaign. This was real war with all its horrors and death.

In 45-degree-below-zero cold, during polar nights which lasted sixteen to eighteen hours, with poor food and equipment, our 122nd Infantry Division battled against terrific Finnish opposition.

I remember our astonishment when we took the first large village—Alakurti. Everything that could burn was on fire. Not a killed or wounded Finn. A cow, freed before she could burn to death in her barn, and an old man were the only living creatures to be found. Not a house survived, not even the bathhouse. Our consolation was that at least the fires protected us from the bitter cold for several hours.

I was amazed, and later overcome by admiration when, after the first week of fierce battles during which the division had many casualties, I learned that our division had been opposed by just one battalion—the 17th Lapland-Salsky.

Our arms did not function in the terrible cold. Our basic weapon was the 1891-type rifle. The basic tactic of the Red Army was to crush the enemy by masses of infantry, following the principle: "They can't kill all." These words were ascribed to Mekhlis, the chief of the Red Army's political department, who was reputed to be one of the leaders in the Soviet-Finnish war. I personally experienced this "strategy" of our military leaders.

Once, our battalion received orders to attack a village across a lake at 6:00 P.M. A second battalion was to advance through the forest from another direction.

Without any artillery preparation, with the support of just a few machine guns, we left our positions.

At first we advanced slowly, then faster, and when the rows of houses were but a thousand feet away we started to run.

"For our fatherland! For Stalin!" someone yelled behind me.

When only two hundred feet separated us from the houses and it seemed that our target would be taken in less than a minute, the space around us suddenly was transformed into an inferno. Small red dots flashed about the houses, bullets hit all around us. Out of breath and hot from running, people dropped and lay still on the snow. Without thinking I followed

216

their example. There was no sense in giving any orders, but I tried.

"Forward! Keep firing as you move!" I shouted and crawled ahead a few feet. None but the nearest to me heard me. To the left Lieutenant Pukhov stood up trying to raise his company:

"Forward comrades! For Sta . . ." the powerful voice died forever as Pukhov fell.

Our men were shooting indiscriminately. I also sent burst after burst from my machine pistol.

Rain had begun to fall. I don't know how long we lay there in the freezing snow. I looked around and saw one of my sergeants turning back. When I shouted at him, he just gave me a look of fear and prayer, and kept crawling as he whispered:

"Please, Comrade Commander, please . . ."

Looking around I understood that the attack was over. Around me I saw only the dead and severely wounded. The rest were retreating.

I saw that I couldn't remain where I was. In order to justify my retreat, I picked up a machine gun and dragged it back to where we had started from.

Lieutenant Chernyk, commander of the third squad, was assembling the remains of my company. Everyone had thought that I was dead or wounded.

The battalion commander, Popov, called all officers together and gave us the following order:

"The attack will be repeated! And let's not lie in the snow dreaming of warm beds. The village must be taken! Company commanders will go in support and shoot at anyone who falls back or turns around."

One didn't have to be a psychologist to know that the new attack, in which the soldiers would have to climb over the bodies of their killed and wounded comrades, would fail.

Retreating a second time, I did not carry a rifle, but just ran, without any thoughts, feelings, or desires. I ran because everyone else ran.

217

As after the first retreat the Finns didn't pursue us. They even discontinued their machine-gun fire as soon as we were out of close range.

Of more than one hundred men of my company who went into the first attack, only thirty-eight returned after the second one failed. All of us wondered and worried: What happens now? As if in answer to our question, the battalion commissar, who had taken over when Popov was wounded, called all commanders to him. He held a field telephone in his hand.

"Comrades, our attack was unsuccessful. The division commander personally gave me the order—in seven minutes we are attacking again. Each of you is responsible with his life for the success of this attack. Any minute now we will be reinforced by two machine-gun squads."

The rest I remember as through a fog. One of the wounded, among whom we advanced, grabbed my leg and I pushed him away. When I noticed that I was way ahead of the men, I dropped in the snow and waited till the line came up to me. There was no fear. A dull apathy and indifference toward impending doom pushed us ahead. This time the Finns let us approach almost within one hundred feet of their positions, but their fire was that much deadlier when it commenced.

I don't remember how I got back after this attack. I awoke either from the cold, for I was sitting in the snow, or from somebody's insistently calling my name:

"Comrade Ugryumov, Comrade Ugryumov, come to the phone."

There I found Popov, who had taken over the remains of the battalion despite a serious wound, and seven other officers.

"We'll have an answer in a minute as to what to do," Popov said.

Everyone was looking with hope in the direction of the telephone operator, who was monotonously repeating the same words:

218

"Eagle, eagle . . . this is falcon. Eagle, this is falcon, this is falcon."

Our hearts almost stopped when Popov was finally called to the phone.

"Yes, this is Popov."

"No, we couldn't even form one company."

"No, we probably wouldn't be able to take half of them out . . . I think Ugryumov . . . yes . . . yes . . ."

Popov nodded his head in my direction and held out the receiver. I immediately recognized the regimental commander's voice.

"Ugryumov, you will cover Popov's retreat with the wounded. Organize a perimeter defense. Lensky will come in the morning. Until then don't retreat without further orders. Understand?"

Two wounded were given into the care of every three soldiers and the battalion withdrew to our original line.

The night was long and terrible. We didn't feel the hunger as it was submerged under the more powerful feelings of cold and fear. The moans and appeals for help by those left behind in the snow made things even worse, especially because we couldn't help them.

After two and a half hours our telephone connection was cut. I went from one soldier to another trying to save in them what spirit and hope I could. I talked to some quietly, helped one to find a more comfortable place, just sat in silence with another one for several minutes. In the middle of the night one of the older sergeants relieved me. I had full confidence in him, knowing that he could approach the men on a much closer plane than I.

Now for the first time since the beginning of the Finnish war, a doubt crept into my mind: Why and for whom all this terror, privation, and sacrifice?

Since the Finns were fighting so stubbornly for what they had, it meant they had something to fight for. That meant they didn't want our system. This thought created a bitterness in me toward those who sent the best people of our nation to die in a senseless war. Why are those hundreds of corpses lying there on the lake? Who is guilty? The more I thought, the stronger my conviction grew: the guilt lay with the Party.

Two reasons

Again Moscow. Again the All-Union Physical Culture Committee. A different office, but most of the people are the same.

But I am not the same. We had finally defeated the Finns but in me there was a deep hurt. Even though I was not guilty of anything except thoughts, I unconsciously became more reserved, more careful in conversations and actions. More than that, whenever it came to accepting any kind of responsibility I simply became cowardly. I understood that if I made one mistake, if I didn't keep in perfect step with the Party—that was the end.

Two events in 1941 served to give me a clear picture of my own situation. It became obvious to me that I, who had climbed more than halfway up the ladder of success, represented but a tiny pin in the wheel that was the Communist machine, working at the expense of the Russian people for the success of Communism throughout the world. Yet when I had begun to work in the All-Union Committee I had felt sure I would have a voice in the administration of the country!

Supposedly, I was in charge of all institutes and schools of physical education, of all finances in the department, appointment and assignment of all specialists in the field of physical education and sports. Actually, I couldn't even transfer an ordinary instructor from one town to another without the approval and directive of Party organs. And if I had made an attempt to transfer anyone, I would have been successful only if the local Party organization did not object to the removal of the man previously assigned to their town.

My only consolation was the knowledge that all other officials, much higher officials than I, whether Party members or

220

not, were also under the thumb of, and completely subservient to the Politburo.

The two examples which I bring below are but two of the reasons why my idealistic belief in Communism evaporated. What I saw and experienced made me break with the Party in spirit. I had to remain a member, but it was only on paper— my heart was no longer in it.

In July 1940, one of my assistants told me that Nikolai Ryzhov, Marshal Budyenny's former adjutant, had appealed to him several times for help in getting a job. Ryzhov had recently been released from prison and was very hard up.

"Would you give permission to have him accepted as an inspector of equestrian sports?" the assistant asked.

I was interested in Ryzhov and requested that he be brought in to me the next time he came to the office.

A few days later a middle-aged man was sitting before me. He wore a well-worn military uniform, without any insignia. He had an unnaturally pale face with serious, intelligent eyes. The calmness of the man amazed me.

"Show me your documents, please," I asked him.

Embarrassed, he handed me two pieces of paper given to him when he was released. One stated that Ryzhov had been dismissed from the Red Army under Article 34. The other was from the NKVD attesting that the holder had been imprisoned from 1938 to 1940 and was freed without forfeiture of his civil rights.

"Were you a Party member?"

"Yes."

"What are you qualified for and what do you do?" I asked.

"I spent my whole life in the army; fought, studied, commanded troops. I have no other specialty. Therefore I do not know what I could do. I would appreciate any kind of work that would help me get on my feet again."

Ryzhov's whole appearance and attitude was so different from the others with whom I had had similar encounters that I wanted to help him.

"Where are you living now?"

"Somewhere on the outskirts. An old friend agreed to put me up for the time being."

"Are you acquainted with equestrian sports?"

A light came into his eyes but died almost immediately, and he impatiently said:

"I think I am. I spent my whole life around horses. . . ."

"All right, I'll try to help you get something. Drop by again in three days. I'll tell my secretary right now so she won't keep you waiting."

"I am very grateful to you. I have only one request to make —if you don't really have any hope of getting me something, or if your attempts are unsuccessful, please let me know immediately. I have been looking for work for quite a while, and everywhere they tell me 'come back tomorrow' or something similar."

As soon as Ryzhov left, I called the chairman of the All-Union Committee and Rudakov of the NKVD. I told them about Ryzhov, saying that since he had spent his whole life in the cavalry he could be of great use to us. I requested permission to accept him, promising to look after him personally.

The chairman of the committee had known Ryzhov personally before his arrest. The approval came through without much trouble, and three days later Ryzhov was accepted as an inspector of equestrian sports.

In the three weeks during which I helped Ryzhov with his new work, and assisted him in obtaining an apartment in the committee building, we became well acquainted. I was attracted by his personality and at the same time earned his confidence.

He worked well and hard. His attitude toward work was much more conscientious than that of any other inspector.

For some time I had been aware that something was weighing heavily on Ryzhov's mind. I wanted to help him, and one day I asked him to stop by and see me. When he arrived I asked him directly:

"Well, let's have it—what's bothering you?"

"I'm glad you asked me. I've been wanting your advice for some time but didn't feel free to approach you with my problem. . . ." And Ryzhov told me the following story:

"At the beginning of the Revolution, when I was seventeen, I lost both my parents and started roaming around the cities in the south. At times I had to steal, but only enough to keep me fed.

"After a while I was picked up by the commander of a troop of the First Cavalry Army. For several months I remained with the unit, was educated by the men, and wore a regular uniform. Then one day General Budyenny visited the troop. When he left he took me along. Until my arrest in 1938, he and I never separated. At first I was his stable boy, then his orderly, and later his secretary and assistant. I am greatly obligated to him. He was father and friend to me at the same time. We fought together, shared joys, sorrows, and danger. I want you to understand that ours was more than just ordinary friendship, although neither of us ever let our close relationship interfere with the performance of military duties.

"In 1937, when Budyenny, now a Marshal, was transferred from chief cavalry inspector of the Red Army to commander of the Moscow Military District, I, being a cavalryman, wasn't transferred with him, but became chief of staff of the Stalin Cavalry Division in Moscow.

"While performing this duty, I was arrested. I won't give you the details of the two years spent in prison. Suffice it to say that when my will was completely broken I 'confessed' and signed anything they wanted me to sign.

"You will understand what I went through when I was forced to sign a statement, without any truth in it, that my Marshal Budyenny had been 'connected with the Marshal Tukhachevsky group' and that he survived only because this

223

connection was not discovered; that through Assistant Foreign Commissar Karakhan, Budyenny was connected with foreign spies and received instructions through him; that he was sending precious stones and gold abroad; and so on.

"After my 'confession' they left me in peace and I began to recuperate. The stronger I grew physically, the stronger my will grew. But any attempts to kill myself were carefully anticipated, especially after Red Army Inspector General Tyupin broke away from his guards when he was being led to the NKVD investigator, jumped down the stairs and smashed his head against a radiator.

"I kept expecting that Marshal Budyenny would be arrested, and hoped that by chance I might see him and be able to call out to him that it was I who had betrayed him, tell him that they forced me to do it, and ask him to forgive me.

"For a whole year I sat without a single questioning.

"In April 1940, I was called again. There was a different prosecutor this time.

"After the usual formalities, I related my story. The prosecutor shook his head, and seriously, even sincerely, in the tone of an old mentor said:

"'You aren't made of very high-quality stuff, Citizen Ryzhov. How could you write all that about a member of our government, a Marshal of the Soviet Union, a man who had raised you to what you were. Why, he was your second father! What can we do now? Of course you know that everything you reported was just a pack of lies. Right? It is true that some of our staff here considered their careers more important than truth and justice. But how could *you* ever sink so low?'

"Tears came to my eyes. I didn't have the strength to reply.

"A month later I was free. Last week I learned that my wife is working in a kolkhoz near Kazan, my daughter has gone blind."

Ryzhov stopped. I could tell by his face that he was under a terrible strain and that he was controlling himself to keep from crying. I was astounded when he suddenly asked for a cigarette

—I knew that he had quit smoking while in prison. He took two long drags and turned to me again:

"I'll have to help them. Have to cure my girl. . . . Actually, I want your advice—should I go to see the Marshal, would it be worth it?"

After a lengthy pause I knew that he wouldn't talk any longer. I did my best to calm him, but my prosaic phrases bothered even me. I naturally advised him to see Budyenny, but not in his office. I promised to find out when he would be home and let Ryzhov use my car to go there, as the Marshal lived outside of town. I told him not to announce his visit in advance.

About three days later Ryzhov went to see Budyenny. He promised to come and see me afterward as I was very interested in the results of the meeting. I had told him that if he didn't feel like it, though, he shouldn't come over immediately afterward and gave him permission not to report to work the next day.

All the more was I surprised when Ryzhov returned in two hours. I was about to ask whether he had found the Marshal home, but when I saw his depressed look, I hesitated.

Ryzhov sat down and again asked for a cigarette. I waited, and gradually I found out what had happened.

Budyenny had met him at the door, kissed him, and led him into the kitchen past a room in which a noisy conversation was in progress. After two or three simple questions, the conversation stopped. It seemed as if they had nothing to talk about.

Then Budyenny reached for his wallet, handed Ryzhov some money, and not looking at him said:

"I'll help you, Kolya, of course I'll help you. Take this now, that's all I have on me. But you know, Kolya, don't come here any more. Rumors, gossip, talk—you understand yourself, I am sure."

There was nothing more to do, so Ryzhov left, leaving the money on the kitchen table.

"But you must understand," Ryzhov continued, "that it wasn't his fault. He is a good, hearty man.

"I am sincerely grateful to him. Yesterday one of my old friends told me about the meeting of the division Communists which took place immediately after my arrest. The question of my expulsion from the Party was being considered. One speaker after another rose to condemn me and accuse me of all possible and impossible crimes, and admit their fault for not sooner becoming aware of 'the enemy who was doing his dirty work' right under their noses.

"The meeting seemed unanimous for my expulsion, when Budyenny rose and asked for the floor. It was obvious to all that the arrest of his former adjutant was quite a blow to him.

" 'Don't you people know Major Ryzhov?' the Marshal asked. 'Why, Kolya Ryzhov fought with us in the Civil War and has been with us ever since. I do not agree with the opinion of the Party Committee. Ryzhov couldn't be a traitor to the Party or to the people. This is a mistake.'

"The silence which followed after Budyenny's words was depressing, fearful. Everyone understood that Budyenny had pitted his authority against that of the Party. Such things don't often happen in the Party.

"The secretary of the Party Committee arose and icily asked:

" 'And what would you propose to do, Comrade Marshal?'

"Budyenny looked around. He hesitated a moment, seeming to make up his mind. Then he quietly said:

" 'Of course we have to expel Ryzhov from the Party. But so far we don't even know whether he is just being held as a witness or has been accused of a crime. I, therefore, propose that we state it thus: expel Major Ryzhov from membership in the Party on the basis of arrest by the NKVD.'

"The meeting breathed more freely, and the resolution, as proposed by Budyenny, was accepted unanimously."

After the visit to Marshal Budyenny, Ryzhov completely turned into himself. I was able to help him get in touch with his wife and send his daughter to the well-known optician Filatov, in Odessa. But Ryzhov met any attempt to help him personally with utmost caution, even morbidly.

I felt that Ryzhov's remaining belief in man was gradually waning, that it would not take much to break him completely. But the Party became aware of this situation in time, and not wanting to lose a capable man like him, went to work for him.

About two months after Ryzhov's visit to the Marshal, I received a call from the army department handling decorations. I was asked to tell Ryzhov to report in order that they might issue him duplicates of the decorations which he had been deprived of upon arrest. After another month I gave him a recommendation for entry into the Party, and not much later he was a full-fledged Party member again.

I remember with what distrust Ryzhov met my suggestion that he apply for Party membership. However, when I confessed to him that the suggestion originated from the Party and that I was doing it under orders, I could see him come to life. Poor Ryzhov, after all he had gone through, he was still hoping, and tried not to listen to the voice of his doubts.

In 1941, two months before Hitler attacked the Soviet Union, Ryzhov came to bid me farewell. The man had changed. Where before there was only depression and doubt, he now believed anew. Believing his country again needed his services, his faith in the Party was renewed. Apparently he had forgotten the ways of the Party: how it had made him turn against his close friend and commander, how the next moment it had blamed him for doing so.

Ryzhov was happy. He told me he was seeing the Marshal again, that their friendship was as strong as ever, that Budyenny was trying to arrange for the return of his gold-encrusted saber, etc. . . .

I hesitated a long time before deciding to write Ryzhov's story. I debated whether it would hurt his standing if I disclosed what no one was supposed to know, and which I had learned

227

thanks to my Party and official position. But I decided that if Ryzhov is still alive and believes as ever in the Party, this account won't hurt him. How was he ever to know that the personnel director of the All-Union Physical Culture Committee, a trusted member of the Party and in high standing with the NKVD, no longer believed in the Party?

The second example of the Party's ruthless use of its members occurred at approximately the same time as the Ryzhov affair.

This case affected me much more than the above, mainly because it involved me personally to a much greater extent—against my will I played a part in the arrest of two of my friends.

"The secretary of the Party Committee would like to talk to you," my secretary said, sticking her head through the door.

"Sure, connect him."

"Hello . . . yes, this is Ugryumov . . . I'm not too busy, stop by now."

A few minutes later Slavny was in my office.

"What is your relationship to Dudin?" he asked me without wasting any words.

"Why, he has been my best friend since we studied at the institute together."

"And with Kozhny?"

"Well, we also went to school together, but we were never very close. I haven't seen him in almost a year."

"Hmm, that's not so good."

"What do you mean?" I asked.

"Nothing. I just think it's bad to lose contact with people."

"What can one do nowadays? You know yourself that our personal life has been neglected. You wouldn't believe it, but during the week I never see or talk to my wife. When I come home she is asleep, and when I get up she has already left for work. With my wife it's not so bad, because we have plenty of time together on Sundays, but it's sort of sad to have your

228

daughter grow up without being able to spare the time to play with her."

"Sure, I know. But did you read the article on the family in *Pravda* a few days ago?"

"I admit that I didn't. But I know what you want to say—that the family is the smallest cell of the state, that we must strengthen it and all that. Isn't that it?"

"You're right, but that's not what I came to talk to you about. How about arranging a little party this Sunday and inviting Dudin and Kozhny?"

"Sorry, but I couldn't do that. First of all, I haven't got the money right now, and secondly, I promised my family to spend the whole day with them."

"Your wife and daughter won't disappear. The picnic is necessary."

"What for? I can rest well enough without a picnic."

"Don't be so difficult. Do I have to chew everything for you before you can swallow it? This is business. Invite Dudin and Kozhny, and I'll come with another fellow. Tell your family that he is my relative. I will bring the drinks and any food we'll need so there won't be any expense to you. And don't dare say anything to Dudin and Kozhny, or warn them. Just invite them for a good time."

At that I completely understood what was wanted of me and who would come with Slavny. My heart beat faster and I wanted to shout that I wouldn't let him make a villain and a traitor out of me but, calling on every nerve, I answered evenly:

"If you say so, I'll invite them."

During the three days before Sunday, the situation pressed heavily on my mind. I finally decided that the least I could do was warn Dudin to drink little and talk less.

Slavny and his "cousin" Svodsky were the first to arrive. Svodsky immediately won the sympathies of my wife and daughter by gathering pine cones for my wife's samovar and paying her several compliments about my daughter, and by showing my little girl several handkerchief tricks so that she didn't take her enthusiastic eyes off him for the rest of the day.

The day and evening went just as our Sundays usually did when we had guests. We went swimming and lay in the sun before lunch. Afterward we played volleyball and ping-pong. Even though I had warned Dudin in advance about drinking and talking, I still couldn't help worrying every time he opened his mouth.

When it grew dark and the question arose whether our guests should stay overnight, Slavny and his "cousin" were ready to go. However, when Dudin and Kozhny and their wives agreed to stay, they immediately changed their minds.

Several days later Dudin was arrested, and not long thereafter they also got Kozhny.

Dudin's wife, who was in her last month of pregnancy, came to my office and in tears asked me for advice and help. My feeling of guilt that somehow I had betrayed her husband, my closest friend, became stronger than ever. I clenched my teeth and couldn't look at her. We both knew that Dudin was honest and true to the Soviet regime, that his record was clean, but neither she nor I could do a thing.

After my friend's wife left me, I locked the door to my office and sat for a long time thinking about what had happened. I attempted to justify myself: my friends were already on the black list and even if I had not arranged a picnic they probably would have been arrested. The only difference would have been that I would have fallen under strong suspicion, nothing else. But another voice within me kept saying: How could you ever agree to such a villainous act toward your best friend who believed in you completely. You should have sacrificed yourself and refused to arrange this meeting, regardless of the fact that it wouldn't have saved Dudin and Kozhny.

I did whatever I could to help Dudin's wife, especially after the birth of her baby. But I couldn't get over the feeling of aversion for myself, and for a long time, maybe unjustly, I kept

230

saying to myself: Help, help, make up for what you have done!

After ten months, Dudin's wife was given permission to see him. I was no less excited than she. What would he say? Would he call me his betrayer?

They couldn't talk much during their meeting because an NKVD man was present. But he was able to tell his wife that he had been accused in connection with the case of Betty Glan, director of Moscow's Park of Culture and Rest. They talked about me, and he had only the best things to say, not attaching any significance to the party he had attended at my house before his arrest. Even so, I can never think without resentment about the part I was forced to play in this affair.

Just before the war broke out, I heard that Dudin had been released. I never heard anything of Kozhny's fate.

The attack by Germany in June 1941 did not take me by surprise. I found myself at the front in the very first month of the war. This time, of course, I did not go as a volunteer, nor with any enthusiasm.

One after another, Soviet armies were smashed during the first months of the war. In October 1941, I was taken prisoner.

13

A LIFE OF ORDEALS

by Oleg Lutkov

My mother was an illiterate peasant from Gomel. I was born out of wedlock.

Mother worked as a servant, and to keep her job she was forced to have strangers raise me. Mother paid for my care, and I lived with several different peasant families in a village twenty miles from Moscow.

In 1910, when I was eight, mother took me to Yekaterinoslav. With some money she had saved, she opened a little shop in the market. I went to elementary school. Because of my illegitimate birth I suffered endless humiliation at the hands of the students. The nickname "bastard" followed me through my school years. Gradually I developed a feeling of hatred for all who were above me in society.

In 1919 I volunteered for service in the Red Army. I fought under General Budyenny through most of the Civil War. I was never afraid of battle, was always among the first, but I was never wounded.

In the Red Army I had no feeling that I didn't belong. Here I was the equal to all. I, the illegitimate son of a peasant, was as good as the next man. Under the slogan: "All power to the workers and peasants!" I fought joyfully.

Late in 1920 I came down with typhus and was taken to my mother in Dnepropetrovsk (the Soviet name for Yekaterinoslav). After I recovered, I reported to the military authorities for re-assignment but was demobilized on account of bad lungs.

Not being qualified for any special kind of work, I became an unskilled laborer on a railroad. Life was difficult. Mother was ill —she had developed typhus while taking care of me, and never completely recovered.

In 1921 I joined the Komsomol. I wanted to learn more, and through membership in the Komsomol there was a possibility of obtaining an assignment to a university or technical school.

I was proud of belonging to an organization that was in the forefront of the defense of the young Soviet state. I sat fascinated at meetings listening to discussions of the theory and practice of Communism. I read much, everything I could lay a hand on. I wanted to know everything, to understand everything, so that I could do my part.

My Komsomol membership, however, did not help me to get into any school.

I continued to work on the railroad. During my free evenings an old Pole, Smelchansky, taught me carpentry. We became good friends. In conversations with the old man I obtained a new view of the situation around me. I resisted his influence, defending myself with the help of phrases from newspapers and magazines, but the seeds of doubt were sown in my mind. That which had seemed highly glorious to me began to lose its glory after Smelchansky's explanations. I quit believing everything official I heard and began to weigh the pros and cons before making up my mind on any question. I suddenly noticed that I was bored at Komsomol meetings, that they talked about the same things day in and day out, that there was no freedom of thought there, that they said what they were ordered to say and thought what they were ordered to think. Gradually my belief in the righteousness of every move by the Komsomol and the Party was extinguished.

I attended Komsomol meetings less and less frequently. Finally I stopped paying my dues and dropped out. Where I hadn't been noticed by the Komsomol while I was a member—when I dropped out they began to interest themselves in me. I was carefully watched and my past was investigated. But what could they find? I was a pure, 100 per cent proletarian, had fought in the Red Army. I knew that I was under constant surveillance; they didn't trust me and were looking for an excuse to pick on me. But here, for once, my childhood helped me. I was punctual and reliable in my work; I was reserved in my conversations.

In 1925 I became a skilled carpenter. My financial situation improved, and the next year I was married. I worked well and was rewarded several times for overfulfilling my production norms. Actually my pay was only eighty rubles a month, hardly enough to live on. Therefore, I worked at home to supplement my income by making the type of wooden suitcases generally used in Russia. My wife and mother sold them on the market.

One day in 1929 I came to work an hour late. For this "crime" I was demoted to the status of unskilled laborer for six months and sent to work on the construction of a new river port near Dnepropetrovsk.

Toward the end of 1929, when I had worked off my punishment, I decided to enroll in night school. I still had a great desire to learn, to make something of myself.

At that time I lived in a workers' settlement near Dnepropetrovsk. I had to take a train to work at 4:50 A.M. Work didn't start till six-thirty, but the ten-mile ride took a whole hour. I worked till four, and then ate supper in the dining hall of the factory.

School began at six and lasted till ten in the evening. One

234

train left for home at nine-forty-five, the next at eleven-forty. I had the choice of missing more than half of my last lecture or sitting through till the end and arriving home much later. I usually chose the latter alternative, not wanting to miss the opportunity of learning anything that could be useful to me. I never wasted the time between the end of the lessons and my train—I read, studied my lessons, and did the homework for the next day. It was almost one when I arrived at home, and the few hours of sleep that I was able to get were hardly enough to keep me in shape for the next day's work.

Despite all difficulties, however, I stuck to this routine for eleven months and became a construction foreman.

My first job following completion of the course was on the construction of the very port where I had previously been forced to work as an unskilled laborer. At first my pay was one hundred rubles a month, but soon after I started working there it was raised to 120 rubles. I liked my work and put all my energy into it.

I had made one very good friend during my Civil War days, Lyova M., and we remained close after the Civil War. With him more than anyone else I had always been frank and open. In the twenties we often discussed the possibility of building socialism in only one country. I didn't believe that this was possible, feeling that the theory was artificial and far fetched. But Lyova avidly believed in the Party dogma and strongly defended it. Despite our political arguments, which sometimes became quite violent, our old friendship continued through the years.

One day in 1931, Lyova came to me and said: "Oleg, you'd better go to some other city. You are being watched here, and it would be healthier for you to move. I'll do my best to help you."

At first I was astonished, but then I realized it was but the continuation of the persecutions that had started when I quit the Komsomol. Lyova helped me get a release from my job and

235

a transfer to work in the construction department of the railroad in Grozny.

From that time on, Lyova became my guardian. He was in a position to keep track of any action that related to me, and despite a potential danger to himself, he always notified me whenever things were getting too hot in any one place.

My forced departure for Grozny precipitated a break between my wife and me. She told me that she didn't love me any more and didn't want to continue living with me. My sons remained with her, as I couldn't take care of them alone in a strange city. I took this break very hard, especially when it came on top of my "political difficulties."

In Grozny I worked on the construction of dormitories and workshops for the railroad. Peasants from White Russia had been recruited as unskilled labor for these projects. They lived in wooden barracks, each of which held thirty-five to forty people. They slept on beds made of rough boards knocked together and burlap bags filled with straw. The barracks were filthy. Overcrowding, absence of soap, bath, and laundry facilities, the constant drying of wet clothes and boots made them smell terrible. Coming into one of these buildings, one's eyes began to smart from the bad atmosphere and the smoke coming from two small stoves at either end of the building. It seemed as if one had walked into a dense fog with vague shadows walking around.

The average pay of these workers was eighty rubles. They couldn't leave the place of work, no matter how much they wanted to, because their passports were taken away to be held until their contracts expired. And where could one go without passports?

I kept in constant touch with the workers and, seeing their life, my disappointment in my own situation was replaced by a strong compassion for these people subjected to inhumanly hard labor, hunger, and cold. They worked on with the apathy of doomed people.

236

After about four years of work in Grozny, I began to notice that the "all-seeing eye" was watching me again. Not long afterward I received "greetings" from Lyova. My departure was speeded by the news that my mother was very ill. I received permission to leave Grozny, and in November 1935 I returned to Dnepropetrovsk. But my mother had already died.

Whereas in Grozny my heart pained looking at the plight of recruited peasants, in Nizhne-Dnieprovsk, where I went to work next, I had my first contact with prisoners being used for forced labor. There were about ten thousand of them, mostly liquidated kulaks. They were employed as excavators. Their daily norm was eight cubic yards, and the digging in the rocky earth was done manually!

Part of the prisoners lived in hurriedly erected, unheated barracks near the job, others were brought in by train each day from their prisons in Dnepropetrovsk, while the rest came by foot from near-by internment camps. They worked under armed guard. I did not associate with any of the prisoners, knowing that it would immediately be held against me.

Again Lyova let me know that I had better get out. Having worked ten months in Nizhne-Dnieprovsk, I left my job under the excuse of being ill. This time I went to Vladikavkaz, again to do construction work. The unskilled workers lived under the same conditions as I had seen before—filth, hunger, poor pay, etc., but this time they were Caucasians. About this time Stalin's slogan: "Life is better, life is happier!" was in high popularity. Who's life became better, who's happier?

Once more "greetings" from Lyova, and in August 1937 I returned to Dnepropetrovsk. This time I went to work for a housing co-operative, doing overseeing and drafting.

After I got this job, things began to go better for me. My wife had divorced me, but I met a woman who had also gone through a personal tragedy, and after several months of acquaintance we were married.

In the Soviet Union a wife can take the name of her husband, but a husband can also adopt his wife's family name. We both felt that it would be better if I were to lose the name under which I had come into disfavor, and I adopted her name.

We lived peacefully thereafter. My wife had just finished the university and was assigned to a position in Zaporozhe. I followed her there, but after a short time we went back to Dnepropetrovsk where we remained till the war with Germany.

I am sure that not only I, but 70 to 80 per cent of the Soviet population, hoped for the defeat of their regime and awaited the Germans, their enemies, as liberators from the Communist "paradise."

I had a chance to be evacuated before they arrived, but didn't go. I, a peasant, of proletarian descent, I, who had come a long way thanks to the Revolution, was a mortal enemy of the Bolshevik regime. They had considered me thus, and so I became.

I won't describe life under the Germans. It was bad under the Bolsheviks, but it became worse under the Germans. Nevertheless, when the Germans were going away I built a hand cart, piled all my belongings into it, and with my wife set out on foot to accompany the retreating enemy. We walked five hundred miles, pulling our cart all the way.

On the sixth of April, 1944, we were in a labor camp in Germany. I knew that the Germans wouldn't last long. Their coming collapse was obvious to us all. Until that time I tried to keep my family alive. I went around to German homes on Sunday, offering to do carpentry work or any kind of odd job. There were few Sundays when I didn't return with a goodly amount of food, received in payment for my work. It was a necessary supplement to the terrible rations we received in camp.

I watched with fear the developments of the war, being afraid to find myself too close to the advancing Soviet troops.

After the war ended, we went through all the horror of the Soviet authorities' free reign in the French zone of Germany, and

238

from there fled to the American zone. Here, in the American section, I lived through the Kempten tragedy. In this horrible affair American soldiers were employed to force Russians to surrender to Soviet authorities. The result was that people cut their throats and slashed their wrists, jumped out of upper-story windows, and used any means they could think of to kill themselves to keep from falling into Soviet hands. Those who survived suicide attempts were nursed back to health and then handed over.

Now I lead the sad existence of a displaced person. I am homesick and love my country, but I fear it also. I live in the hope that the tyranny will fall and that my people will awake from the heavy sleep.

CONCLUSION
by Louis Fischer

The conclusion is clear: a dictatorship fails with the individual. Dictatorship means compulsion and coercion and therefore the individual is not free and therefore the individual suffers. In a dictatorship the state grows strong, the national economy can expand, but persons are expendable. This is not the way to make a new human being.

A dictatorship is equipped to deal with things and masses; the Soviet dictatorship placed a hundred million peasants on collective farms. It could no more solve the problems of the men, women, and children on those farms than a warden does the problems of his prisoners or a lieutenant the problems of his soldiers.

The agricultural communes in Palestine are voluntary groups moved by high idealism; a new type of person has emerged in them. But the Soviet press is continually complaining of stealing, malingering, malfeasance, bureaucracy, and inefficiency in the Russian collectives. How could it be otherwise?

Years ago many Soviet workers believed that since the capitalists were gone they were the owners of their factories. The divorce between government and people has shattered this faith.

240

There was a social incentive in the Soviet Union; the dictatorship killed it. Now all employees work, as they do in capitalist countries for their pay envelopes. When these are thin in terms of goods, the work lags.

Dictatorship lays a dead hand on everything and everybody, including the dictator.

Success in a dictatorship comes to the most brutal, the most cynical, the most immoral. The others are the victims. Since the victims are completely helpless the brutal-cynical-immoral agents of the government succeed easily in erecting buildings, in publishing many books, in digging coal, in obtaining unanimity, in running the state.

All dictatorships, Hitler's, Mussolini's, Franco's, Stalin's, now Prague's, pay subsidies to young couples that want to get married and want to have babies. The state provides "from the Cradle to the Grave." But on what standard of living? And what kind of person emerges?

The thirteen who fled knew about or went to prekindergarten crèches, and kindergartens, and primary and grammar schools, some to high schools and colleges. Those institutions are shells, frameworks. What do they teach? What of the human being do they produce?

Why do Americans, Englishmen, and western Europeans, so skillful in building walls and making electricity, become impressed when the Soviets do the same things with less skill? Aren't we critical of our civilization because of its deficiencies in morality, spiritual content, and intellectual honesty? Why should statistics and military victories impress? What of the costs?

Unconsciously, but in some cases consciously, the sympathizers of Soviet Russia, of whom I used to be one, learn to judge Bolshevism by its own standards of morality, and its own standards of achievement.

Approval of a dictatorship has a corroding effect on democracy and decency.

Attitudes in the Communism versus Democracy issue vary from:

Communism is completely right and Russia can do no wrong, to:

Moscow is to blame for everything and there is nothing bad about democracy except that it isn't conservative enough.

Between these extremes are those whose fear of being taken as Communists keeps them from criticizing capitalism, and those who are so afraid of being classed with "Red-baiting" tories that they are silent on the evils of Sovietism.

The perspective I now have of Soviet history leads me to believe that without freedom there can be no good. Bolshevik treatment of national minorities has been regarded as a good. Yet several national minorities were disloyal during the war and sympathized with the Nazis. Moscow suppressed their autonomous governments and banished large sections of their inhabitants. Due to Kremlin encouragement of Russian and Ukrainian nationalism in recent years, racial antagonisms, including antisemitism, have been revived. Moreover, what value has freedom for national minorities when no member of a national minority enjoys personal freedom? The same relative, restricted value attaches to such Soviet goods as vacations, medical care, broad educational facilities, and social security. Let a person deviate one iota from the official political line, let him be suspected of the slightest doubt about government policy, and he loses all privileges. There are no rights under Bolshevism, there are only gifts from the state, and the state can withdraw them and has withdrawn them not only from individuals but from the entire population. A dictatorship seems to be so steady and permanent, so clear and firm in its procedures; actually, it is the most nerve-racking kind of government because the people never know what ukase or decree or policy reversal will descend upon them tomorrow. All the cradle-to-grave provisions in the world do not bring a sense of security when the government is not subject to democratic checks.

It is difficult for a person who has not lived under a dictatorship to realize how tense and trying the life is. Thirteen Who Fled gives a graphic description of what would happen to Mr. and Mrs. America, or Monsieur and Madame France, or Mr. and Mrs. Briton if their countries succumbed to dictatorship.

A true picture of Soviet Russia should not conduce to complacency about democracy. If democracy's current contest with Communist totalitarianism leads to the curtailment of democratic rights, what has been gained? The test of democracy is the existence of the freedom to struggle for more democracy; a Soviet citizen is denied this possibility. There is complete freedom in Soviet Russia, there was complete freedom in Nazi Germany, to agree with the dictator. Democracy is the right to disagree. The punishment of, embarrassment of, and intolerance of dissenters is a serious attack on democratic freedom.

Nor is democracy complete or safe when some citizens are not allowed to vote, are not allowed to serve on juries, do not get fair trials, cannot find jobs, cannot obtain free education, and have limited economic, social, and political security. Fear is the enemy of freedom. Fear of the lyncher, fear of arbitrary action outside the law, fear of unemployment, fear of war weaken democracy.

In the long run—and if there is no shooting war—the cold war between democracy and Communism will be won by the side that is superior culturally, morally, technologically, and economically—by the side that grants more liberties.

Poverty and riches, progress and backwardness, war and peace, good and evil, learning and illiteracy, religion and immorality have co-existed for ages. Of course, dictatorship and freedom, Communism, socialism, and capitalism can co-exist. But in present circumstances they co-exist and compete. Each tries to demonstrate its superiority.

The purpose of the Iron Curtain is to keep the people of the Soviet Union and of the Soviet Empire from knowing how much worse off they are than the inhabitants of free countries. It also serves to prevent the outside world from realizing the extent of the terror, repression, and poverty inside Russia. If Stalin were convinced of Bolshevism's superiority the doors of his country would be wide open for the foreign observer to come in and the Soviet citizen to leave. The Soviet citizen would not want to leave. But we know now that the moment the door opens Russians escape to the West. This is the lesson of the Soviet refugees, hundreds of thousands of whom have preferred a strange world to their own country.

To confuse and mislead its subjects the Soviet government preaches Russian superiority: not the Wright brothers but a Russian was the first to fly an airplane, not Edison but a Russian invented the electric bulb, not Marconi but a Russian invented the wireless, and so on. Suppose they were first. Why are they not first now in the use and development of scientific discoveries?

This Soviet propaganda is designed to prove to the Soviet people that Russia is better and, above all, that Russia can get along without the West. It is a weapon to further isolate the Soviet Union from the outside world. In stressing alleged Russian superiority the Kremlin actually reveals its fear of exposing the Soviet mind to evidence of foreign superiority.

Russia fears the superiority of the democratic world. Superiority in all fields, not only in technology, is democracy's finest weapon against dictatorship. Russia's great challenge to the non-Soviet world should be an added incentive to improve democracy.

Ultimately, the truth will penetrate the thickest iron curtain and bring changes in the Soviet Union and in the Soviet Empire. Efforts to hasten those changes are the biggest contribution to world peace.